Saw the House in Half

A Novel

Saw the House in Half

a Novel

Oliver Jackman

Howard University Press

Washington · 1974

An excerpt from this novel appeared in *Amistad I* as "A Poet of the People," published by Random House, 1970.

Printed in the United States of America.

LIBRARY OF CONGRESS CATALOGING IN PUBLICATION DATA

Jackman, Oliver.
     Saw the house in half.

     I. Title.
PZ4.J124Saw3   [PR9230.9.J3]   823   73-88971
ISBN 0-88258-010-8

To my wife, Annie, and my son, François Ayodele

What it have across the sea?
You leave something in Africa? . . .
Is there you going?
And furthermore I can't swim.
You can swim, Papa?

Derek Walcott:*The Sea at Dauphin*

West Indians have no inherent values of their own; their
values are always contingent on the presence of The Other.

Frantz Fanon: *Black Skin, White Masks*

*. . . I don't really see how
I can explain to the reader in a brief
note all the images and symbols that I
see in the verse of the Barbadian folksong
from which the title comes:
    "Saw the house in half
        And give me the chamber part."
It is my idea that West Indians still
live in a half-house, and that half of
that half is African and the other European. "The chamber part": that's the
comfortable part; Dacosta Payne thinks
at the beginning that the European part
is the chamber part, then he thinks that
maybe the African part is the chamber
part; finally he goes back to the West
Indies; is that the chamber part? Now,
how the hell does one explain that to the
reader? Let him figure it out, I say,
and I hope you agree.**

                    *Sincerely,
                    Oliver*

              *Note from author to editor

Chapter One

I still have the engraved calling card which Dacosta Payne gave me on that yellow autumn day in 1949. The card reads:

Wilfred Dacosta Payne, M.A., M.Sc. (Leeds), B.Com.,
Fellow of the American Institute of
Business Management

He explained that it was "only copperplate engraving; when one is leading a life as essentially itinerant as mine, one would have to be an absolute Rockefeller to be able to afford a steel job." To underscore his point he produced from a calf-leather card case two other cards, one bearing a New York address, the other a Geneva address. "Copperplate again," he said. "Not many people can tell the difference, Brathwaite, but one knows oneself."

I didn't feel that he was making a particular effort to impress me, but I was more than ready to be impressed, being in that state of shock and hypersusceptibility which classically overtakes the young man come for the first time to the big city. For I was then in my third disoriented day of trying to cope with the phenomenon of London, that gargantuan agglomeration of mist and myth which had always been totally alive and complete in my colonial

1

imagination, but now had to be accommodated in my actual life. Real Burberrys; genuine coppers who actually said "'Ere!" to my face; palpable October fog; the stony, audio-visual reality of Big Ben unrefracted by *oratio obliqua* or the cinema screen—it was as if on waking from one of those recurrent dreams of flying one discovered that one could, in fact, fly.

But I *was* impressed by the liquid, drawling vowels of his English upper-class speech which, never mind the black face, went perfectly with the slim, tall figure, and the accouterment of double-breasted camel's hair overcoat, tight cavalry-twill trousers, and dark brown chukka boots. If there was a slightly false note it was, perhaps, the unkempt overgrown mat of tightly curled black hair on his head: It looked aggressively "African." Was he, then, one of those dissolute African "princes" in whose misdemeanors the *News of the World* periodically took such profound and disingenuous delight?

"I'm Barbadian, actually," he intoned, so obvious was my unasked question. And then, blocking the access of patriotic pride that this piece of news had produced in me, he added, "Originally." Of course, I thought, deflated, that must have been a long time ago.

"We're cousins, you know," he went on, and I wanted to hug him. For how could I be the utter nothing which London had begun to make me feel I was when there were cousins like this about?

"Actually, Brathwaite, we're related through your mother," he said, and went on to explain with loving precision our relative positions on two family trees.

We were standing in the vestibule of the large, bustling student hostel to which the Colonial Office Students' Division had assigned me. On the white ceiling above us, Cupid had been arrested in white plaster in the act of chasing four white plaster nymphs around a white plaster circle; from their midst the innocently phallic shaft of a chandelier emerged to light, by means of a cluster of spear-ended miniature bulbs, a severe arrangement of a dozen overstuffed brown armchairs and half-a-dozen high, marble-topped coffee tables that served as a reception area. Dacosta Payne smoothly piloted us over to one of the tables and sat me down.

"I pop in here from time to time to see if there are any faces around I recognize," he said. He was sitting on the very edge of the chair, his hands clasped on the ferrule of a tightly rolled umbrella which he rocked gently back and forth on the floor. For me, the very posture bespoke his status as plenipotentiary of that complex, subtle, and elegant world outside Barbados to the conquest of which I had so optimistically dedicated myself. Manifestly it could be conquered; Dacosta Payne had done it. But could I? "Today," he went on, "the head porter mentioned to me that three gentlemen, *gentlemen*, he said, had arrived from Barbados a few days ago. I suppose you've noticed by now how frightfully polite the English are *in England*. He let me have a look at the register, and your name struck a chord."

He set about questioning me very closely, with almost avuncular concern, about my plans for study. The news that I was on my way to Cambridge in a few days moved him to a faint sigh—of nostalgia for the delights of beginning?

"Tremendous temptations to muck around in those places," he said, but it seemed to be the voice of one who regretted not having mucked around enough.

"I came up in the early days of the war, put in a year in the arts faculty at Leeds, and then enlisted in the air force. Best thing I ever did. Worth a hell of a lot to me."

"That must have been quite an experience," I said, awed once again.

"Mmh, well, yes, I suppose it was. Not certain that that was quite what I meant, but *passons*. Where was I? Yes.

Well, I got myself invalided out, end of forty-four; was doing one of those retraining larks on one of the new kites they were serving up about then. Pilot put us down in a wheat field and I got some bits of glass and assorted stuff in my eyes, d'you know? Left eye went for a complete burton, for a while, anyway. I'd had enough, frankly, wasn't at all sorry to get back to university. Weren't very many of us at university in those days, you know, a few beat-up veterans like myself and lots of pimply-faced young chaps straight out of grammar school. But they gave me a year's allowance and I swotted day and night and was lucky enough to pick up a first. The rest of that stuff," he waved toward the card which I found I was still clutching as if it were a good luck charm, "all that was icing."

"But what do you do now?" I asked, with the directness of my twenty years.

"Bit of this, bit of that, d'you know? I'm a kind of consultant, really. You see, English businessmen haven't the foggiest about business management, brand-new over here. It's the Americans who've really got it taped. I cottoned on to that pretty early in the game, so I suppose you could say I'm blinding them with science. I do management surveys, efficiency analyses, bit of time and motion study, that kind of thing. Mostly with small firms; they're having a hell of a time getting back on their feet, you know, shortages, rationing, government controls, lack of staff. I go along and give them a few tips on how to save money, cut some corners, streamline, find new markets, that sort of thing. Management consultant, d'you know? But the English don't like you to use that sort of title. Too pompous, they say. The fact is, they're somewhat ashamed to admit that anyone can teach the shopkeepers of the world anything about business, specially a ruddy foreigner. That's were my time in the RAF comes in useful. I may be a bloody nig, but I *was* one of 'the few.' "

It was my turn, then, to give him news about Barbados, tidbits of gossip and political scandal, who was where, and the rest of it. He surprised me by the minute interest he took in it all, cross-examining me about the names of people's babies—and their legitimacy, if any. How could he care about a world that already seemed so Lilliputian to me?

"Do let me take you out one of these evenings before you commit yourself irrevocably to the cloisters of Queens," he said as he was about to leave. "Might show you a thing or two, what? London's a charming old place once you find your bearings. Shall I give you a tinkle some time soon?" I was delighted at the prospect, and said so.

Then he was off, leaving me, on the whole, more hopeful about England, a little less confused; maybe, after all, I should be able to find an accommodation with it, though surely never that mastery which he had so clearly acquired; already the porter seemed to be looking at me with slightly less pity and contempt than I had seen in his eyes these past three days.

The tinkle came two days later. He offered "a spot of dinner and a cabaret, if you care for that sort of thing, and maybe a nightcap at the house of a friend of mine afterwards?" He collected me in an elegant black machine of the kind the English call a town car.

"Just a little Jaguar I picked up from a contact second-hand. It was a snip. Would have been a crime to refuse it at the price." He didn't mention the price, as I recall.

"Would you mind terribly if I brought along the friend I was speaking about?" he asked, as we drove off. "Turns out she'd nothing on, so I thought we'd have a crack at her liquor cabinet first, and then pay her back in provender, so to speak." I had already divined that the friend would be female, perhaps from something in his voice when he had spoken to me on the telephone, and, certain that she would be as spectacular in her way as Dacosta

Payne was in his, I was more than ready to spend the
whole evening in her company.

As we drove through a maze of back streets toward
the flat of Dacosta Payne's friend, I found myself simultaneously wondering about both the friend and Dacosta
Payne himself. About Dacosta Payne I had the unaccount-
able feeling that if I looked away from the figure who
was skillfully and knowledgeably guiding us through
alleys and lanes, some of which seemed just to miss being
cul-de-sacs, he would no longer exist; I apprehended him
no more vividly than if he had been someone I knew only
by description.

But the girl I hadn't met seemed more present and real.
I had a ridiculously precise picture of her. She was bru-
nette, with soft hair cropped close to her ears, soft brown
eyes set wide apart over a little nose, and a hint of
freckles beneath the first, translucent layer of skin. I
know that this image had not sprung full-grown from out
of nowhere, and we had reached the house, a three-story
brownstone building in a mews, yes, a mews, somewhere
off Piccadilly, before I identified the provenance of the
picture; it was part Deborah Kerr, part Ingrid Bergman
of *For Whom the Bell Tolls,* and part Kathy, the freckle-
faced waitress who served at table in my section of the
dining hall, and who was the first white woman with
whom I had ever conversed on terms of equality—she
called me, and all the other students, for that matter,
"Sir." In a totally unconscious spasm of gratitude I had
apparently given her the accolade of beauty. (To this
day I don't know whether she was even good-looking;
nine months later, when familiarity had bred detachment,
I returned to the hostel to find that she had been sacked
for making an offensive remark to a Gambian student
about his color.)

The real Gillian—I never learned her surname—was, of
course, far different from my patchwork image. She was

blonde, for a start, her head a fluffy, and probably un-
fashionable, mass of light golden hair; she was tall, with
incredibly dark eyes that dominated a face that was too
long to be oval; I suppose the black beauty spot and the
tan must have been artificial, but for me they were pris-
tine. Was she really all of a piece, as I remember her, or
is it memory that distorts for simplicity's sake? I remember her voice as being like her hair, which is manifest
nonsense; but that is what I remember. More objec-
tively, I recall a pastel wallpaper and high-backed chairs;
a carved wooden chest which she said came from Eastern
Nigeria; a large gilt mirror (in which I watched her out
of the corner of my eye) standing above a mantelpiece of
stippled gray marble; a line of crystal decanters from
which she offered me a choice of sherry, whisky, or six-
year-old Barbados rum.

I was enchanted, and it is a fact that for a long time
afterwards Gillian occupied one-half of the scale in which
I weighed the good looks of any white woman I met. If
it is true, as it probably is, that the Gillian of my memory
never actually existed, the same is no less true of most
of the reconstructions of memory.

Where was Dacosta Payne in all this? Foursquarely
there, make no mistake about it. Amused in a detached
kind of way, like a man watching—and admiring—a film of
himself, elegant, courteous—a swift opener of doors for
ladies, a debonair bearer of trays, a dab hand with a soda
siphon, a conjurer with his gold Ronson whenever you so
much as thought of having a cigarette—slightly, but not
offensively, patronizing to me, as he had every right to be.

In the car, on our way to dinner, he would lean over
his shoulder from time to time to bring me into the conversation, or to make comments, some of which I remember to this day: "There's a very thin dividing line between
Soho and Mayfair, you'll notice, and it isn't only a matter of topography, either. . . . They don't care for black

people in the X Club, over there; but I could never afford to go there when I was black. . . ."

Dinner was probably excellent; it seemed to me to be exquisite. We went to the X Club; being with Dacosta Payne, I, too, was not black. Typically, the management favored black entertainers; the American Negro folk singer who was in vogue at the time was there for a season. He saw Dacosta Payne and waved to us in the middle of a song. Later he came over and joined us, kissing Gillian on the top of the head and calling her honey-lamb; Dacosta Payne he called boy-chile.

That year I got a Christmas card from Dacosta Payne, posted in Rome; he enclosed a note saying that he'd be out of England for most of the winter, but would drop me a line when he got back. The following spring I received an invitation to a reception he was giving at the Carlton in honor of a visiting team of American Organization and Methods people. On the back of the card he wrote: "Do you ever come up to town? Should love to see you if you could pop up for the weekend of this shindig; we could run down to the country the next day and lunch with some people I'm sure you'd love. W. DaC. P." But exams loomed, and common sense just prevailed over the attractions of a posh do in town.

When I did get to London that summer I missed Dacosta Payne; I phoned Gillian, who told me that he'd gone to Finland on business. Would I care to come round for a drink, anyway?

I hedged, said I'd like to very much and would call her back. I didn't go, and I didn't call her back; the self-assurance I thought I'd acquired after nine months at Cambridge simply melted away at the prospect of confronting, alone, this paragon of London sophistication.

Dacosta Payne and I met again that winter in London; this time it was Gillian who was missing. "She's popped off to Davos with some chums for a fortnight," he explained. But I did see the flat once again. We were going to a West Indian bottle party and we stopped in there to pick up a bottle of rum. He had a key, of course.

The party showed me more plainly a side of Payne which I had barely glimpsed at our first meeting, when he had been so hungrily curious about what was going on in Barbados. The gathering was a mishmash of students, current and superannuated; a few professional men who had "made it" in England; one or two entertainers who had not made it; plus one exiled calypso king. It took place in a grim, flaking, semidetached Victorian house in Chiswick. Chased inside by the cold mist that emanated from the river and clung like a miasma to the street, we edged past the disapproving glances of two or three white residents and crowded into a large, bare, pathetically badly heated room that was shared by two Trinidadian students. After Cambridge, where the top of the voice was used only for the exchange of intimacies or for drunken altercations, the noise was deafening; everyone seemed to be shouting for no reason, more loudly, I thought, than one would in the West Indies; newcomers were greeted with an impartial effusiveness that I found alien—and even somewhat shocking. Exile seemed to bear more heavily on my London-based compatriots than on those of us who inhabited the serene world of Cambridge. In order to stay alive in London it was perhaps necessary to enact a caricature of liveliness.

In all this, Dacosta Payne seemed to drink more, argue more, tell more jokes, laugh and talk more loudly, and eat more rice and peas than anyone else, all the while holding firmly to his English mannerisms and accent. Clearly, he desperately wanted his credentials to be acknowledged, but he had a double set and this confused some of his interlocutors.

That was to be the last time I saw him for six years. I continued to receive postcards and Christmas cards from him while I remained in England; but now his base of operations was more or less definitely on the continent, somewhere between Geneva and Rome.

In my last year at the university, I received from him a reprint of an article, "Quelques considérations sur les problèmes d'industrialisation dans les pays sous-développés, par W. Dacosta Payne," which had appeared in a learned journal in Switzerland. On a card, which described him as "Conseiller industriel," and which bore a Geneva address, he had written, "Still blinding them with science. W. DaC. P."

Chapter Two

Payne, Brathwaite and a dozen other West Indians, three of them students, were sitting in a large high-ceilinged flat shared by Trinidadian twin brothers in river-bound Chiswick. The dank, dark Thames made itself felt as an invisible intruder in the room, a personage in the employ of the Enemy. The Enemy was the weather, that much chronicled and romanticized weather, the weather of Wordsworth, of Sherlock Holmes, of Dickens, that turned out, once you came closer than literature or hearsay, to be a vicious, all-pervading, anti-West-Indian agency. It drove you indoors, diminishing your society to fortuitous miserly handfuls like this one, so that you were absolutely compelled to live each contact to its fullest, whether bitterness or joy was the outcome.

Perhaps that was why the three students had turned on Payne so sharply, not knowing when they would see him again and unwilling to take chances—as you could at home—on hearing just these words again, on treading just this ground again. It was the weather that had them huddled, most of them still wearing their coats, around this futile spitting fire of coal dust; and the dank Thames, seeping through crevices under the doors and through the

11

poorly insulated windows, was able to insert a frigid curtain between them and the fragile warmth that issued from the fireplace. But the Enemy was above all the great juggernaut mass of white humanity that surrounded you every day, everywhere, that smiled at you and put you in the wrong. That sent his women to tempt you into confusion and softening of the heart, and, in the very schools through which you hoped you might acquire enough of his skills to give you a chance to win your emancipation, insidiously pumped into you a venomous skepticism about emancipation itself; so that like a man responding to a posthypnotic suggestion you found yourself asking yourself in unguarded moments, what *is* this emancipation? Isn't the world all one? Good God in Heaven above, what an effort to keep up your guard!

Payne had heard them out in silence as they developed the thesis of the Enemy. He knew he was on dangerous ground when he made his plea for objectivity: That was enemy language. "The thing is," Payne said, "you must resist the temptation to simplify. At your age, of course, it's so devastatingly attractive to simplify."

"Oh, shut your ass. You been up under white people crutch so much their shit smell like roses to you. I telling you they're all the fucking same, education or no education, you hear? Where do you think I does go every blasted day? Sweeping the underground? No, man, I sitting with the cream of the British educational system. . . ."

"And *we're* supposed to be cream, too, don't forget it. . . ."

"Evaporated milk, you mean. Specially processed overseas. . . ."

"*Condensed*, man, *condensed!*" Laughter surged through the room now, displacing the beginnings of bitterness that hung like smoke in the air. As if a little embarrassed by their harshness the three men—boys, really, none of them over twenty—who had jumped on Payne now moved simultaneously to offer him a cigarette, a drink, anything that would pass for a gesture of peace. Payne, absurdly grateful for the token, countered by offering his own thin pigskin caseful of Balkan Sobranie. It came back empty.

Payne desperately wanted to reach them so that he could tell them a few things he knew they needed to know. But first it was necessary to communicate, and so far he had been totally unsuccessful. He looked over at Brathwaite, who was sitting cross-legged on the floor with a glass of cider in his hand. Brathwaite had not spoken once in the time they had been there. Payne could not decide if this was from sheer lack of interest, or whether it was a Cambridge pose of god-like detachment which Brathwaite had picked up with his bow tie at a fashionable bespoke tailor's. Whichever it was—and one was not better than the other—it was certain that Brathwaite would be of no use as an intermediary. He decided to try shock tactics.

"Look here," he said, jolly but firm, the intonation of the indulgent philosophy don, "you can't seriously pillory a whole nation. Some of the people you run into don't even know that Britain *has* colonies. Are you blaming *them*, too?" He had meant it as a rhetorical question, but this was a luxury this gathering didn't permit. Three or four voices erupted simultaneously:

"Every last fucking one," said a Jamaican voice.

"Remember Nuremberg!" said a law student from Trinidad.

But Payne, accustomed to audiences, felt confident that he was on his way to capturing this one. "And the babies?" he asked, this time not waiting to be interrupted. "Let me tell you a story, happened to me just a little over a year ago, when I was living in some dreadful digs in Notting Hill Gate. Landlady made a big fuss about let-

ting me have a room. Said I was the first of 'my people'
she'd ever had, and, depending on how I conducted myself, I might or not be the last. The old story. Claimed
she was moved by true Christian spirit, that sort of thing.
She charged me fifty percent more than the man next
door in exactly the same room. She didn't know I knew,
she didn't think I'd ever talk with him since he had been
one of the first to complain about having a wog in the
place. She didn't know that I also knew that a famous
child-murderer had lived there two years previously.
Highly respectable, my arse. So I'm around the neighborhood shopping one day when I see this truly delectable
bint coming into the grocery attached to one of those well-
clipped toy dogs. Whore, I thought right away. Lana
Turner sweater, ski-pants very tight on the haunches, big
artificial mole on the cheek. All the signs. But then, on
closer inspection, I'm not so sure. Listening to her talking
to the grocer I think she's too educated for your common
or garden whore, and Notting Hill isn't quite the place
for the better class pro. And the quality of the clothes
she was wearing. Although you never know, of course,
quality costs money and whores coin the stuff. Well, she
catches me at my investigation, and before I could turn
away and pretend I was studying the spuds she gives me
a smile. A damned nice smile. It says something on the
order of, 'Hello, fellow human being. Here we are, both
alive on a nice summer day.' Absolutely nothing whorish
about it. A marvelous, straightforward recognition of common humanity. I respond in kind, and we start talking.
She lives in the building two doors from mine. She invites me to tea. Smashing place. Pye Black Box, hundreds
of records, books all over the place, half a dozen very
decent-looking contemporary paintings of which two are
autographed and addressed to her, the whole thing looking as if it had been put together by an editor from
Vogue as the ideal pied-à-terre for a gay young aristocrat.

"What do you do, I ask very directly. Oh, I thought you knew, she says. I'm a prostitute. Obviously very successful, I say, cool as a cucumber. Yes, she says, I specialize. Rich old men who like to be beaten or to watch others fucking, that sort of thing. It's not such hard work as the regular kind and it pays loads more. Would you like to work for me, she asks. I ask her to explain. She wants me to screw her for her old men to watch through a peephole. She shows me the peephole. Very clever. Imported from the States, where they're standard issue in apartments so that the tenant can check whether he's letting a Mafia agent into his abode. I was game. I hadn't too much doing at the time, to be absolutely truthful, and she was eminently screwable. Eminently. We made an appointment and old Dacosta was there at the appointed hour ready and eager to earn his fee.

"I wasn't supposed to see the client. That's normal practice, she told me. But she let me see him, anyway. A token of her confidence in me. Through another peephole which she didn't tell her clients about. Very proper city gent, bowler, tightly rolled umbrella, and, I swear it, the *Telegraph* under his arm. He spoke to her in a very civil way. Businesslike.

"'Everything in order?' he asked. She reassured him, and he handed over five lovely large notes, tenners, one of which was marked Dacosta Payne. Beautiful. Then she comes back into the bedroom, and the city gent takes up his position. She strips, very slowly, corny stuff, the kind you get in the cheaper striptease joints. Lots of diaphanous underwear. I'm sure he couldn't have been watching with more interest than I. She was sensational. Pearly skin, like the conch shells you find at Crane Beach, smooth as a baby's arse, *pink* nipples I swear! Pink! The size of a shilling. Payne drools. She lets down her hair, great quantities of technicolor gold hair which she divides in two and strings around either side of her neck so that it comes to rest between two Mother Earth breasts, and she does a kind of Lena Horne stride over to the bed where yours truly is about to come on himself. As soon as she flops on to the bed in what I suppose is a classic movement in the game, the instrument that has been eagerly rearing up between my legs flops too. Flops and stays flopped. Never budges, no matter what she does. And she does everything there is to be done. For all of ten minutes. And then she produces this big laugh, like a tomboy, leaves me on the bed, and goes out to the gent. She apologizes very sweetly, like a grammar school mistress regretting the indisposition of her star parallel-bar performer, and hands him back the fifty quid.

" 'These things happen,' he says, very philosophical, and off he goes."

"Is that the end of the story?" one of the twins asked, a wicked but not unfriendly grin on his face.

"Yes, more or less," Payne replied, "but . . ." He was interrupted by the Jamaican again.

"What's the moral? Every story got to have a moral."

Payne was clearly upset now. The taut line that creased the skin of his forehead might have been a sign of anger with great difficulty suppressed. It might have been panic: There is no infallible dictionary of facial expressions.

"Of course there's a moral, if you would only give me half-a-chance." Again Payne was cut short, this time by laughter, the kind of laughter that precedes a booing, although this time no one spoke. Now he seemed to be pleading to be heard, as if he could feel the laughter eating corrosively away at the structure of his confident exposition, and he must hurry before it tumbled down on him. "The moral is, don't categorize. Don't simplify. You risk cutting yourself off from too much that you need to know. Suppose I had succumbed to the temptation of dismissing that girl as a hoity-toity English whore? I would have been cutting myself off from any possible under-

standing. She wasn't your 'typical English whore.' Your
typical English whore or your typical Jamaican whore
would have thrown me out on my bum right there and
then. This girl simply laughed. She had me in the most
humiliating of all possible situations, and she simply
laughed. Don't you see what I'm trying to say?"

"What you're trying to say is that everything was all
right afterwards?" It was the twin, a brown young man
cut after the lanky pattern of Brathwaite, who wrote un-
rhymed poetry during classes at the London School of
Economics and pulled his thin lips tight when he wanted
to imitate Payne's languid intonation. "The old cock remembered how to come to attention? And all was forgiven?" He waited for Payne to respond, but Payne was
impassive now. He saw he was fighting a losing battle.
"I suppose you would like us to love the man, too, the
client, a human being like us, we shouldn't be contemptuous, there but for the grace of God, dust to dust, all is
vanity. Boy, you is bullshitter fatha!"

"I'm trying to say," Payne began again, speaking like a
man chinning himself for the eighteenth time, "that the
human condition does not admit the possibility of the individual dealing with his fellow human being in the mass.
That it is the duty of people who have a little sophistication or education to take his fellow human beings one by
one. That is all I'm really trying to say." He had miraculously managed to recover a good part of the dignity
which had been finely shredded and tossed around that
grim cold cell and Kevin, the vocal twin, now looked at
him very intently, as if suddenly two or three familiar
sounds had issued from a man who all along had been
speaking an obscure Tibetan dialect.

"But, man, *they* don't see *you!* They don't see us,
Brother Payne. For them we are indivisible and invisible
to rass!"

"Tell him, Kevin, tell him!" It was the Jamaican again,

a six-footer who was built like a stevedore, a student at
the Royal Academy of Dramatic Art. "Tell the rass man
wha' really happenin' in Babylon." The Jamaican spoke
with leaden irony, his smile like a whip upraised.

"The Saga of Thames Ditton, you mean, Rasta Man?"
Kevin asked, "That is heavy stuff, man, heavy stuff."

"Tell him!" the Jamaican insisted.

"It's your story, Rasta Man. But if you really want to
have it told by a spokesman worthy of the tale, I'll oblige.
Very well, then. Our big-boned friend here has a professor of speech and deportment and suchlike things who is
pining after our friend's ass, right? I mean the broad
backside you see spread-eagled on the ground here before you. It is quite an expanse of ass, you'll agree. But
gadzooks and odsblood, the aforesaid professor has in his
home on the Thames a *truly delectable* bint whom he took
to wife by some glorious misfeasance of providence lo
these four or five years. The plot thickeneth? What can
a professor who really prefers big-assed Jamaican men
do about his slim-shanked Scottish spouse?"

"Open season on Scottish spouse!" somebody shouted.

"Oh, shut your ass," said Kevin without rancor. "The
professor went back to the pre-Keynesian norms. Barter.
You see my drift? Thus, after much circumscription and
many private, extracurricular meetings which he arranged
with our hero in order *soi-disant* to help him out with his
difficulties of adaptation to the requirements of RADA,
the old prof arranged to have our hero spend a weekend
at his house in Thames Ditton."

"Man, you're spoilin' the story. He ain't use no circumscription or no circum-nothing to speak of. Him tell me
plain one afternoon say make we go down to Thames
Ditton spend the weekend and him ready to *guarantee*
him wife go find me as captivating as him already tell
me him find me. You want him give me an engagement
ring make the thing clearer than that?"

"Is who telling this story, brother man? As I was saying, our hero accepts the barbed invitation and hies him
to Thames Ditton."

"Matter of absolute fact, I hadn't too much doing at
the time," the Jamaican broke in again, mimicking
Payne's speech almost as well as Kevin.

"Sooo, the Creature is something to behold," Kevin
continued.

"Juicy, man, *juicy!* Wastin' away by the river," the
Jamaican added.

"And *ready!* No sooner his foot hit the threshold than
the prof claims he has some shopping to do in the village
and he leaves our hero alone with the maiden. And it
isn't long afterwards that the prof-ess. . . ."

"Two minutes afterwards, man. Two minutes. A few
remarks on the weather and WHAM!"

"The prof rapidly, very rapidly, dispatches his shopping,
whereas our Jamaican friend is still in the middle of his
merchandise when the prof returns, *whereat* the prof
catches him. Right in the middle of the whereat."

It was obvious that the story was known to most of the
others; there was something of ritual in their laughter
and their muttered comments as Kevin spoke. The Jamaican himself followed the recital with impatience, his head
cocked at a mock angle of critical attention like an experienced acolyte at a rehearsal for Palm Sunday service.
He broke in again now, his whole body shaking under an
implosion of sacred laughter.

"Him open the door *with a key,* man. The whole thing
look as if it planned. Timing perfect. Every movement
blocked by a master. I hear the noise and I turn me head
sharp-sharp and there he is in his form-fitting tweeds
looking down apologetically at me from the door. 'Pray
don't let me disturb you,' he say, 'just wanted to see if
everything was all right. Could I . . . might I . . . join in
the . . . ah . . . fun?' Me done catch on long time, so me

tell him no, not just yet, very polite. Him go out with tail between him legs." He broke off as the laughter burst out of him in a paroxysm that doubled him up on the floor. Kevin, who was sitting next to him, patted him on the back with the negligent gesture of a mother burping her seventh baby, and continued speaking through the spreading crisis of laughter.

"That, me dear sir, was the pattern for the whole weekend, Rasta brushing the Creature and the prof pleading vainly for an ancillary role in the celebrations. We don't need to seek far to imagine the precise configuration of the role the prof had in mind."

"Punchline, Kev, give the man the punchline," Rasta said through his laughter.

"Well, a few weeks later, Rasta overhears the prof at a party saying that all the West Indians and Africans in the school ought to concentrate on *dance,* not drama. 'Drama calls for too much subtlety,' the prof says. '*Their* forte is *movement.* They're so utterly *animal!'* "

"So true," said Rasta. "And, as the man said, *il faut cultiver son jardin.* That is why I had no problems of, shall we say, an erectile nature." He was looking straight at Payne as he spoke. "If my memory serves me. You see, being what I am, I have a rule. Whenever you see pussy, whichever side it coming from, my rule is to Think Big." He kept his face rigid with solemnity as he spoke, and Payne felt himself impaled on a spike of ridicule and humiliation far sharper at that moment than when, an incalculable fraction of a second later, the great raucous hurricane of general laughter broke upon him.

Chapter Three

It was a job that took me to Nigeria in 1954. Which is to say that I was offered a junior editorial post on an English-owned, English-language newspaper. Which does not by any means explain why I should have gone to Nigeria in the first place. I am, of course, hedging, begging the question, chinxing—as they say in Trinidad. Because I am not sure that I know the answer to this question that I have asked myself so many hundreds of times.

All the same I wasn't the only West Indian of my generation making some sort of pilgrimage to West Africa in the 1950s. . . .

Answer the question.

A fortuitous combination of curiosity and opportunity. . . .

What kind of curiosity?

Er . . . um . . .

Answer the question!

A kind of gravity pull of atavism . . . ?

ANSWER THE QUESTION, MAN!

A growing suspicion that, contrary to the information

I had received, human perfection might conceivably be found elsewhere than in the person of the Englishman; a growing uncertainty about the concept (absorbed as easily and automatically into my Barbadian consciousness as solar vitamins were absorbed into my body) that the highest form attainable by the black human being was that of the black Englishman; an inexplicable (*EVERY-THING IS EXPLICABLE, DAMMIT!*), well, a desire not explicable in orthodox terms of enlightened self-interest, economic or career benefits, or personal ambition to experience existence in the place where most of my forefathers experienced their existence. . . .

"Most" of your ancestors?

After three hundred years who the hell knows where *all* of his ancestors came from? To continue: . . . their existence, and to see some of the undetribalized descendants of those ancestors in their native social and geographical setting. . . .

A kiss-me-ass back-to-Africa romantic, in other words?

Ah, well, if you put it that way. . . .

Answer the question!

Well, if you insist, yes, dammit. But, I mean, I wasn't the only one. . . . *You went for the money, man. For the comfort. In search of ease. Catching your royal ass in freezing London, cooking on a shilling-meter one-burner stove, smarting in your hypersensitive soul from the slings and arrows of racial contempt in the white man's country, shit-scared to go back home to face the uncertainties of starting a career, you plumped for what you hoped would be the fairly fat life of the semi-imperialist, the black "expat" who lived almost though not quite as well as the white expat (ready to console yourself with the fiction that the difference made you a martyr—a shameful, filthy moral plaster for your festering cowardice) with the result that you were right back where you started, playing your old role of near-Englishman again.*

GET OFF MY FUCKING BACK!

Chapter Four

I arrived in Lagos with a list of "useful people to know." At the hard core of this roll call were, for good and sufficient tribal reasons, the names of three prospering West Indians, two lawyers and one businessman. One of the lawyers was in Warri, which, when one is in Lagos, is farther away from Lagos than when one is in London. The businessman, a lean Trinidadian in his sixties, who had made a small fortune in the dry-cleaning business, invited me to luncheon on my first Sunday. His house in Yaba, a two-storied affair of massive appearance, was built, I guessed, to no more demanding specifications than that it be bigger than anything else in the neighborhood for at least thirty years after construction. In its half-acre compound was a single-story complex of garages and servants' quarters about six times the size of the room and parlor that I had taken at 10 Alade Street. His name was Alexander Quesnel, and the initials AQ were filigreed in stone along the length of the first-floor verandah of the house.

"I hope you don't think this is any picnic here in this country, boy," he said when we were seated at the long, solid-shanked mahogany table in the dining room. "I been catching my royal ass in this country for thirty years

just trying to keep my head above water." His voice retained the singsong Trinidadian intonation with which he
had arrived. "When the white man ain't jumping in your
skin, it's the African. I don't know which one is the
worst." His wife, the plump Yoruba-speaking bastard of
an even earlier West Indian diaspora, was not sitting with
us. She waddled around, a smiling headslave, making
certain that the right quantities of food were being dished
up to us. Quesnel and I were the only diners, and only
half the table was covered by a spotless damask cloth.

"The West Indians here ain't a damn bit better, believe
me. All they got is envy. If they see you with a shirt a
little better quality than they wearing, they ready to tell
the world you taking bribe. A jealous bunch of bitches.
Soon as I catch myself, I packing up everything here, and
I gone back to San Fernando."

That left me the Lagos lawyer. He came to the *Sun* to
see me even before I got around to telephoning him.
The first word that came to my mind as he walked in was
"jolly." He was a man of about thirty-five, the kind of
brown-skinned West Indian mixture that I always imagine as belonging in a white tussore suit and a panama
hat. But for the slight negroid wrinkle in the hair and
that special untannable yellow in the skin, he might have
been one of those Hollywood figures who flit from bar to
bar in some steamy Central American republic just before the banana boat departs and the revolution arrives.

"Brathwaite! How're you, boy? Auguste!" He pronounced his name as if it were spelled O'Geese. We
shook hands and he sat down in my lone visitor's chair.
"Eustace wrote to say you should be here about now.
How you settling in?" He seemed very pleased with himself, and quite pleased to see me.

"Can't you get out of this office for half-an-hour? Let's
go and have a drink in the Embassy."

We walked the three hundred yards to the accompaniment of a tourist-guide commentary from Auguste. He pointed out Ayo's Bar and Refreshment Center and told me in lowered tones and without a trace of jocularity that Ayo had two air-conditioned bedrooms above the bar that could be hired at an hour's notice. I said I knew. He burst out laughing and slapped me on the shoulder.

"Boy, you only been here a week?" He pointed now to the lush compound of the Alatishe family which nestled incongruously between the magistrate's court and the Methodist church.

"I suppose you know all about that, too," he said. I told him I knew only the name of the owners, the Alatishes, and the name of the house, Mango Lodge, which was written in enormous gilt lettering on the iron gate, taller than a man, which stood open before us. Thirty yards of lawn, scarcely wider than the gates, ended at a small fountain, around which neat beds of zinnia and marigold fought a losing battle with the heat for their dignity. The house itself, well-protected by giant mango trees with leaves black-rimmed by anthracnose, was a brave old relic. White, wooden trellises covered a deep verandah. A brass knocker stood gleamingly at attention on the polished mahogany door. This and the four windows of the upper story, white and with deep ledges, made for sitting and sipping on, was all one could see, yet it all made a definite three-dimensional impact so that you could almost see the heavy old furniture and the faded daguerreotypes and the fragile maiden aunts behind the façade.

"The Alatishes, that is real African class, boy. You don't believe it, eh? This town has one or two people with real class. You're surprised? Man, when you really get to know the African here, you'll be even more surprised. Talk about aristocracy! Not like England, I don't mean that. But people like the Alatishes, that's the real thing here." We moved slowly through the morning heat, engrossing as a bath, to the dark frontage of the Embassy.

Auguste ordered two beers as expansively as if they were magnums of champagne and continued his exegesis.

"This is a hell of a country, boy. You have to sweat just to breathe! People like us, people like us, we should get pioneer status the way industries get it. I mean, you look back—you must know this already, you're a journalist—the West Indians have done a hell of a lot to build up this country. But don't fool yourself. They ain't grateful. Far from it. People like the Alatishes, one minute they're telling you how you're an *omowale*, that's Yoruba, 'child who has come back home,' but just you look as if you're keeping your head above water and, bam! They're ready to tell you how you're a foreigner just like the *oyibo*, worse, man, worse. You have to watch yourself around here, you hear what I tell you, Brathwaite, boy. The English out for you, and the natives out for you."

In his first briefing, the day after I arrived, Kippins, my baby-faced English boss, had said to me, "On this newspaper we never spell 'jail' g-a-o-l. Always j-a-i-l. And we never use the word 'native.' Not even when it would be perfectly correct."

Chapter Five

Auguste was pompous. It went, in a way, with his physique, florid, running precociously downhill into obesity. I had the fancy that his body was assiduously transforming into carbohydrates all the protein it ingested, much as his spirit appeared capable of converting into banality every element in the surely extraordinary life he was living in Nigeria.

It was one of the Alatishe family who impaled him on a definitive adjective. With due irony, this was on the first evening he took me to their house. Auguste had prepared the occasion with great *brio*, warning me about a week in advance that a possible invitation was in the wind, and then calling up in the early evening of the very day for which it had been issued.

"Can you come to my place in half-an-hour?" he asked on the phone. "Properly dressed," he added. He explained that Lady Ogunbiade, who was one of the Alatishes, was having a "levee" in honor of one of her daughters who had just returned from England. The day had been fixed, with an imprecision as great as "the-sighting-of-the-new-moon" at Bairam, in relation to the arrival of the mailboat from Liverpool. The guest of

27

honor was returning from a three-month holiday, he explained, and the Alatishes always had a levee when one
of the family returned from abroad. He made it clear that
he was doing me a very great favor in slipping me in almost literally on his coattails, and I very nearly refused
the backhanded invitation. However, reflecting that he
didn't have to ask me, I agreed.

Penetrating the house was an exercise in déjà vu. Behind the mahogany door I did indeed find the heavy mahogany furniture, the fading, rather authoritative-looking
rugs, the oval photographs of bespectacled Edwardian
black men and beruffled Victorian black women, the
white-gloved serving men, that I had sensed from thirty
yards away.

But the identification did not lessen the shock. It
seemed to have a liberating and lightening effect, the
equivalent, I suppose, of two quick doubles on an empty
stomach. Everything seemed not quite life-size, whether
larger or smaller I cannot say. It was as if I were seeing
an extraordinarily realistic play in which I was taking
part from within the audience.

There was even a maiden aunt, frail enough to seem
part of my personal fiction. Her name, like that of my
grandmother, was Matilda. It seemed a delightful and
almost bizarre coincidence, and my voice must have rung
with a somewhat childish wonder as I told her of it, for
she looked at me as if uncertain of my sanity.

"There were many women named Matilda in the last
century. There are many women named Elizabeth in this
century." It was not dismissive; the tone was that of
someone who, while not capable of bearing fools gladly,
was prepared to wait a few minutes before deciding that
one was a fool. I perceived this from afar and knowing,
this evening above all, that I was a long way from being
a fool, persevered.

"My grandmother's name was Mary Anna Matilda," I

said. "It isn't just a question of one name, but how the names are put together. Elizabeth Anna Matilda would be a nineteenth-century combination, but Susan Elizabeth would be definitely twentieth century. That's the kind of thing I meant."

She laughed, and gave herself away. She was probably nearly seventy, a little woman with hard bones that showed through the lace dress and a frizzly white top for a head, hair shorter than my own. But that laugh was the laugh of a woman laughing with a man, the laugh of a seasoned sex conspirator. Somehow I felt certain that through the thickets of age and menopause and culture I had flushed out the woman her contemporaries had known. I could have said anything to her at that moment, including an invitation to go to bed. It was an intimation of intimacy that made me feel both uncomfortable and triumphant. How can there be any human experience more exciting than the shock of making contact with another human being? If it is not possible to say that we fell in love with each other at that moment, I am not responsible for the circumscription of language that makes it so.

"My names are Matilda Ayodele Olashade Oluremi Alatishe. You wish to offer an interpretation of that combination?" We laughed happily together. "You like champagne?" I made a face to show that champagne didn't especially move me. "There is some that is very good. That is not what they are serving. Come with me and we shall find champagne that you will like." She took my arm and we walked along a corridor to a huge kitchen. Two waiters were standing patiently while their trays were filled with glasses and canapés. Matilda spoke in Yoruba to a large woman in a high-collared black dress who was obviously a kind of housekeeper. A bottle was produced from one of the two man-sized refrigerators and opened.

"Don't sip. You must drink mouthfuls. That's better. Cheers. Bola, tell these people to serve this master from that bottle, *sh'ogbo?*" Bola gave a brief nod which assured me that my special status was registered for all future occasions. She was clearly accustomed to Matilda's steely caprices.

"The story is that my father and my mother gave me the three Yoruba names at the naming ceremony," Matilda went on, leading me out again. "But my father's brother was an Anglican deacon. So he wanted his brother's child to have a Christian name. Christian? What I should say is that he wanted to baptize me, he wanted me to have an *oyibo* name. So this man, he not only gives me this *oyibo* name, he makes it the *first* name. My father was properly vexed! But he had to take it. What could he do? Make a scandal in the big European church and disgrace his poor brother?"

We were back in the concourse. The band had started to play a fox trot in a rigid Germanic rhythm and with fairly approximate harmonies. It was ridiculous, but I wanted to dance with Matilda and, looking at her, I knew that she wanted to dance with me. Of such is the Kingdom of Sex.

"Have you met the guest of honor?" she asked. I had not. "There she is, dancing with your friend Auguste. I went to boarding school in Sierra Leone, from the age of eleven to eighteen. That's why I'm never too sure of my Yoruba. I think my English is pretty good. Is it? You should know. You don't have an African language to confuse you."

"Your English is West African. But it's rather good, of its kind," I said judiciously, like a highly paid wine taster.

"*Om'ota!*"

I didn't know what it meant. "It's unfair to insult me in a foreign language," I said.

"I can say it in Yoruba, but a lady would never say it

in English. Mrs. Weekes's school in Freetown was called
'The Ladies' Academy.' We learned sewing, deportment,
English, Latin, French, and arithmetic. But sewing and
deportment came first. I have done many things, but I
cannot say the word for *om'ota* in English. In Sierra
Leone we would call your friend 'a consequential man.'"

Without knowing the nuances she implied, I found the
word to be totally apt. His choosing to dance a fox trot
was "consequential"; the way he moved was "consequential"; I suppose even his being at the levee was a "consequential" act.

"The Alatishe family is consequential, if you wish an
idea of what I mean." She laughed. In truth, her laugh
was like a cackle. "Not all. I was considered a bad girl in
my day." She pulled me down to whisper in my ear. "I
once ran away with a man. A Danish seaman. We lived
together in Cardiff for two years. A bad girl!"

It didn't surprise me, of course. It was obvious that she
was not consequential.

"I should not tell you this, but I think Tola is like me."
She indicated Auguste's partner. "I don't know. I don't
know her well. Her mother Morenike is my niece, the
daughter of my brother Segun. That Morenike was a very
consequential child, fat and extremely greedy. After her
husband died she came back here to live, but we cannot
bear each other. She finally withdrew to one of her husband's properties. The result is that I scarcely know her
children. I don't know any young people at all. Except
Tola. A little. She chose to live here when she came back
from England. That's why the levee is being held here."

The dance ended and Auguste came over to where we
were standing.

"Hello, Miss Matilda," he said in his jolly way. "You
letting all that good music go to waste?"

"When I used to dance that would have been too slow
for me," she said. "Tola, this is Mr. Brathwaite. Another

ajerike like Mr. Auguste. My niece, Mrs. Ayodele." Before our handshake was finished Miss Matilda said, "I am going to my bed. Enjoy yourselves."

"Thanks for the champagne, Miss Matilda," I said. "It is certainly different from the ones I've tasted."

"That is because it is much, much better. Goodnight." She went off through the single corridor.

"She's a fabulous old lady," Auguste said. "You know what *ajerike* means? Sugar-cane eater. That's what they call West Indians."

"Yes, I know," I said. It was true, but I was not above taking pleasure in irritating Auguste even though, consequential as Miss Matilda and I might consider him, he was making a real effort to be my friend with no motive, so far as I could see, beyond that of friendliness.

"How long have you been in Lagos, Mr. Brathwaite?" It was a banal enough question, an elementary gambit of meaningless social intercourse. I cannot explain why it seemed to me to be one of the most important questions I had ever been asked. I started to answer, but the simple words of response seemed to clash together in my palate and refuse to come out in the order I wanted.

"He's a newcomer, Tola, a Johnny-just-come. Two weeks, no more. I bet you didn't know that there were *ajerikes* as black as Brathwaite, did you? He could be a Yoruba, don't you think?" Auguste had taken charge, with a jolly joke, and I could have hit him in his fluent, jocular mouth.

Chapter Six

It didn't take me long to find out about Tola and Auguste. Bits and pieces of gossip, sometimes disguised as news, come to journalists in the ordinary way of business and without one's actually noticing cohere into useful formations. So I learned that Tola's husband was a perpetual law student and had been an acquaintance of Auguste's at the Inns of Court ten years before; that Tola had graduated from university in London and taken a diploma in journalism while her husband "ate his dinners"; that their marriage was more or less at an end on the (to her husband and his family) face-saving grounds of *her* barrenness; and that Auguste would not be averse to joining the Alatishe family when the marriage was officially declared at an end. And all this without a word from Auguste himself.

My reaction to hearing his name coupled so casually, so naturally, with hers was not just surprise, which would have been normal enough, but indignation, a sense of a grave, almost intolerable affront done to me, personally. I remember this now with perfect clarity, and it is easy, now, to see with perfect clarity what it signified.

Auguste and I continued to meet frequently enough. He

sought me out with that surprising unselfishness he had shown ever since my arrival. Taking me almost casually under his wing, he introduced me into the large demi-monde, that half-submerged social milieu that is to be found in all large cities where the displaced bachelors of both sexes seek, at differing prices, their differing kinds of accommodation.

Auguste was a member in excellent standing of the milieu. At the Imperial, one of the most popular centers of this thriving subculture, the girls would come to his table and bring their own drinks. Two or three of them would sit with us, and there was never any sense of even latent competition. They were simply pleased to see him and sit with him.

"So, Lati, your friend lawyer Ogun done married *pata pata* and left you. *O ma she o!*" He was a master of pidgin English and night-club Yoruba.

"No mind am, Mr. Auguste. That no be marriage proper. I done know that titi wey he marry *ti pe, ti pe!*" She clicked her thumb and middle finger above her head to emphasize the scarcely conceivable duration of the acquaintanceship. "She get breasts small, small so, like a puppy!" Lati and the other girls bent double laughing, hands pounding the metal table in ecstasy. "You know when puppy born, male, female, all get breasts wey look like spots on half-caste face? Na so she stay!"

"*O ma she o!* Na lie, Lati!" said one of the girls through her laughter, more to provoke than to contradict.

"To God! She navel big past she *omu!* She pappy get money plenty. Na that wey catch Ogun. He still know wey my house dey."

Auguste obviously had a good reputation at the Imperial. The girls trusted him and would sometimes ask advice on all kinds of topics about which a lawyer and sophisticated man-about-Lagos could be expected to know, about a young sister in nursing school, about land-

lord problems, once about an offer from a Frenchman to
a girl called Abike that she come and live in his house in
Dahomey while his wife was on six months' holiday in
France.

Abike was, even for the girls of the Imperial, rather
special. She was a tall, big-boned, copper-colored woman
of part-Fulani descent, who had been brought to Lagos
from the North by a young English district officer about
six years previously. He had soon learned that what was
good enough for Kabba was not quite good enough for
the Lagos European Club. He dropped her as he was
bound to, but Abike had decided not to go back to Kabba
just yet. She must have been about thirty when I first saw
her; the hips and waist had thickened and altogether she
was a little too solid for my taste. But this very solidity
gave her an air of great dignity; she was the only one of
the "girls" whom one instinctively thought of as a
woman.

She seemed to exert a particular spell on the English.
She was always slipping away with some pale-faced
bachelor who was on his first tour of duty or some
middle-aged business executive whose wife was "away in
England putting the children to school." Her diffident
swains would come and sit in a corner with the slightly
cringing demeanor of vegetarians obliged to be present
at a barbecue. A message would be given with great cir-
cumspection to the waiter, who would in his own good
time go over to Abike and announce in ringing Yoruba:
"Abike, that white man over there in the corner with goat
features wants you to go and sleep with him tonight."
The table would laugh, Abike would look over at the
man for a while, and, if she liked his face and was free,
she would say, "Tell him that I drink whisky and kola
tonic." The drink would be served, Abike would drink it
deliberately, accept a dance or two from other men if
asked, and then get to her feet with a bit of a swagger,

unwind and rewind her *lappa,* and say slow goodnights to her friends at all the tables on her way to the exit.

This queenly woman seemed to have tremendous faith in Auguste. He met my curiosity about their relationship with a series of bland explanations that left me unconvinced. He claimed that he had never slept with her, which was quite possible, since it was a claim which he made about few of the girls I met at the Imperial with him. He had done her some unspecified "good turn" when she had first come to the Imperial. But he was always doing the girls good turns. He could frequently and without meanness have told them that he made his living from the kind of advice they were asking and invited them to come to his chambers where his iron-hearted clerk would have extracted the usual substantial fees. The most revealing remark he ever permitted himself was a model of ambivalence: "Abike ain't like the rest of the girls. She has class. You see that color she has? That's Arab blood." A surprising delicacy kept him from pursuing this line of thought. I, after all had the same "blood" as "the rest of the girls." He ended by saying that sometimes he had to stop himself from thinking of her as a "lady."

It wasn't long before I became a full participant in the double life of the semi-expatriate community we West Indians constituted, with one foot reasonably planted in the levee-giving, bridge-playing, English-educated, Lagos bourgeoisie, and the other in that half-lit *banlieue* of clerks and club-girls which centered around places like the Imperial. I visited the Alatishe house on my own. I went to the Imperial on my own. There were one or two girls who brought their drinks to *my* table. Miss Matilda now spoke of Auguste only as "your consequential friend from St. Lucia," giving me the feeling that I had my own *locus standi* at Mango Lodge. Tola's laughter when his name was mentioned seemed deliciously disloyal to a

man who was almost a recognized, official suitor. I had
no sense of myself being disloyal to him. No doubt some
psychosexual calculus was at work, some absurd amal-
gam of my Barbadian puritanism and the aboriginal ruthlessness every man has from the moment the chase
begins. After all, what right had he, a hardened habitué
of the Imperial, to the friendly decencies when a girl like
Tola was in question?

Abike had gone off to Dahomey. Auguste had told her,
"Girl, I don't know. I got French blood. My father's
father came from Marseilles. Them French don't play! If
that man takes you to Cotonou and his wife was to come
back suddenly and catch you in the house, you never can
tell what might happen. The wife could give you one hell
of a beating-up and *then* call the police. And you don't
even speak French. You wouldn't even know how many
months in jail they give you by the time they through."

The counseling session took place in full conclave.
Everybody knew about the offer that Abike had received,
and they all knew that she would ask Auguste's advice
as soon as he came in. There were about six girls at the
table, and one of the older waiters was half-pretending
to wipe around the glasses.

"That's what I done tell am, Mr. Auguste," the waiter
said in a low voice. "I see them French people too much
when I was working near Idiroko. The black ones just as
bad as the white ones. That no be country for Lagos people to go. Trouble dey too plenty!"

"Eh, heh! I done tell am so!" said one of the girls.
"This Abike, she like white man too much!"

"*Dake' mbe!* Shut your mouth! Excuse me, Mr. Auguste, these people too ignorant! Aie! Festus, him dey
talk like a proper Bushman. No mind am. Na Ibo man.
You don't know they speak Yoruba for Dahomey?
T'olorun! If to say the white people speaking French,
that is no problem!" Abike spoke with more animation

than was usual with her, but on this point she was right.
She could at least make herself understood among the
Yoruba diaspora on the "French side." But the members
of the counseling group would not give her a hearing.

" 'That is no problem!' Eh, heh, you think say you be a
Volkswagen? 'No problem!' Sissy, hear the lawyer, I beg
you, *e'jo!*"

Auguste was very judicial. He admitted that Abike had
a point about the language. But he pointed out that he
had *not* said that she ought not to go. "It isn't for me to
tell you to go or not to go. That is your own decision."

"Eh, hehhh!" A deep sigh of triumph and vindication
from Abike accompanied by a look that called for con--
tinued silence while Auguste spoke.

"If you go, ·it won't take long to find out if you like it
or not. If you don't like it, you come back. Matter finish!"

"Eh, hehhh! Thank you, Mr. Auguste. These girls. I no
know say what them dey think. I no be little pikin just
come out for bush wey dey fear the first rabbit wey jump
in the grass." Abike stood up, pushed her chair back, and
unwound and rewound her *lappa*. "Thank you, Mr.
Auguste. When I done make up my mind, I go let *you*
know." She came down hard on the "you," shook· Auguste's hand and then mine, and walked with regal gait
to her table.

She went. It was possible that she had something of the
same affinity for white men that they had for her. Perhaps it was an aesthetic quirk, of the sort some men have
about redheads or tall women. Or some sentimental
hangover from her days with her district officer in Kabba.
Perhaps it was no more—or no less—than a tendency to
professional specialization.

She went at a time when my relationship with Auguste
was in one of those periodic troughs which occur even in
real friendships when one or the other partner, con-
sciously or not, is reassessing—to put it no higher—the use
of his time.

Auguste and I had literally not seen each other for weeks; I cannot recall which side had initiated the infinitesimal chill that lay on the routine of our acquaintanceship. I still frequented the Imperial, but so much in my own right now that none of the girls felt called upon to remark on Auguste's absence on any night I might chance to drop in. That was a private concern; the waiters and the girls were conscious of my private and separate existence, and had, I supposed, elevated me from the status of "that other *ajerike*" to that of "Mr. Brathwaite," something almost equal—but, of course, not quite equal— to "Mr. Auguste."

Abike was in the public domain. Thus it was Maria, the statuesque Itsekiri girl whom I liked because her pockmarks made her shy and therefore far less formidable than she looked, who told me about the departure in a serial recounting that lasted through a session at the Imperial practically until the very moment I clicked home the fasteners on her Maidenform brassiere the next morning.

For Abike's departure to Dahomey had, necessarily, the quality of legend. Other girls had gone off before; Maria herself, still a convinced Catholic, had been "housekeeper" to a Jesuit priest in the Gold Coast for more than a year. "I go take a taxi to Kano" was the girls' classic way of saying that they were on the point of finding a wealthy protector in some far-off place. But everything about Abike's departure was on a different scale.

"I do not understand the girl," Maria said to me. She spoke better English than most of the girls at the Imperial. "If you see the loads she pack to the French country! Aie!" She clapped her hands softly in wonder. "And the man, the Frenchman, he say, my wife is returning in four months; you will come with me for that time, finish. *Aburo,* she have provision for four *years!*"

The man sent a black Citroen with chauffeur across the border to take her to Cotonou. "The loads fill the car, eh! The driver has to tie some on the top of the car!"

Abike had also given a farewell party, for women only. "Chicken, goat, steak *beaucoup!* She bring one *agidigbo* band from Ikorodu. You know Taiwo? That is the one. Gin, whisky, beer! I never see that! Everybody say it better past *komojade*. Lande make a big joke. 'Wey side the baby?' she ask. Eh! I never laugh so!"

The laughter did not last long. By Maria's account the whole affair had been stage-managed to a degree of almost professionalism. "Everybody get very happy, they say how it is good to have men but better to enjoy yourselves without them, and all that. The party was fine, fine! And just when we are enjoying the thing Abike stop the music. She make a speech. I for done leave the place one time. I know she want to spoil our happiness." I swear that, retelling this part of her story, Maria made a *moue*. I thought of girls in a convent, at high tea, nuns even, forgetting for delicious minutes the rigors of daily life, suddenly brought back to earth—or is it heaven?—by the Mother Superior's call to prayer.

"She begin one long speech about how life is a road full of corners. Plenty Yoruba proverbs. 'Only the man at the top of the palm tree can see the lion two miles away.' *O ma she o!* When she finish, eh, heh! everybody is crying. It is like a funeral for a young man. All this time the chauffeur is waiting not far away. And, just like that, Abike disappear, and we don't know where she is. She is gone! She leave ten pounds in the parlor and she is gone to Cotonou! She never say goodbye self!"

Abike knew her friends, of course. The ten pounds was more than enough to pay the rent and the orchestra, and it was left to the girls to take care of chairs and dressing tables and the goat, and to pay the boy who cleaned the rented room-and-parlor. But even Maria, who thought Abike rather tended to give herself airs, never expressed anything but admiration for the *style* of the thing.

"That Abike!" she said more than once, shaking her head the way a mother might do at the exploits of her delinquent genius son.

Chapter Seven

Abike's return to Lagos followed with passionate fidelity the scenario that Auguste had sketched out at the Imperial. She came back by mammy lorry, she was almost in rags, she was dirty, and she bore the marks of a fair amount of brutality.

"It was the wife of that Frenchman. Just as Mr. Auguste done say." Maria clapped her hands softly several times in quick succession as she said this. It was a gesture of wonderment I had seen my mother make in faraway St. Michael, Barbados. "Some of the woman's friends wrote to her and say how the husband has an African woman living for the house. So she came back secretly and she go to the Governor self. Softly, softly, the police came to the house and they arrest Abike." She spoke of these doings in a foreign land as she might have recounted a folk tale to a child. For an instant, an indignant, middle-aged Frenchwoman was transformed into a pale, vengeful ghost riding the airwaves from a distant land of snow and slipping by a secret passage into the Governor's castle at dead of night. She hisses spitefully into his ear and, lo, come daybreak, trusty beadles, the terror of the countryside, go forth bearing a magnificent scroll upon which

42

Abike's crime is penned in the severe cursive of the medieval Italian chanceries.

"She was in *jail* for *four days!*" Maria had, unprecedently, come to 10 Alade Street, breaking the unwritten rule that the Imperial girls so rigorously observed of never visiting a client except by express invitation. Monday, my houseboy, had visibly sniffed. Maria, at 6:00 P.M. when the sun is still a sizable red ball over the Marina and the light meter reading in my room-and-parlor is f5.6 at 1/125th, is a rather fat young woman whose fish-tail dress is whorishly tight around the hips and the too-ample belly, whose calling is obvious in every hobbled, slightly knock-kneed step she takes. But she had made the journey from her thin-walled room on the Ikorodu Road to tell me of Abike's misfortune, and I refused to be an accessory to Monday's sniff because I thought I understood why she had come and was flattered. She was telling me that I was her friend, her Auguste, and if the day should ever come when my greater knowledge of the world, of Frenchmen and other phenomena, could be of use to her, then she would hear my words and value them.

"Four days!" she reported. "Yay! I cannot tell you the things those French have done to my sister. And the black ones are the most bad," she added, as if stating a fact that she knew was obvious to me but had only recently been brought home to her. "In the end the man, that man with his Citroen, he send her some money and the police take her to the border and give her ten shillings and say 'Go!' as you say to a dog." Having transmitted her communiqué, she accepted a demure vermouth and left for work.

Abike had, of course, gone straight to Auguste's house. I wondered, futilely, about his reaction that evening when he opened the door; futilely because I simply didn't know the man well enough. I had not the slightest clue about his feelings toward Abike before, none about his whole conception of himself. Did he feel in some perverse way responsible, did he wonder whether he had owed it to himself or to her to advise her unequivocally against the Dahomey experiment? Or did he feel some sense of triumph—surely a permissible piece of perverseness—that his implied warning had not been heeded? Or—this was the wildest sort of speculation—had he with Machiavellian subtlety somehow planned it all this way?

Auguste's demeanor with me positively provoked speculation. Having stayed clear of me for all of three months, he chose a time about a fortnight after Abike's return to come to my office. He was his jolly, bland, complacent self of old, a fairly spectacular achievement for a man who was currently starring in one of the juiciest scandals in years.

"Brathwaite, boy, what's happening? What's become of you these days? You must be up to no good!" He was in excellent spirits, and there was not a trace of irony to be detected in his hearty cross-examiner's voice. Without pausing to give me breath, he swept me off to the Embassy remarking as we passed the Alatishe house that I must know the place like the back of my hand by now. There was something like resignation in his voice, but this may have been my imagination.

At the Embassy he proceeded to tell me about Abike's return as if it were no more than one of his more interesting civil cases of recent days.

"She turned up at my place in a terrible state, appalling! She wasn't even wearing shoes! Can you imagine that? Abike? Boy, they gave her a real rough time over there."

"Is it true that they messed her about in the jail?" I wanted gory details; he was making it too everyday for my taste.

"Oh, I suppose so. I mean, she's a damned attractive

girl. I don't imagine they get one like that every day, do you?'' The jocularity seemed a little forced, a concession made to the public image of himself. I was immediately ready to relent.

"She's pretty tough, don't you worry. I'll bet you she took care of herself." He had obviously not wished to probe too deeply into that aspect of her sojourn in Dahomey.

"How is she now?" I asked. It looked as if he were determined to pitch our conversation on this delicious topic at the very lowest level of bromidic blandness, and, after my first sallies had been patted back over the net, I thought I might as well play along. He seemed terribly pleased by the simple question.

"Oh, boy, in great form! Great form! She is one hell of a cook, that girl. Haven't eaten like this for years. And she has those houseboys of mine well in hand. These days the house is as neat as Government House! She's fantastic!" If I let him go on in this vein, he'd soon be telling me what salary he paid her. But I couldn't now ask him outright if he'd learned the secret of her irresistibility to the flower of Great Britain and Western Europe. He hadn't even admitted that he was sleeping with her.

"She's so grateful to me it's embarrassing," he went on. "She says I shouldn't change my life because she's there." I suppose it was then that I realized that Auguste had disappeared from my sight about the time that Abike had "packed to Dahomey." And, really, if he was not to be seen at the Alatishes, at the Imperial, or at the Embassy, it meant that a radical change in his social life was taking place. So I speculated a little more. Had he been more truly in love with her than with Tola? Had Tola been simply a "correct" target for a man who considered himself eligible?

"Don't you like that? 'Don't change your life because of me.' You know, boy, I ain't tried anything, you know what I mean, but I have every reason to believe she means exactly what she says." His "I have every reason to believe" sounded mysterious rather than pompous, suggesting dimensions to their relationship that a mere journalist could not conceive. Had he had a dry run, bringing home a girl for drinks, say, and finding that Abike had faded out on cue? Had he sent her off for an evening with no explanation to see how she would take it? Had he tried a day of calling her "You whore!" without ill effects? I have never known anyone so apparently open and uncomplex as Auguste, so capable of inducing uncertainty about his superficies.

On this occasion, he drove me not only to speculation but to real rudeness as well.

"The story at the Imperial is that Abike has a very special muscular system. I hope you're coping alright," I said and instantly wished I hadn't. It was obvious that I had hurt him deeply, and it was suddenly obvious, too, why he had come to see me at this time. Despite the thick tissue of self-satisfaction that enveloped him, despite all the evidence that we were far from being kindred souls, he had felt a very particular need to talk with me, almost regardless of the price he could expect to pay for my company. I was, after all, a fellow West Indian, a fellow tribesman. His quiet reply made me feel even more stupid.

"Boy, if you had ever run into a real clutch pussy, you would know it's something to stay away from." The logic of what he said and the unaggressive—almost apologetic—way in which he said it made me wonder which of us was really the more insensitive. Naturally, I responded angrily.

"Why do you always call me 'boy'? Do I look like a boy to you?"

"I'm sorry, I'm sorry. Just a manner of speaking." My God, I thought in some more rational part of my being, I must really be the only person he has to talk to, if he's apologizing to me for that. We sat in silence for a while; I was unwilling to move or to withdraw what I had said and he, I suppose, to let go of me, his last hope of a sympathetic ear—or accent?

"She's real class, do you know that, Brathwaite?" he said after a while. "Not like some of these so-called aristocrats. Real class inside, from the marrow. You must have seen that, how she was different from the rest of the girls at the Imperial. Just from the way she walked, you could tell it." I nodded agreement. It was the least I could do, since I didn't yet feel I could go all the way to an apology.

"Do you know what she did coming back here from Dahomey? When they left her at the border with ten shillings to her name? She turned down an offer of twenty pounds for one night from the customs inspector! Twenty pounds! She said she would rather walk to Lagos! Can you beat that? Pride. My God, that's a twist, isn't it? Somehow she felt she had to come to me exactly the way she left Dahomey, so I could see just how far she had fallen. She wanted *me* to be the one to pick her up." He shook his head slowly a few times, and then grandly, back in character, ordered refills for our glasses. As we drank I had the surrealistic suspicion that he was silently drinking a toast, something like "To the Health of a Great Lady."

Chapter Eight

I suppose that by 1956, which was when Dacosta Payne swam once more into my ken, it could be said that I was *settled* in Nigeria. At least I had discovered there a few certitudes of the kind that are necessary to give minimal shape to one's life, and was living according to a rhythm that was to an agreeable extent of my own choosing and to a large extent agreeable. In the two years since my arrival I had become a competent, confident journalist, read and sometimes quoted, often recognized in public places, and once or twice mentioned by name in the debates of the House of Representatives. I was also the recipient of a charming species of begging letter that seemed to emanate exclusively from the fourth forms of secondary schools and usually began:

> Dear Mr. Brathwaite:
> Could a journalist of your eminence spare a few minutes of your doubtless valuable time to consider my case . . . ?

The "cases" were almost invariably based on a desire to know "my professional secret." I enjoyed the hint of uncertainty in "doubtless," and was touched by the as-

sumption that to every profession there is a "secret"—
one secret—susceptible of being revealed to interested in-
quirers on one half of a self-addressed (unstamped) post-
card.

Dacosta Payne's reappearance was heralded by an item
in the French agency file. "Dr. Wilfred Dacosta Payne,
the British industrial consultant" was in Togo advising
certain French-based companies on the expansion of their
investment in industrial undertakings in West Africa, a
growing field. He would be stopping over in Lagos for
discussions with "leaders of industry" in Nigeria.

I knew then, without the flicker of a doubt, that Dacosta Payne was and had all along been a fraud. The
"Dr." might have been a transmission error, or a Paris
subeditor's late-night fancy, or a genuine title *honoris
causa* from some worthy institution in Geneva or Bern.
But I knew it was phony. And the "British industrial consultant" bit: That, too, could be subeditorial slackness—
Payne is not, after all, a Hungarian name, and the man
had had some connections with Great Britain; yet, somehow, the combination of the two inoffensive elements
was for me definitive and conclusive.

What was worse, I realized that I had always known
that Payne was a fraud, a perception dating in a way
from the earliest days of our acquaintanceship, but suppressed through a childishness—and cowardliness—in me
that I was apparently only now outgrowing. Payne had
been such a glitteringly perfect piece of bronze that in
my boyish avidity to see and enjoy real gold—at almost
any cost—I had been all too ready to accept the fiction he
proposed and represented. Now, I was bitterly disappointed in myself and lavished upon the twenty-year-old
Brathwaite an outpouring of contempt such as only the
twenty-six-year-old Brathwaite could have been capable
of. Naturally, I did not know what kind of a fraud he
was, but in the broad moralistic sweep of my new-found
revulsion that was a detail to which I gave no weight.

I would have to see him when he came through Lagos. That was clear. There would have to be a showdown, though precisely why, and precisely how, was somewhat less clear.

I learned of his arrival from our port reporter, found out that he was staying at the Embassy, and with a full head of truculence went to find him.

It was just after eleven in the morning, when the hotel was full of guests and journalists and businessmen escaping gratefully from the heat into the dark, high-ceilinged vault of the lobby bar for a cuppa or a beer. As I walked in I immediately recognized the back of Dacosta Payne's head rising out of one of the heavy overstuffed leather chairs that stood in the passageway to the bar. With annoyance it occurred to me that I would have recognized it even if I hadn't been expecting to see him.

Suddenly uncertain of what I was going to do, I stood for a full minute near the mahogany cage that imprisoned the receptionist. Then, like an avenging angel who has lost *en route* the sacred scroll whereon the purpose of his mission is writ, I moved over to Payne's chair, and, coming up on his right side, leaned over and spoke.

"Yes?" he replied, a little startled, "yes, you wanted . . .?" Then he recognized me, made to get up, and started what would surely have been a smile of genuine delight. Both muscular impulses must have been arrested by what he saw in my eyes and he sank back into his chair, still looking at me, not speaking. With some surprise at my own detachment I noticed that his hands were tense on the arms of the chair. He looked straight at me with the tired, experienced expression of a man who recognizes an unpleasant corner when he sees one, but is no longer overly excited by the phenomenon as a phenomenon.

"What do you want?" His voice was cool, polite, distant, a stranger's voice. He might have been addressing an emissary from a public opinion poll. I knew that we had gone too far too fast. Whatever message—oh, so garbled in transmission!—my intuition or my newly acquired "maturity" had been trying to send me, this was still the Dacosta Payne who had opened his heart, or something wondrously like, to me back in those chill days in England. That Dacosta Payne, let the record show, had never defrauded me of anything. If some years back he had captured my imagination, it had been a poor enough prize and an unresisting prisoner. Yet, now, here I was, literally looming over him, all self-righteousness, and incredibly enough appearing to constitute some kind of threat to him. This, there was no mistaking. He had withdrawn into the waiting, defensive posture of a man who knows that the opposition has the ball. But what ball? I was thinking. What did I, in fact, have *on* him? And what did I have *against* him? And for all that, the situation had already developed its own insidious momentum which I simply didn't know how to turn aside.

But Payne, of course, had seen all this, and it was he, typically, who saved me.

"Well" he said, his voice low, "cat got your tongue?" Spoken in purest Bajan by this adept of purest Mayfair, this broke me up into laughter that was fifty percent relief. He joined in.

The *détente* gave me a chance to draw up a chair, to compose myself—a little, at least—and to begin to prepare a tactic of withdrawal, for there was really no alternative to withdrawal.

"This is one hell of a reunion, isn't it?" he said when I had settled down in my own overstuffed chair. I could only nod. "What's it now, five years? Six? Since we were last in touch? What're you up to in Mother Africa, working for Interpol?"

"*Touché*," I said, feeling not unlike the decapitated fencer in the Thurber cartoon. "Six years, I think. Lots of changes in six years." I scarcely knew what I was saying.

"Of course. Everything changes. People change. I should jolly well hope for you, for one, have changed. Shouldn't like to think that you were still as wet behind the ears as you were back there in 'fifty, was it?" The tone was right. We were doing fine. "What've you learned since then, a certain modish cynicism, no doubt? Anything less negative along with it?"

"The difference between Caslon and Bodoni typefaces, for one thing. I prefer Bodoni. It has a clean-cut elegance that will outlast fashions."

"Oh, I'm glad you're on the side of elegance. The only 'ism' I really care for, if you see what I mean." Yes, we were doing fine. Already we had exchanged some very useful signals. To start with, we had said goodbye to the days of our patron-client relationship, and there was a chance that one of these days we might be friends.

We talked history, our personal histories. I told him about my two years in Nigeria and he talked about what he called his "Europeanization." He was seldom in England these days, he said. Everybody was "on to" management studies; there might even be a faculty at one of the larger universities before long. "Not dear old Oxbridge, to be sure; sometimes I suspect that they're teaching economics in *Latin*, the way they resist the twentieth century. But I suppose I mustn't say anything offensive about your dear old alma mater." Europe, he said, was still virgin territory, except for West Germany, which he described as being simply an extension of General Motors. "I've got very keen on the economics of industrial development these last few years. Especially in our poor countries. That's all very new, and I know whom to read." He gave me a half of a wink. "On the management side there's *nobody* to read. In my small way I've been trying to fill the gap. I make no pretense at being an academic, but I'm literate, and I can add two and two together. The Italians and the French are *very* keen. Especially the Italians. They feel that since they have no more colonies nobody can question their good faith.

"What I'm really getting worked up about is Africa. This West Coast particularly. The potential is fabulous. There ought to be a university to teach West Africans nothing but management. When all the Europeans go, who are going to be your managers? Have you thought about that? Seems nobody has."

Then it came. He didn't "rule out" establishing himself in West Africa in the near future. Probably right here in Lagos. That was why he had come, to test the terrain. He would know by the end of the week whether what he had in mind was feasible. And he would give me a tinkle before he left.

I started preparing to leave. I didn't want him to begin to suspect just how uncomfortable this news made me. Already visions had flashed through my mind of being assigned to a "Dacosta Payne story" one of these days, a "story" in which one or more of the many highly colored balloons which Payne trailed behind him burst with a loud bang and an infernal stink. "What? In *my* house?" Lady Macbeth had said. I felt the same way, and was ashamed of the feeling. But once more Payne was too quick for me.

"Look here," he said as I shifted my hips for the move, "we have to talk. Seriously. Before I go. But, for the nonce," he rubbed a forefinger along his upper lip and gave me a look that could only be described as roguish, "will you accept that some of my papers on management are used as teaching materials in good schools in the States, and that I *was* at Leeds and in the RAF? Will that hold you?" It was so nicely calculated, this confession that confessed nothing, this reassurance given where none had been asked, that I could only laugh. He joined me. Laughter, ambiguous unguent, to the rescue once more.

I offered him the use of my car should he have transportation difficulties, but the Leaders of Industry had apparently taken care of that detail. So we said goodbye —or, rather, *au revoir*. I didn't in the event see him before he left for Geneva, but he did give me the promised tinkle.

"My Nigerian deal has come through," he said. "I just wanted to let you know, and to tell you that it's really awfully important to me. Not the money side of it, although I don't expect to starve. But I think I can do some good. Should be about three months. We'll be in touch."

Chapter Nine

The thing about Charmaine and Myron," Auguste said, his head held at the angle which is traditionally associated with judiciousness, "is that you just can't figure out what the hell they doing together in the first place. I mean, if you want to see a juicy piece of tail, well that is Charmaine. A real juicy piece of English ass." He slapped me on the leg with honest-to-goodness masculine glee in his eyes. "All real, man, all real. But the husband," he now shook his head from side to side, from court of first instance to appeal court and back again in complete bafflement, "the husband I don't understand at all. First to begin with, the man never in town. If he spend one week out of four in Lagos that is a lot. I mean to say, man, when you got a thing like that in your yard you have to be a goddamn fool to be running round the place, Aba, Onitsha, Warri, all over the country. And I'll tell you the truth, even if he was on the spot twenty-four hours a day, he still don't look to me like he up to it, you know what I mean?" He slapped my leg again.

We were "on terms" once more, Auguste and I, not good terms but his terms. Once more he was taking the initiative, calling me up when he had a free moment, and insisting on paying for the beer at the Embassy. On this particular morning the cool inner bar was more than usually agitated; the unoiled street door swung with an irritating frequency, each swing a gratuitous reminder that outside the cool, dark enclave in which we sheltered there still existed a hot, sweaty world of appointments and deadlines, of writs served and unserved, of dock labor and farm labor; of unquenched thirsts and tools that could not be laid down. I envied Auguste the self-employed status which clearly insulated him from the slightest twinge of guilt at our idleness.

It was Charmaine herself who had provoked his remarks, a slightly overweight silhouette of a woman with what seemed to be blondish hair who had made an apparition at the cashier's desk, asked in a ringing English whisper whether the girl would be so awfully kind as to cash a check for fifteen pounds, and left shortly after with loud protestations that she didn't know what she would *do* without the darling people at the Embassy.

"She's pretty vulgar, isn't she?" I said, partly out of conviction, but also because I seemed unable to stop myself from needling Auguste. His enthusiasm offended me for some obscure reason, like gross balloons inviting puncture. It was much too early in the day for gusto. In truth, the very rapid impression I had gained of Charmaine as she entered, transacted, and departed, was one of loudness, of a certain arrogant crassness. I suppose I liked my Englishmen and Englishwomen *piano*. (Long afterwards it occurred to me that Dacosta Payne was my kind of Englishman, not quite as ridiculous a formulation as it sounds: a foreign language I don't know well is more understandable when spoken badly by a West Indian than spoken by a native speaker.)

"Vulgar?" He was incredulous. "You ain't hear that accent? Boy, that is English aristocracy you just see there. Pure blue blood." From his own account, Auguste's acquaintance with the English aristocracy had been min-

imal, its members not being much given to hanging round
the Inns of Court where he had studied, apart from
some rare deviant intellectuals. He had, therefore, not
had the opportunities that had been more or less forced
upon me of studying at close quarters the speech and
manners of the breed. Thus he couldn't appreciate the
importance of the vowel "o" in the ordering of British
society. As unforgiving as any shibboleth ever invented,
for my relatively more educated ear it had served to place
Charmaine, briefly overheard at a distance, in a category somewhat distant from "English aristocracy," and I
took some pleasure in setting him right.

"You're right about one thing, though. In the colonies,
even the cockneys get on as they had been born in Buck-
ingham Palace," I said, to soften the little lesson.

"It's a hell of a thing, boy, the way they have us all
brainwashed. I don't really give a dam' if she's an aristocrat or not. That's their problem. Far as I'm concerned,
they're all the dam' same when you get down to it."
Auguste was always surprising me. He now went on to
talk about Charmaine and Myron, and the more he talked
the harder it was to envisage them as actual flesh and
blood. He made them sound, rather, like some improb-
ably exotic double bloom implanted on Lagos as epi-
phytic orchids are implanted on trees. ("Well worth a
visit," the guidebook would say, and people would get up
charabanc parties on long weekends to go and see.)
Auguste scarcely bothered to attribute distinguishing
characteristics to Myron or to explain how such a non-
entity had been able to capture the extraordinary creature ("somewhat vulgar, a little overweight, and blondish," ran my stubborn mental shorthand note) who had
made a brief appearance against the light at the Embassy's cash-desk and who was, in Auguste's dictionary,
tremendous, glamorous, gorgeous, fabulously endowed,
and no nun.

"She knows everybody. . . ."

"She has fantastic taste, clothes, everything, wait till you see her house. . . ."

"If somebody was to tell me she used to be a really big-time actress, I would believe it. Style, man. . . !"

"Somebody must be getting some, I sorry it ain't me."

Months later, making an entry in a newly acquired "commonplace book" which I occasionally employed as a buffer against forgetfulness, I wrote the following:

> Charmaine is one of those people who could quite believably have sprung full-grown out of the head of some present-day deity. Have seen others of this kind (are they all only-children?) with personalities that strike one as being perfectly whole and perfectly free from the markings of change, adaptation, adjustment which are as visible on most people as the rings on trees. At ten she must have been very blonde indeed. At forty(?) the blondness is darkened(!) by a little graying at the front and—presumably—by the chemical residue of the exertions of a hundred hairdressers. Is there some law of pigmentation which decrees this evolution for blondes? (Cf. green eyes and freckles and red hair, not to mention albinos. The word in Yoruba for white man, "oyibo," was invented to describe albinos—"scraped-skin-man." I remember a red-haired, freckly-red-skinned Nigerian center-forward in the barefoot soccer team that beat England in 1949.) I can see Charmaine at age ten, long pigtails and blue polka-dot dresses and exquisite public manners constantly on display. I have seen her lineal descendants by the banks of the Cam in summer, with mummy and daddy being punted on the river and a young undergraduate making passes at Nanny. "I'll just run over there and talk to those children in the garden, shall I, Nanny?" she asks, more knowing than complaisant Nanny would ever guess. And off she runs to dazzle a clutch of less adventurous, less assured, and certainly less beautiful playmates, smoothing her hair with precociously sensuous fingers, commanding their resentfully fascinated

attention by means of just that assuredness and
beauty, transporting them unwilling but unresisting
still into realms they are not quite ready to visit:

"What are you going to be when you grow up?"
she asks.

"A nurse."

"An engine driver."

"I'm going to be a . . . a . . . a POSTWOMAN!"

"Silly, there aren't any postwomen! I'm going to
be a . . . a . . . a bus *conductress!"*

And Charmaine:

"You're all really much too silly for *words"* (her
voice already carefully modulated, every word fat
with deliberateness). "By the time I'm eighteen I
intend to be a film star. Not an actress. A star. My
father thinks I have the most beautifully textured
blonde hair he's ever seen. He says it must be due
to a recessive gene, as both he and mummy have
auburn hair. I bet none of you sillybillies has any
idea what a recessive gene is. I have magnificent
hazel eyes, and Daddy thinks I have definite star
quality. That's what I'm going to be, a star." (Or it
may have been "the leading woman writer in the
English language. Daddy says I have a *natural* gift
for language." Or both.) And no one present dares
to doubt, much less contradict, her. She is a witch,
and this may very well be the same thing as a star.

Now, she is a little overweight, and a little puffy
at the chin and under the eyes: fading, not faded.
The face is held together by an infrastructure of bone
as firm and immutable in its symmetry as the under-
pinnings of that immaculate psyche. The body,
when conventionally clothed, is almost unremark-
able, with the conformist imprint of middle age
upon it, but at closer quarters you are nagged by
those magnificent hazel eyes into further scrutiny,
and this is submission. So you are bound to register
that regardless of age she is a splendid female of
the species, generously equipped by nature with all
that is most appropriate and poignant in bust, legs,
and the kind of pearly-pink flesh that never tans

and never burns, but which in Lagos graduates to a
shade which is not quite olive and not quite pearl
and which one had always thought as existing only
in the rotogravure blandishments of cosmeticians.

Charmaine is, unquestionably, a witch.

In the event, it wasn't Auguste who brought Charmaine
and me together; it wasn't even Kippins, although it was
he who provided the occasion. Charmaine picked me up
at the Mainland Club about half-an-hour after I first set
foot in the place. The *Sun* had recently decided to pay
subscriptions to the club for all its more senior editorial
staff on the very reasonable grounds that the fee would
be recuperated many times over in terms of the information and contacts which could be obtained there. Kippins
thought that the time had come for my induction, and he
duly escorted me there, duly bought me my first drink,
and duly exchanged small talk with me while duly introducing me to those denizens whom he thought worth the
Sun's concern. It was very clear to me that he was performing a duty; his natural Saturday afternoon habitat
was elsewhere, the Colony Club, to be precise, which was
as indubitably the "European" club as the Mainland was
the "African" club, Preamble and Article One of both
Constitutions notwithstanding.

We stood up at the bar, an elbow-worn mahogany
crescent over which a wizened, soft-spoken Ibo named
Pius presided. The small clubhouse was crowded with
earnest and noisy drinkers who wove a heavy net of boisterous conversation in three languages from end to end
of the bar and out into the billiard room. Kippins,
squeezed up against me by the press of jostling bodies,
shouted a commentary on the play.

"The Freedom Party swear the Mainland is a NANI
den, but the place is always full of FPs." NANI was the
National Alliance for Nigerian Independence, currently
the government party. "Once they get to the Club you
can scarcely unstick them from one another." He was dy-

ing to get to the Colony Club where, no doubt, his wife
awaited him by the side of the Olympic-standard swimming pool, and where rumor had it that there was a
billiard room where you could actually hear the click of
the balls over the voices of the watchers even at noon on
a Saturday.

"It's quite impossible to unstick *anybody* from *anybody*
in the Mainland," a woman said behind us in one of those
effortlessly audible English voices that can freeze an
errant colonial at two hundred paces, "and I'm not sure
that you should be encouraged to try, Mr. Kippins." We
turned. It was Charmaine. Kippins did the introductions,
and she stuck herself between us, her left buttock lavishly massaging my right thigh. Kippins offered her a
drink.

"Do order one for me, but it goes on Myron's bill. He
was supposed to be here ages ago, but he's never on
time. Serve him jolly well right if he has the biggest bar
bill on the West Coast. And a refill for these gentlemen,
Pius dear, if you please." For Pius already had a pink gin
on the bar before her before Kippins had had time to
speak. She squashed the mumbles we both uttered. "Do
be quiet. Myron puts it on expenses, and oil companies are
filthy rich, anyway. So's Myron. Down the hatch."

"So, who're you, Mr. Braithwaite?" Seen this close, her
face appeared larger than life-size. Egged on by the heat,
elaborate tracings of blood vessels eluded the carefully
posted cosmetic sentinels.

"It's *Brath*waite in Barbados," I said.

"Don't tell me you're one of the gang at the *Sun?*
Where did you find him, Mr. Kippins? He's gorgeous!
What do you *do?* Do you *write?* You could do with some-
body on that newspaper who can *write*, do you know?
Tell me about yourself, go on."

"Why don't you tell me about yourself? I'm sure that
would be a better story."

"Touché; touché. But it wouldn't be, really, you know. *Anybody* in Lagos can tell you about me. I'm quite *notorious.* And that's rather dull."

By and by Myron came, giving Kippins his chance to escape to the calm certainties of the Colony Club. Myron was a surprise to me. Unconsciously I had pictured him as a little man, short-sighted, perhaps, who would follow the bewildering contours of Charmaine's being with amazement and a humble gratitude that fate had permitted him to be quite so close. Or else a big man, beefy and dumb, a butter-and-eggs man from Texas, overwhelmed by the Sussex- or Surrey-bred sophistication he had purchased. But Myron was neither. He was a wiry, crew-cut man in his early forties who looked to be eminently in his senses, with that quiet look and manner I have since seen in men with a judo Black Belt, or ten million pounds, or a secret certainty of being in direct communication with the Savior, or some other species of ace permanently up their sleeves. At the time I didn't quite recognize this quality for what it was, since I was too taken up by my surprise and, I suppose, too young to see more in him than the perfectly ordinary, unbizarre *persona* he presented to the stranger.

"Myron, love, Mr. Brathwaite, *Brath*waite, not Braithwaite, is coming to have lunch with us. He's the new West Indian *star writer* at the *Sun.* He's rather a darling, don't you think?" Her voice dropped perceptibly as she spoke to her husband. The crush at the bar was thinning out as the lunch hour approached, and you no longer had to shout to be audible to your neighbor. But I was immediately certain that Charmaine's tone of voice was always different when she spoke to her husband. There was, incredibly, a whisper of deference in it.

"Marvelous. I promise you you'll enjoy it, Mr. Brathwaite. Charmaine keeps the best table in town. She actually stole the cook from the Chambord in Cotonou. One eats like royalty at our place."

I wanted to say something about this being the first I had heard about lunch, but even if I had been crass enough to utter the words I would not have had a chance as their interchange and intimacy rolled over me. I was relegated to the role of object, quickly and kindly disposed of. They talked *at* me with easy, marital unanimity.

"Myron's utterly devoted to me, aren't you, love?" To my amazement, she kissed him below his ear. "He's always paying me the most outrageous compliments. Go on, Myron, tell him who's the second-best cook on the West Coast. Go on, tell him!"

"Oh, Charmaine says that Philippe is the best cook on the Coast, but I keep telling her he's only the second-best. When *she's* in the mood she's Number One." Although it was a speech he must have recited a thousand times before, he tossed it off with a carelessness that was quite persuasive, and she kissed him again. It was play-acting, I felt, but performed before the Saturday lunch-time multitude with such aplomb it had a quality of art, almost, that was confusing and tantalizing, suggesting some hiatus in my understanding of them that I could not quite identify.

"Myron, you're a love. You're a shameless liar, but if God doesn't forgive you, I will."

"Mr. Brathwaite, I tell you no lie. The second time you come out to our home you'll be able to compare. She does things in a kitchen that make strong men weep."

"Do you know, this ridiculous man of mine once nearly wept—literally!—over a nonsense of a *mousse au chocolat* I made him!"

"That's enough, darling. Mr. Brathwaite's mouth must be watering. Don't worry," he patted me on the shoulder, "Philippe's no slouch. You'll get the best meal you've had since you got to Lagos."

I followed their Buick into that world of well-coifed lawns and disciplined hibiscus hedges that "Europeans" had reserved for themselves in the golden days before political parties and "agitators" had begun to suggest that the natives of the country had rights. The suburb had, nevertheless, kept its distant air of a reserve. Here the grass was greener, the gardens neater, the children sleeker, and the dogs better-nourished than in any other part of the city. Quite a few Africans, civil servants and doctors, had breached the invisible barrier that quarantined Ikoyi from the noisy, filthy, and lively heart of Lagos; drumming was barred by a municipal ordinance.

Their house was one of the largest and newest in the suburb. It had been designed by a company architect and landscaped by a company expert. It was a low, sprawling affair, wide at the front and narrowing away to a two-storied tower that held the living quarters. The effect, in the midst of the solid fieldstone horrors that honest Lancashire foremen had pounded together for the earlier colonizers, was gay almost to the point of hilarity. Inside, it was obvious that someone had kept the company decorators firmly at bay. The house itself, despite its air of a somewhat jokey excrescence among the sturdy, unimaginative structures of serious British colonialism, had an awe-inspiring pedigree, the aristocratic credentials of twentieth-century American architecture. Once inside, however, I was aware not of a lineage but of a personality, that of Charmaine. It was the first time I had ever been made so conscious of the capacity that the individual possesses, if he is willful and wealthy enough, for molding his environment around him like a placenta. I can pick out particular details that impressed me at that time, the great openness, for example, of the sitting room, which did not for all that diminish the sense of intimacy, little short of overpowering, that I felt when we sat, the three of us, drinking one more gin and tonic before going in to eat Philippe's avocado salad and groundnut stew. There were pictures all over the walls and a few Nigerian sculptures in wood and bronze on stands, and each single piece aroused in me a very particular curiosity, even though at the end of the afternoon I would have been hard put to describe any one individual piece. And then there was the furniture. It was obviously of Scandinavian provenance with some curved, form-fitting pieces comfortable as a womb, and others austere, tubular, and of curiously puritan aspect, which turned out to be quite as accommodating to the body as those of the welcoming contours. Somehow it was obvious that each single chair or side-table or sofa had been chosen without regard to price, with regard only to the very individual desires and tastes of the occupants. The whole place reeked, discreetly, of money rigidly harnessed to sophisticated idiosyncrasies.

"Myron, love," Charmaine said as soon as we arrived, "you look after Mr. Brathwaite, while I go and *beard* Philippe in his den to see what *miracle* he has in store today. And, darling, if you *must* show off your photographs of me, do make certain that you're selective, won't you? Myron has done some terribly *revealing* studies—*he* calls them *studies*—of me. I'm not sure we know you well enough, Mr. Brathwaite, to let you see them. Not yet, anyway. They're frightfully artistic, though. Karsh saw one of Myron's portfolios a few years back, and he was absolutely green with envy, wasn't he, love?"

"It wasn't Karsh, darling. It was the man from *Life*, you know who I mean, Mr. Brathwaite. Goldblatt. I don't know that he changed color quite so dramatically. He was kind enough to say that anytime I got bored with the oil business he could easily get me work in magazine photography."

The photographs of Charmaine were magnificent. They covered, I suppose, the eight or so years of their married life, but were only incidentally a record of the passing of time and the changes it had wrought on her. The majority were in black-and-white, great stark abstractions of these colors and the tones between. Those in color were pieces of technical virtuosity in formal portraiture. He showed me the old-fashioned, prewar Leica he used and said that he never did any of his own processing. "I just try to find the best people for that sort of thing and let them get on with it. The mechanics of the thing just leave me cold." When I told him that Cartier-Bresson had exactly the same approach, he put his hand on my shoulder and said, "Why, that's a darned nice thing to say!"

And, of course, he showed me the photos of Charmaine in the nude. These were all black-and-white and, even more than the heads and busts, had the impact of abstractions, dazzling conglomerations of shapes and tones which could be reduced by a determined eye to representations of a blonde woman with the configuration of, say, Charmaine. If you insisted on seeing them as objective reproductions, then you saw a woman in all her ripeness, a creature of classically lush contours, from the great mound of firm breast to the tumescence of the *mons veneris*, from long softnesses of arm to the arrogant muscled cheeks of her bottom.

After this, lunch was an exquisite anticlimax. Yes, Philippe was an extraordinary cook. If the groundnut stew was a little frenchified, it was an undoubted improvement on the robust peasant dish of the same name that Monday concocted for me from time to time; there obviously could be no other way to eat avocado. But Philippe's art took second place to all that had gone before. Which was what, exactly? I decided eventually that the word I wanted was "luxury." That sense of intimacy I had experienced was really an outcrop of luxury, which is one of the intensest forms of privacy. Luxury extracts you from a world where your desires are in conflict with everyone else's—and therefore unrealizable—and deposes you in another where your desires are fulfilled as soon as —and, sometimes, even before—they are formulated. On later visits to this house I had none of these sensations, perhaps because on those occasions the house had been turned into a magnificently functional machine for entertaining; that first day it was a preserve into which I was temporarily admitted on equal terms with the inhabitants.

Going through the ritual of good manners and paying correct compliments on the house and the food I felt as inadequate as a first-year undergraduate making an impromptu speech before the Royal Society. Myron was gracefully offhanded.

"Oh, I told you. Philippe's a very decent cook, indeed. But wait till you sample the Mistress' handiwork. That'll throw you for several loops."

"Well if she's as good a cook as she is a decorator . . . ."

"Better, my boy, even better. A paragon of the womanly arts." I thought of the photographs and was glad that my pigmentation could not visibly advertise my thoughts. And it was quite clear that Myron's remark was meant to be taken literally.

"Well, I'm ready to be dazzled," I said. The image was to return to me later.

"I hope you're not running away now," Myron said. "Do stay and have a brandy or something." The "brandy-or-something" proliferated all over the remains of the afternoon. Myron proudly showed me Charmaine's collection of teddy bears from thirty countries.

"It's unique. One or two of them come from royal families who had a rough time in the last war. Got them for next to nothing. After all, who collects teddy bears?" He laughed happily at Charmaine's originality. "Did you know that teddy bears got their name from a President of the United States, Theodore Roosevelt? Curious, isn't it? I've never been able to figure out why she chose teddy bears."

"But I've told you, love. I *adore* them. What is there to figure out?"

It was nearly sunset when I left, and when sunset came, a drunken mauve projection splashing on my windscreen and forcing me to drive with octogenarian, curbhugging caution, I decided that the whole afternoon had been dazzling in a rather menacing way. Thinking of that house, that food, those photos and sculptures and paintings, the teddy bears, the overdemonstrative marital devotion, I felt as I supposed a jungle dweller might feel after a half-hour in bewildered contemplation of a partial eclipse of the sun. Monsters! That's what they are, I thought, revelation dawning as the sun set. In this light the display of Myron's nude portfolio was clearly obscene. Monsters, I thought, with visionary alcoholic clarity. Obscene, too, all that opulence, all that luxury, for the exclusive delectation of two persons. Its very existence is an obscenity.

It was only afterwards, sober, that I began to suspect that I might not have reacted so violently had Charmaine alone been there. And I couldn't for the life of me, understand why this should be so.

Chapter Ten

Payne was back in Lagos, as he had forecast, three months after our last meeting. He didn't get in touch with me immediately but inevitably within twenty-four hours I heard about his arrival. I soon learned that he had taken a top-floor in central Lagos, with Swedish intercom system, air conditioning, wall-to-wall carpeting—the works, and would be operating under the name of "Africonsult, Inc., Industrial Consultants."

About a week after his return he telephoned. "I didn't call earlier as I've been rather tied up with all the piddling details of settling in. Not that I'm by any means over that hurdle, but I'm beginning to get things more or less sorted out. What say we have a session some time soon?"

It was a fortnight before the session materialized, lunch —at the Embassy, of course; there was nowhere else. He was one hundred percent himself, again, already on first-name terms (their first names) with the waiters, and even rating a "Good morning, Mr. Payne!" from Rees, the unconvivial, alcoholic Welshman who managed the hotel.

Over lunch we chatted amiably and aimlessly about the banalities of life in Lagos; about his settling in, about the apparent technical incompatibility of his specially imported

telephone system and that of the Nigerian Posts and Tele-
graphs; about the problems of finding the right kind of secretary—he was probably going to have to engage a married
Englishwoman, although hiring a white secretary in
Nigeria went against the grain; about the question of contacts of various kinds—"I'm expecting more than a leg-up
from you there, old man," he informed me, leaving no
doubt in my mind that this was the last thing he either
expected or needed.

It occurred to me that in some ways I now knew him
too well, and that to this extent Dacosta Payne was becoming a bit of a bore; for I knew that all this was preamble; he wanted to say something fairly specific, and
was probably keeping it until the coffee came. I was completely right.

"Sugar for you?" Yes, I said, two lumps.

"None for me. At thirty-five you have to begin to think
of the old waistline. You've got a while yet before that
kind of thing starts to bother you."

We sipped at the watery Embassy brew, he smoking
some expensive-looking gold-tipped cigarette, while I
puffed on a cheroot, cheap, local, and foul, but, like my
bow tie, an essential part of that year's Brathwaite image.

"D'you know, it's occurred to me that you might just
conceivably find our rather curious relationship a little
embarrassing from time to time. . . . I mean, in your line
of country you don't want the idea to get about that you're
too close to any particular businessman, that kind of
thing. So if you feel that you'd prefer us not to see perhaps as much of each other as we might have done if
this had been London, well, quite frankly, I think I'd
understand."

It was spoken with the elaborate casualness of a speech
which had been meticulously rehearsed. To this extent it
was not well done, but that it was done at all was a trib-
ute to a sort of honesty and delicacy in Dacosta Payne.

For what he was clearly saying was that the nature of his activities was such that one day a balloon might well burst and this was a friendly release from any friendly obligation I might feel to stay in the vicinity of the explosion. On the moralities of friendship, at least, he was impeccable. He was also something of a master of the unspoken word.

Chapter Eleven

Not long afterwards, Charmaine invited me to a buffet supper, confirming the summons with a card that stipulated "Dress, Very Casual." At the time of the party I apprehended Tola in a quite three-dimensional way, and I had no illusions about the nature of my attraction to her. It was still a case of wanting to get her to bed, to "make" her; she was still the object of a "chase" that might or might not be "successful." And yet, as I could learn only in retrospect, I was already on the devious, inadequately signposted road to love.

For one thing, I was now happily certain that she had never taken Auguste's lumbering courtship very seriously. She appeared to treat it as she might one of those minor ills to which women are normally subject—a slight menstrual pain, say, which incommodes but does not incapacitate and certainly doesn't call for major surgery. And, of course, as was inevitable in that sounding-box of a town, she had heard about Abike. On the one occasion she had consented to go out with me—cinema, a late drink at the Mainland Club, and home—she had mischievously asked how Auguste's housekeeper was working out.

Since, from the moment I saw her in the Mainland, I had also wanted to get Charmaine to bed, I came to the party positively aglow with gay, unclouded lust.

There were thirty or forty people already there when I arrived, many of them faces I recognized from the Mainland, where I was now a regular, a brandy-and-ginger man, whom Pius would see and serve fairly swiftly even in the more hectic crushes.

The long living room had been partitioned into two salons, in one of which there was dancing to recorded music by the light of one heavily shaded lamp, while the other section with Pius presiding at a well-stocked bar was given up to milling and drinking. I quickly saw that the form was to make an appearance in the second section, and only then, if one chose, to pair off and retire to Section One.

There was no sign, immediately, of Myron. I greeted Pius, got a drink, and asked Charmaine to dance.

"Sinclair, darling," she said in her loudest voice, "I can't possibly dance with anyone now. I'm the *hostess*. Myron's nowhere to be found. He was supposed to be here hours ago but heaven knows where he is. He's probably *locked* into air pockets somewhere in the East this very minute. No, what you must do, just look around a little harder and I'm sure you'll find some complaisant little thing just dying to go off into the dark with you. Anyway, I'm far too *old* for what you have in mind." She put her hand flat on my chest and pushed me gently backwards, and moved off to go to the door to meet new arrivals. A cluster of faces that seemed to have been transported *en masse* from the Mainland bar laughed at me loudly and unmaliciously.

I did not feel at all put off by Charmaine's dismissal. I was convinced that there had been a definite message in her speech, to wit: Myron's not here, and likely to come very late, or perhaps not at all. Meanwhile, mill around or find someone else to dance with until I can conveniently get around to you. The rest had all been grace notes, the performer showing off his fingering technique long after the harmonies have been resolved. I had no reason for this conviction; but I was like a batsman in form who has no explicable reason for knowing that a particular ball is really a half-volley and not just cleverly flighted, yet he knows, all the same. So I milled happily, absorbing this new and quite special experience, a party by Charmaine.

The party was exquisite in all its appointments, including the human. Charmaine and Myron knew "everybody worth knowing" in Lagos; they—rather, she, since it was already obvious which of them was responsible for every detail of the interior decoration of the house—had constructed from among her acquaintances a very personal anthology for this evening.

There was Campion, the blind labor manager of African Holdings. Some people said he was British Intelligence, and not quite so blind as he would have you believe. And Bijou from the Gambia who told me, quite truthfully according to Auguste, "I used to be one of the most expensive harlots on the West Coast. Now I am in the transport business. I am fucking only for pleasure." And there was Prince Adeleye, the reputedly communist heir of the richest traditional chief in the country, arrayed in silk shirt and a silk ascot with the colors of Magdalen, Oxford. And Binns, the lanky American consul from North Carolina, who spoke the clipped Durban English he had acquired when his father was in the consular service in South Africa, and who liked to send to his friends in the southern parts of the two continents specially mounted picture postcards which showed him arm-in-arm with Africans. And Angus Jones, the Governor-General's Private Secretary, giving every appearance of enjoying his assignment as the social eyes and ears of Government

House. And the austere lone-wolf nationalist, Adu Adumuyiwa, with the thin, prematurely worn face of a John the Baptist adrift in a wilderness where the locusts and wild honey were reported to be poisonous. He was supposed to have said at one of his meetings, "If the bloody imperialists will not depart peaceably, they will be driven out bloodily." It had become the favorite slogan in radical circles throughout West Africa.

And there was Tola.

After a little exertion I got her away from Jones and took her into the dancing section.

"You seem to be finding your way around Lagos quite well, Mr. Brathwaite." Her voice had quite a harsh timbre, reminding me of Yoruba marketwomen and the white-robed girls who sang in shrill revivalist choirs at Victoria beach on Sundays. Yet she had very little of what could be called a "Nigerian" accent.

"You sound almost ironic," I said, surprised that I had provoked so intimate a reaction as irony. She made me quite uncomfortable even as my mind was composing the outline of the campaign that would be waged in due time.

"I'm sorry, I didn't mean to," she said. "All I meant was what I said. You haven't been here all that long." It hung together, all that she said, by every semantic test, but something was saying to me, "More grace notes."

Meanwhile we talked, easing the conversation on to safe topics where subtleties of inflection were of no importance. We talked about her Aunt Matilda, about Auguste, about the factitious rivalry between the two newspapers we worked for, which she described as a luxury import. Around us bodies were making compacts, threatening stable marriages, giving consolation, offering themselves for tribal admiration, to the music of Lord Kitchener's "Small Comb," E.T. Mensah's reconstituted calypsos, and Louis Jordan. But we were just dancing, working hard at the pretense that we were not in the middle of a whirling tide of sex and intimacy. Talking and dancing, we moved soberly against the tide. And then, when the music stopped for longer than usual, we found ourselves grounded, standing at arms' length waiting for the music to begin again. But not only was the music not beginning again; there was an explosion of light, and Charmaine's voice, just as explosive in the muted room, shouting, "Come on, you lovers, the food's ready!"

Tola excused herself quickly, almost brusquely, and disappeared into the depths of the house, and I found that Charmaine had me by the arm, piloting me into the dining room.

"I see you took my advice very, very literally. She's rather striking, isn't she? Myron's quite dotty about her. So am I, really."

"She's a smasher," I said, a little sulkily. I was very put out by Tola's disappearance. I felt absolutely certain that if we could escape the false atmosphere of the party, with its public intimacies and its insistence that everyone play some particular convivial role, we could somehow find our own idiom. Charmaine's hand on my arm was an irrelevance.

"A terrible bore," Charmaine said as she guided me to the buffet table. "Myron's called to say his plane's grounded at Enugu with engine trouble. He'll have to come up by road in the morning. Isn't it just *too* irritating?" She turned to repeat the information to the people just behind in line. "Isn't it too *infuriating?* I made the *quiche Lorraine* especially for him. He adores *quiches.* He says mine are the best outside Lorraine. He's the most *shameless* liar!"

During supper there was no sign of Tola, nor was she visible afterwards when dancing started. There was no one to whom I could turn to ask about her. I felt disoriented and even more sulky than before, and now I could do nothing so long as she chose to remain invisible; and what could I do later, call her and say that I had detected that her indifference to Sinclair Brathwaite was less than absolutely total?

So I milled some more, and stole another girl from Angus Jones. Large and jolly, she was a cousin of the Governor-General's wife, in Lagos on her first African visit, and danced everything as if it were a mazurka.

Charmaine, meanwhile, was about her obsessive business as hostess. I saw that the party, which seemed from the very beginning to have gone with an easy, disjointed, natural swing, had, in fact, been ruthlessly orchestrated down to the tiniest detail. Thus, for example, she had fed Angus Jones with an unending stream of people he didn't know well and who wished to talk to the Private Secretary, Government House. Thus, at no time did I hear one of those loud denunciations of some offending Englishman or American for which Adu was renowned. Charmaine had kept him fully occupied with Bijou. And, afterwards, I realized that it was no accident that I had such hard going to find someone to dance with. Everyone, except me, was "suited." But my turn was coming.

"I hope that I don't have to prostrate myself to get you to dance with me," Charmaine said, coming up behind me at the bar. She had changed from the almost formal black frock in which she had begun the evening into *aganyin*, the blouse-and-wrapper combination from the Gold Coast which was becoming increasingly popular with Nigerian women. I had occasionally seen white women wearing various kinds of African clothes; without exception they looked self-consciously "dressed-up." But Charmaine was, simply, elegant; on her the *aganyin* looked like a highly original piece of couture especially designed for her. The skirt part, a figured green cloth wrapped tight around her hips, dropped sinuously down to her ankles; the blouse was very décolleté black lace and strapless; her shoulders glowed pearl in the dim light.

"That's sensational!" I said when I turned around and saw her. She really was magnificent, a sex goddess from before the Fall. Some of the people at the bar, including Bijou and Adu, applauded.

"You're such darlings! Terrible flatterers, all of you." She took my arm for the second time. "Come on, let's get away from these *wicked* people. They're laughing at me." We went on through to the dancing section. I couldn't be absolutely certain about that last remark; it sounded like no more than words, a traditional formula of English modesty. And yet I wanted to reassure her.

"It really is magnificent," I told her. "You look stunning. That's the only word for it. Look at Bijou. She's wearing *aganyin*, too. She looks very good, but that's all. On you it looks like something that was specially invented for you." We had started shuffling in time to a slow highlife. In the flat sandals she was wearing she came up to my ear, which she now kissed lingeringly.

"I don't believe a word you say," she said in something approaching a whisper. I leaned to return the compliment on her now invisible pearl shoulder.

Charmaine's dancing reminded me, anatomically, of the pale blonde suburbanite lady who had for a fee initiated me into the slow-slow-quick-quick-slow mysteries of English ballroom dancing. "Contact must be maintained at the level of the thighs, Mr. Brathwaite," she had said, in the fluorescent desert she called her "studio." She had then hermetically affixed her long shapely thighs to mine and, in a triumph of pedagogy over real life, had taken me through chassés and half-chassés, through the whole theory of the slow fox trot, quickstep, and English waltz, without once permitting my imagination to conceive of thigh-contact as anything other than the key to the Bronze Medal of the British Ballroom Dancing Society. Charmaine held herself like a silver-medalist, contact uninterruptedly maintained from waist to knee. And she danced superbly, dominating the rhythm so completely that her body seemed at every move to be inventing a truer version of it, dedicated to the greater good of both our bodies. In this she danced like a West Indian or African.

I told her this, and she kissed my ear again. "I hope I'm not wiggling my bottom too much," she said. "It does give one away so."

"I don't understand."

"If you want to tell if a white woman's been sleeping with Africans, just watch the way she wiggles her derrière. It speaks *volumes!* Luckily, you can't see mine, can you, darling?" She laughed and kissed me again.

"Miss Hightower never told me about that," I said.

"Who's Miss Hightower?"

"A blonde I used to know who believed that thigh-contact was the key to success."

"I don't think I want to hear a great deal more about Miss Hightower." She hardly spoke again, seemingly quite content to dance and to let the party take care of itself now that she had set it on the right paths. But after half-an-hour, at a break in the music, I spoke out of the sweet agony of a groin stretched beyond endurance by the lazy insistence of those thighs.

"Charmaine, if you don't mind, I think I'll stop for a while." She did not disengage herself from my inflamed thighs and belly and diaphragm but smiled up at me and said, "Why, I thought I was making no impression *at all* on you," an obvious and undisguised lie that made me angry, for it seemed to say that we had been playing a game of which we both knew the rules, and that I had been caught cheating, taking the game for the real thing. Now, I wanted Charmaine, and I was no longer sure that I could have her, so coolly had she manipulated me. This was not at all what I had envisaged; my scenario had starred a self-possessed Sinclair Brathwaite who would casually and in his own due time set about plucking an overripe fruit for leisurely consumption. In this revised version Sinclair Brathwaite was the fruit.

I said the obvious things against the background of a new record on the electrophone, and, before I was conscious of the tableau I was creating, Charmaine, the hostess, moved back into my arms and we were dancing again.

"I forget how young you are," she said. I said nothing.

"Don't sulk! After this dance, we'll stop. Then, if you really want to tell me off for the awful cock-teasing old woman I am, we'll go to my sitting room upstairs, O.K.?" In a few minutes we drifted through the bar, which was now sensibly less populated, and went up to the first floor of the tower where there was indeed a small sitting room, stark white with kente cloth hangings, which housed an uncluttered assemblage of sofa, coffee table, black Kano pouffes, recessed bookcases, desk, sewing-machine table, and one tall candle-like standard lamp which Charmaine switched on as we entered.

Once inside, the sounds of the party were lost to us, transmuted in the passage out of ground-floor windows through the humid night and over the roof into a gentle murmur like distant waves on an island lake. We stood looking at each other, on my part, at least, uncertainly. She turned away without a word and went through a door set between the bookcases. I walked around and looked at the shelves, trying to find the link between Charmaine and Elizabeth Bowen, Jane Austen, Simone de Beauvoir, D. H. Lawrence, Katherine Mansfield, bound copies of *Vogue*, picture books of Cezanne's and Augustus John's works, a book of Henry Moore's drawings, and loose copies of the *New Architectural Review*, feeling for all the world like a visitor awaiting his hostess at one o'clock in the afternoon. It was, of course, nearly one o'clock in the morning and I suspected that I was shortly to go to bed with my hostess on the backless but rather wide sofa in front of me.

In a short while she reappeared in her bare feet. The blouse was gone, and her wrapper was tucked under her armpits in the style of the women of Isaleko.

"There's a bathroom through there if you want to use it," she said.

For no reason that I can convincingly explain to myself I burst out laughing. She joined me, and our amusement shattered the tight-strung atmosphere of uncertainty and discomfort like a stone against a glass pane and we were through, two contented burglars looting to our heart's content. She was a generous lover precisely as a prostitute is a mean lover. She could not disguise her experience, but she used it to please and flatter me, and so she pleased herself, moving in soft, swooping stages into the ultimate egotism of climax. As we continued to make love it seemed to me that there was no way in which we could not please each other. When we stopped, and she fetched cigarettes and a drink and came back to the sofa, even the quietude was an extraordinary erotic experience.

When Tola walked in, Charmaine saw her first, as she was sitting up with her back against the kente cloth that covered the wall above the sofa. I was lying at right angles, my head nestled in her lap, smoking and looking up at the scarcely pendulous globes of breast above me, and still marveling at the virginal smallness of her nipples. I heard a short strangled "Oh! Oh! I'm sorry!" in a voice that reminded me of Tola's and I jerked up and around to see that it was, indeed, Tola who was leaving by the door that we hadn't closed.

"That's a bit of a mess, isn't it?" Charmaine said. She was apologizing to me.

Chapter Twelve

The Dacosta Payne boom was now in full swing. There were his "official" receptions—part of the contact-making process—that always developed into parties which people talked about for days afterwards; there were the Sunday luncheons which soon got the reputation of providing the best palm-oil chop in town; there were the "coffee breaks" at 11:00 A.M. at the Embassy, with a score of civil servants and businessmen and journalists, ostensibly doing precisely the same thing they had done before Dacosta Payne's arrival, but somehow finding in him a focus and an ornament. It was very chic to know and be known by Dacosta Payne; and, willy-nilly, I found that it was even more chic to have known him longer than anyone else in town.

In any event people assumed that, coming from Barbados myself, I was naturally an intimate friend: Nigerians frankly considered West Indians for most practical purposes to be an expatriate tribe with all the solidarity of the native tribes. So reporters, as well as people outside the business, would frequently question me or gossip to me about Payne; one of our younger men who never did anything for the twice-weekly column I ran suddenly be-

gan offering me stories about the new "industrial consulting magnate" ("magnate" being a word very much in
vogue at the time for anyone in industry or commerce
from Henry Ford II to the owner of four leaky canoes
plying the lagoon between Apapa and the Marina), and
was flabbergasted when I refused to use them on the
grounds of their triviality. I am certain that it was he who
started a rumor in the office that Dacosta Payne and I
had fallen out, which had the curious effect of increasing
the volume of gossip I now heard about my compatriot.

It was he, too, who dropped the first hint about Dacosta Payne and Funke. He stopped by my cubbyhole one
day about six months after Dacosta Payne's arrival and
said, "I hear your countryman is negotiating with one
of the big American hotel chains to build a luxury hotel
in Lagos. Is he having any success?" I told him I knew
nothing about it; I didn't get around town as much as he.

"You mean you are still not speaking to him?"

"Olapeju, why don't you go and buy some more fried
plantain and leave me alone?" I said, wearily. His mouth
was still not completely empty, and there were palm-oil
stains on his handkerchief that betrayed the menu of his
last snack. Totally unabashed, he came and sat on my
desk and leaned over my typewriter with an air of one
about to impart a great confidence.

"Listen, oga, you know who he is entertaining these
days after all the parties are finished?" he asked, his long,
thin, foxy face further elongated by the conspiratorial look
it now wore. I shook my head.

"Funke!" He opened his arms wide, in a gesture of
triumph; this wouldn't get into my column either, but it
was certainly news. He got down off the desk and went
out the door jauntily, saying, "Trust Olapeju to get the
real news."

I didn't know what to make of it. Funke was a Lagos
institution; although I had seen her close up only once in

all the time I had been in Lagos, she was, like an institution glimpsed frequently but never visited, almost three-dimensionally familiar to me. In a town where sexual prudery was unknown and would probably be incomprehensible to most people, she had made a name for blatant, even flamboyant, venality and sexual opportunism, and for shifting from patron to patron as her bank balance moved her. The series of patrons had been spectacular, and it was no exaggeration to say that there was not one—at least of those about whom I had heard—who had not left her better off and found himself worse off. There was the young Scottish solicitor who was discreetly repatriated to Glasgow before he could be charged with embezzlement; a timber merchant from Warri who had cut a swath through Lagos social life for a whole year and had afterwards simply disappeared; one of the first Nigerians to be made an assistant superintendent of police who was summarily dismissed for corruption about six months after he took up with her—and six months after his promotion; a painter who had refused a scholarship to the Slade because of her and was now reduced to carving so-called Benin busts for the airport trade: these I knew of, and although reason cautioned that there were probably more sides to all these stories than the one I had heard, the statistics were pretty impressive.

And yet, who better to lock horns with the local *femme fatale* than a Dacosta Payne, I thought, and more or less left it at that.

Payne and I didn't see a tremendous amount of each other; sometimes he would invite me to the smaller parties, and I can vouch for the excellence of the palm-oil chop. More pertinently, he would call me up from time to time, "keeping in touch," occasionally giving me useful tips on what was happening in that part of the city's business life in which he was involved. He did this, I felt, out of a sense of duty, that surprising sense of duty which I had seen at work before; for by now we both knew that we didn't actually like one another a great deal; he found me too staid, too verveless, and I had become impatient with his unremitting black Englishman act, once for me a thing of elegance and beauty, an outward symbol of a fine sensibility, now no more than an exquisitely fashioned carnival costume worn out of season.

His industrial consultancy was genuine enough, it appeared. He was making something of a living—though it could hardly have been on the scale of his spendings—by advising small industrial firms on productivity, marketing, and advertising. He even ran, with the blessing of one of the international organizations, a well-publicized seminar on manpower training. By the end of that first six months there was no question but that Dacosta Payne was definitely somebody in Lagos, not a heavyweight by any means, but a widely known and respected welterweight in the world of commerce and society, one of the people, to boot, about whom it was felt that they "contributed something." Despite Funke, he was on the secondary Government House guest list, invited frequently to receptions and the larger dinner parties. Funke was not. Sir Femi Oladairo, the Queen's Counsel whose brother was Oba of Lagos and who was perhaps the most influential Yoruba in the West, said one night at a party that Dacosta Payne was an *omowale,* a child who had come back home. The remark was widely repeated, not least by Dacosta Payne himself; it wasn't long before all references to him in the newspapers read, deadpan, "Mr. Dacosta (Omowale) Payne."

Chapter Thirteen

You pay a price for everything. The thought flashed through Funke's head, uninvited and without comment. Now I will have to let the white man fuck me. Thank God, he is quite nice-looking. And he is not crude like some of the others. Like some of the black men I have had to deal with. Some of those policemen! *T'olorun!* Funke laughed within and the news of the laughter reached her face very quickly, so that when the white man came back out of the inner office he was confused. She should not have been smiling, since she was in something of a predicament.

"I'm afraid it's going to be very difficult, Miss Adedeji. Your cousin has failed the Part One exams twice now, and the policy is very clear. In special cases we allow two attempts at Part One, and it seems that he has already had his full allowance, even though he doesn't seem to be what we normally call a special case." Proverbs found himself faltering. Funke was still smiling. What the hell did she have to smile about? He had gone into the inner office for pure form. He knew the policy perfectly well; he could have told her at the beginning of the interview. He also knew the loopholes, and had taken

86

specially favored applicants through them more than once. But form *was* important. This he knew down to the marrow of his bones. His little act of leaving her waiting for ten minutes while he ostensibly consulted higher authority and precedent was part of the daily, unrelenting performance of authority, less spectacular than the changing of the guard at Government House, but even more crucial a part of the ritual of power. And now the woman was smiling, when she should have been wringing her hands. She seemed neither anxious nor perplexed. She could not know that he was going to let her cousin through one of the loopholes, since he hadn't known it himself when he had left her in the outer room. But, having made up his mind, and having already composed the minute on Babajide Adedeji in his head, he would have to go through with the third act.

"We notice that in your letter you say your cousin has had troubles over money. Could you be more specific?" he pursued.

Funke's expression returned to normal. The frown came back, two thin creases in her forehead that Proverbs had already fallen in love with. As when he had first seen them, he wanted to touch the two extremities with his forefingers and trace the short line down the side of her head to join with the straight slashes her tribal marks made on her cheeks. The profession for me is gynecologist, he thought. But I'd be struck off the register in three months.

"Yes, sir. The boy has had bad troubles. His mother is my junior sister, and she does not understand the cost of living in London. She thought she had enough with what the father gives her and that Jide was being wasteful. It was pure ignorance, sir. She did not come to the family until too late. We would have helped if we had known. Now it is all right. We will send the money, and he will be able to study properly again." She was earnest again, but Proverbs felt something was missing. Behind the polite, almost obsequious, language, he sensed a confidence about the outcome of the interview which did not jibe with the facts as he knew them.

"I'm afraid it isn't quite as simple as that," he said. He was acting again. Of course it was quite as simple as that, since his recommendation would be accepted, and he already knew what his recommendation would be. "What the Department must have is some quite irrefutable evidence that his failures have been due to circumstances beyond his control; we must know that he is intellectually capable of undertaking and completing the course of studies for which we are paying a substantial subsidy. And it isn't just the Department. The Chief Secretary has never been very keen on scholarships for law studies, and every award has to be justified down to the last detail." He was laying it on very thick, even though it was all true in a narrow sense of the word "true," but he was damned if he was going to let her get away with that smile and, now, her not altogether convincing deference. He passed his hand over prematurely thinning fair hair; a straggly phalanx of freckles marched in an ostentatious parade up his face and lost themselves in his scalp. Corruption of the flesh. Freckles and albinism. The word in Yoruba for a white man had been invented to describe the albino. He was a true *oyibo*, then. It gave him, when he was drunk or overtired and in a mood for fantasy, a mad sense of authenticity. *Oyibo* actually meant "scraped-skin man." So, if you scraped the skin of Miss Adediji, you would find a Proverbs. Oh, if his aunt could know what was passing through his head right now, could know that he was seriously contemplating a technical betrayal of Empire for the price—the unguaranteed price—of a tumble in bed with a black woman, ah, Ye Gods and Furies!

At this point his own internal laughter seeped through

to his face. The muscles of his cheeks, caught unawares by the message from his brain, lifted as directed ever so slightly, creasing the flesh under his eyes into the comfortable, accustomed lines of a smile. Miss Adedeji saw, and he saw that she saw. There was no explanation to be given.

Chapter Fourteen

The garden was ringed by several dozen palm-oil lanterns which someone had cleverly attached to the hibiscus hedge at strategic points. They gave off a powerful, but somehow somber, light, casting capricious shadows as the fist-sized flames shifted this way and that in the light evening breeze. Brathwaite had seen gardens decorated with palm-oil lamps before, but it had taken a Dacosta Payne to conceive of using them as the sole illumination for an entire party. So much about Payne betrayed an obsessive interest in the decorative, in design, in making an external impact, that Brathwaite would not have been surprised if in his next temporal incarnation Payne became a couturier or a landscape gardener.

A big man wearing an *agbada* with gold thread embroidery at the neck and sleeves came up to him holding a glass of champagne between his thumb and forefinger.

"*O da go ni!*" the man said. Brathwaite knew that this meant that it was a good party, but he said, "Excuse me?" to discourage the man from continuing in Yoruba.

"I'm sorry," said the man, "you're not Nigerian?"

"No, West Indian."

90

"An *ajerike* like our host! Ah! Which island? Barbados as well?" Brathwaite nodded.

"Delightful!" the man said. "You know Mr. Justice Franklin of the Barbados High Court, I'm sure. We were called together. That's quite a little while ago." He looked at his glass and then twirled it thoughtfully. "Then one day I saw in the *Times* that he had 'taken Silk' the same week I did. Quite a coincidence, eh?" The champagne and the gesture reminded Brathwaite that he had seen the man before, at the party at the Alatishes, and had immediately consigned him to Aunt Matilda's category of the consequential. But they had not been introduced. "Oladairo," the man said, holding out his hand. "Brathwaite," Brathwaite said. He knew that this was Sir Femi; if Sir Femi ever wanted to know *his* given name, he would have to get one of his clerks to find out.

"Franklin, de Caires, Baird. We and the West Indians were very close, you know, in those days. Just a handful of black colonials who had been fortunate enough to scale the heights, so to speak. We stuck together. As a matter of fact, we rather looked up to the West Indians, they seemed so much more sophisticated than we savage Africans." Brathwaite didn't know whether Sir Femi was being ironic or merely bantering; in this light it was impossible to discern the expression of his face. "We still exchange Christmas cards. Every year without fail. We manage to keep in touch. I toured the West Indies some years back and Franklin was very decent to my wife and myself when we stopped over for a few days in Barbados. Very pleasant little place. Your countryman is doing very well for himself, I must say. Payne. He certainly has ideas. Very much a man of the twentieth century. Very much so. I'm delighted to have met you." Sir Femi moved on with a just perceptible twitching of the muscles of his face that was meant, Brathwaite supposed, to be a gracious smile.

Brathwaite felt anger rising in him as the distinguished

Queen's Counsel, Leader of the Nigerian Bar, and pet African of the British Establishment moved away. It was as if Sir Femi had somehow measured him and found him to be worth precisely two minutes of ruminative monologue and no more. The consequential son of a bitch.

"Mr. Brathwaite! How *marvelous* to see you! Isn't it a *super* party? Darling, you remember Mr. Brathwaite, *Brath*waite, don't you?"

"Of course I do. How are you, Mr. Brathwaite?"

"Hello, hello. How are you. Nice to see you. That's a very attractive dress, Mrs. Dryfoos."

"Do you really think so? You are a flatterer. I rather like it myself, but to tell the truth I wondered if it wasn't a little young. . . ."

"Do stop it, Charmaine! You know perfectly well you wondered no such thing. My God! Just imagine if some other woman had made that remark! You're too insincere."

"Myron, love, I've told you again and again. There's no point expecting a woman to be *sincere* about her appearance. It's as much as I can do to be sincere about my bank account."

"Your countryman is making quite an impact in Lagos, Mr. Brathwaite. Very attractive personality. . . ."

"A frightfully attractive *man*. And elegant! Such a joy to see a man who can be elegant and still look *virile*. He's frightfully virile-looking, isn't he? And that get-up he's wearing. So *original!* He's given me an idea for a dress."

"Very sound man, too. He's been talking to me about some of his ideas, and I must say I was impressed. He's going to run into trouble with some of the fuddy-duddies around here, I'm sure. But I've told him he mustn't let himself get too discouraged too easily. You two are good friends, I take it, Mr. Brathwaite?"

"Oh . . . we've known each other for years. Since my student days, as a matter of fact."

"He's a comer. Good man. Very sharp."

"What was that marvelous crack, Myron? Do tell Mr. Brathwaite."

"You mean about fences? Oh, yes. He said that since my business is to take wealth *out* of Nigeria while what he's trying to do is to find ways of keeping wealth *in* the country, we're on opposite sides of the fence. . . ."

". . . but you can often get quite fabulous results through judicious use of holes in fences! He really is devastating! Aren't you proud to be from the same country, Mr. Brathwaite?"

"He certainly is an extraordinary man. . . ."

"You can say that again. If I thought there was the faintest chance he'd be interested I'd try to get him into our organization, but I think he prefers his side of the fence. Oh, I perfectly understand what he means when he talks about 'opposite sides of the fence.' It's perfectly true that we bring jobs, what is called progress, all that, when we introduce modern industry into a country like this. No doubt about it. We can quite honestly say that we're doing something for Nigeria. But, when you get right down to it, that's not what the shareholders look forward to hearing at the annual general meeting, is it? What they're holding their breath for is the dividend announcement. I'd be kidding you if I said otherwise. I know what *our* priorities are. And there has to be another side. Payne sees this. And he's tackling it from the right end. These programs he's been working on. Especially the training. Just what's needed. It's what companies like mine ought to have started on way back. I told Payne that as far as I'm concerned something has already passed through the hole in the fence. I'm going to be plugging for our organization to start its own programs along the general lines he's working on. What he's seen is that it can't cost all that much, and it'll likely get us some good will we may need one of these rainy days."

"Does everybody feel the same way as you?"

"My God, no! Even in my own company, it's far from being a pushover. *'Tempora mutantur, sed nos in illis non mutamur':* translated 'The times may change, but damned if we will.' That ought to be the motto of a lot of the so-called modern businesses operating in Nigeria."

"Darling, you mustn't bore Mr. Brathwaite with all this dreary shoptalk. That isn't what he came to this party for, is it Mr. B.?"

"Oh, I'm far from bored, Mrs. D. . . . ."

"Please call me Charmaine. Everybody does."

"And call me Myron. You mustn't let the British brainwash you into taking on their horrible formality. Do you know, Charmaine was the first Britisher I ever met who didn't literally freeze me into incoherence with petty formalities?"

"That's why he married me. The other Englishwomen he met—I do wish you wouldn't say 'Britisher,' Myron—the others said yes the first night out all right, but the morning after they called him Mr. Dryfoos!"

"Oh, come on, Charmaine! You'll make Mr. Brathwaite blush . . . so to speak. . . ."

"Myron, love, you're sparkling tonight! 'So to speak'! Positively brilliant! You mustn't mind us, Mr. Brathwaite. We're both perfectly dotty."

"It's rather useful not to be able to blush. It's one of the few social advantages of being black."

"Mr. Brathwaite! I think we're all being *infected* by the atmosphere around Mr. Payne. You sounded almost exactly like him just then."

"I would say a splendid man to imitate, if you must imitate somebody. The best."

"I *absolutely* agree. There ought to be lots more Dacosta Paynes in this world. We need them badly, Mr. Brathwaite."

"Call me Sinclair."

Sir Femi moved with prehensile deliberateness away from the bar and made for the small fountain, a plaster statue inspired by the Manneken Pis, which was the center piece—and a sure-fire conversation piece—for the otherwise dull expanse of neat lawn that was the garden of Payne's rented villa. A handful of guests were sitting on the circular seat beneath the fountain. Even in the flickering light of the palm-oil lanterns Sir Femi recognized the woman who was sitting with her face turned in his direction as Funke, and he walked purposefully toward her as if that had been his sole intent and goal from the moment he left the bar.

"Little sister," he said in soft Yoruba, "you are well?"

"Well," Funke replied, using the shortest permissible response. Before the full antiphonal exchange of greetings could be completed, she switched abruptly to English. "Mrs. Scott, you know Sir Femi Oladairo? Mrs. Scott." Sir Femi started perceptibly and shook hands with the stout Englishwoman who was sitting beside Funke.

"Of course." Jock Scott was one of the "development solicitors," a lawyer who was making such a killing on land speculation that he scarcely bothered to appear in court these days. Nigerian firms never got the apparently open access to bank vaults that their British counterparts seemed to have, and there was no love lost between them. "Of course, how are you, Angela? I didn't recognize you. . . this light. How's Jock? He here?"

"Yes, he's over there somewhere," she said, waving a sausage-like finger to her right. "How's Ti Ti? She here, too?"

"No, I'm afraid not. Her old school association's having a business meeting tonight, and she's the treasurer. Nothing gets in the way of that." He laughed briefly and made a mocking gesture of a man surrendering in the face of inhuman odds, and Angela Scott laughed with him.

"But I should be moving on," she said, rising. The top of her head, its integument of straight dark hair so rigidly swept back that it appeared a bodiless pigment, met him at eye-level. The little pearl-encrusted bag that she carried looked in her huge hand like an accessory for a doll's house. Sir Femi mouthed a protest at her departure, but she ignored it with a wide smile full of innocent camaraderie. "Ta-ta, Funke. See you all later," she said, patting Sir Femi on the shoulder and walking sturdily away in the direction where she had said her husband could be found.

"May I sit down?" Sir Femi said to Funke. Without answering, she moved, unnecessarily, to make room for him on the padded bench. "I must say," he went on when he was seated, "you don't seem too pleased to see me."

Funke shifted very slightly away from him. She said nothing.

"Do you know," he went on, "I really didn't see Angela Scott there? Oh, I saw there was *somebody*, but my mind really didn't go beyond just registering that fact. I wonder why she went off so quickly? Does she know something about us?"

Funke laughed, a small explosion of breath through her open mouth that she bit off before the sound was completely expelled. "What is there to know? That I was your mistress two years ago?" Still under the influence of Angela Scott's recent presence they had been speaking English. Now Funke said in Yoruba: "There is no market for yesterday's fish or yesterday's gossip." She looked up at him now, waiting. He couldn't see clearly enough to read the expression on her face, but he recognized the gesture and could deduce the rest. The eyes would be crinkled, the mouth slightly pursed and asymmetrically upturned at one corner. It was part of the common vocabulary of expression. On a schoolgirl, with teacher's back turned, it would be no more than cheeky. He had seen it on the faces of old women at a *komojade* dancing to the *gan gan;* there it was the permitted coquetry of the dancer. But with Funke the expression was, as it were, withdrawn from the common currency and given a quite particular value. He had seen it on her face for the first time the first time they had made love, and it gave him the fright of his life. Laboring between her murderous thighs with the knowing fury of his forty-eight years, he had cracked the tight nut of her canny sensuality no less than three times, each time contriving —only just— to rein in his own ecstasy as she splintered in trembling orgasm around his prick. He had been caressing her head, which she had turned away from him, her teeth spastically clenched, at the moment of climax; his body was full of the tingling joy of virility and anticipated release. When, suddenly, her head turning with that same spring-taut jerk to face him, he saw *that* expression on her face. It told him (and he took full responsibility for the translation) that he was doing a marvelous job, really marvelous. But *she* was having the orgasms! Don't build up a great head of illusion about your virility, it said, about the conquest and reduction of Funke, because Funke is ready to go on like this all day. And you, Olufemi Oladairo? Are you ready? Well, climb right back in there and show me.

She had, of course, disowned the expression. "You please me very much. That is obvious to you, isn't it? I know *I* please *you.*" And would discuss it no more. What was there to discuss? Ti Ti, with her good Second in Modern Greats, would have understood him. She was the only person with whom he could have talked about it, if it had been possible to talk about it. She would have diagnosed it as arrogance, he guessed. "The traditional sexual arrogance of the prostitute. It's the only defense they have against the daily diminution of their integrity." She would probably have cited Sappho, and the hetaeras

of Athens, who took refuge in lesbianism out of boredom
with the limitations of the heterosexual relation. "After
all," she would have said, "when a woman has been having orgasms at the rate of twenty or thirty a week from
age fourteen, there must come a moment when she feels
that an orgasm is an orgasm is an orgasm. And, by the
same token, think of how much worse it must be for those
who don't have orgasms. Humiliation without recom-
pense." And she would probably have added something
about the rationale behind female circumcision in some
tribes.

"Angela is very clever," he said now. "Perhaps she
knows even more than that. Perhaps she knows that I'd
like to start it all again." He was speaking in a low voice
from customary motives of discretion, but in his own ears
he sounded like a man pleading. He was astonished at
this. His voice seemed to have been taken over by an
emotion of which he had been quite unconscious only five
minutes before. And he couldn't honestly repudiate this
oh so impolitic, uninvited impulse.

Funke laughed that grudging laugh again. "You must
be joking, big brother," she said. "What is finished is
finished. I have never gone back to a man yet." She said
this with simple, unarguable definitiveness. Now it was
Sir Femi who laughed, a short burst of sound directed at
himself.

"Do you think anybody looking at us could guess
what we're talking about?" he asked, half to himself.

"Your wife. She knows about us, and she knows about
you."

"So right, so very right, Funke. Perhaps that was why
she didn't come tonight. She's got my measure, even better than I've got it myself."

"But I thought you said. . . ."

"Oh, that was an excuse. I knew it even then, but I
didn't think it important enough to make an issue of it.
I'm sure that she foresaw this. What does the *ajerike* song

say: 'Woman smarter than man in every way.' There's something which I really believe. Always have. Do you know, I think that the only really stupid things I have done in my life have been connected with women.''

"Well, the stupidities with Funke are over, that is sure."

"Are you being faithful to Payne? Is that the problem? You weren't faithful to me, you know. I didn't find out until afterwards, but everybody else knew. Even Ti Ti. Now, all of a sudden, you've changed? What is it, old age?'' Again his tongue had run ahead of his judgment. He couldn't understand it. He was not a man given to unconsidered statements. His reputation at the cutthroat and not always jurisprudentially distinguished Nigerian Bar was one of soundness, coupled with a kind of almost Anglo-Saxon intellectual dandyism. He had taken Silk at 34, the youngest King's Counsel in the colonies. Because, above all things, he always knew more than he said and said only exactly as much as was strictly necessary. Now, meeting Funke in the accidental intimacy of Payne's garden, despite the fact that for two years he had had not great difficulty in keeping the dead past decently buried, despite the transcendental fact that Funke was now notoriously unavailable, he found himself saying a whole series of unsayable things. *"He isn't himself."* Or: *"He hasn't been himself for some time."* The familiar old wives' diagnosis of all ills from diarrhea to drunkenness appeared uniquely apt for his state; not being himself, being other than himself, falling out of character. A mild onset of schizophrenia provoked by Funke's proximity. A small part of his mind lightly touched; one of these days the biological chemists would discover that women like Funke actually emitted electrical energy that could have the effect on the chemical substances in the brain that vinegar has on milk. (The old wives would say that he was "addled": How amusing if they turned out to be right!)

It was clearly time to pull back, to make a gigantic

effort to suppress the memories of her body that had surged to the top of his consciousness. (A body that, as he remembered it, was capable of retaining even the faintest light so that he could see the precise shape of her breast in a room lit only by starlight. Very irrational, all that.) He must also dismiss from his mind the most erotic image of all, the image of a Funke he had never possessed, a Funke he was always one orgasm away from possessing. One of the most effective of all aphrodisiacs did not figure in the pharmacopoeia: pride.

"Please ignore what I just said," he told her, his brain righting itself like a plane that clears a spot of un-expected turbulence. "As you said, what's finished is finished. But, tell me, is this *omowale* going to marry you?" He told himself that the question was measured and canny and kindly. Concern about Funke's evolution—she twenty-eight to his fifty, still an adventuress without resource but her body, but with a legitimate claim on his concern since she had patently taken possession of some tender part of him—in a deadheat with concern about business. Was Payne planning to be something of a fix-ture in Lagos, or was he just passing through, spoon in hand, interested only in the cream he saw on the surface? If marriage was in his mind it was an argument for some stability of intention. Sir Femi had made his own assess-ment already, but evidence was evidence.

"What are you asking, big brother?" Funke said, resting her hand on his shoulder. "You know that I am not one for marriage. '*Omowale*'! Ah! You think he is an *omowale?* Where is his home? He is like me, you hear? We do not know where home is until we put on the sleeping-cloth!" She laughed now wide and frank and shook his shoulder in an invitation to laugh with her.

"But he is a serious man, Funke? You're not wasting your time with him?" The pressure on his shoulder changed. Still holding him lightly, she leaned back a little and looked questioningly at him.

"If my father asked me that question I would not answer; if you had asked me the same question five minutes ago, I would not have answered. Yes, he is serious, *for me* serious. He does not want my soul and my body for one price. You understand?" She shook his shoulder gently. Sir Femi gave no sign that she had said anything of particular significance. "He does not care about the other men. For him it is as if I was born the day we met." Sir Femi shivered very slightly at the words. The first time he and Funke had made love, some lines of John Donne's learned at school and happily forgotten ever since came rushing into his mind as if they had been waiting for one occasion and one only.

> I wonder by my troth, what thou, and I
> Did, till we loved? Were we not weaned till then?

Was life so inevitably banal and unoriginal? He must ask Payne if he knew the poem. "When he is with me," Funke pursued, "he is with me. He is not thinking about business, or half-thinking about some other woman. He is all with me."

"He has no wife." Sir Femi spoke in English, a little ruefully, a little absently as well. He was thinking: Not once, in all the five or six months of our affair did I hear Funke speak with such passion, such single-minded passion. I ought to be grateful to Payne. I owe it to him, to whatever gifts he has in bed and out of bed, that I'm saved from making much more of a fool of myself over Funke.

Funke said, in English, too: "I am his wife! He does not have to take me to church. But, *egbo,* you are a real *oyibo!*" She laughed again, and clapped her hands.

"Not a real one, *aburo.* A toy *oyibo,*" Sir Femi said. One more unfiltered thought slipping past his tongue.

"And Dacosta is *omowale!* Yay! I will tell him that you
have christened him."

"Yes, tell him. I'm sure he will like that."

Payne, princely in a gold-embroidered black *danshiki*
of his own design and cream tussore slacks tailored for
him by an ancient Jew discovered off Shaftesbury Avenue, offered a glass of champagne to Adu Adumuyiwa.
Adu accepted it as he might have accepted a piece of raw
seal meat from an Eskimo host. He had come to Payne's
party out of curiosity, as he might have accepted an invitation to visit an Eskimo igloo if by some chance it had
arrived in Lagos, intact in every cultural and climato-
logical detail.

He had been introduced to Payne at one of those morning sessions at the Embassy. Adu disapproved of morning
drinking, and only business—and the insistence of the
other party—had persuaded him to go to the Embassy. He
was comprehensively suspicious of Payne because he
found it hard to understand what the man was doing in
Lagos; even when he was forced to admit to himself the
viability of a small industrial consultancy business, he
came up against another question: What had brought
Payne to Lagos of all places? He clearly couldn't make
half the money he would make in Europe; equally clearly,
Payne was a man to whom money mattered. And, frankly,
Adu did not particularly like West Indians. As a student
in London he had found them unbearably supercilious
toward Africans in general, and after a while he had
simply not bothered with them. The English were bad
enough, but it was their country, and you had no choice
but to deal with them. When the traumatic experience of
England was over, distance had permitted him to indulge
in some tentative rationalizations about his black and
brown cousins from the Caribbean: Had they succumbed to
the human need to have someone to look down on, the

house-slave/field-slave syndrome? Or was it an even
deeper need, the need to shut Africa and all things African totally out of their consciousness? Adu had little pa-
tience for this kind of speculation. Sometimes he wished
that it were possible for his mind to take a binding, once-
for-all, sovereign decision as to those things which were
peripheral to his life, and, acting thenceforth with inexo-
rable logic, to shield him completely from the peripheral.
But, alas, the peripheral was too often only too attractive.
So, here he was, drinking the *ajerike's* champagne, a cog
in the wheel of the man's ambitions whatever they were,
serving no purpose of his own but the highly peripheral
purpose of social intercourse. Worse, really, was the fact
that he was quite enjoying himself, taking pleasure in the
relaxed arrangements Payne had made within the essentially flamboyant, ostentatious terms of reference of his
life.

Payne was tackling him now, in a light-fingered manner
that Adu rather envied and rather distrusted, about his
political ambitions. "Aren't you getting a bit cheesed off
with being perpetually on the sidelines of the political
struggle?" Payne asked, gently agitating his glass so that
it picked up orange glints from the palm-oil lamps. They
were standing alone at the bar looking out onto the lawn
where people were forming and reforming themselves
into little groups according to some indecipherable atomic
system of social intercourse. "Chessed off," "sidelines";
Payne's choice of the two pieces of British slang seemed
somehow to reduce the great, bitter complex of the country's political life to *manageable* terms, a rugger game,
say? Terms that could, anyway, be dealt with at a party.
Caught uncomfortably between amusement and annoyance at the concept, Adu had replied that you had a much
better view of the game from the sidelines than from the
middle of the scrum. Immediately he was annoyed with
himself for being so easily caught in the meretricious

game of metaphors. "Politics is scarcely a rugger game, anyway," he said, trying to be cutting but succeeding only in sounding plaintive. "There are those who think it's a matter of life and death." Now, that sounded pompous.

"Oh, it's a matter of life and death alright," Payne said. "I haven't any doubt about that. But, if you don't mind my saying so, you are at once the most trenchant and the most detached commentator on the country's politics that I've run into, and I'm simply surprised, that's all, that you're not into it deeper than you are. Is it too presumptuous of me to say so?" My God, Adu thought, the man's giving me a lecture. I ought to ask him straight out what's it got to do with him, Mr. Detachment himself. So I'm a *trenchant commentator*. It sounded suspiciously like a shorthand way of calling him a bitter do-nothing loudmouth. He found that he didn't know how to answer Payne. The man had got directly under his guard by means of an approach he had taken to be both light-fingered and lightweight. The question was an old one: His father asked it at least once a month, and the reply *to his father* was easy—and true—enough; that the time isn't ripe. It was too intimate and truthful an answer to give to Payne. Further, he wouldn't understand; a whole background would have to be explained to him, about tribe, about constituencies, about certain personal relations with members of the two main parties. Not that his father knew the precise prescription that he had written for himself, the exact mixture of the various components which would precipitate Adu's decision, but he understood that there had to be a prescription and he could identify the components if they were put before him.

"You must come to one of my meetings," he said. "Perhaps you'll understand it all a bit better then."

"I beg leave to doubt it," Payne said. "I've already been to two of your meetings and I think you make tremendous sense in practically everything you say. I think you're especially right when you talk about the need for really indigenous training programs with a twenty-five year perspective. But your kind of thinking should be available to the Government, don't you think?"

"Well, they could follow your excellent example and attend my meetings, for a start."

"They're well attended by the Criminal Investigation Department, at least."

"Then they should *read* the reports." They both laughed, conscious that they had reached a stalemate. Adu, feeling friendlier now towards his host, broke the short silence that followed.

"You have been questioning me very directly. . . ."

"And getting no answer."

"Well, I wouldn't quite say that. Anyway, now I want to ask you a very direct question."

"Why did I come to Nigeria?" Payne forestalled him. Adu smiled and nodded. "Oh, I thought you would get round to that sooner or later. It's not an unobvious question, after all. Of course, you don't expect a comprehensive answer. That would take a month, including Sundays. But I'll gladly give you a few, shall we say, headlines? No particular order of priority. Here goes. Plain curiosity. The kind that takes unaccompanied maiden ladies to Katmandu. But, of course, I'm not too curious about Katmandu, whereas I've always been curious about Nigeria. Have you ever heard of King Ja-Ja? Of course you have. He spent some time in Barbados, at least according to one story, and he was certainly incarcerated in St. Vincent. I grew up hearing great baroque tales, there's even a song about King Ja-Ja. The concept of an African king, you'll probably appreciate, is fascinating, tantalizing when you've been brought up in a colony and brainwashed into assuming that 'regal' automatically equates with 'white.' But right in the middle of my folklore there was black royalty, a historical Nigerian king. And a king the

British feared so much that they had to hide him away in the most remote place they could think of, the West Indies. It's not very coherent or logical so far, is it? None of it is, especially if I'm going to tie it up into a neat little packet for you and have time to look after my other guests as well. So, from very early on there is lodged in my consciousness the image of a Nigerian king. And he is just as fabulous in the best sense of the word as all the other majesties. I must have said to myself at some stage in my dream-starved youth: One of these days I am going to see an African king, a *Nigerian* king. It's not a deeply shameful ambition for a young black boy in the colonies to have, is it? Oh, and then Africa, the whole thing in capital letters, Africa my home, dark forgotten continent of my unconscious. And then, of course, opportunity. A series of accidents occurred and all of them pointed in the same direction, Lagos. So I followed the directions. It's not much of an answer, I know, but will it do for the nonce?"

"It will do." Adu shook his head like a parent affectionately despairing of a mischievous child. Payne had paid him back in his own coin, had done better, in fact, because he had taken the trouble to provide the facsimile of an answer, an elegant little creation like the pseudo-*danshiki* he was wearing. He had of course not answered the real question, which was: Why had he chosen to come to Nigeria to do what he was doing? Didn't the West Indies need industrial consultants as well? Adu realized that it had been naive of him to expect that in return for nothing he would receive an outpouring of truth, that Payne's fluent lips would bubble over with the secrets of his heart in return for Adu's own gruff evasions. At least Payne had been neither gruff nor measly with his evasions; he had given them a decent enough garb of myth, frankness, and charm. A man like this was made to be a politician. If only he had Payne's gift of anesthetic glibness! There was nothing for him to do but pretend to be persuaded by Payne's prestidigitation; it was as near as he would ever get to the "real thing." It was as near as he deserved. "Oh, yes, it will do," Adu said, thinking: I wish I had run into you in England, I would have got your measure. For England was like a mammoth white cricket sight-screen against which the figures of black men stood out in sharp relief. He wondered why no one of his acquaintance seemed to have known Dacosta Payne in England, and a curious thought, the ultimate in cynical pessimism, struck him. Was Payne, could he be, a political agent for the British? It was far-fetched. And, yet, was it all that far-fetched? It was the kind of job a West Indian would take; it would fit in with the confusion he had noted in them as to who exactly they were, the confusion that led them to lust after British honors (whereas even the Sir Femis took them for nothing more than their genuine commercial value); the confusion that had had West Indians volunteering in droves for service in His Majesty's Armed Forces during the Second World War and proudly wearing regimental colors afterwards despite the discrimination and contempt that ninety per cent of them had endured as an unscheduled addition to the absurd cruelties and suffering of war. Yes, it would be like a West Indian to take on the work of political spying for the British in an African country; it would help to confirm in him the near-certainty that he was "different from" (an attractive euphemism for "better than") the natives, and thus nearer to the British. It would be a modern extension of the tradition that had brought West Indian missionaries to Africa a bare thirty years after the end of slavery (*Missionaries!* What an absolutely ironic, practical gorgeous joke to play on the recently enslaved!) and West Indian brakemen and railway clerks to Nigeria at the turn of the century to occupy an indeterminate status between "native" and "European."

And wasn't there a very close parallel between spying in the nineteen-fifties and preaching the Christian gospel in the eighteen-sixties? Couldn't a clever War Office man persuade a Barbadian ex-serviceman that there was a noble job of work to be done in the African colonies helping Her Majesty's Government to a better understanding of the political movements, an "intellectually challenging job," a "rewarding job," a job in which one would be "on history's side"? The only question was whether there were people in the War Office quite clever enough to see the possibilities. Remembering the first rule of successful conflict: Never underestimate the enemy, Adu concluded that his far-fetched idea was not at all, not in the least, far-fetched after all. He patted Dacosta Payne amicably on the shoulder, and they moved off toward the other guests.

Chapter Fifteen

It was obviously difficult for Tola to find the right tone of voice, much less the right words, when I phoned her a few days after Charmaine's party and asked her to come for morning coffee at a little bar that lay about halfway between our two offices.

"What are we going to talk about? Why are you asking me?" The questions were not logically connected, and I interpreted them as a noise she was making in preparation for saying no as politely as she could.

"Don't just say no," I begged.

"I can't think of a good reason to say yes." But she had now found a tone. It was mocking, but gentle enough: the tone you might use with a froward child who has worked himself into a not too dangerous trap.

"That we like each other and this makes us quite curious about each other? That would be a good reason, if it was true. Isn't it true?"

"Do you always give in to your curiosity? Would you be prepared to satisfy my curiosity completely? Would you?"

"In twenty minutes, at Harry's. Try me." I put the telephone down quickly to stop her from having to choose between the difficult word "yes" and the far too easy word "no."

She was at Harry's before I got there, installed in a booth drinking orange juice.

"Is it fresh orange juice, or out of a tin?"

"Fresh. Very good."

I ordered a glass for myself and sat down.

"I don't want to spoil your triumph. . . ."

"Triumph?" I interrupted.

"Oh, yes, triumph. It's quite an achievement getting me to come here. You damned well ought to feel triumphant."

"Alright, I feel triumphant."

"But I came on one condition."

"Did we talk about conditions?"

"Oh, this is a condition I set myself, a promise to myself. I'm just informing you, it's not a threat. I'll come and have coffee with you and talk with you anytime. But the moment you make a pass at me, that's the end. You see what I mean, don't you?" The harsh and rather pompous speech was offset by the tone of her voice, pleading, excusing itself, hoping that the suggestion would be seen as reasonable. God knows it was reasonable enough; she was entitled to at least one gesture that would give her some slight protection for her self-respect.

"What do you expect me to say?" I asked. "Do you want a notarized pledge?"

"Oh, please! If you're going to make jokes about it, let's forget it."

"Forget you've said it?"

"Scrap it as a subject of conversation."

And at that time, what with the sense of triumph which she had so accurately diagnosed and the pleasure of actually seeing her there, I felt generous and terribly powerful. Let her have her fig leaf, I said to myself. She knows I know.

I asked her again the next week, and she came. We talked easily, in a comfortable exchange of autobiographical data. No further commitments were asked or given. We met twice for orange juice in the following week and once a week over the next month or so. We talked ravenously about everything, but we talked, really, about nothing, since we kept scrupulously clear of that area she had designated as being out of bounds. But we went on meeting, because there was nobody else that either of us wished to spend an hour with drinking orange juice at eleven in the morning. We were capable of—there was no way in such a small town to avoid—mentioning Charmaine's name, without really discussing Charmaine. And, of course, never a mention of that most special and most unavoidable concatenation of Charmaine, Sinclair, and Tola. Once she even brought me an invitation from her Aunt Matilda to drinks after dinner but insisted, nicely, that I tell her if I was going to accept so that she could be away from the house on that particular evening.

"You know my aunt's very fond of you and not at all fond of my husband. She's always telling me I should divorce him and make myself free for some eligible young man. I know she would take a particular delight in playing that record in your presence, and I really couldn't stand that." It was a plea that came near to being flattering, and I felt a quite illogical sympathy for her predicament.

The situation was intrinsically ridiculous. We were like two people at either end of a perfectly serviceable bridge who have solemnly signed a pact to communicate with each other only by means of an elaborate system of smoke signals. I wanted to hear, from her, not through the one-dimensional Lagos grapevine, just what was wrong between her and her husband. The grapevine had it that their childlessness was the problem, that his family was convinced that it was her fault and was as eager as

Tola's Aunt Matilda that the marriage should be ended. But this was the taboo ground of genuine emotion; her aunt's invitation had forced her to tread on its outskirts, and that was as far as she would go.

There were inevitably a number of other narrow escapes, moments when feelings on one side or the other burst out from the constraint that was put upon them, when I was offered a glimpse, plain as daylight, of that perversely suppressed layer of Tola's psyche that wished —I was sure—to be unsuppressed, that wished to come out from the steel casing of her will and meet me head-on. It was on the existence of this layer that our whole relationship was predicated, but it was hard, sometimes, in the bland commerce of orange juice and impersonalities we conducted, to believe that it truly and necessarily existed.

Tola's Aunt Matilda, whom I now visited at least once a fortnight for tea and cakes or sometimes sherry or palm wine, without ever discussing Tola, had clearly decided to take an active role in shaping the friendship she knew to exist between us. She continued to try, without success, to bring us together in the old house in Balogun Square, but she was foiled by my own perverse determination to play the game Tola's way. Now it was I who warned Tola in advance of my dates with the wily Matilda, with a scrupulousness that was in the circumstances almost surrealistic, but which was probably based on a kind of Machiavellian Old Testament ethic which promised that these careful sacrifices would be rewarded in good, carnal kind when the audit was taken.

There was a small, immediate reward. Tola felt obliged to recount to me the mild tongue-lashings her aunt meted out to her about her unreasonable chastity, never once mentioning the name of Sinclair Brathwaite. Matilda's favorite line, Tola reported, was to accuse her niece of belonging in spirit to the nineteenth century and of wasting the opportunities and facilities offered by the twentieth. I delighted in this roundabout process by which an aged "maiden" lady took up arms on my behalf; she had far more opportunities than I to press my suit and from what Tola said did not miss a single one.

"I think the truth is that Aunt Matilda is mad because she can't have an affair with you," she said one day. It was a grotesque thought, but I couldn't help showing my pleasure. Matilda had finally nagged Tola into employing a part of her vocabulary that had been totally excluded from our encounters at Harry's. I pictured Matilda as a kind of sandwich-board man marching patiently up and down the street in front of Harry's carrying a placard with all the words that Tola had declared taboo between us. It was time to stop the delicate double talk.

"If I had been around forty years ago, even thirty," I said into my glass, "that would really be a terrific piece of news. I want to have an affair with you."

"I asked for that," she said. "I'm sorry. I'd better go." She was a genius at exits.

I wasn't surprised that she "couldn't make it" the following week, and the week after that. The third week, by a tremendous effort, I didn't call. Another week passed and then she called up, the first time she had ever done so. She wanted us to meet in the evening near Victoria Beach. A half-dozen wisecracks were aborted in my throat: Victoria Beach was the classic nighttime rendezvous for lovers who had no safe bed, for foreigners who preferred to take their chances in the spaces between the coconut trees rather than face the indiscreet lighting of the clubs, for all the furtive of the city.

"There's something I want to say to you that I don't think Harry's is quite the place for. Can you manage it, about eightish? By the first beach house after the fork?"

I permitted myself to say that it sounded a curious place to meet.

"It's the best place I can think of. You don't mind it that much, do you?" There was really nothing to mind, if she didn't mind.

In the event, the beach road and its approaches were fairly bare. Unseasonable rains had whipped the Atlantic into a fury, and in the light of a half-moon you could see the white caps ending their timeless ferrying from the Brazilian coast with a great thundering descent upon the shore. The beach reappeared in swift glimpses only; the long strand that had accommodated so many random lusts and perhaps even a measure of love was now a pale pool reflecting a rather tentative moon. It was the off-season for lovers.

A few cars, Tola's little drophead coupé quickly recognizable among them, were parked at the fork in the road that led to the two arms of agitated beach. I stopped not far from her and was just getting out to go over when I saw her coming toward me, her head held slightly forward in that characteristic pose of women who have never been quite able to accept the large-breastedness that nature has ordained for them.

"Your car's more comfortable, isn't it?" she asked.

"Well, it does have a bench seat." My car was about a half-inch wider than hers. She got in and started speaking right away, her voice pitched a little higher than usual, as if what she had to say was pressing unbearably on her vocal cords.

"I want to tell you that we can't meet anymore. Our sessions at Harry's. I'm sorry, but we'll have to stop." She was looking straight ahead through the windscreen, already misty with the fine Atlantic spray.

"Why?" Perhaps I repeated the automatic question two or three times, partly to myself, for I realized then that I had known ever since the phone call that something like this was inevitably on tonight's agenda.

"Why? Well, where are we going?" The question was

asked with impatience and some bitterness. "Where the hell are we going? Haven't you asked yourself, Sinclair? We have to stop. I'm sorry," she said again. She got out of the car, walked over to her own and drove away. I didn't try to argue with her, much less stop her, since I had indeed asked myself a thousand times where the hell we were going in our flagrantly *demi-vierge*, teasing, masochistic relationship, two overgrown American juveniles honing our sub-petting techniques to a fine edge of despair and mutual frustration. It should have ended long ago, I thought, as I watched one more disappointed car nose up toward the beach, discover that the tide was running against love, and turn away in an angry squeal of tires. I had been the accomplice in an act of blackmail against myself, engaging myself to pretend, week after week, to a woman who had seen me naked and detumescent that I had no organ of sex and that she was equally bereft, a mere voice, chic couture, and a happy combination of plastic effects. It was a relief to be free of the cold, complex-ridden bitch.

Chapter Sixteen

The next time I was bidden to a party at Charmaine's was a little more than a month after my beach rendezvous with Tola. The invitation was delivered in fairly dramatic fashion. The hostess herself came to my cubbyhole at the *Sun*. My door was permanently ajar, its unpainted plywood frame "sprained"—our carpenter's word—in a position that forced the adult visitor to enter sideways. I recognized her hip as it came through the opening and had an unreasonable spasm of anxiety. "You must fly! My husband knows *all!*"

"So this is your lair!" was what she said, putting her behind on precisely the corner most favored by Olapeju. She was wearing white, a man's white shirt pinned back at the cuffs with gold stickpins and a white twill skirt. She brought into that mean little office, with its stale odor of ten thousand cheap cigarettes and yams fried in last week's palm oil, a whiff of cool lawns sloping down to a river where idle young men harmlessly punted idle young women to and fro.

"What brings you here?" I asked. The question was meant to be light and friendly, but it must have sounded ungracious, to put it no higher; for she rose immediately as if I had struck her.

116

"Well, well! You might at least make me feel a *bit* welcome! You don't imagine that I'm in the habit of spending my morning in printing establishments, do you?" I relaxed, because I knew that she wasn't really angry. "Printing establishments" was the giveaway, one of her private affectations about which I had already begun to tease her. She loved to pretend that she was of the generation that called a brassiere a "bust-bodice" and a car a "motor." Good mood or no, she still managed to make me feel a little like one of those sad creatures in nineteenth-century lithographs who assembled pages letter by letter.

I apologized quite sincerely. "You don't imagine I'm in the habit of receiving elegant and beautiful women in this hole every day, do you?"

"I could forgive you almost anything, you're such a flatterer!" She bent over to kiss me on the nose and I saw, low in her full, white brassiere, the sharp division of white skin from bronze of her latest suntan. Flattery—I had by now discovered that it was as simple as that—was an instant dam to Charmaine's anger, capable of converting those violent cataracts into the most placid of lakes. I had not meant to flatter, and that is the very best sort of flattery.

"Why are you such a bastard when you can be such an absolute sweetie with no effort at all? I came to invite you to a party, but I was damned close to scrapping the whole idea just now, let me tell you." She leaned over again as if to bite me and I backed away, remembering the thinness of the barrier between my office and the newsroom, and certain that it couldn't be long before Olapeju's instinct—or network—hurled him like a projectile into my sanctum.

"Charmaine!" I said, almost hissing. I gestured with my hands to warn her that we were practically in a thoroughfare. She understood immediately.

"I had better be as demure as I can manage, then. I

suppose you want me to sit on this dreadful chair," she said in a histrionic whisper that must have been audible beyond the newsroom. I laughed out loud, defeated.

"Well, I want you to get this straight, Sinclair. I'm having a few people round for supper tomorrow evening," she went on in her normal voice, "and I'm only asking you to make up the number."

"I'm not coming, then," I said. I wasn't offended in the slightest by her bluntness. We had long since entered on that fairly comfortable, post-coital ground which is not quite true intimacy, but very different from friendship. The time for skirmishes of pride, we both knew, was past; when the swords were out now real blood was drawn. "What's the matter, one of your oilmen from Texas got stuck in a barge in the Niger Delta? You really have a nerve!"

She laughed her loud English laugh. "It's Myron who's stuck. But he's nowhere near your Delta. Even though you're such a worm, I've come all this way to *beg* you to come. But you'll have to behave. Tola's going to be there." Her voice dropped as she mentioned Tola's name, and I could have sworn that it was involuntary. For whatever reason, it was a word Charmaine did not pronounce lightly. "No hanky-panky," she said, wagging a finger at me in mock remonstration. "I had a hell of a time getting her to agree to come. It's the first time since, well, since you-know-when."

"Why did you ask her at all? What's so special about bloody Tola? And why ask *me?* Can't you find some underfed stag out at the Rest House?" If she wanted to arrange a straightforward dinner she needn't have asked Tola at all, so I knew that she was cooking up something, one of her *cordon bleu* parties in which guests were not people so much as ingredients. I had always read that the genus Party-giver was composed of frustrated widow-ladies who obtained a quasi-sexual satisfaction from the social intercourse of others; the diagnosis certainly did not fit Charmaine, but I was at a loss for one that would.

"Darling, you know how I *detest* dull parties." Her smile was one of open conspiracy, for she knew she had me. The whole proposition was risqué, which made it that much harder to resist. No doubt Tola's first instinct of resistance had melted too before the hot challenge implicit in Charmaine's invitation.

"I suppose you're going to tell Tola that you've invited me."

"I've told her already. I have to play *fair!* After all, *you* know *she's* coming. We couldn't have the poor girl walking through the door and fainting at the sight of you. There's no point in a *climax* at the very beginning of the act, is there?"

In her own devious, manipulative way she was right. Tola wouldn't faint, but if she felt that she was being made a fool of she'd leave so quietly soon after dinner that the shock waves of her departure would be felt almost as much as if she made a scene.

"If you come, you must *behave*, Sinclair." She was insisting on this so much that I was no longer sure I knew what she really wanted. We were lovers—or, rather I was Charmaine's current lover on occasion. The occasions had almost to be manufactured because we could not, or did not sufficiently want to, transform our different but equally obsessive patterns of living to the point where our affair could become more than just that. Charmaine had her "waifs" to look after, this being the name she gave to the disoriented tribe of company wives whose mornings and afternoons were a desert of inactivity with husbands at work, children at school, and gangs of servants at their beck and call. She beat them consistently at bridge and used this moral superiority to bully them into good works—"I even get some of the more promising ones to read!" she had once boasted. And she had her

house to look after. And her cuisine. And the occasionally
visible Myron. And I had my great, pointless, untamed,
man-eating desire for Tola to look after. (Aunt Matilda
continued to invite me to teas from which Tola continued
to abstain.)

When I had telephoned Charmaine the day after you-
know-when she had laughed at me quite a lot, repeating
her remark of the night before: "I forget how young
you are!" She had expected, she said, that I would have
waited at least a few days, and she certainly hadn't expected that I would sound quite so shell-shocked—and so
eager.

"I'm a *married* woman," she had said. "You recall having met my husband. I hope you don't imagine you've
seduced some *simpering* virgin who's going to be running
after you night and day begging to be screwed again."
The tone was much less abrasive than the words. I felt
that she meant no offense, but I knew that she meant
every word. "Didn't I see you nuzzling away at Tola before you came upstairs to . . . use the bathroom? Well,
have you called *her* up today? Imagine what a fascinating conversation you could have!" She was reading my
mind like a gypsy. I thought I was in love with Tola; and
I was certain that I was bewitched by Charmaine; I saw
the gravitational pull of each as quite separate and au-
tonomous. Tola's magic was love, Charmaine's magic
was sex. Almost as I spoke to Charmaine I was polishing
gambits for use in the conversation I was planning to
have with Tola before long.

I suppose I could have followed my instinct and lied,
but it seemed quite as futile as it would have been to
lie to a real witch. Charmaine had brusquely taken our
relationship out of the traditional battle zone; there were
to be no espionage, no skirmishes, no phased withdrawals,
no hostages, no white flags, no capitulations. There was
to be no sex war between us; we were almost allies, if I

read the signals right, possibly even against Tola. Charmaine and Sinclair had gone to bed with each other, would go again as often as they both liked (and their engrossments permitted) until the day came when it was no longer true that they both liked it. At no time was dissimulation, that dread venereal disease, to be let into our relationship.

I was not sure that I could sustain the role she was thrusting upon me; it seemed to call for a kind of emotional abstinence of which I had had no experience. No jealousy, no fits of rage, no moments of near complete abandon to the illusion of one self disappearing into the other; only pleasure, uninflected pleasure, was left. It had seemed a terribly austere discipline. But it was a challenge, a dare, and I responded as one always does to this kind of test. I was rather pleased with the speed of my reaction, the rapidity with which I seemed to hit on a style.

"Actually, you're right. I'd love to talk to her," I had said, showing guile out the door like a compromised daughter, "but I can't even think how I would begin."

"Don't expect me to give you advice," she had replied. "I like Tola too much." I was confused as I suppose she meant me to be; her liking Tola should not have been in the script. Indifference, yes; but liking? But she stuck to her guns: Tola was, she said, quite vehemently, exceptional. She didn't care what I did, so long as I did not— to her knowledge—"mess about with Tola." Still intoxicated with the strong odor of honesty that had been in the air, I had come near to explaining to her that I was in love with Tola.

"Myron's gone to the States," she said now, "a dreadful place in New York called Albany that seemed to be populated by faceless tycoons the one time he dragged me there. All buttoned-down and *promoting* something or another. Quite nauseating, really. He'll be away for quite a while. There's some kind of business deal in the offing. All the same, I don't want you doing the slightest thing that will set her to thinking about"—she hesitated, and then poked me on the shoulder with a long finger— "about you and me on the sofa. Not the teeniest *gesture.* You mustn't hang around so long that she'll imagine you're waiting to jump into bed with me. And I don't want you ostentatiously running off too early; she'll only think you've gone away to come back again. I simply won't have you putting a foot wrong."

I felt like exploding in the small office, but was only too conscious that anything above a normal speaking tone would have been like sending a printed transcript personally to every subeditor in the *Sun,* not to mention the telephone operator, whose cubbyhole was immediately behind my own.

"You-and-me-on-the-sofa! You-know-when! Look, Charmaine, keep your bloody party! What the hell do you take me for?" It was difficult to keep my voice down. "I tell you what. You go home and get on the phone and get your bloody 'spare man' where you usually get them." I was really angry at her for the manipulative bitch that she was. She knew I was dying to see Tola, although she could scarcely know exactly why, and, after dangling the prospect before me like the simplest of procurers, she was now making it impossible for me to come by trampling over my self-respect. "What kind of game are you playing with me, Charmaine? What are you up to?" She was toying with me as a child would with a yo-yo.

"My dear boy, I know you don't mean a word you say. You wouldn't miss the party for all the tea in China, because your dear Tola is going to be there. It must be ages since you drank an orange juice at Harry's Bar with her." There it is, I said to myself. That's what it's about then, Lady Macbeth! You fabulous phony, with all your disdain for jealousy, all this performance to let me know that you know I've been seeing Tola. Too bad, too bad; you could have saved the revelation for the party. It would have been so much more effective. Would have knocked me out completely. "Had any orange juice at Harry's lately, Sinclair?" I would have gone straight home, maybe flabbergasted, completely off-balance. But not a word will I say to you now, not one word. And if Tola decides to be cool and distant, as is most certainly in the cards, I will hang around and gorge myself on that luxurious body of yours, dear old bird-in-the-hand.

Chapter Seventeen

Tola was wearing red, a long wine-colored sheath with bobbles at the hem that seemed at one moment severely formal and at others almost frivolous. I saw her before I saw Charmaine—or anyone else—because she arrived barely seconds before I did. Jumping out of my car almost before the engine had quite died, I opened her door as she carefully swung her legs out from under the steering wheel, the dress riding almost up to her knees with the tight maneuver. She took the hand I offered, a cool, distantly friendly smile on her face. If I pressed her she might even dance with me.

"Hello, Sinclair, I see all the best people are here again." Walking through the door ahead of me, as custom demanded, her slim legs almost touching as she moved in the tight dress, she managed to make it quite clear to all who saw us that the only connection between us was one of time. I was, therefore, immediately behind her as Charmaine enveloped her with a hug; by the time I had performed my statutory peck on Charmaine's cheek, Tola had completely disappeared, and I could not help wondering if she had simply gone out through a back door, got into her coupé, and gone away home. It was exceedingly improbable, I knew, but she had perfected, in this house at any rate, the art of total withdrawal.

I sank quickly into the comfortable contours of the party, keeping an anxious eye out for Tola as I drank and talked and danced. There were enough people I knew and enough whom I didn't, to divert me; Dacosta Payne and Funke, of course, looking so completely part of the scene that it was difficult to believe that Payne had not been in Lagos since the beginning of time.

"Charmaine always gives smashing parties, doesn't she?" he said to me. This was only my second experience, but "my countryman" had obviously been to parties to which I hadn't been invited. Trust Payne, I thought. "She's a perfectionist, that one," he went on.

"Like you," I said.

"Do you really think so?" The phrase, the intonation, the little wrinkling of his face into a half-smile, all came out of that secret book of good manners to which only the English middle and upper classes seemed to have had access—until Payne came along. "If a thing's worth doing, it's worth doing well, the old saying goes," he added for good measure. He was fast developing into a walking British cliché in blackface.

Angus Jones was there again, with yet another female guest from Government House whom he was, as usual, skillfully deploying in his very serious game of getting-to-know-new-faces-on-the-Lagos-scene. This one was rather better-looking than the standard Government House issue, though, as usual, a little on the large side. Perhaps there was for female guests at GH, as for policemen, a minimum-size entry qualification. Having nothing better to do, I took her off him for a set. She danced better than might have been expected, moving easily to rhythms with which she must have been unfamiliar, with none of the graceless, frenetic contortions that so many English and North Europeans seemed to think *de rigueur* when "exotic" music was being played.

"You dance very well for a visitor," I said to her. "Visitor" was an inspiration; I couldn't very well say "foreigner." And I couldn't very well say "for a white woman."

"Thank you. I love to dance. Thank you," she said. She was pleased by the compliment, but clearly did not think it extravagant.

"It isn't everybody who loves dancing that can dance," I said, without too much asperity.

"Oh, I'm not sure I'm doing the right things, but it seems so easy to follow the rhythm. And *you're* easy to follow, as well."

Deuce.

"We have the makings of a very successful mutual admiration society," I said. "Anyway, I suspect that you've been a professional dancer or something like that."

"Oh, but you *are* clever. You're not quite right, but you're very, very close. I spent eight years studying ballet. It turned out that I wasn't made for ballet and ballet wasn't made for me. Too big in the hips for one thing. Then I started having trouble with my metatarsals. I had to give it up when I was eighteen. But it didn't put me off dancing, thank heaven."

She was one of those myriad guests who pass through the mansions of colonial governors, the daughter of an old friend and colleague of the Governor General's. A few years back she would not have been permitted to visit a house like Charmaine's, which the Lady of Government House would certainly have considered "bohemian" if not downright "bolshie." Now, independence was casting its special and indecipherable shadow before it, and it was considered, if not safe, at any rate an acceptable risk in these uncertain days for this daughter of a retired half-colonel from Berkhampstead to dine and dance at a house where at least one-third of the guests might turn out to be African.

Her name was Pamela St. Aubyn, she told me. I guessed that she was about twenty-five. She was dark-haired and a little thick in the calves—the hips were fine by me—with a bell-clear Roedean voice and the smell of good soaps and lavender water about her. Yet as we talked and danced I became less and less confident about fitting her into that easy groove of insouciant privilege to which everything about her, except what she said, screamed that she belonged.

"If I'd known Government House was going to be quite so stuffy, I don't think I'd have agreed to stay. But I was dying to see this part of Africa and everyone said I couldn't stay anywhere else."

"Why not? The hotel isn't bad. The lift's usually stuck, but it isn't too many flights to the top floor . . . ."

"Oh, I don't mean that. I couldn't just have slipped into a hotel like that. H.E. would have been livid! He'd probably have made sure that there was some great conspiracy behind it all, somebody in London intriguing against him, oh, you have no idea! But you probably know how devious all these old Colonial Service people are." I didn't; secrets of that kind never filtered quite so far down. All the English I had ever met in Nigeria spoke of G.H. and H.E. and H.M.G.—to me, at any rate—only in tones of bated reverence. Daddy, she told me, had been with a line regiment and only went into the Colonial Service because Biffy had persuaded him to when they met in some Middle-Eastern post where Biffy was an administrative officer. "They've known each other since Cambridge, but to this day Daddy isn't quite sure if it wasn't Biffy who sent in a report on him that held up his promotion for two years." Seeing my bewilderment, she explained that "Biffy" and "H.E." were one and the same person. "Even down in sweet old Berkhampstead where everybody's supposed to be retired, you can still feel absolute ripples of suspicion whenever somebody mentions an old colleague who's done rather well. It's amazing the number of proper old gentlemen I know who turn out to have put up some quite devastating black in Poona or Dar es Salaam or some other such place."

For all her detachment the magic, or the mystique, or whatever it was still had a hold on her; the Governor General was "Biffy" only in reported speech. Still, she wasn't totally witless, she danced beautifully, and whatever her ballet teacher might have said I was not inclined to dismiss hips like those too lightly.

"What do you do when you leave here?" I asked. "Back to sweet old Berkhampstead?"

"No. Off to jolly old Jo'burg. Haven't you noticed?" She brought her left hand round and a stone flashed on her ring finger. "I'm getting married in a fortnight. To a South African."

"Oh, really?" I said. There was nothing else to be said.

I amused myself with the thought that this was the kind of line with which a diabolically clever chatelaine at Government House might equip the more attractive female guests in these difficult days when it was perfectly possible that they might find themselves the object of the unwelcome attentions of, well, *African* men. It was a sure-fire show-stopper. But I believed Pamela St. Aubyn, and I returned her intact to Angus Jones at the end of the dance. She ought to have been obliged to wear a sign in sixty-point capitals. Still, I knew about "Biffy." It might come in useful in a column one of these dry days.

I danced with Charmaine and was made to feel like a cork in the sea of her sexuality. Having reasserted her considerable power over me, she left me and resumed her performance as the perfect hostess.

Tola suddenly reappeared out of some quirk in the architecture that was apparently known to her alone, and was immediately captured by Angus Jones and introduced into the circle he had gathered around him. I saw that Payne had joined the G.H. crowd, but there was no sign of Funke. After a decent interval I went over to ask Tola to dance. She smiled and came with me, but as we passed the bar she touched my arm and said, "Would you get me a drink, please? I don't really feel like dancing just this minute." I was a little taken aback, but there was nothing to do but comply. At least we would talk while she drank.

"Mr. Payne is your countryman?" she asked. I nodded. I was beginning to feel oppressed by the insistence of practically everybody that because of geography I had some special responsibility for or expertise about Dacosta Payne. "Are you good friends?" she went on.

"Not really," I said limply, "although I think we're cousins."

"You 'think' you're cousins? You mean you really aren't sure?" Her voice was astringent, if not exactly caustic, and I took this as a sign that we were going to be friends again. "But you *ajerike* people are extraordinary! You don't even know your own family. *O ma she o!*" I must have looked upset, because she abruptly changed the subject. "Who is the large girl Angus Jones is offering tonight? Another Government House in-transit passenger? He just mumbled a name to me. I suppose he doesn't see any point in introducing his women to other women. Angus is going to get his CMG before he's thirty-five." She was in excellent form.

"You're right," I told her, laughing, "another Government House passenger. Pamela St. Aubyn, daughter of Lieutenant Colonel Giles St. Aubyn, formerly of the Grenadier Guards, the King's African Rifles, and the Colonial Service. MC with bar, twice mentioned in dispatches, OBE."

"Oh, are you doing a piece about him? What's he famous for?"

"No, I'm just joking. All I really know is his name. I danced with her while you were invisible. What were you doing, showing Philippe how to cook the African dishes? I'm sure he's been so brainwashed by the French he can't put boiling water to *garri*."

She laughed without constraint. "No. Not that. I'm sure Charmaine would shoot any woman she caught just talking to Philippe. No, actually I was reading." We were now sitting at the bar. Tola had chosen the corner which was hugged by the doorway that led to the living quarters, so that very little light shone on her.

"Reading?"

"Yes, reading." I couldn't see her face too clearly, but I could make out that she was smiling. "I always read at Charmaine's parties. She gets all those lovely American magazines you never see anywhere in Lagos. Haven't you noticed, up there in her sitting room? The big metal rack? I can't resist sneaking up there and getting in a quick read." I could tell from her voice that she was enjoying every bit of this little by-play.

"I suppose the sofa is your favorite spot in the room?"

"How did you guess?" She was almost gleeful now.

"You're in a very good mood this evening. Has Aunt Matilda been at you again?" I asked. She sipped at her drink and didn't answer immediately.

"Don't you think," she said after a while, "that it would be quite beautiful in a strange sort of way if we made love on that sofa in Charmaine's sitting room? Quite poetic? I've thought about it quite a lot, you know. It's the sort of thing Aunt Matilda would approve of."

"I wouldn't disapprove of it myself," I said very quickly. I wasn't going to be shocked speechless. "When? Now or after dinner?" Pretty slick, Brathwaite, I thought, great ingenuity and resourcefulness under fire. What was she up to? I didn't stop talking while I wondered. "Either would be beautiful. But why do you say 'strange'? I can't see how making love to you could be strange. I've been thinking about it for months. It would be beautiful no matter where."

For a long moment, in which I had time to conclude that she wasn't—couldn't be—making an elaborate, teasing joke, and to draw all the most optimistic inferences from this, she remained silent. Pius filled our glasses and withdrew the yard or so which was all that separated the bar from the wall behind. I suddenly realized that he must have heard every word we had said, but his face was a complete blank as behooves the professionally deaf.

"I'm going home," Tola said, "as soon as dinner is over." I waited for her to continue, to put this remark into some context, but she said nothing more.

"For God's sake, why? You are a damned abrupt woman, Tola. If I had the nerve, I'd get up and leave you right here." Everything she did or said to me was an emotional rabbit punch aimed at the very slackest and softest muscles.

"Please don't," she said, leaning over and taking my arm as urgently as if I had actually made the move to go. "Please, don't go before we've talked. I talk very badly. I know." Her grip was very far from token; I would have had real difficulty in escaping it. For form's sake I strained a little against it although I hadn't the slightest intention of leaving, especially after her plea. She had never before pleaded with me for anything and it was not at all disagreeable to have this physical proof that there was something she wanted from me.

"Sometimes I think there's something wrong with the machinery in me. Things I want to come out get held back and a lot of other nonsense comes out. You know what I mean? I'm just bloody inarticulate." "Bloody" in her mouth sounded frivolous, a child's imitation of vehemence. "But I don't write too badly, do I? I don't have any trouble getting what I want to say onto paper." In fact, she wrote very well. Her pieces in the *Dispatch,* whether she was writing on politics or food or clothes, were the best things in the paper, always sharp and witty, and full of that mysterious journalistic charisma that has an impact even on cynical practitioners.

"I think I'm in love with you, Sinclair. I'm sure I shouldn't say that. You see what I mean. I said 'think.' That makes it sound so tentative. And maybe I shouldn't even be saying that, in our . . . in our circumstances. But I said that very silly thing just now about Charmaine's sofa, so I have to keep talking until I get to what I really want to say."

"What you said about Charmaine's sofa was 'silly'? You didn't mean to say it? You didn't mean it?"

"Oh, no, that isn't what I mean at all! *T'olorun!*" She let go of my arm completely now. "I give up. Let me write you a letter." She laughed. "That's what, I'll write you a letter."

"Come and dance," I said. She got up immediately, still laughing.

Chapter Eighteen

I can see Tola now as she stood by the street window of my flat at 10 Alade Street on the evening of her first visit. It would have made, I think, a rather striking photograph with one of those super-wide-angle lenses, and I remember it almost as if I had indeed photographed it, picking up the upturned toes of my brothel-creepers as the large, comically irrelevant foreground image that draws the eye magnetically to the elongated, sculpted black figure of the girl standing slightly to the right of the frame. She is elegant and lost; the very posture, half-profile toward the camera of memory, with half-a-frown visible in the tense flesh at the corner of one eye, bespeaks bewilderment; her hands, caught in a moment of unclasping, are clearly going to be clasped again.

"How did you find this place?" she asks. She makes a sweeping motion with an end of the mammy-cloth curtain that is tucked away beside the window.

"In the columns of the *Dispatch*. How else do you find a flat in Lagos?" My flat sits atop a record shop in a fairly squalid part of the city, noisy with the dysharmonic ebb and flow of men and machines. Above all, Alade Street is decrepit, the decrepitude of a back street in

133

a rebuilding city in that sad interlude between decay and
the arrival of the bulldozers to stake a claim on behalf of
the current town-planning theory. To the northeast is the
carriageway that daily sweeps thousands of vehicles on
to the mainland, going east, going north, having got what
they wanted from the city. To the southwest is the business end of the Carenage. On both sides the buildings
scrape the skies or pretend to, carrying faintly, as if it
has come by wireless and not been apprehended in all its
clarity, the imprint of Le Corbusier or Frank Lloyd Wright
on their lean, boxy frames.

"The street is named after a member of my family, did
you know that?" She speaks wonderingly, as if there is
some lesson in the information that she cannot quite
fathom. "This is the first time I've ever been inside a
house here."

"What was he, your ancestor, some politician?"

"Oh, Sinclair, don't be ridiculous. An African politician
in the nineteenth century?"

Already there is a special tone to everything she says
to me, a mixture of reproach and resentment. Everything
comes too easily to you, Sinclair, it seems to say, including confused grass widows like me who would be far better off maintaining a polite but watchful distance. It seems
to me that she takes a particular pleasure, for example,
in picking me up when I mispronounce one of the more
common Yoruba words or when I make in my column
those small mistakes of detail that everyone makes from
time to time. It is more than just school-mistressy; it is as
if at the same time she is chastising herself for caring.

"One of my great-grandfathers was a factor. He had a
business in this street. I suppose he must have been pretty
conspicuous in those days. He was even literate! There's
a Bible in the old house with a great Ex Libris and an
elaborate kind of bogus family tree on the fly leaf." She
tells me what she knows of that early black capitalist-

Christian. Alade Street would not have been much different; there would have been the same weatherbeaten stone warehouses with their rickety upper stories. But the warehouses of today had been the business headquarters of the few Africans who had wangled their way into the favor of the English monopolies and into the strange new world of commerce that had come with—some say brought—British rule. She makes me see them, sweating in their heavy frock coats of best imported stuff, making their ambiguous living from the minuscule percentages the English left to them, not unlike the blackbirds of my Barbados schooldays which stayed sleek on oats they gleaned from the horse droppings in the streets. I guessed that these harassed men would have wrought a terrible revenge on their women and children and servants in the need to compensate for the daily lacerations their dignity and *amour propre* had to suffer in that new jungle of British culture and commerce in which they were the beaters and bearers. And what dreams must they not have dreamed as they sat down to their weekly game of whist and brought off, as perhaps the Queen's Commissioner had never done, a Vienna coup or an end play! No wonder they sent their children to school in Sierra Leone, for that was nearer to England; and England, whatever its sons might do in Africa, was still the place where at least one black man of quality was reliably reported to be practicing at the Chancery Bar and to have been received by the Queen.

Tola's recital momentarily turns my drab, seedy, little flat into some sort of historical monument; but she speaks of these frock-coated Victorians she has re-created, her own flesh and blood, with such detachment and irony that the aura of romance is quickly dissipated; the flat is once again its pathetic, makeshift self, blank side on to the prevailing breeze, airless, with the sullen reek of night soil in its pores, brave enough with its one black wall all tarted up with key-lighted airport sculpture and imitation kente-cloth drapes. But in the end it is stolidly unsusceptible to the cosmetician's art, a warehouse that had once played host to a handful of sweating, pretentious, despised, black-skinned scavengers.

"Charmaine is your decorator?" Tola asks, precise as an acupuncturist's needle.

"Is it all that obvious?"

"Oh, she gives herself away, the black wall, this curtain. It's the kind of thing she's done with the servants' quarters at her house. She's done much the same in Angus Jones's little bungalow at Government House."

Bullseye! Except that I didn't know about Angus Jones.

Tola has come to 10 Alade Street by way of Harry's Bar. That is to say that we have started to meet again for orange juice. Without having to put it into words we both know that we shall become lovers; but we also know that there has to be some intermediate epoch between the pronouncing of the words at Charmaine's house and the rite itself.

Never before have I been so conscious of the fact that mating is a rite, be it as commercial as it is at the Imperial or more fraught with social consequences as it is in less forthright circles. For us the ceremony is almost unbearably weighted; all around our coupling hover gods and demons of pride, family, and the future. It is one thing for Tola to propose that we fuck on Charmaine's sofa and quite another that we fuck anywhere at any time. Will it be the last time, this first time? Or shall we fuck again? And again? And if we do again where shall we be at the end of a particular evening or afternoon? Irretrievably locked together in a complex of emotion and continuing desire and Aunt Matilda's dreams and solicitors' instructions?

She is bewildered for good reason; and were she looking straight at me she would see that I too am bewildered. I know (I am certain) I am in love with her and I know she is certain that she is in love with me, otherwise, of course, she would not be here.

So I know that the remark about Charmaine's interior decorating clientele is not bitchy; it is one more of those precise translations of thought into words over which she has already shown that she has less than perfect control.

By chance the street window is opposite a gap in construction that runs thinly down to the Carenage itself. As I stand behind her I see, through the tunnel of buildings, a stray launch chug past, its statutory lamp just recognizable in the strong glow of a sunset that reaches us over the roofs all diffused and softened by the permanent gray cloud that covers the city at dusk. Tola's black skin glows purple in this light; forgetting that she is here on an assignation, that we have waged an elaborately verbal, articulate campaign of mutual seduction, I kiss her on the cheek that points into the sunset, out of nothing but inarticulate delight. She starts, surprised, but does not turn away, and all is well.

We made love urgently, as if we were afraid that our conviction, like anesthesia, might wear off. The explosion came shattering us back into aloneness, bringing a self-contemplating calm that was to me quite unprecedented; out of this we surfaced, very gently, to contemplate each other.

The Tola I now consider, who lies head cupped in clasped hands upon her pillow, is a quite new person. She seems longer on the bed than standing; I imagine that miles of muscle which hold up her public, upright personality like steel ribs in a corset, are relaxed, readjusting balances in her body in a process that is the precise reverse of *rigor mortis—extensio vitae*, I work out in fifth-form Latin. She, too, is appraising me.

"What do you see?" I ask.

"Complacent detumescence," she replies, grinning.

"My God, you've used that before," I say. She points to my penis. "You've used *that* before." The new Tola is, clearly, above all things, not solemn. (The old Tola most certainly was, if not solemn, frequently too sober and too introspective for my taste. When there is so much unspoken and unconsummated between two people, does it form a kind of ballast that will not permit things as light as gaiety or humor to become airborne?)

"Are you always so literary in bed?"

"But you started it. You're the one who introduced the four-syllable words. I would have thought that this was more of a four-letter-word context."

"You *are* complacent. And you *were* the other thing, but now I'm not so sure any more. In fact, there are signs of, ah, retumescence?"

It is only when we have made love again, with nearly all the comfortable rhythm of old lovers and all the delighted exploration of new lovers, that I see her truly relaxed. The first time may be an accident, or a tremendous mistake you regret immediately; the second time is something massive and unequivocal, the cornerstone of a granite construction.

"Am I good?" she asks, simply. There is no longer the net between us over which we have been sharply batting balls of repartee.

"I don't know, I never know if a woman is 'good.'"

"But if she's bad?"

"Oh, well, I suppose so. Yes. A woman *can* be bad. But I'm never quite sure it isn't my fault."

"Or the wrong woman."

"Or the right woman at the wrong time."

"Am I the right woman at the right time?"

"Yes, very much so."

"I knew it. I shouldn't say that, either, I suppose. But I can't bother to edit now. I've been accused of being a holder-back.'' She stops and laughs. ''Bolaji swore I never gave myself to him completely, that there was a kind of valve inside me that I couldn't unlock, or wouldn't unlock for him. In a way I think he was saying that this was why we have no children.''

''Sounds very poetic to me.''

''It's a lot of nonsense. But, all the same, he had me halfway convinced. I mean, they don't mention a valve in the anatomy books, but haven't you heard of couples who couldn't have children, yet the moment they adopt a child the wife starts producing like a housefly? Don't you suspect there could have been something in the woman, a blocked passage somewhere, that held back the process? How else can you explain it?''

''Accident. Coincidence. But I like the idea of the valve. It seems to be working quite well today. I got the impression it was wide open.''

''But that's what I thought with Bolaji. You know what I mean. Perhaps it wasn't, after all. Anyway, which is more important, what I feel, or what he feels?''

''What I feel,'' I say, as unemphatically as possible. I fully deserve the apologetic kiss she gives me.

Chapter Nineteen

About a month or so later the *Sun* decided to send me to the Gold Coast to cover regional elections, and later, to report on the visit of Baron Moon, the great jazz figure whose reign—and range—bridged the unbridgeable gap between New Orleans and cool jazz.

"Why don't you take a holiday and come for the second week? I'm sure the Baron is going to be fabulous," I said to Tola.

"Leaving you a week to see if what they say about Accra girls is true?" They said that Accra girls "moved better" than Lagos girls.

"You know I can't stand wild generalizations," I said.

"So you can't miss this chance to get in some empirical work." Since we had become lovers, Tola's manner had changed. Where she had been awkward of speech and often constrained in manner, she was now quick and darting and, to a surprising degree, given to sudden precise flashes of fantasy. She could be set off by a telephone pole. "Sinclair, look at the poor thing! It's pine, probably from Norway. They stripped it down to the bone and dragged it away from its family and from that nice, crisp weather up there to bring it to this sweaty town.

140

It's probably crawling with those enormous maggots right this minute. Doesn't it sadden you!"

Once, after we had made love in the middle of the day, she jumped out of bed to go to the refrigerator for a drink. All of a sudden she shouted, "Sinclair! Sinclair! Come quickly!" I scrambled a *lappa* round me and rushed out to see her, naked as a statue, standing at the window that was in full view of the street. "Look at them, Sinclair," she said, pointing down into Alade Street. All I saw was the usual complement of sweating men in torn khaki shorts pushing high-laden *omolankes* on resistant wheels made of solid rubber, tally clerks carrying ledgers and wearing the traditional five or six fountain pens in their shirt pockets, Moji at her stand at the corner frying plantain and having an argument with a policeman. "Isn't it terrible?" Tola asked. "Why couldn't they be doing what we've been doing?"

I dragged her away from the window.

"My God, Tola, don't you know you're naked?"

"Nobody out there would recognize me," she said, smug in her impeccable logic. The change was not, it seemed to me, just the normal progression of intimacy; it was abrupt, overnight. She no longer had the trouble in "getting things to come out" that she had spoken of. As things came out I found myself face to face with a very different person from the one I had pursued through orange juice and distractions to this place. Where—and why—had all this impulsiveness and humor—and warmth! been hidden?

She came to Accra, having persuaded the *Dispatch* that they should have some coverage of the first African visit of the legendary Baron. The paper generously agreed to pay half her travel costs, and all "legitimate expenses."

I had gone by car as it was clearly going to be useful to have independent means of transportation. By the time she came, my first assignment was finished; I had inter-

viewed chiefs and bosses, drunk my way through cases of
unchilled beer and unchased schnapps, as well as enough
palm wine to fuel a flight from Kumasi to Kano. My body
felt used and stale; in one week I had driven a thousand
miles through savannah and rain forest; I had talked with
devious men and with direct men; with dapper men in
nylon shirts who hated the British as they would hate the
keeper of a brothel twice as successful as theirs; with
half-naked men sweating into hand-woven kente the
thickness of a Shiraz rug who hated the dapper men; with
courteous Englishmen who took none of them seriously
and me even less so. I had slept in the car, on mats in
guest huts, one night on a magnificent four-poster in the
mud palace of a northern chief, and two nights not at all.
I had starved and feasted alternately, had rented one
girl and been lent one. At the end, none of the "machines
inside me," as Tola would have said, was working right;
I was constipated and could not sleep although I desperately needed to sleep, because my body was not quite
sure what it was expected to do next. I offered it an
afternoon at the sea at Labadie basking—not swimming,
nothing so violent was indicated—in the tepid Atlantic,
sandwiches and cold beer, and then led it very gingerly
toward sleep again. After a little initial bucking and
shying, it accepted.

Tola arrived the next day and registered as Mrs. Brathwaite. We were staying in a small hotel that maintained
an old-fashioned dignity in service and façade despite the
rapid encroachment of one of the more flourishing red
light districts. The main verandah looked grandly onto
the Atlantic; a "sundowner" here had a cinematically
lush sunset as accompaniment most days of the year, and
some of the older coasters still came ritually for their
pink gin before, and gin and tonic after, the green flash
that came when the orange ball of sun extinguished itself
in the Atlantic.

Tola and I went there just before sunset. Our love-making here seemed to both of us quite special, and neither could quite define or explain this.

"It's just Accra. The air. Maybe that's the answer to the riddle about Accra girls. It isn't the girls at all, it's the air," she said as we dressed. "Every woman who comes to Accra is an Accra girl."

"I think it's the signature in the hotel register: 'Mr. and Mrs. Brathwaite, Lagos.' The aura of legitimacy. Marriage is obviously the greatest aphrodisiac of all."

"The pretense of marriage, maybe. All the Mr. and Mrs. Smiths who've been having it so good all these years, and nobody understood why!"

Out on the verandah we felt like honeymooners. Everyone else seemed middle-aged and sexless, from the silent English with their newspapers and pink gins to the Africans, mostly bespectacled and solemn, who drank beer and kept their conversation to a low, decorous, and un-Nigerian buzz, making me feel that, come Independence, they would start to drink pink gins, too. We were scrutinized from all angles by glances so rapid and so swiftly withdrawn as to be almost surreptitious. I was sure that our love-making clung to us like a perfume, an animal musk that stirred discontent and a vague resentment in the breasts of these earnest tipplers whose only interest was a precise mead of daily anesthesia.

As we sipped our first drink the sun put on its act, a slow immersion that left the sea and sky and the bottles at the bar a confusion of orange tints. The green flash seemed to be a hallowed signal; the bar became animated as newspapers were laid aside, drinks changed, and little plates of plantain crisps and peanuts appeared. Two men who had been sitting in silence opposite each other since we came in now began to speak in that loud, confident voice which in England is a prerogative of the upper classes but is arrogated by all classes of Englishman in the colonies.

"Tremendous fuss they're making about this Baron

chappie, is he supposed to be any good?'' one asked. Tola
and I looked quickly at each other and away again in a
complicity of suppressed laughter.

"They reckon he's the best thing to come out of America since Louis Armstrong," his companion replied in a
staggering display of expertise. "They say he can electrify
a crowd like those gospel preachers, you know. Be very
curious to see how he goes down out here. Not quite the
same thing as New York or New Orleans, is it?" He
turned quite deliberately and smiled in our direction,
unmistakably tendering us an invitation to join their conversation. We smiled back, taken by surprise, but we had
no wish to be included; neither of us was quite ready to
start work. But the Englishman's gambit inhibited our
conversation, and we quickly finished our drinks and left.

The Baron's arrival had more panache than he might
have anticipated. The DC-6 landed at just after eleven on
one of those mornings when the sun had retired behind a
mass of smoke-gray cloud to bathe the earth in heavy,
humid, secondhand warmth. About four thousand people
were held behind rope barriers surrounding the arrivals
shed by a patrol of amiable mounted policemen who rode
up and down in a jerky little gait, half-walk, half-trot,
flirting with the women. Everyone was dressed as for a
festival, except the press. In our minuscule enclosure to
the left of the immigration section only Tola and a girl
from the broadcasting station looked as if they hadn't
slept in their clothes for several nights running.

"Gold Coast people are very consequential" she whispered. "Look at all the *broderie anglaise.*" And there
were acres of kente-cloth and gleaming black torsos that
gave the crowd the look of a flowering hedge in some
science-fiction land where the plants have subjugated the
human beings.

The trouble started, strictly speaking, with the press.
The local authorities hadn't bargained on having so many

reporters to deal with. News agencies which "covered" Africa from Rome, newspapers like the *Sun* which had scarcely ever used the word "jazz" in their columns, learned quarterlies from the universities in French-speaking Africa, all wanted to be represented at this first confrontation of native and expatriate black culture. Nearly thirty of us were squeezed into a space designed for a dozen.

What caused the breakdown and the blow-up was the "pool." At the last minute, an arrangement had been hurriedly put together by which two photographers, one for stills, and one for movies, were to be allowed to move around freely at the arrival; their output was to be the common property of all other photographers and newsreel representatives.

As the plane taxied onto the parking apron the Daimler of the Premier drove out through a special gate. The Premier, a squat man about forty whose hair had receded almost to the tip of the parietal bone, jumped out and started shaking hands with the people in the receiving line. Neither of the photographers—both of whom were English—paid any attention, both being busy shooting the plane and all the preparations for the descent of the visitors.

"Get some shots of the Premier!" someone shouted from the press enclosure. One of the photographers made a "get lost" gesture, the other simply ignored the request. Then one of the photographers who had been shooting from the enclosure jumped over the wooden barrier and ran to the field just as the Baron started coming down the gangway. An affable mountie immediately gave chase and felled him with a blow of his whirling baton. Another policeman joined in the attack, but soon a third, who looked like an inspector, intervened. The offending photographer and his offending camera had by this time sustained quite severe damage; the press enclosure was abuzz and aclick with the cursing of the writers and the shutter-buttons of the photographers; the crowd behind the barricades, shocked but uncertain how to react, held their banners emblazoned with AKWABA!—the Ga word for welcome—absolutely still, flags caught in the winds of equal force blowing from opposite directions. The welcoming party and the guests of honor were frozen into a tableau that Tola and I were to laugh about wryly for months. There was the Baron, two-thirds of the way down the steps of the plane inaccurately resplendent in a *danshiki* and *sokoto* that would have been sensational had he been visiting Nigeria. He stood, feet distributed over three steps, immobile for the time it took me to look around to my left at the multi-colored, rigid crowd, to my right at the hapless photographer in the grip of a now dismounted policeman all crimson flashes and black uniform, and back again toward the plane. One of his hands gripped the rail of the steps as if he were afraid he might fall, the other was trapped at shoulder height into a caricature Nazi salute, in truth nothing more sinister than an uncompleted wave that was meant to be all exuberance and brotherly love. Behind him, in like immobility, crunched with the momentum of a too-rapid descent ended by the too-sudden halt of the Baron, was Smoky Lestrade whom I recognized from pictures on the backs of record jackets. He might have been paralyzed for all I know by the sudden violence, and probably, to judge from the permanent cringe I was to see later in the visit, by his own memories of other violence official and unofficial. In the doorway of the plane stood Bill Weinstein, the Baron's manager, a tall, florid man under whose left arm a briefcase snuggled as if held there by magnetism; he looked as if he might have been calculating the pros and cons of not leaving the plane at all, continuing to Monrovia and cutting his losses. Behind him and just visible over his left shoulder was the blue cap and fair hair of an air hostess; I couldn't see her face, but I had a strong impression of innocence, Suffolk or Essex, trapped in the ninety-degree angers of Songhai.

On the ground the Premier caught the eye for the good reason that he was the Premier; from him, first of all, would have to flow the warm, unfreezing current of command or of action. But he seemed as shocked—for this moment that I recall as clearly as if I had a panoptical photo before me—as we. The gesture in which he was frozen was two-armed; completed, it would have portrayed bewilderment, the arms spread out, the eyes (which were three-quarters on to us and to the crowd) unfocused, the tail of kente-cloth fallen from the shoulder, all asking to be delivered from this moment of uncertainty, the classic pose of the follower looking for a leader. Around him the welcoming party, a half-dozen men and women highly placed in the world of official culture, a Parliamentary Secretary in the Ministry of Community Development, the President of the Musicians' Union, the President of the Circle Beautiful with a ten-year-old schoolgirl carrying a bouquet of what the press would certainly call tropical blooms, all stood in attitudes of interrupted deference, all half-inclined toward the plane and the honored guest. Even the photographers were stunned; the movie man swung around to the noise of blows and the loud grunt of his black colleague as he fell, his camera sliding down his shoulder pad to be caught and to lie still in his neck harness; the still man turned, too, but seemed to be awaiting the command of some absent director.

The Premier duly broke through the icy wall of shock. His arms seemed to twist his body round toward the plane and he started to move with a shout that was thunderous in the hush that had come upon the airfield.

"My friend!" He moved, fast and suddenly, squat legs powerfully swishing toward the steps; the Baron, with more deliberateness, unfastened himself from the rail, and the two men met before the Baron's second foot had touched African soil. The Premier clasped the Baron in his arms and the crowd gave a great roar in which relief must have had at least an equal share with welcome. Over to the right of the aircraft a pickup band made up of leading Musicians' Union officials, who seemed to have been chosen on strict trade union, rather than musical, criteria, broke into "You're My Everything" ("with intent to commit a felony" Tola suggested when I used that phrase in my report to the *Sun*) which the Baron had recorded in a dozen best-selling versions over the years. The fallen photographer dragged himself back towards the press enclosure with his dented Rolleiflex and bloody head. A busty woman wearing a Red Cross uniform came across from an unseen hideaway and led him, unresisting, away.

As we were leaving, a thin, sandy-haired Englishman of about fifty, followed by a younger man, equally thin, but black, came bustling toward us.

"I say, do you mind? Could you just hold on a bit there?" It was the Englishman who spoke in a pleasant, unaffected voice that had Southern England and a minor public school branded upon it. He was elegantly dressed in a tussore suit and wore a regimental or old-school tie pinned to a beautifully pressed cream silk shirt, which bore not the slightest trace of the perspiration that was pouring down the back and sleeves of my open-neck shirt.

"I'm frightfully sorry, but there's been the most awful confusion about the press arrangements this morning. Do you think you might come along to my office for a chat about threeish this afternoon so that we can try to set things just a bit straight? It'd be awfully good of you. You'll scarcely be filing before then, will you? We should have something of a program worked out by then, shouldn't we, Willy?" He turned to the African, who replied, rather languidly in a rather English intonation, "Oh, certainly, Trevor, by three, certainly."

"I'm sorry, we haven't introduced ourselves. I'm Trevor Woodall-Smith from Comdev. Willy Boaten, my assistant." Willy smiled sweetly.

"Are you going to wait until afternoon to file?" Tola asked as we drove away down the hill back into Accra. I hadn't an answer. I wasn't really thinking about matters like filing; I wasn't sure that I was thinking or even that I was thinking about any particular subject at all: I felt quite numb and inoperative. Tola's question, making me focus on specifics, also made me realize that I was extremely angry, in a useless, grandiose, inchoate way. I wanted to flay and sequestrate premiers, policemen, polite Englishmen, and pansy Africans; to burn DC-6s and plow up airfields; to piss on pool photographers, especially white ones; to tell the *Sun* go screw itself, never to write another trite, comprehensible phrase. I wanted to drive my Peugeot in a straight line until the petrol ran out and then walk through villages, hostile or welcoming, announcing myself as No One, because the world seemed quite definitely populated by a tribe of Cyclopes whose single eyes seemed turned permanently inward. Since Tola was the lone exception, I said, no, I would write my story and wait to see what turned up at Woodall-Smith's "chat."

"Everything's a bit of a mess, I'm afraid," Woodall-Smith said when a dozen or so of us were seated in an airy lecture room at the Adult Education Center late in the afternoon. A blackboard behind him bore monosyllabic witness to the normal function of the hall, and we sat at desks that had all the stigmata of pupilage upon them save only that they were free of the carving, sometimes crude, sometimes of an inspired elaborateness, that is *de rigueur* in a real school. Adults, clearly, behave better in school than children. "Everything's frightfully scratch. I'm not sure even why they roped *me* into the exercise." He smiled in a self-deprecatory sort of way. The well-meant gesture was lost upon us. There is a bitter hostility *de métier* between the PRO and the press, and the amateur PRO does himself no good by claiming to be amateur, since all PRO's are by definition amateurs in the eyes of the press. But Woodall-Smith continued to play his part. "As far as I know, this visit has nothing to do with Comdev at all . . ."

"What's Comdev, anyway?" The speaker was from an Australian magazine; he was on a round-the-world jaunt and happened to be in Accra by the sheerest accident, although from his aggressive tone you would have thought he was working against the harshest deadline. "Where do you guys come from, anyway?" Willy was also there seated beside Woodall-Smith, who had changed into a bush jacket from Fortnum and Mason, looking at us with great kindness.

"I'm sorry," Woodall-Smith said, for the twentieth time, it seemed. "Community Development. It's so easy to fall into this dreadful habit of abbreviations. What I'd like to do is this. First of all, I'll tell you about a few things we've arranged, and then you must let us know what you think we've done wrong by way of omission or commission." There was an almost audible sneer all round the front row of desks. Someone took a picture of Woodall-Smith and Willy with a loud flash-bulb explosion as if determined to preserve these incredible moments for posterity.

"First of all, the program for the next few days. Part of Mr. Moon's activities here are, well, frankly, commercial. He'll be playing to paying audiences and so on. That's nothing to do with us at all. I assume Mr. Weinstein has all the information about that. What we're interested in is the charity shows, and a few special appearances up-country in local communities, that sort of thing."

Once more he was interrupted very brusquely by the Australian. "Yeah, yeah, Trev," he said, sounding more and more American by the minute, despite the tight cockney vowels, "that's great. But what we want to know is, are we going to get our heads bashed in and our cameras smashed every time we step outa line? Like that poor bastard native this morning? We're big boys. Tell us what the score is and we'll act accordingly." His voice was booming and harsh although he had the small, wiry figure of a ballet dancer topped off by ash-blond hair and baby-blue eyes. "What I mean is, who's really running the show? You or somebody else? You're a dandy apologizer, but I want to get out of here alive with a story. I got four kids back in Sydney, right? You can't buy groceries with an apology, right?"

Even Woodall-Smith joined in the general laughter. We were all pleased to have such an unorthodox spokesman, since he managed to say, with a nice turn of violence in the bargain, much of what we wished to say.

"I'm not quite certain I can answer *all* your questions, but as to who's in charge of press relations, that's what they call it, isn't that so, well, Willy and I are the ones in charge." There was loud laughter once again, led by the Australian. Laughing myself especially at the coupling of the bland, effeminate Willy and the bland, effete Trevor in a responsibility of any kind, I found myself oddly feeling a little sorry for Woodall-Smith. It *was* possible that he had been thrown unwitting and unwilling into this mess, that he had nothing but good intentions toward those who were driven by professional exigencies to clamor for exactness, for precise information, and for the kind of quasi-diplomatic treatment visiting journalists get —and need—when involved in this kind of coverage. Good intentions weren't enough, I knew, and when they voyaged alone, as here, could be as dangerous to life and limb as a gang of virgin teen-aged boys in a convent; but they were at least marginally better than bad intentions. More-

over, it seemed that this was all we were likely to get.
Also, there was something too practiced in the Australian's needling; this poodle was still excited by the smell
of game.

Willy distributed to us a handful of leaflets: on one of
them was written THIS IS ACCRA; FIFTY QUESTIONS
AND ANSWERS ABOUT THE GOLD COAST; and one
was a program of activities from which we learned that
the first Comdev show by Mr. Moon would be two days
hence.

"What's this, then?" our spokesman boomed. "Nothing
doing until Thursday? What are we supposed to do until
then, sit twiddling our thumbs?"

"I believe Mr. Weinstein has a suite at the Palace
Hotel. The telephone number is 4242. If I were you I'd
give him a tinkle and see what he has lined up for you."
Woodall-Smith sensed that everybody had had enough of
the Australian and the "little chat"; like a professional,
he took this wind in his sails and started picking up his
pieces of paper. "Well, gentlemen, I'm afraid that's all
we have for you today. You have our phone numbers.
Do get in touch with us if there are any problems." Without waiting for the Aussie to catch his breath, Woodall-
Smith sailed out of the room with Willy in his wake. I
slipped away at once: the post-mortem, which was already
beginning, was certain to be both boring and unproductive. And I had to get back to report to the other half of
the Tola-Sinclair pool.

Weinstein had had the brilliant idea that the Baron
should play in two or three clubs in one evening on those
days when he wasn't booked for some elaborate affair.
It meant that he got two separate "gates" each time, club-
owners had a good bite at the money that was being spent
in Accra, and the real aficionados had a chance to have
a whole night out in pursuit of the Baron. It was a triumph
of commercial ingenuity.

On the first evening Tola and I, having taken Woodall-Smith's tip and telephoned Weinstein, reserved a table at the second club where the Baron was going to perform. It was an open-air place very close to our hotel, that we reached by walking through a street that was no more than an alley between warehouses, surfacing on the main thoroughfare that linked this reeking, crumbling, unplanned part of the city to the carefully zoned and manicured East Side. The "Weekend in Bahia" was a cement-floored tennis lawn behind a warehouse. Leaving the street at the invitation of a flickering neon sign which said:

WE COME TO
WEEKE D IN AHIA

you went under an awning of palm leaves to a wicket gate where a fat girl with enormous gold earrings collected entrance fees—under a hand-painted sign which said LADIES IN FROCK FREE and meant, as Tola carefully explained, that ladies in native dress had to pay an entrance fee but ladies in European clothes could enter at no cost.

No one had heard of our "reservation"; but it didn't matter, since there was at least an hour to go before the Baron and his group arrived. All Accra seemed to have gone to the first club at which he was playing, a sedate institution on the East Side frequented by Englishmen and the more successful whores. Its name was the Hibiscus; but it was known to all Accra as the "Weekend in Willesden."

"Do you love me, Sinclair?" We had ordered our first drink and were arranging our bottoms on the familiar metal chairs on the edge of the dance floor when Tola asked me the question. We had made love, awkwardly but on irresistible impulse, in the shower just before leaving the hotel, from where we had walked, hand in hand, feeling like the honeymoon couple we were taken to be, to the Weekend in Bahia. It had been, perhaps, a good twelve hours since I had told her that I loved her and could really not conceive of a life which did not contain her and my love for her. So the question was not idle and certainly not ritual.

"Yes, why?" I said. I was both impatient and curious.

"Yes, why," she mocked me. It was true that what I had said sounded dismissive, but she should have known better. She knew all that I knew. "I want a better answer than that. I'm thinking of all kinds of things. Those blasted curtains at your flat. 10 Alade Street. I like your calling cards. 'Mr. Sinclair Brathwaite. 10 Alade Street, Lagos.' There's something very precious about you, Sinclair, and yet you can be, well, quite crude. Which of the girls in this club did you sleep with before I got to Accra? You do want me to be honest with you, don't you?"

"How can I stop you? That's the answer to the last question. You'd better make out a list. In triplicate. Tola, what are you up to, for Christ's sake?"

"Oh, it's the atmosphere. Don't you feel it? How would you write up the atmosphere at the Weekend in Bahia?"

"Right now? 'A brooding silence filled the air at Accra's premier night club, the Weekend in Bahia, as aficionados awaited the arrival of America's greatest living jazzman, Baron Moon. The house orchestra, idling at the circular bar, spoke in singsong Fanti voices as a handful of jazz lovers sat patiently at metal tables around the oblong dance floor. Sullen waiters moved sluggishly from bar to table serving watered drinks to their captive clientele. Any minute now. . . .'"

"Oh, shut up. Do you love me? What would you do to show how much you love me? Would you come back to our room right now if I asked you?"

I ignored the last question; it was not meant to be answered, just as she did not really want or need an answer to the first.

"There isn't a word for 'love' in Yoruba, do you know that? The word we use means 'want.' People like me who live between two languages, we have a made-up word we have to press into service. 'Fefe.' 'Want-want.' You know what that means: I can only love in English." She was wearing red once again, what they called in England "pillarbox red," the red of a GPO van, which is, I suppose, a vulgar color, public, for carpets on which gross dignitaries walk and for waiting rooms that would be grand. But it looked original, very intimate and warm on her black skin, making the skin almost blue in this garish fluorescent light. It also made her seem larger in the way a mirror makes a room seem larger; the eye, coming to the edge of the red, was drawn as if by an effect of refraction back to the black.

"Don't sound so sorry for yourself," I said. "Enjoy your double-take existence. It gives you an unbeatable excuse. You can always say, 'But Sinclair, I didn't mean what you thought I meant!'"

"It's an excuse you can use, too."

"The verbs are 'excuse' and 'use,' and the nouns are 'excuse' and 'use.' Hard 's' for the verbs, soft 's' for the nouns. You teach me Yoruba, I teach you English." I had to move very very fast to avoid the small stream of beer that she aimed at my trouser leg under the table.

The club was filling up quite rapidly; big parties were coming in, bringing with them a boisterousness and gaiety that had clearly been a little time in the making. It was easy to sense that the big moment was not far away.

"Tola!" A woman's voice from over my shoulder. "Aburo! I don't know that you here for this town!" It was Bijou from the Gambia who leaned over our table, black lace and aganyin and dangling filigree gold and much perfume. "You have brought your own man, just like me," she said. Adu was indeed standing a few paces behind my chair, not quite certain, to judge from his tentative stance, that he was ready to advance and be recognized. There was nothing tentative about Bijou; she had already kissed Tola and sat down before I had managed to stand. Adu joined us, mumbling a greeting as if performing a distasteful but unavoidable duty.

"Well, my sister, I do not know that this is your man," Bijou said, gesturing quite kindly in my direction although she had not actually spoken to me so far. "This is the one you were meeting at Harry's Bar, *abi*. I hope you and Charmaine no go fight when you reach Lagos." She spoke with much gesture, her face pushing its way into Tola's face, her hands gently thumping the table, palms upmost, for emphasis. Because she was so direct she seemed without malice, and it could only have been this, together with some old habit of intimacy, that held back Tola from the explosion I expected.

Tola spoke quickly in Yoruba, too quickly for my dwarf vocabulary and lame ear, and even Adu joined in the laughter. I knew the remark had been ribald, even vulgar, from the quality of their amusement, and I felt excluded, further outside the magic circle of their instant communication than even Bijou, the foreigner whose native language was Wolloff and whose Yoruba was probably as pidgin as her English. It was Adu who tried to explain.

"It is a play on words," he said, still smiling. Laughter seemed to come easily enough to his prematurely worn face. I realized that I didn't know him at all; he was a "political figure" who was worth a varying number of inches on our news pages from time to time, whom I saw at the Mainland Club or at parties invariably laying down the law of anticolonialism with a rigid dogmatism that seemed to leave no room in him for something so inessential, so dialectically unproductive as laughter. "It could not really be translated. There are two words that have almost exactly the same sound. One means husband and the other means the . . . the male reproductive organ."

"Oh, Adu, you're making it sound so heavy!" Tola came to the rescue of her witticism. "I just said I was happy with what I had, and I hope she is happy with what she has." Bijou and Adu burst out laughing again.

"You're not doing yourself justice, Tola," Adu said. "It's much better than that."

"I've just been telling Sinclair about things you can say and things you can't in Yoruba. This is one of those things you can say in Yoruba that you can't say in English." All in all she seemed more pleased at being able to put me in my place as a non-initiate in the mysteries of tonal languages of which Wolloff, I learned, was one— than she was upset at being discovered more or less in *flagrante delicto* by one of Lagos's most famous loudspeakers. But this was in its way reassuring; she was now taking our relationship for granted and was quite agreeable to us entering the public domain.

The house orchestra had now withdrawn from its post at the bar and was settling down to the traditional loud, disjointed search for E-flat and G-natural. After a while, they played a very tolerable highlife to which nobody danced, so unanimous was the sense of approaching events. And, indeed, halfway through they were brusquely silenced by a sign from some unseen authority. Over the public address system a voice, high-pitched with the effort to sound American, announced, "Ladies and gentlemen, the one and only Baron Moon!" We all stood and cheered the name of this black man who had been a guest on Mrs. Simpson's yacht when no black man in Africa, America, or the West Indies could be sure of getting a room in the meanest hotel in London or Chicago. We cheered him because the white world told us that he was great, that all-powerful white world of consumers and publicists which set for the black man not only his image of "the world" but also his image of himself. One of the Rothschilds, the *New York Times*, the *Neue Deutsche Zeitung*,

and Electrical and Musical Industries, Incorporated, bade
us cheer the greatest living jazz musician, and cheer we
did, with a good will and a thrill of pride, to boot.

"Hi there, everybody," the Baron said. He stood in the
uncertainly focused spotlight at the entrance, a black man
of medium height, broad with hard fat, perspiration
gleaming from the edge of his slicked-back, thinning hair
and on his round knobbly face. The smile, a caricature
rich with gold-capped incisors, showed a residue of real
pleasure through the lines of tiredness and habitude;
through how many thousands of nights, how many thousands of "Hi there, everybody's," did that nugget of
pleasure have to fight its way to make its appearance on
this night?

The band started to play, fairly accurately, an up-tempo
version of "You're my Everything"; as it stumbled less
certainly into the middle-eight the Baron, who seemed
never to have problems with his reeds, was there to steady
them with the big booming tone that has never quite been
matched by any other tenor saxophonist. He made the
music suddenly sound exceedingly real; the forcing of
syncopated sounds through metal and reed ceased, as he
started to play, to be a commercial stratagem to lure people on to dance floors. A person, a very particular human
being, was now commanding our attention with a declaration couched in music. The local musicians faltered; they
wished to listen. All except the drummer who, it seemed
from the activities now discreetly in train on the stage,
should have been the first to move so that the Baron's
own drummer could set up his glittering battery of equipment. But the Baron turned and smiled at this foolhardy
man and made signs to his own drummer to set up further
downstage; at the same time, with a wave of the trunk of
his saxophone, but not interrupting the stream of sound
that came from it, he invited the galvanized house
drummer to continue. It was so graciously and so spon-

taneously accomplished that there rose from us a cheer which was orchestrated by none other than the Baron himself. In a twinkling the photographers were upon the brave transported drummer, to whom the Baron, with another wave of his horn, now awarded a solo. It was a frenzied performance on instruments that were old and of poor quality by a man whose technique was later to be bested by the merest flicking of a wrist of the Baron's New York drummer; but it had an authenticity of inspiration that nobody could beat.

The Baron, that graciousness again, did not take a solo himself; after the drummer's break, he whipped through a mandatory chorus to end the piece and turned around to shout, "That's my boy! Stand up baby, let the people *see* you!" He seemed just the tiniest bit troubled at not knowing the drummer's name; but this was one of those occasions so full of magic and power that it was no surprize to hear someone in the crowd shout, "Bobby Dadzie! Bobby Dadzie!" as if in response to the unarticulated question in the Baron's eyes. The Baron, his saxophone swinging loose in its harness and picking up random glints of fluorescent light as it moved, sweat running in bubbling rivulets down his temples and into the collar of his cream silk shirt, was smiling a smile of childishly pure pleasure. "Come on, Bobby! Ladies and gentlemen, Bobby . . . DADZIE!" Bobby Dadzie came forward, a little shy now, his drumsticks held like talismans in one hand. He bowed awkwardly; he knew the correct gesture, but it wasn't in his normal repertoire. The applause was a roar that seemed too solid and integrated to be composed of single voices, and yet there were single voices to be heard. They called for "The Baron! The Baron!" and very quickly everyone seemed to be shouting, "The Baron! The Baron!" so that it was difficult to imagine that there had been any other object of our applause. The Baron had us all ready to eat out of the palm of his hand.

The rest of the evening was much the same. There were no more Bobby Dadzies; we were bathed, without benefit of fortuitous sentiment, in streams of passionate jazz played by musicians for whom technique was something taken contemptuously for granted, a question no longer posed. Music, the abstractest of arts and the rigidest of disciplines, assailed us with emotions that should have been foreign to us, foreign and unidentifiable and certainly incomprehensible, but which were insistently recognizable. They had to do with the complex mystery of being a black man in a white world; they had to do with banalities drawn from the soap opera of daily life, with terror, with the unremitting search for poetry which is an integral part of the soap opera. Beauty, oh, yes; afterwards we were all saying that difficult word without apology, and, with exclamations of surprise, discovering that the Baron was, with his music and through it, himself beautiful.

"When I was a harlot I was very conservative," Bijou said to the Baron later that evening in his suite. We had flowed without quite knowing how into the party that was being given there. It may have been because I was among the journalists who had rushed up to the stand after the too-brief, nonstop ninety-minute show, clamoring for an interview, for some words in which to imprison at least part of the experience. Or perhaps because Tola was so gorgeous and so exquisitely visible when the Baron's eyes followed me back to my table. Or because Bijou wished the evening to end in that way and had sent out powerful sex vibrations toward the ringside table where Weinstein sat not far from us with Willy and three Accra Bijous. Whichever it was, Willy had lounged over while the packing-up was taking place and the club was still full of stunned people trying to reconstruct out of the scarcely animate residue some image of the recent past. In a drawl that sounded even more effeminate and English than it had some hours earlier, he had inquired whether "you people would like to come on to Mr. Moon's hotel for a nightcap. Just a handful of friends, that kind of thing. *Do* say yes."

The Baron and his manager had adjoining suites. With the communicating doors opened there was a miniature ballroom which was packed to the windowsills when we arrived. Bijou was now to be seen in a score of younger, more frenetic reproductions. But it was to the original that the Baron gravitated as soon as he arrived. Behind him came a half-dozen club girls, handpicked by someone mandated to furnish a cross-section of local pulchritude, tall girls with slim, Formula-One hips, and buxom girls whose flesh giggled invitingly as they walked. Seeing Bijou, they pouted, recognizing in her, I guessed, all the signs of a Sister Superior.

"When you young you no fit to be harlot, I tell you." Bijou was looking straight into the Baron's rapt face; her palms came upwards and her lips curled in remembered horror at the ineptitude of her youth. "This one? You, Mr. Baron?" Her right hand reached out to slap the Baron's right shoulder with a thud that was wholly unfeminine. "I could make you fuck me for my ass! Now! Now self! Eh, heh! Believe me. But when I was younger? I no have the sense to know that." The girls screamed, two of them clapped their hands to their mouths and ran laughing with mock embarrassment to the far end of the room.

"Baby, let's go *now!*" the Baron said. Despite the wide-open windows and the breeze that was blowing in from the sea, the Baron was still sweating into his shirt, his third since we had first seen him. A monogrammed white handkerchief fluttered in his right hand like a flag of truce. "I ain't making no conditions!"

"Mr. Baron, believe me, I for done come with you one time, but I have this my man here." Adu, standing with

Tola and me at a respectful distance behind Bijou like
the official entourage of a princess, was actually smiling
again. Bijou leaned forward, drew the Baron towards
her, and kissed him full on the lips. "Yay!" the girls
shouted. The Baron was disengaged only by the firmest
pressure from the same hand which had engaged him.

"Come on, let's dance," he said to Bijou. "Somebody
put on some records. Some highlife records. I wanna dig
the *African* jazz, you know what I mean?" He rolled his
eyes the way black men do in white men's films and tried
to draw Bijou towards him. But she kept him still at that
ambivalent arm's length.

"I no like dry fucking, Mr. Baron. I'm sorry. Make you
dance with these young titi here. But not too much dance,
you hear? African girls no like tired men." Bijou's tone
was so gentle, almost tender, there was in it such a mixture of lovingness and admiration and wisdom that I
trembled in the microsecond between her words and his
response for fear that he might not understand. How was
he to understand, I asked afterwards, unconvinced and
unconvincing in my role of devil's advocate when Tola
and I talked about that evening. They were speaking two
vastly different vernaculars when they thought they were
speaking the same language; nothing in the Baron's experience could have prepared him for the complexities of
a Bijou, all luxuriant expert flesh with a "For Sale" sign
marked on every inch exposed or unexposed of her ripe
body. ("What a lot of nonsense you talk, Sinclair," Tola
says. "Harlem must be full of retired whores." Yes, but
when you make the journey from Harlem to *Africa*, do
you come expecting to find exact reproductions of the
fauna of 125th Street and Lenox Avenue? I'm not saying
I have a watertight case, but I have a case of some kind.)

The Baron's round, hard body seemed to expand and
stiffen in the same instant. Quite slowly he pulled Bijou's
hand off his shoulder and turned round to face away

from her. His eyes met the eyes of Smoky Lestrade, his wiry, wizened drummer, old before his time with the terrors of his "habit" and other frights which seemed to leave him completely only when he was seated on his saddle.

"Smoky!" The Baron's voice boomed from his basso's chest.

"Yeah, Baron?"

"Smoky, baby, what's worse'n a nigger whore?"

"Baron, baby, ain't nothing worse'n a nigger whore."
(In the fields in Barbados, when I was a small boy, and a grown man worked for a shilling a day from seven in the morning until five in the evening with a one-hour break at one o'clock, a gang would always work to song after the lunch break. "You digging?" one man would chant. "I digging," the others would reply. "You digging good?" "I digging good." "Dig the cane hole," "I digging the cane hole." "Dig the white man cane hole," "I digging the white man cane hole." Years afterwards I read that this was a "residual Africanism.")

"Smoky, baby, you ain't know nothing. You just ignorant, man, *i*gnorant." Late, oh, disgracefully late, I picked up the parody, the Sam Spade films with Bogart, the tough guys; I had had no trouble picking it up in his music which had been joyously full of parody. Perhaps this was a major tool in the Negro's America, the ultimate weapon of the victim. "Man, I'm telling you, there's one thing worse'n a nigger whore."

"What's that, Baron, baby?"

"Man, a nigger whore from Africa. That's what's worse'n any nigger whore you ever see. Dig?"

"Well, how about that? Shit. A nigger whore from Africa. If that ain't the *most!*" Smoky made his observation fluently but without emphasis, like a man repeating a rhyme he had learned in elementary school, looking with his yellow, pinched eyes at no one in particular. The Baron, his back now completely turned to us, was shouting, "Bill! Anybody see Bill?" "Bill" was Weinstein, who was standing by a window not five yards away with his arm around one of the girls, involved in a conversation that seemed to have completely blocked out the rest of the room. He looked up on hearing his name, a tired, what's-up-now-for-Christ's-sake expression on his face. Interrupted in the middle of what appeared to be a pleasant passage, he looked to be a warm, boyish person, who might have been proposing a nude swim at Labadie followed by a good, rousing game of hide-and-seek among the coconut trees. He didn't belong in the atmosphere of sophisticated, bitter violence that the Baron had just unleashed.

"Bill baby, what this party needs is some *white* chicks, dig? Some *white* chicks, man. You dig?"

Chapter Twenty

We returned to Lagos to find the rain in full possession. During the rainy season, the city showed its most infuriating and ambiguous face. The days would be covered by an unmoving tent of cloud gravid with moisture which might spew out great refreshing showers that seemed to open up large holes in the thick atmosphere, or else clammy exudations that rimmed your shoes with mildew overnight and clothed you by day in an inescapable integument of sweat. It was a languorous time: Sounds were muffled in this thick air, vehicles and people sloshed heavily and reluctantly through streets that often filled shin-high with rainwater; life became half as intense and yet somehow twice as demanding.

"Everybody" knew that Tola and I had been together in Accra. It was not likely that Adu had been the reporter; this wasn't his sort of thing. It was also difficult to believe that Bijou could have summoned up the energy—and the literacy—to send the news on ahead of us. She was not a true gossip; her contributions to the art were based on the fact that she was genuinely interested only in people and money, and that her train of life had never demanded that she put a premium on verbal discretion.

165

The day after our arrival, Olapeju, his backside at its usual angle on my desk, congratulated me on my coverage.

"I did not know you were such an expert on jazz music," he said, sounding quite sincere. "Everybody in the office was reading your copy." He paused; he knew a great deal about timing. "The *Dispatch* also had very good coverage. Is it true that the Nigerian correspondents collaborated very closely throughout their assignment? In *every* respect? That's what we hear." I found myself smiling at him. I really didn't care if he had a portfolio of infrared pictures of Tola and me making love. My insouciance was something quite new. Olapeju's great gift of transforming practically any piece of information he gleaned into a potential menace—the born blackmailer's gift—was now quite ineffectual. Nothing outside ourselves could menace Tola and me. The very worst the Olapejus of this world could manage would be to write to Tola's husband informing him that his wife had publicly taken a lover, naming Sinclair Brathwaite as the lover. Watching Olapeju with the secret glee with which a cornered mouse with a concealed automatic pistol might watch a cat, I calculated that the most predictable result would be to speed up the formal break, the divorce, the consummation so devoutly wished by Tola's own family, her husband's family, and me, the consummation which she would scarcely discuss with me.

"Why should we talk about marriage, Sinclair?" she asked once more when, that same evening, intoxicated with the revelation that Olapeju's questioning had brought about, I asked her the question once more. Once more she recited her litany; I was not only being conventional but unimaginative as well; I knew nothing about her except our mutual delight, I knew nothing about marriage except at secondhand; people should get married only when there was *nothing else left for them to do;* we had time and scope we hadn't begun to use yet; also, if I were understanding enough, I should realize that she had a problem to which she didn't yet know the answer. I should also realize that my "solution" was not the best possible way of helping her to find the answer.

"And if I really loved you, no doubt, if I wasn't just trying to pin a Brathwaite label on you, I wouldn't have any problem about simply continuing to love you. I should be quite happy to go on this way *ad infinitum.* There's one thing you haven't yet got around to putting into words: I should think of the scores of men in Lagos dying to be where I am." As soon as I had made this last unnecessary remark I regretted it; I really did not feel half so bitter as the words sounded.

"Sinclair, darling, if that is really what you think, I should either be flattered or damned angry. I choose to be flattered. I'll be flattered." She had a mock pout on her lips that suddenly made me imagine her as she must have been as a teen-ager, tall for her age and with unmanageable legs. She must have been the class clown, out of self-defense, so that she should not be the butt she feared she was. Now she had the strength to resist the temptation to be insulted, and that other less resistible temptation to quarrel with a lover when you feel that you may be ever so slightly in the wrong. She *was* in the wrong by every test of logic, but this strength—and grace—clothed all that she had said before in love and washed my logic, irrelevant and graceless as horse turds on a white gravel path, out of the way.

The rain kept Lagos alternating between moments of stifling steaminess, when it seemed that the smell of charcoal smoke and last night's swimming, uncollected night soil would never go away, and moments when the volume of water in the shallow gutters seemed to be precisely right to drive the city's banana skins and milk tins and old shoes and bits of cardboard clear through to the sea, leaving behind a surprising, earthy fragrance that belonged to the farmland thirty miles from the town.

It was time to give a party, Tola and I thought, as we lay listening to the rain falling like hailstones on the galvanized roof of 10 Alade Street and the buildings around it. We were happy with each other, happy as children playing on a beach; we built perfect sandcastles of love, and as the tide of time washed them away we built more. The castle was the thing, not the time.

"We have to have a party!" Tola had found another castle, more elaborate, involving more hands in the construction; it just might turn out to have its own kind of perfection. "We'll have your flat bursting at the seams. Nobody will know whether they're having a good time or not; it'll be too crowded to think." "Our" party was going to take place at my flat; there was a Rubicon here, somewhere.

"I'll steal half-a-dozen bottles of Aunt Matilda's champagne. She has a small cellar that she opens only for special people. She won't mind, especially if she knows it's for your party."

"Tola, champagne isn't liquor! Have you any idea what people drink at parties? And how much? My God!" "The party" was in danger of becoming one of Tola's fantasies.

"The champagne will be for you and me. Maybe Bijou. Every time somebody recognizes Charmaine's handiwork in the decoration, I'll give you a sign and we'll slip out onto the steps and sneak a drink." Already she sounded high.

"Are you planning to ask Charmaine?" We had seen nothing of her for some time. More precisely, not since Tola and I had become lovers. It had not been deliberate, but I couldn't believe that Tola would deliberately seek her out now. I certainly wouldn't have.

"Oh, Sinclair, so you've slept with her. You've slept with her in this bed. . . ."

"You don't know that. . . ."

"Of course, I know it. I could smell her in the flat even before I saw her trademark on the walls and curtains."

"Oh, Tola, that's a lot of nonsense. You make a wild guess and you want me to believe it's intuition."

"I *smelled* her, you idiot. I knew that she'd been in your bed the moment I opened the door." This was sheer fantasy now, and there was nothing to do but let her ride. "I could *sense* that your Charmaine had been *performing* in this bed. *Performing*. That's what she is. A *performer*. She probably scratched you, deep weals on your back, big claw marks, and next morning I'm sure you thought of yourself as one hell of a man when you felt the burning under your shirt. That's your Charmaine. She leaves marks, bloody great big unmistakable marks. That's your Charmaine." She had built up so gently to the tirade that it was almost over before I realized how violent it had been. When it was finally over there was nothing to say; there had been this between us, so long unspoken, this ghost which had to be exorcised. Instead we had ignored it.

"I'll flirt with Myron," Tola said after we had been silent for what seemed a very long time. "He'll adore that."

"No doubt I'll adore it, too. What about my consequential friend Auguste? I haven't seen him for a long time. He'd adore it if you flirted with him, but I could always make sure that he brought along Abike."

"That's the name of his mysterious girlfriend? He never takes her anywhere. You must invite them. I hear she only goes to big public things with him, like the races, and international tennis tournaments. Some people say that he chooses things like that to show how tough he is. I'm sure she's the one who makes him take her. It's the easiest way to show herself off to the largest possible clientele. I mean, she must realize it's going to end one of these days. You *must* ask them. She's a terrific-looking woman. Doesn't she remind you of those colored women you see in French magazines, from Martinique or French Guiana? Don't you think she's very West Indian?" I pondered all this for awhile, including the unmistakable dig—but at what, precisely?—contained in her thought about Abike's "West Indian-ness." It was true that Abike had upon her the imprint of mixed race that was more common in the West Indies than in most other places. But Tola had not meant to be merely descriptive.

We passed on to her next inspiration. The party was planned in leaps and bounds to her fantasy; it was to be pointless and unorchestrated (neither of us mentioned Charmaine) and would have to find its own rhythm without too much intervention from the joint hosts. We would provide the food and drinks, the music and the site; we would guarantee only that there would be enough to eat and drink and too many people for too many people to be with. They would make of it—and of us—what they could. For we admitted that the party was a kind of celebration of this new "thing," the Sinclair-Tola thing, which was clearly becoming an entity in the Lagos equation. Lagos—the Lagos we knew and the Lagos which knew us— was going to have to come to terms with Tola-Sinclair, and it might as well do so in circumstances over which Tola-Sinclair had some measure of control.

The evening of the party was humid and heavy with the residue of the day's rain and heat; a film of mildew seemed to hang in the air and flying ants swarmed around the street lamps in Alade Street performing their short, frenetic dance from which they dropped, wingless, into the enamel pans of gourmets waiting below. People tramped into the flat dragging off their plastic macs and dripping street effluvia into corners. An amplifier which I had rented from the Imperial battered our ears with the music of the Black Beats and Ayinde Bakare. From the beginning, people had to shout to hear each other. "You

have to have terribly loud music," Tola had said quite
anxiously a few days before the party. As the event became more actual, with flesh-and-blood people specifically
committing themselves to attend (Adu was passing up a
family affair the same night simply because Tola had
asked him), so the gay, fantastical irresponsibility she
had affected began to dissolve; the instructions she gave
to Monday were as detailed and immutable as a nineteenth-century battle plan, no matter how hard she tried
to make it sound casual, no matter how much she pretended—by using the "we-might-do-this" formula—to disguise instructions as suggestions.

Wearing tight black pants and a ruffled *aganyin* shirt
and resolutely refusing to speak too often or too obviously
to Monday, she looked deceptively like a guest. I actually
felt like a guest; she had taken over so thoroughly the
logistical ordering of the occasion that I could find nothing host-like to do. It was Monday, drilled, brainwashed
almost to zombie-hood, who was the surrogate host.
Decked out in new sandals, a gleaming white shirt, and
a modish pair of blue slacks, he seemed a different man
from the inefficient, short-tempered servitor I knew him
to be, serving the drinks with a flourish and occasionally
introducing guests to each other.

Parties, even my own, excite me. Where two or three
are gathered together the dynamics of the thing are fi-
nite; there is interplay or there is none; that there is a
time to go elsewhere is the primary truth. Tom and Jerry
both wish to go to bed with Angela, or to take her out
dancing; Jerry and Angela find Tom a bore or like him;
Angela and Tom think Jerry is the most interesting person
in town and spend the evening basking in the glow of
his presence. But multiply by ten; it's not infinity,
granted, but Tom, Jerry, and Angela are at full stretch
by the mere combination of neuroses, intellects, preoccu-
pations. Call it a forcing-bed, I won't quarrel with that

metaphor. I began to sympathize with Charmaine's elaborate "arrangements." Perhaps invitations should read: "A party has been *arranged.* . . ."

Afterwards it was impossible to say whether it had been a "good" party or not. People danced, drank, ate, talked in corners, and drifted away at what seemed normal intervals to the accompaniment of what seemed normal excuses. There were some beautiful women and some interesting men; there were bores, and there were fat girls with square, uninteresting faces. There was an Englishwoman whose husband was an acquaintance of mine; she visited Lagos for two months every year, spending the rest of the year in England "looking after the children." She had been warned against the *efo* (which she persisted in calling "palaver sauce") but her pride compelled her to ladle out two large spoonfuls onto her rice. I guessed that in the bleak suburb where she mourned her marriage for ten months of the year she was the resident African expert; it would never have done to funk this esoteric culinary hurdle. For her pains and pride she had the roof of her mouth nearly reduced to ashes by the sauce. "Delicious, delicious," she lisped with undying British courage: For months to follow this was to be an ironic password for many of those who attended "our" party.

I suppose that it was Adu's party; it was he who, suddenly showing a side that was almost flamboyant, pulled the evening along a track of his own making. It started when he caught Tola and me drinking Aunt Matilda's champagne out on the landing in an unspoken toast to Myron. He and Charmaine had arrived late, wearing evening clothes, having come on from a dinner party. Immediately Myron had stiffened like a gun dog which smells game in the air but is confused as to direction because of rapidly shifting wind currents. He had walked around the room, absently patting Tola's arm, sniffing at the tantalizingly familiar but unidentifiable scent. Seeing the tour in progress, and recognizing that vague, wondering expression on Myron's face for what it was, I went out and opened a bottle as quietly as I could, knowing that Tola would be coming as soon as she could disengage herself. As we drank, Tola with mock-modestly downcast eyes and I, half-laughing, half-embarrassed, hoping that the champagne would now forever drown the subject of Charmaine and all her works, Adu had wandered out onto the steps.

"I don't care what you're celebrating; if you don't give me some of that champagne I'll tell everybody what you're up to." His unexpected voice behind us made us both start; it was Tola who recovered first. A little high from the alcohol she had actually imbibed and from the other elevating elements in the atmosphere, she laughed outright. "*Sham*pagne! Adu," she said. "If you can't pronounce it right you shouldn't be allowed to drink it."

"However you pronounce it, I want some. Come on, start pouring. What are you celebrating?"

"We're celebrating international understanding. Finally this *ajerike* understands that a Nigerian woman understands him. We're not giving you any champagne unless you have something equally worthy to celebrate. Tell us and we'll see if you qualify."

"I'm not bluffing, *aburo*. If you don't give me a drink, I will inform everybody that while they have been drinking cheap whisky and local beer the host and hostess are gorging themselves on champagne." It was not possible to be absolutely certain that this was a joke. But this was Tola's game. I said nothing.

"Not a drop until you prove that you're worthy to join this select company."

"Well, what if I tell you that I've been asked by both parties to be their candidate in the Lagos by-election?"

"Both parties?"

"Both. Officially. In writing. The letters came in one after the other today. Eisenhower never had written invitations from both parties. Do I deserve a sip of champagne for an achievement like that?"

"My God! You certainly do! *Olorun pa mi!*" She gave him a beer mug and started to pour. "Which one are you accepting?"

"Neither. Neither, my dear. But I thank them both very sincerely. They have forced me to make up my mind. I will run as an independent."

"That's marvelous! Marvelous!" She threw her arms around him and delivered a loud kiss. "That is what you should have done long, long ago. I never said anything, it's none of my business, but if you really want to know, I've always thought that you were a bit of a fraud, really, going about the place laying down the law about what everybody's doing wrong but never getting into the thing yourself. Do you mind my saying that, Adu? I've said it, anyway." Tola was fast approaching euphoria; strands of her wiry hair lay limp on her forehead pinned there by the unseen cement of her sweat. She was now gesturing with those generous sweeps of the hand that in a closed space knock vases from tables and other people's drinks from their hands.

"I don't mind you saying it. My father has said it—to my face. I've been saying it off and on to myself. But on the other hand you might say it was a strategy that worked, eh? I wouldn't have got these offers if I hadn't frightened both parties a little, would I?" He looked downright smug. Putting down his beer mug, he suddenly grabbed Tola and hugged her; it was as if he was congratulating her on *her* political astuteness. They broke into Yoruba, kissing each other, breaking away, and gesticulating with hands thrown wide in those eloquent gestures which are as much a part of the language as the verbal vocabulary itself.

"We must make an announcement," Tola stated grandly.

"It had better be a discreet one," I suggested. "There isn't all that much champagne."

"Well, go and get Bijou; we'll let *her* have some champagne, and *then* we'll make the announcement. Everybody can go on drinking what they were drinking before." Adu's news seemed to have become her news; once more I was being made to feel irrelevant. But at least I had been chosen as the courier of their joy.

Getting Bijou wasn't quite as easily done as said. She was presiding over a section of the party in which Myron was prominent, and was shouting quite effectively over the top of the noise of the amplifier and the scrape of dancing feet that there was no reason why Adu should "run" when the object of his "running" was being offered to him on a plate by both the leading parties. If Adu had any plans about keeping the latest developments secret, he had obviously not communicated them to Bijou.

"But *is* he going to run or not, Bijou?" Myron was the questioner, and there was such resignation in his voice that it was clear that he had asked the question a dozen times before without getting anything like a straight answer. Bijou's contempt for discretion obviously had some bounds.

"Myron, darling, it is not my business if he go run or not. If to say he go run, the whole world go know." She was saying, loud enough for the dead to hear, that it wasn't Myron's business either; Myron gave no sign that he had received any particular message. In the pause, I whispered that Tola and Adu wanted her to come onto the landing.

"Tola and Adu are calling me," she informed everyone in her normal voice. It was stupid of me to have upgraded the perfectly ordinary message to the status of a secret.

"We're drinking champagne," Tola said. "Why didn't

you tell me that Adu was going to run in the Lagos by-election?"

"You go run, Adu? You done decide?"

"Oh, Bijou, you knew very well I was going to run. What else is there to do?"

"I know, yes, but you never tell me."

"Stop being so subtle, Bijou, and have some champagne," Tola said quite sharply, handing her a beer mug.

"Your friend Myron was questioning me as if he was the police. He very interested in your political evolution, he say." It was only then, hearing the unmistakably ironic inflection in Bijou's voice, that I realized that she was angry. I scarcely knew her—or Adu, for that matter, although with him something of an acquaintanceship had developed since Accra, the only thing we had in common, together with our mutual recognition that Tola was in different ways quite special to both of us. In Accra, without doing a great deal (and with invaluable help from the Baron) Bijou had acquired a new stature in my eyes. I was still a little frightened of her, and I had never quite understood why Adu, a good seven or eight years her junior, and a man with something of a reputation for austerity, should have chosen this uninhibited, scarcely literate, downright notorious woman as his companion, or why she should have acquiesced in a relationship that on the face of it anyway had so little to offer her. There was nothing, as far as I could see, that she could need from a man who at the age of thirty had more enemies than most people amass in a lifetime. Adu was, moreover, one of the most unconvivial men in Bijou's quite large catchment area, an introvert, a man who would evidently never make money in any substantial quantities. They made altogether the unlikeliest and most "incompatible" couple in Lagos, our own eighth wonder of the world; yet, within the short space of time that they had been together, even acquaintances had acquired a complacency

about them that the residents of Pisa would have envied:
It was banal now to consider them bizarre. I had made
several guesses at the secret of their relationship, none
particularly convincing. Oedipus complex? Fading Siren
Catching Desperately at Youth? Cash? Like all Lagos, I
suppose, but with far less grace and ease, I had found
myself thrown back on the simple supposition that they
liked each other very much.

Certainly Bijou's anger at Myron's persistent questioning impressed me as genuine and disinterested, even
though what I had actually heard of the exchange had
not seemed to warrant it. I was ready to assume that
Bijou had picked up in Myron's questioning something
more than the normal, social curiosity I had diagnosed
from the fragment I had heard. It was a marvelous thing
to have loving guardians poised to snarl at the remotest
whisper of a threat to the loved one.

"If we go drink champagne, make we drink champagne,"
Bijou said, draining her beer mug and changing the subject with the same abruptness. "I can't stand dribdrabs.
Make everybody drink champagne. We go celebrate the
political evolution of Adu Adumuyiwa. Bring out the rest
bottles, *aburo*," she said, addressing me. "I know say you
get more than one bottle."

"We don't have enough champagne for a general celebration, Bijou," I said. The six bottles of rather good
champagne which Tola had filched from Aunt Matilda
deserved something better than the anonymous and un-
discriminating consumption a "celebration" would entail.
Most of the people would not have known the difference
between Veuve Clicquot and Spanish cider, and wouldn't
really have cared. But I cared, and I didn't mind if I
sounded as mean as an Ijebu man. "Six bottles won't go
very far," I said; "everybody will have dribdrabs." It was
a plausible cover-up. Tola looked at me and smiled like a
wife.

"Well, let's go to my cousin's place," Adu said. "They always have lots of champagne at a *komojade*. That's what everybody drinks at the beginning, for show. Later on they go back to their normal drinks. There should be plenty left. Come on. Let's go."

"Oh, we can't break up the party like that, Adu," Tola said. "You see what you're doing, Bijou, with your crazy ideas?"

But nothing came of Bijou's crazy idea in the end. We finished off two bottles of the Veuve Clicquot without interruption—everyone must have assumed that some highly secret conversation was taking place on the minuscule landing—and returned discreetly to mingle with the others.

The party had long since created its own momentum and style. The loud music and Monday's assiduity, new as his clothes, had maintained it at a high level of decibels and animation. In the comparatively small space that was available a number of separate groups had somehow managed to form. By some curious social alchemy this seemed to make the room larger rather than smaller. In almost every case there was a particular woman who appeared to be the fulcrum and center of the group, around whom the gathering hermetically formed itself. In the midst of all this were the dancers, that single-minded tribe you see at every party, for whom music is an environment in itself. A dozen of these possessed people revolved in a narrow circle bounded by the limbs of the talkers seated on the floor, and contrived to expand the dimensions of my cramped parlor even more. Watching it all from the entrance, I felt a little godlike—a visiting god, it would have to be, not a resident one, so distantly founded my powers seemed. In a place like this I had ordained a party; I had commanded the presence of people like this at a time like this. But it was clear that this time and place and these people took their being and authority from other gods but me. I was content.

The dancers soon showed whose party it was. While they functioned, all went well. They plucked partners out of the sealed talking groups and returned them revivified, even though the talkers pretended that it was really *their* party and the rest was just noise and mindless movement.

But then the amplifier started to buzz, making a low-pitched rasping sound that blotted out the music at shorter and shorter intervals. Someone stopped the record player to look, and in the relative silence tailends of conversations enunciated in loud and almost frantic voices fell on us like hailstones from a blue sky. I heard "MAKE HER DO IT. MOST WOMEN ARE BLOODY COWS ANYWAY . . . " and "FOR THE NINETIETH TIME. THE KIND OF THING YOU COULD HAVE PICKED UP AT A BATA SALE . . ." and "SITTING RIGHT IN THE CENTER WITH HER LEGS SPREAD OUT. . . ."

The electronics expert said that a tube was blown, and there was nothing to be done about it. "You mean no more music?" the dancers asked. That was indeed the case. The party collapsed quickly but quite gently, like one of the more sophisticated sorts of inner tube. It was already nearly one o'clock, the dancers recalled that the next day was a workday, and the non-dancers found themselves an isolated majority, as it were. The animation they had thought of as mere background had, after all, been much more, as a typewriter platen is much more than a paper-rest. The goodbyes were kind but firm, and within fifteen minutes we found that we were down to a hard core of not more than a dozen, among them Bijou and Adu, of course, Myron and Charmaine, and, somewhat to my surprise, Auguste. He had come alone, mumbling for form's sake an excuse about Abike. Now he was very adequately equipped, his partner being a very attractive junior reporter from Tola's newspaper, a slim girl with unstraightened hair and small, aggressive breasts, who had until recently been top student at the Anglican Convent School just outside Lagos. Everything about her made it clear that she did not plan to be a junior reporter for very long.

"But this is *dreadful*," Charmaine said, rolling the whites of her magnificent eyes and holding her handbag lightly by the tips of her fingers to show that she was ready either to take a firmer grip on it and go or let it fall onto the nearest table and stay. "All those *people*! Where have they gone to? It's been such a *marvelous* party. I was having a *fascinating* conversation with a rather gorgeous young man and then he was snatched away by some *harridan* who said she was his wife. She said something indistinct and quite unbelievable about the baby's one o'clock feeding. She looked at least fifteen *years* older than he. I'm sure she's *had* her menopause *years* ago, poor thing. They all just *rushed* off. I can't imagine where some of them can be going so early in the evening." We all laughed as we were meant to; this was one of Charmaine's more unearthly flights; you could practically see the milkstains on Bisi Shomoluade's dress. But Charmaine had made her point, and Adu was not slow to pounce on it.

"Exactly what I was saying. It's too early to pack· up. I know what we must do. Everybody's coming with me to the house of my cousin Kayode. I'm sure there's still a lot of activity there." He explained about the *komojade,* which Charmaine deemed to be *irresistible,* and in a few moments we were out in the Lagos night, leaving a slightly frustrated Monday to clear and lock up. "Our" party had been cut off in its prime, but I didn't really care. That was as good a point as any other at which to end a party.

Chapter Twenty-one

Kayode's house was in the heart of Isaleko. We drove there through streets bathed in that special luminescence that neon imparts to dampened tarmac. The town was silent now, the few policemen in their wet-weather gear looking furtive and at bay as they cowered under the galvanized overhangs of jerrybuilt textile shops. We crossed a narrow bridge that forded a reeking swamplet which seemed to have strayed inadvertently down the lagoon into this overbuilt urban slum, and we were suddenly there, out of Bakare Street of the sleeping shanties into Olabisi Street bright as the day with arc lamps and the throb of *gan gans* and the voices of revelers.

Cars were parked on both sides of Olabisi Street, leaving a passageway for pedestrians only. We stopped where we could, disembarked, and trooped toward the lights. I was quickly swept up in the physical enticement this midnight street was offering to all comers at the top of its lungs. We all seemed to hurry, impatient to merge into this organism that Kayode's *komojade* had become through a long day's maturing.

There was a marquee surrounded, like a king's palanquin, by a phalanx of people who were obviously residents of the neighboring streets and who had as obviously received no invitation to attend the festivities. They were dancing, some quite formally paired-off in all three possible permutations of gender, others solo and almost introspectively. Casually, indulgently, they parted ranks for us to pass through and gain the enclave where the official festivities were taking place. Under the bright hot lights toward which a thin cloud of cigarette smoke ascended as if guided by a sort of photomagnetism, a woman of about sixty danced alone to the playing of a lone drummer. Her hair stood in a hundred rigid black-and-white stalks upon her head, and rivers of sweat ran in the canals between the tightly threaded plaits as she gyrated; her nylon blouse, heavily figured to imitate brocade, swung loose about her midriff with the weight of her slack grandmother's breasts. "Yế! Yế!" the audience intoned as she made her pattern, arms, hands, torso, waist, hips, legs, and feet responding to the pattern of sound set by the drummer. "Yế, yế!" they said, staccato as handclaps, as the drummer formulated his plaintive, glissando queries, and the woman's supple body told its complex tale, romantic, sensual, sometimes brutal, and all poetry, of the human being as flesh. We all stood bunched at the entrance to the marquee, stock-still and frankly hypnotized, like tourists at a shrine, perhaps, who suddenly feel as if they are being transformed into votaries.

Adu was recognized by a woman standing at the far end of the marquee at the point where it joined up with the main door of the Kayode house. She signaled silently to us, gesturing extravagantly like an usher in a cathedral, to make a circuit of the marquee floor and join her. Adu, going first, started out on tiptoe and then realizing how ridiculous he must seem had to hold his hand over his mouth to stop himself from laughing out loud. Inside the house we found ourselves in an element so different

from the one we had just left that they might have been
two totally separate countries. Except for the inescapable
throb of the *gan gan,* and the insistent—but now muffled—
"yé, yé" from the marquee, we might have been in Aunt
Matilda's drawing room. On the polished hardwood floor
a worn but very respectable oriental rug bore witness to
a measure of long-standing affluence. Everywhere there
were inlaid tables and elaborately worked brass trays on
collapsible legs, and the walls were covered with a score
of oval-framed photographs of black Victorian ladies and
gentlemen faded now to a mendacious pallor. I thought I
recognized at least one face from the Alatishe drawing
room. But it might have been my imagination. Here a
ceiling fan stirred up the stifling air and redistributed it
over a gathering of prim ladies and proper gentlemen,
all dressed in traditional Yoruba clothes. Again, it might
have been nothing but fantasy, but I had the feeling that
I had come into a room populated mostly by persons in
fancy dress who were dutifully playing along with someone else's sense of occasion and hoping against hope that
their tolerance would not be stretched too far.

Adu was now greeted by several people all of the age,
I imagined, of his father; indeed, we soon knew that it
was his father to whom he spoke first, as he completed
his round of greetings, and Tola set off on hers.

This was my first meeting with Adu's father, but by
now I knew, of course, who he was. There was, in a very
thin file at the offices of the *Sun* marked ADU (ADU-
MUYIWA) ADUMUYIWA the passing and almost contemptuous phrase ("Father: OLAJIDE ADUMUYIWA,
trader, Isaleko, b. Ijebu-Ode 1889?"). Sheer curiosity,
almost of the tourist variety, had taken me beyond this
curt parenthesis even before it became clear that because
of Tola Adu was likely to be a sizable factor in my life
in Lagos, and long before our casual, post-Accra acquaintanceship had begun. Adu excited this kind of curiosity

among the most incurious people; to claim to be "independent" in Nigerian politics was provocative enough, for there was a sufficient variety of parties to accommodate every kind of ideology—and idiosyncrasy; but Adu stretched one's interest almost beyond bearing by being without visible means of political support. He spoke at meetings sponsored only by himself, meetings which had no discernible goal in view. Yet he possessed a surprising and articulate following among taxi drivers, barmen—and bar girls—and musicians of my acquaintance. Moreover, he earned his livelihood in what journalists delighted in calling a "sensitive" profession; he was an insurance underwriter, having chosen this quite heterodox field when everyone else who had a chance of higher education was studying medicine or law. At some remote period of his life—perhaps when his contemporaries were planning nothing more far-reaching than their attack on the English Language paper in the School Certificate—Adu must have started to plan his attack on selected orthodoxies.

Adumuyiwa Senior had once been a "trader" in the received sense of the word, and had once lived in Ijebu-Ode; but this was as near as the note in our files came to the truth. He had actually been born in Isaleko, the heart of "old" Lagos, in the days when the sense of family could send a man and his two sons in a canoe on the three-day journey to Cotonou to spend "a little time" with an uncle, say, a month or two years, a journey from which he might return with a new wife and two more children in a larger canoe. He had been born into a family of drummers, and had the largest *gan-gan* of all beaten into his ears for fifteen or twenty minutes each day until the day of his *komojade*. His escape from the rigid mold which centuries of tradition had cast for him was due to the fortuitous combination of circumstances in which on one side the facts of twentieth-century life and on the other the corrosive juices of a very individualistic personality found themselves in league. A time came, in his son's words, when "the old man ran away in search of the twentieth century." With a proper cynicism, I had asked whether the journey was worth making, and had received a short, sharp lecture for my pains. "You West Indians," it began, always an ominous beginning, presaging that most intolerable chastisement of all, the chastisement you suspect you deserve. "You West Indians, you're so sophisticated that you do not know if it is proper to shit!" I argued that I was not a representative sample. "Oh, I've seen enough of your brothers, here and in London. You look down on Africans because we don't brush our hair twenty times a day with English brilliantine and because we don't speak English as well as you think you do, and you are all very proud of your literacy statistics, but now here you are suggesting that my father should have remained a drummer all his days. *O ma she o!* May God spare your corrupt souls!" I had no defense; I couldn't, in the face of his passion, claim that I was making a lighthearted sally.

The runaway worked as a houseboy, went to school, was once sold into slavery to a devout Moslem making the *hajj* on foot, escaped again shortly before the party crossed into French territory, worked on the railways— where he was befriended, as Adu admitted with a peculiar smile, by a West Indian brakeman—saved money, set up in trade dealing in everything from cattle to enamel bedpans, read obsessively, and "fell into the transport racket" during the Second World War, out of which he made a minor killing. A wife, three daughters, and a son joined him along the way.

"I think he looked on us as baggage, frankly," Adu told me. "Oh, very important baggage. But the baggage is not the destination, if you see what I mean. He is really a very selfish man who is considerate of other people. But he makes a clear distinction between himself and others. I have perhaps inherited that from him. Perhaps I learned it from him; perhaps it is a necessary distinction that society is always trying to obscure because it is afraid it could not survive if everyone appreciated the distinction."

"Very anthropomorphic view you have of society," I teased him.

"Everything is anthropomorphic," he replied seriously.

"So what did he do with all the money?" I asked. Adu was not noticeably a rich man's son; he drove a small car that was always being repaired, and wore the most un-adorned *agbadas* of all the people in the "circle" in which I now found myself moving in Lagos. He was known to give away a great deal of money, spending lavishly only on his unceasing one-man campaign. It was an axiom of Lagos gossip that he must be on bad terms with his father; other fathers were in perpetual debt in order to meet the exigencies, including six-cylinder cars and "story-houses," of their sons' political careers.

"I think he spends a lot of money on my sisters. They all went to England to study nursing. It was the fashion-able thing to do at the end of the war. None of them has ever come back. The eldest one is married to a cousin of Tola's husband. He studied economics and is a big ex-patriate nationalist. You know the type: He has been president of the UK branch of NANI for five years, but has never come back to Nigeria since he left nearly ten years ago, and I'll bet anything he will come back only on 'va-cation.' It is an expensive business for the old man. The other two are working in hospitals. The salaries in hos-pitals here are not up to their standards, so they can't come back. But England is expensive, so the old man has to help out." He spoke ironically, but without the slightest trace of malice in his voice and I guessed that he too had "helped out." "And, then, the old man has a great obses-sion about schools. If you want to get a few hundred out of him, just tell him you're *thinking* of starting a school somewhere. He'll 'advance' you a hundred and fifty pounds to buy desks or books or whatever you say you need most. A few innocent people have repaid him. The others knew better. He still writes long letters to the newspapers about education which he sends to me to correct the English. You must have seen them at the *Sun*. They're always signed 'Son of the Soil.'" I had indeed seen them in manuscript, but the *Sun* never published them, as the writer refused to follow our rule about pseudonymous and anonymous letters and send us his name and address. I explained this to Adu. "That will not stop him sending them. He probably hopes they will have an educational value for your subeditors."

My first sight of "the old man" was a shock. Having inevitably constructed a physical image of him based on the information I had acquired about his life-style as well as on some unconscious extrapolation from his son's slight physique, I found myself shaking hands with an enormous man in his early fifties, a prototypical "rain-forest Negro," the spitting image of the mythopoeic "buck" of the American South, well over six-feet tall and possessed of a Pantagruelian physique bespeaking a man who had discovered at birth that some things were pleasing and others unpleasing and who had decided—and had been able—to eschew the latter and cleave to the former. It was extremely difficult to imagine this splendid monument to the virtues of hedonism engaged in the ascetic and laborious task of examining the pace and quality of educational reform in Nigeria, and engaging in passionate public discourse on this abstract subject.

"Mr. Brathwaite, I am *very* pleased to meet you. I have been reading your articles in the *Sun* for a *long* time and when my son tells me you are his friend, I *nearly* ask him to take me to your office. But I did not. I know you journalists are *very* busy men. Welcome." Beneath the affability that seems to go with great girth I thought I detected the same kind of toughness I saw in his son. The voice was Adu's. Hearing it emanate from this frame was like seeing an heirloom restored to its original setting. He did not let go of my hand as he spoke; holding it gently and invisibly in his own great fist, he worked it up and down in harmony with the emphasis on his words. It occurred to me that the definitive attribution "trader" in the *Sun* files was, in its own way, true. He looked and sounded like some of those spectacularly successful traders who were then in the process of beating their lavish and loud way into the public consciousness. But it was an inescapable fact that I had never seen his name in the press as the donor of fabulously endowed scholarships, or ever remarked him in the back of an air-conditioned car with his arm around some beauty of the moment, as was *de rigueur* for Lagos' chartered *nouveaux riches*. There was an austerity in this man that did not go with his appearance, as Adu's voice did not go with his.

Inside, at least, in this still center of propriety and decorum, our arrival caused a stir. We were looked at out of corners of eyes—and from behind fans—with curiosity and perhaps some alarm. The thin aunts and buxom matrons had retired here to trade past family lore and to speculate about the future of the child to whom they had given thirty or forty names and as many pounds sterling that day; the occasion was essentially a family affair, knitting the past, the present, and the future together in many symbolic ways: Was the child born soon after the death of his maternal grandfather? Then his first name had to be Babajide. Was he the first child after several years of marriage? Or after a miscarriage? Then it was fitting that he be called Ayodele—"Joy Comes to the House."

Our group, casually dressed, cosmopolitan and unrooted in the essence of what was taking place, was an intrusion, the presence of Adu and Tola notwithstanding; they, indeed, by bringing us, had demonstrated that they were already corrupt, or being corrupted, losing their way and their touch. The strong smell of accusation was in the air, despite the warm Yoruba formulas of greetings that were to be heard, the warm embraces, the respectful genuflections and the grace with which the elders acknowledged them.

Adumuyiwa Senior clearly came and went on his own terms in this circle, and, for whatever reasons, his presence even on those terms was desired. So it was he—and it could have been only he—who pulled us loose from the quicksands of this encounter, pulled us loose with the brutal casualness of a gentlemen-farmer cutting short a visit to his prize pigs.

"Come on," he said, in that throbbing voice he had incongruously implanted in the featherweight frame of his son, "come away from these old people and get something to drink." He put his arm round Charmaine and said, "You have to give the child a name, an English name." He ignored the unmistakable gasp that came from one of the "old people." "A name from your family. Someone you really love."

Charmaine, that perfect hostess, was also, *a fortiori,* a perfect guest when she wished to be. Now she wished to be, so she moved with Adumuyiwa's arm, but gently guiding it and its owner toward the door to which he had inclined his head when he made his suggestion about leaving "the old people." Behind them we followed; there was no place for us in this musty room.

"I would *love* to give the baby a name," we heard her loudly whispering to Adumuyiwa, "but would it be *proper?* It sounds frightfully *untraditional,* but I'm sure you know best."

"Of course I know best," Adumuyiwa said. "I educated his father. He ate my *garri* like my son there. When I ask you to give him a name, it is the same thing as if I give him a name myself."

"May I call him 'Aidan'? It's the name of my mother's eldest brother, and it's such a darling name. Our Aidan's a terribly famous man, an explorer. Do you think that would be alright?"

"It's a very nice name. But you must come and see the baby self." He started to lead her away, and then remembered the rest of us. "Go on, boy, aren't you going to give your friends a drink? There is champagne." He, like his son, gave the *ch* the same value as in "chocolate." "I'll send Kayode out. He has been with the baby all day. Worse than a woman." Adu winked at us and led us out in the opposite direction toward the marquee.

The scene there had changed; the *gan-gan* player had melted anonymously into the band; a popular song was being played; and the social dancers were at it. The contrast was not in their favor; inevitably, I thought of the couples who had been dancing satirically in the street, and for a fraction of a second the quite irrelevant picture of the slaves imitating the quadrilles of their masters (a composite picture from Martinique, Louisiana, Bahia, Monrovia) flashed into my mind.

Kayode came out to join us, a big, broad-shouldered man who would more credibly have passed for the junior Adumuyiwa than his cousin. He was wearing a heavily brocaded *agbada* with gold thread at the neck and sleeves; its splendor was considerably diminished by the haphazard pattern of creases that seemed to spill over from the garment onto his face and betrayed the shameful fact that the proud father had been fast asleep at the shrine of his first-born.

Tola greeted him with a kiss and a loud, indiscreet laugh which completely demolished the little shreds of dignity that he was frantically trying to throw around himself. "Kayode, darling, your devotion shows in your eyes! We didn't mean to wake you up on a day like this!"

"Oh, stop it, Tola," he said, but with a laugh. He

seemed in a way relieved at being so summarily exposed, and frankly rubbed his eyes as he was introduced round.

"So this is your *ajerike* boyfriend," he said to her as she presented me. I didn't mind being called *ajerike* in these circumstances; there was no malice, only the teasing that he felt Tola deserved. "My brother, trouble dey plenty for that woman," he said to me in pidgin and a mock-whisper.

"*Om'ota*," she said. (This was best translated as "bastard," Aunt Matilda had finally told me.)

"I know the woman well," he went on unabashed. "We were at school together. When she gives trouble, you come and see me. I'll give you good advice." She pushed him away with friendly violence.

"'The woman'!" she exclaimed. "Listen to him!"

"I'm listening," I said. "God knows I need advice." It was all good clean fun at one o'clock in the morning.

Adumuyiwa Senior came out, preceded by his booming voice, and holding Charmaine by the arm.

"Aidan's a *darling* baby," she said. It was typical that Charmaine should wring every ounce of value out of her name-giving. Kayode's quizzical look made it plain that Adumuyiwa had awakened him and shooed him out to join us without even mentioning that a Gaelic name was in the offing for his child; even now, the old man did not seem to think it worth bringing to his attention.

"All babies are darling," the old man said, shortly. "*Komojades* are not for the babies. They are for the parents and grandparents so that they can congratulate themselves on their fertility. I am glad that you had the sense to get some sleep, boy," he said, turning to Kayode, who smiled at the unorthodox compliment.

The people we found in the marquee were different in one immediately noticeable respect from those inside the drawing room: They were all much younger, mostly about my age. And they were nearly all—the men, at least

—well along the road to inebriety. This was understandable enough. The *komojade* had begun at midday.

Our own group was none too lively now. We drank our champagne like hired revelers on contract to be jolly. Charmaine entertained us with a graphic description of the size of "Aidan's" penis, her voice sinking to a husky stage-whisper: "Myron's always talking about companies with *growth potential*. Well if you want to see *real* growth potential, you go and have a look at Aidan." But it was all a little desultory and mechanical, the last polite flowering of animation before the time came for those furtive little exchanges of glances between partners which presage a general departure.

But it was obvious that old Adumuyiwa was on a different time-scale. For him, our arrival—and particularly the presence of Charmaine in our party—had brought new life to the dying *komojade* and he was not going to let it slip easily out of his hands. He took Charmaine off to dance, to the delight of the unaccredited dancers outside the marquee. The *gan-gan* drummer reappeared and beat some lingering, slow phrases on his drum. Old Adumuyiwa detached himself from Charmaine and, holding his sweeping *agbada* aside with his two arms, described a formal step that was all bows and elaborate traceries of toe and heel which seemed to mirror exactly the sound that came from the drum. Charmaine, imitating his dipping and swooping design as if she had done nothing else all her life, earned a phrase of her own from the drummer, and gave him back in movement the facsimile of his music.

"*E'wo oyibo! E'ku jo! E'ku jo!* Look the white woman! She can really dance!" The limers gave her the accolade. The old woman we had seen dancing when we arrived suddenly materialized from the crowd, entered the marquee, and stuck a shilling onto Charmaine's forehead. "*E'ku jo!*" The entrance to the marquee was packed now, as the changed accents of the music penetrated the crowd.

Everyone was shouting encouragement to the white woman who was dancing like a Yoruba. Old Adumuyiwa straightened from his dancing to paste a pound note on Charmaine's forehead, and in a minute she had received about ten pounds in ten-shilling notes and half-crowns and florins that came from inside and outside the canvas circle. It took a little time for Charmaine, committed to the music and the movement, to realize the magnificence of the compliment that was being paid her. When she did, straightening up suddenly and noticing for the first time the confetti of banknotes that was blowing about her, she immediately stopped dancing and came back to the table, head bowed, her hair streaming lankly on either side of her face. I looked at the perspiring face and saw that she was an aging woman.

We all rose as she returned. It was Bijou who went on to the floor and collected the money.

"*E'ku jo*, Charmaine!" The compliments were repeated at the table. Old Adumuyiwa gave the drummer some notes and then joined us.

"If I had known this woman before," he said in that voice which was audible without effort even over the music, "she would be my wife." He looked at Myron with a smile that I would not have thought reassuring if Charmaine had been my wife. In the old days, it was said, when an Oba received a visit from a woman he found especially desirable, as she made to rise from her prostrate pose of obeisance he would lightly place his foot on her neck. Married or not, she would remain in the *afin* that night. At that moment, I could see old Adu's metaphorical foot on Charmaine's neck. But Myron was delighted.

"You pay us both a great compliment, sir," he said.

"Oh? I was not complimenting *you*. I envy you. I envy all men who have beautiful women. It is a good thing I am not God. I would ruin many marriages. I envy you, Mr. Brathwaite, but not for myself, for my son. If I was as young as he I would certainly take Tola from you. Let us have some more champagne." The old man's directness was like a detonation in our midst. It made me look sharply at Tola who happened to be sitting next to Adu on the other side of the table to my left. My look bisected that of Bijou who was sitting to my right beside Myron, and perhaps it is no more than hindsight which invests my memory of her face with something like pure terror. Adu and Tola were looking at each other, smiling a smile I translated simply as the there-goes-the-old-man-again smile which the two cousins must have exchanged hundreds of times before.

Suddenly everyone wanted to go and Charmaine, who had not spoken since her return to the table, was the first to rise.

"You're all too, too marvelous," she said, displacing a large swatch of blonde hair from her eyes with the back of her right hand and tossing her head back in a gesture that seemed coltish or skittish or coquettish and at any rate false until I saw that she had been weeping and that even now lines of mascara-tinted moisture lay like eccentric railroad tracks on her cheekbones.

Chapter Twenty-two

To Adu, idly going through prospectuses while waiting for Myron, his office seemed momentarily scruffier than usual. The hard wooden chairs bought six years before for economy and function looked just what they were, cheap and rickety and uncomfortable. The battered filing cabinets acquired at bankruptcy auctions screamed their provenance from every rusting and peeling pore. The piles of policy folders gathering dust and a little mildew in the corners of the room rebuked him for a black impersonator in a white man's milieu, first cousin to those secondary schoolboys who on prize-giving days painstakingly murder the music of Shakespeare with the tonalities of Abeokuta.

Adu often had moments like this, moments of self-deprecation that, he supposed, served as a necessary antidote to the arrogance of which he was often accused to his face by his Nigerian friends and behind his back by his British and European associates. If he was truly arrogant, he thought, it came from his father, from whose precept and example he had early acquired the combative notion that any single human being was equal to anything and everything in creation. Those files on the floor were, of course, dead, awaiting transportation to the incinerator; inside those beat-up cabinets was probably the best filing system in Lagos, one he had devised himself—with a slight nod to the Dewey Decimal System; his business was so healthy that the powerful African Commercial (General) had first tried to suffocate it and later to acquire it, offering the impersonator a seat on the ACG board in the bargain. The same "arrogance" that had made it impossible for him to accept this offer had also made it impossible for him to mention it to anyone except Tola.

The truth was that Adu was a highly efficient operator in the esoteric field of *oyibo* enterprise he had chosen, who had achieved in six years exactly what he had set out to achieve, a considerable reputation in his profession and just enough money to permit him to indulge that ultimate idiosyncratic luxury, an independent line in politics. He was the only multiple-line underwriter on the West Coast and he was very, very good. The manager of the ACG had said to him during their abortive negotiations: "You get away with murder just because Lloyd's of London loves you." He had savored the alliterative remark: It offered, as he had said to Tola, at least three layers of ironic enjoyment.

More recently he had been savoring another kind of pleasure, also heavily charged with irony, the pleasure of refusing a spate of invitations he had begun to receive to be an honored guest at conventions of insurance underwriters in places like New Orleans, Louisiana, Seattle, Washington, and Norfolk, Virginia, where his exotic name and innovative derring-do in the staid field of shipping insurance were well-known in "the industry."

Myron arrived with Anglo-Saxon precision just as the clock in a nearby tower struck ten. On such a scrupulous respect for the distinction between one particular sixtieth of an hour and another are civilizations constructed, Adu thought, seventy-five percent seriously. Through the open door he saw Myron, stingy-brim Adam hat in hand, wasting a smile on grim-faced Charity, the seventh in the line of secretary-receptionists that Adu had employed since the opening of his office. (He had had endless trouble with pretty, pliable girls who simply could not understand his capacity for dissociating what was done in bed from what had to be done in the office; Charity, lean, hard-boned, bad-tempered, and ugly, seemed to be a case of natural selection: She was impeccably efficient.)

Although Myron could see Adu perfectly well from where he stood, he pursued the ritual of "going through the receptionist" so Adu let him play the game. When Charity shouted, "Mr. Dryfoos to see you, sah!" Myron was visibly taken aback and stood uncertainly as if waiting for a more familiar cue. "Go in! Go in!" Charity told him in a loud, impatient whisper. He did.

"I'm glad you could see me at such short notice," Myron said.

"No trouble at all. I couldn't resist. I am dying to know what Worldwide wants with me. A formal pledge not to nationalize oil when I become Prime Minister? How much would that be worth? At least fifty thousand pounds in cash or a villa in Antibes, I would guess."

"Oh, come on, Adu. You should know me better than that."

"No, Myron. I don't really know you all that well, when you get down to it. And I know Worldwide not at all." Myron, discreetly squirming round in a vain search for a comfortable posture, looked at Adu with obvious surprise.

"I must say, you don't sound very friendly, Adu," he said.

"I'm sorry about that. Did you really expect me to look on Worldwide as an intimate friend?"

"But why do you assume right off that I'm here on Worldwide's behalf? I'm not, you know. I'm here on my own hook. Although I'll tell you, it's beginning to look as if I've come on a fool's errand. What I want to discuss with you has nothing whatsoever to do with Worldwide. This is strictly Myron Dryfoos, III. Now that we've got that straight, will you listen to me?" Myron had spoken quickly, his thin hands nervously chopping away at the air before him, and Adu found himself unwillingly impressed by the tension and urgency that emanated from his visitor. He nodded briefly for Myron to continue.

"I don't know who's been offering you villas on the Mediterranean. That's way out of my league. I have a more modest proposition. It's in connection with your campaign. There's no point beating about the bush. I would like you to accept a donation of five thousand pounds toward campaign expenses. Absolutely no strings attached."

Adu felt his stare freezing on his face like a cosmetic mudpack. A swift montage of reactions raced through his mind: Physically kick the bastard out of his office—first a push, then the kick. Call the police—but what's the charge? Call the American Consul General? Write a letter to the *Dispatch;* laugh in Myron's face. The thick cake of tension on his face cracked, and he leaned back in his chair and laughed.

"Myron, this is really . . .," he searched for a word and found it. "Delicious. Five thousand pounds. It's a nice figure. I could buy two loudspeaker vans. . . ."

". . . with battery-operated tape recorders. Put your speeches on tape and saturate Lagos. . . ."

". . . twenty thousand posters."

" . . . four-color offset lithography. None of the others has posters in color. And you could hire some full-time canvassers to cover out-of-the way polling areas the others haven't even touched."

"And what do you get out of it? That is the missing link. What is your interest in a successful Adumuyiwa

campaign? And what will Adumuyiwa be called upon to
do in return for this prodigious piece of generosity?"
Adu was all smiles now. He was sure he understood what
was happening, and there was really nothing to be upset
about. Myron, collector *par excellence* of *objets d'art*,
wanted to move into a new field, to add a new dimension
to his hobby. He wanted human objects. And, Myron
being Myron, the objects had to have that ineluctable,
indefinable something called class. So Myron had decided
to collect an independent politician. In its particular way
the idea was a credit to both of them.

"Nothing, Adu, I want absolutely nothing. When I said
no strings, I meant no strings." Myron was smiling now,
a generous little connoisseur's smile. The rare piece was
his: Only the formalities remained. "Believe me, I don't
even want to know how you spend the money. And if
you think you would be more comfortable about the whole
business that way, for all I care you could stop speaking
to me the day after you cash the check. The point is,
you're far and away the best candidate around. Nigeria
needs you. But, as of now, anybody can see that your
campaign is running out of steam because you simply
haven't the money or the organization you ought to have."

"And it's worth five thousand pounds to Myron Dryfoos, III, to see me take a seat in Parliament? That is
strange."

"My God! What's so strange about it? I've been living
in this country, how many, five years now? I shouldn't
have to be telling you that I've developed a very real
feeling for Nigeria. Another thing, I haven't exactly hidden the fact that I'm one of your greatest fans. I know
you can shout slogans with the best of them, and there
are silly people who get palpitations whenever an African
dares to say that he wants his country to be really free.
But you surely know that I'm not one of those." Myron
shook his head a little dolefully as if he were truly sad-

dened by the plight of "those." The interlude suddenly ceased to amuse Adu. Afterwards he would be pleased that Myron had contrived to make such an ass of himself; this had removed from a menacing, demeaning situation most of the odor of menace. All the same, there was a Yoruba proverb: "A vulture is a vulture even when his wings are golden in the rays of the setting sun."

"Myron, I think we had better end this conversation right here," Adu said. He spoke calmly, but there was a constriction of the muscles in his upper body which was doubtless on its way to his face. "I don't want your bloody money. And I'll tell you something. If this was an independent country there would be ways of having you kicked out. Unfortunately, all I can do is to ask you to leave my office."

"What the hell do you mean, Adu?" As he spoke, Myron made an involuntary backing-away motion that made his chair buck and scrape its feet loudly on the wooden floor. His Adam hat slipped from its perch on his knee and he bent to pick it up.

"Get out! That is what I mean. Out of my office." Adu rose from his chair and waved a hand toward the door. Myron, straightening up, looked as if he was about to reply, hesitated, and then turned and walked out. But he stopped at the door and made a half-turn toward Adu.

"As long as I live," he said, "I'll never understand you people." Then he turned again, and went past Charity's desk and out of sight.

Chapter Twenty-three

Dacosta Payne was by now a distant figure seen only occasionally at other people's parties. I was content. Indeed, it was he who made the unilateral effort to keep our separate worlds thinly linked by a series of telephone calls, which, as time went on, increasingly acquired the aspect of a tribal ritual long devoid of real substance. He had even tried once to arrange—"stage," Tola said—a luncheon for Auguste and me, on condition that we bring our respective girlfriends. I had been willing enough, but both Auguste and Tola had balked.

"Who the hell he think he is, some kinda tribal elder or something?" Auguste had said rather indignantly. I suppose that he felt that he would have the senior claim to any such post. "That's the trouble with all you Bajans. You always looking for somebody or something to organize. That's why half the traffic policemen in the Windwards and Leewards used to be Bajans."

"And three-quarters of the teachers," I said, a little tartly.

"But it's true. Even during slavery days they used to specially recruit slaves from Barbados to be foremen in the Brazilian jungle. All-you born policemen."

Tola had not liked Payne from the start. "There's something rather unhealthy about that elaborate mask your countryman has designed for himself," she had said not long after she met him. In her mouth he would, of course, always be "your countryman," ever since she had learned that the term made me uncomfortable.

"What does he want, a public exhibition of the irresistibility of West Indian males to Nigerian womanhood?" she asked when I mentioned the luncheon. I was surprized by her vehemence.

"Why are you taking on so?" I asked.

"'Taking on'! Aren't we British today!" But she must have recognized that she was being unduly sharp; she apologized quickly. "That your countryman is such an obvious operator that I suppose I'd be suspicious if he sent me a Christmas card. He's just too consistently bogus for me, that's all." Then, apropos of nothing at all, she added, "I know Adu can't stand him." The subject was dropped.

Payne phoned the week after the party at 10 Alade Street, but this time it wasn't quite routine.

"Look here, old sport," he said, "I think I may be able to put you on to something fairly interesting. D'you think you could pop round and have a chat fairly soon? Preferably today, if that isn't too much of a bore." The voice sounded even more languid than usual as it deposited its anodyne message in my ears. But somehow neither the language nor the exquisitely pitched tone of detachment could hide the fact that Payne was more than ordinarily excited about something.

"I'll come over right away," I said.

"That would be frightfully good of you, if you're sure it's not too inconvenient. I know you newspaper chaps have rather a frantic time of it. . . ."

I found his iron-faced English secretary-receptionist presiding over the northern elegance of his waiting room.

She informed me, in an accent that originated a few degrees west of her employer's, that he was expecting me.

He met me at the door, greeting me with a two-handed grip on my forearms, excitement flowing like an electric current through his limbs, and sat me down in a form-fitting Scandinavian armchair. He remained standing, his back to a large executive desk that was as antiseptically uncluttered as any movie tycoon's.

"Listen, Sinclair, I'm afraid even to put this into words, but I think I've got it. I *think* I've got it. Just listen to this, and maybe you'll be able to give me a few pointers." There was certainly something extraordinary in the wind: I had the impression that he genuinely wished my help.

"Anyway, it's the kind of thing you'll almost certainly be wanting to do a piece about when the time is ripe, *when* the time is ripe."

He moved away from the desk now, a lithe, predatory figure whose present unease did not blot out a certain natural elegance, a fineness of physique that seemed to complete and continue itself in his surroundings and in the clothes he wore.

"Look here," he said, but was moving away from me toward the blue wall to my left which displayed an enormous black and green abstract by Funke's discarded painter, "you know there's been an awful lot of cant about shortages of managerial skills in countries like Nigeria. Parrot stuff: Why are there no Nigerians even in the middle echelons of business, why do these firms bring in expatriates at astronomical cost to do jobs that Nigerians should be doing? Practically every time I go to Government House H.E. takes me off into a corner and tells me how ashamed he is that nothing is being done by the Colonial Office or by the big business houses to put the situation right. If you tackle the businessmen, they give you the old dead-end answer: Simply haven't got the chaps, they say; it'll take decades to train the right sort of people, dida dida dida. Well, I think old Dacosta Payne's found the answer. Just listen and see if you find any holes in it."

For some months now he had been working on a number of foreign businessmen and he had finally got eight of them to agree to recommend to their offices a scheme for training a limited number of their middle-level Nigerian employees: First there would be an intensified in-service orientation period of three months; this would be followed by a six-month academic-type course in general business management, economics, and accountancy, all to be topped-off by assignments in relevant branches in the various head offices overseas.

"It's so damned simple it's a wonder nobody's thought of it before," he said. "Of course, it took some persuasion to bring them round; all the old prejudices came out about what the 'natives' can do and what they can't. I think that the magic word 'independence' did the trick. They simply haven't got around to thinking out some of the implications of independence; I pointed out to them that we'd be getting independence sooner or later, within five years at the outside, and that life might just not be as simple for them as it is nowadays. You could see the little wheels turning around in their heads each time I brought this up. On the positive side, of course, they could see that it wouldn't do any harm in an independent Nigeria to be considered as pioneers in bringing Nigerians into management." He told me that he had kept Sir Femi informed about all these developments, and the scheme had his blessing. Payne would, of course, be a consultant to the various managements concerned, and would help in arranging the training program.

On my side, his idea was that I should get up the background on the employment situation in commerce in Nigeria and prepare a couple of articles to be published as soon as the formal agreement was signed.

He was full, as the French say, like an egg, and I knew that he had really called me in because he wanted some-one to overflow onto. *"We'll* be getting independence within five years at the outside," he had said. I was sure that the thought had come gushing out in all spontaneity from the depths of an unconscious that we partly shared.

For a little while after that interview, I felt very close to Payne.

"You must admit that I'm handing you a scoop on a silver platter," he said. I agreed, but pointed out that one didn't say "scoop" these days: The word was "beat."

Chapter Twenty-four

Martin Heal had his office on the third floor of the Edwardian building which houses the Lagos headquarters of the African Commercial (General), a vague title behind which lay a tradition of fifty years of import, export, retail, wholesale, extractive enterprise that encompassed practically every aspect of the country's commercial life from coconuts to coffins. Heal's office had been the general manager's office for nearly forty years, and it had apparently never been altered in any material aspect. Forty years ago, three-quarters partitioning had been the latest thing in practical office design for the tropics; now that air-conditioning was becoming standard for executives, it was something of a shock to Dacosta Payne to find the most powerful man in Nigerian commerce anachronistically sweltering under the creaking ministrations of a ceiling fan in a room into which noises from the street, from the lagoon, and from other offices homed as if drawn there by some principle of sonar attraction.

Heal rose from behind his cluttered desk of heavy, hand-crafted mahogany to greet Payne. He was a big man, over six-feet, with the rawboned frame of a Australian pioneer. Payne had met him before at Government

House and at other official gatherings. The man Heal had been totally invisible behind a thick mask of professional Anglo-Saxon affability. Often enough, Payne knew, behind the mask there lay only an empty space. But with Heal he wasn't so sure: ACG was too full of bright, thrusting young men and too close to the centers of power in England for empty men to reach the top.

Heal sat him down in one of the two sweat-darkened leather armchairs before the desk and took the other.

"Your letter was very explicit, Mr. Payne," Heal said, plunging right into their business. "A model, if you'll permit me to say so. All the questions that would have occurred to me were answered almost as soon as I thought of them. I gave it to our people in personnel, and they had the same reaction. The proposal is watertight, so I shan't waste your time with silly questions. What I want to know is, what's in it for you?"

Payne had been expecting the question, but much later in the interview, and certainly not couched in language quite as direct as this. It was the obvious question when all was said and done; it went to the heart of his whole existence in Lagos. For these reasons it could be answered, in any real sense, only in the privacy of a confessional. Payne didn't quite know the answer yet, and he decided to be as direct as Heal had been.

"Frankly, Mr. Heal, I don't quite know the answer myself. Off the top of my head I'd say, some prestige and some money. The money I hope to get as a consultant to the scheme, and what you businessmen call 'good will.' That's the same thing as money in the long run, isn't it? Also some personal satisfaction of a sort that you may or may not understand. How close does that come to the sort of answer you wanted?"

"Oh, it'll do. It'll do. Well, ACG will go along with it. I've had the green light from London. Whenever you're ready, we're ready. There's only one thing. You speak of a consultative group. I assume you've reserved a place for yourself on it?'' Payne nodded. He even knew what was coming next. "Well, the ACG representative on the council will have to be chairman. That is, if there is no *technical* objection." He made the word "technical" sound pornographic.

"Well, it would be up to the group to elect its own chairman. But I scarcely think they would ignore the fact that outside Government itself ACG is the biggest single employer of labor in the country. I shouldn't worry if I were you, Mr. Heal."

"Oh, I'm not likely to worry. But I don't want to be misunderstood. ACG won't be lobbying for the chairmanship. I just think everybody would be more comfortable all round if at the first meeting there was absolutely no doubt in anybody's mind as to who was going to be in the chair. Let me give you a far-fetched example of the kind of thing you would want to avoid." Heal leaned over and poked a finger toward Payne's midriff. "There are a handful of African employers, nothing big, but not altogether negligible, you know what I mean. Now it would be a very bad idea, indeed, if the council were to be suddenly faced with the idea of 'Nigerianizing' the chair. You see what I'm driving at, don't you? You could run into some real trouble there. Could be jolly awkward, what? And we don't want to get off to a bad start, do we?'' How many times, Payne thought, how many hundreds of millions of times by now has this scene been played out since white men first trained their guns on coastal villages in Africa? How many white forefingers have been poked at the short ribs of how many black men in America, in the West Indies, in Africa? Was that to be the eternal symbol of black-white relationships till the end of time? Would it never be possible for some black hand some day to take firm hold of that white index and carefully twist it out of its socket, disabling it for at least as long as it took the black man to get up off his knees? For himself, he would willingly have taken that particular finger, with its fine brownish whiskers sprouting just below the crease of the knuckle, and snapped it backwards until he heard the satisfying crack of breaking bone. He let himself savor the totally impolitic thought for a second or so before relegating it to its place in the rubric of unrealizable private dreams which all men carry as insurance against a total breakdown of communications with what is called the real world.

"Oh, I think that can be taken care of easily enough, Mr. Heal." Payne said. He couldn't quite manage the smile that ought to have gone with the assurance.

"Well, that's settled, then," Heal said. "We shall be depending on you, Payne." He stopped and looked at Payne with an expression that said as plainly as words: "Surely there's nothing more to be said?" Payne, who had not failed to notice that he was no longer "Mr. Payne," stood, shook hands, and went through the outer office and down the three traffic-laden flights of stairs to the street. Idiotic as the sensation was, he felt definitely cooler in the glare and violence of the eleven o'clock sun.

Chapter Twenty-five

"Dacosta Payne has done it!" I told Tola the evening of Payne's announcement. "Information reaching me from unimpeachable sources, etc. The mouth of the horse." She had come to Alade Street as usual just after seven. But for her curiously puritanical insistence on not actually sleeping overnight at Alade Street, we had in every respect the domestic rhythm of a married couple. Late business calls were routinely transferred to my number; if she was going to be late she telephoned—our way of indulging Monday in his fantasy that it was important that he know to within ten minutes when dinner was to be served. (One night, returning very late from a club-crawl in the suburb where several hundred people from Monday's hometown had reconstructed a facsimile of far-off Umuahia, I had recognized him sitting under a street lamp reading. To his great embarrassment I stopped and saw that the book was the algebra textbook for the West African Examinations Syndicate. On the pavement beside him was a pamphlet entitled "Fifty Incomparable British Recipes.")

"He's given me what amounts to an exclusive on the story," I said, "but if you're a good girl for the next week or so I'll let you have a look at my notes."

"Oh? That sounds very good. I'm filthy. I'm going to take a shower before we eat." I noticed then that she was wearing the same shirtwaist dress she had worn when we met for a sandwich at Harry's Bar early that afternoon. Normally she went home after work to change.

"I'll come and talk to you in the shower, then," I said.

"All right, but no ogling and no passes. I started my period last night, and, the way I feel now, sex is strictly for the lower animals." It was perfectly true that when she was showering I was given to both ogling and instant erection. The sinuous motions of showering, the stretchings, the fluid alternation of limb movements, the saponaceous caressing of every inch of the body, I had told her, added up to an autoerotic dance. My presence as spectator raised the level of the whole exercise and converted it into an elegant prelude to consummation. Was it just coincidence that the Goddess of Love was supposed to have risen out of the foam? And take the whole history of the word "bagnio. . . ."

I gave my report on my session with Dacosta Payne to a Tola balletically gyrating in the shower. When she was dry I waited for her comment, but she was silent as she dressed.

"Well, aren't you pleased?" I asked. "You have to admit that it's pretty spectacular for a mere operator. Even if he does come out of it with a nice piece of change for himself. Who would have thought that Nigeria would be brought into the modern managerial age by none other than our old friend Dacosta Payne? I don't know about you, but it certainly restores my faith in the power of sheer nerve. Not to mention style, bullshit, and cavalry-twill trousers."

"Oh, Sinclair, I don't know. It sounds good, no question. But I don't think I'll ever be able to summon up a great deal of enthusiasm for your countryman, even if he does bring off this marvelous coup. Somehow his soul and mine don't seem to meet. But if you're pleased, I'm pleased." She had perched beside me on the bed and was lightly brushing away at the front of her hair where stray globules of water from the shower had found purchase. The quiet dismissal of Payne and all his works, good or bad, was delivered not so much to me as to her reflection in the cheap five-foot mirror on the wall opposite, and it took me a long moment to realize just how total it was.

"My God, Tola, you mean you don't even give the man credit for this? What does he have to do to win your approval?" Was I defending Payne or did I somehow feel that I, too, was under attack? Monday interrupted the paranoiac train of thought by knocking loudly on the half-open bedroom door.

"Dinnah sahved, sah." He was very peremptory. There wasn't a moment to be lost.

Dinnah (unchewable cubes of meat floating in an undefinable brown liquid ensconced in an impenetrable crust) seemed to loosen her up a little.

"I've had an impossible day," she said, not quite looking at me. It was not an apology but one of those delicate submissions at which she was so expert. "Aunt Matilda. She's gone into politics."

"What do you mean?" I asked. Tola didn't seem to be joking, and I had to take her at her word. It was unlikely, but not altogether inconceivable, that Miss Matilda might decide that Nigeria needed her more than she needed the morgue-like tranquillity and shelter of the Alatishe mansion. "Where is she going to run? Against Adu?"

I must have sounded particularly startled, all the same, for Tola laughed for the first time. "No, no, Sinclair, I don't mean in that way. She's decided that all the Alatishes should do something to help Adu get into Parliament. Those who feel they can't go out and make speeches are to give money, write letters to the newspapers, canvass their friends, that sort of thing."

"What are you going to do? Sneak the letters into the

Dispatch? Or are you going to take charge of his public relations?" Now she looked me full in the face, and I saw no conciliation in her eyes. She lifted her knife a few inches off the plate and waved it very gently, introspectively, up and down.

"Sinclair, you're a genius. That is exactly what is going through my mind. Exactly"

"Adu's public relations?"

She nodded. "I'm thinking about it."

"You haven't much time."

"That's what Aunt Matilda says. She summoned a kind of family council this afternoon. My mother was furious, but even she had to come. Aunt Matilda is a very senior person in the family. She tore into us. She said that the whole Alatishe family, young and old, was becoming a bunch of relics. We come to the house once every month and complain that the country is being ruined by incompetent and corrupt politicians, but not one Alatishe is doing anything about it. 'You're not even smart enough to recognize when God gives you a chance to redeem yourselves.'" Tola mimicked Miss Matilda's speech which still retained the uvular "r" she had picked up in her Freetown days. "She told us we should be working for Adu, who, after all, is a cousin. My mother promptly said that she had a YWCA committee meeting and had to go, but that she would give twenty-five pounds to the campaign fund. Aunt Matilda asked for a check on the spot and Mother actually paid up. Everybody took his cue from her and started flashing checkbooks. Then they left. But I live there. Aunt Matilda had me all to herself. I'm not saying there was a big struggle. I agree with her. Anyway, I promised that I would see if I could do something really useful. The alternative would be having to hear myself called a 'relic' three or four times a day."

"So when do you start work?" I dearly loved Miss Matilda, and her handprints were clearly recognizable in

Tola's story; but no amount of refracted charm could obscure the simple fact that Tola was contemplating—had perhaps already decided on—giving up the next several weeks to furthering Adu's political career.

"Oh, Sinclair, I haven't even talked to Adu yet. Give me a chance, luv." The inhabitual cockney endearment, the lightness of heart it conveyed, made it clear that there was nothing for me to say, that she had in fact decided what she was going to do and was, if anything, quite relieved to have gotten it off her chest.

"You'll have to resign, won't you?" I asked, trying to be matter-of-fact and cool.

"You know the *Dispatch*. One hundred percent NANI. I'll offer them my resignation. They'll accept it. The editor will say that if the final decision had been his he'd keep me, but, unfortunately blah blah."

"So what happens after the election? They'll scarcely take you back. What'll you do?"

"Oh, how do I know? I told you. I haven't even spoken to Adu yet. Who's to say he even wants a public relations quote specialist unquote?"

It was hopeless. The by-election campaign was no longer the peripheral thing it had seemed just a few days before. It was swamping my life. We talked through dinner, meticulously building barricades against the inevitable quarrel. She inquired about my piece on the Payne Plan, told me jokes about her consequential mother, and filled me in on *Dispatch* gossip about the NANI candidate. Then she said she was tired and would have an early night. We kissed. She left. We had not "quarreled."

We had not quarreled, but we were clearly losing contact, and it was shattering. After she left I felt as I had often done as a child in that split second when you see the blood actually flowing from the cut finger or the bottle of jam from which you were stealing one small spoonful lying on the floor with its contents irretrievably spilled:

O, you lament silently, where is that beautiful moment, a whole lifetime ago, when I was standing here quite entire? I tried to read, but couldn't concentrate. There was nothing for it but to go to the Mainland Club and take out my frustrations on one red and two white billiard balls.

The club was usually deserted at this time; even the light over the nameboard at the entrance seemed dimmer. Pius was not on duty; one of the younger barmen served me and told me that the cue boys were not available, but both tables had been ironed late that afternoon. I heard the sound of balls being struck just as introspectively as I planned to strike them, and was almost pleased to recognize Auguste as the lone player; he was immersed, as I had planned to be, in that quite unique atmosphere that is a deserted billiard room when there are no partners or opponents, no score, and, most of all, no audience. The only light in the room glowed single-mindedly from the chimney-like housing suspended directly above the table. The balls flowed across the table, cannoning, creeping with counterspin along the cushions, or screwing back into immobility like red and white punctuation marks on the perfectly tended green cloth lawn. From the obscurity beyond the table I watched Auguste silently for a good ten minutes. He was an excellent player and to be a lone spectator of his skill was almost as satisfying as it would have been to play myself. His game seemed a succession of easy shots of silken tameness, but I knew enough to see the great delicacy and sureness which were at work. I could have watched longer, despite the itch to unrack my own cue and set it to work on those intractable spheres, but at the end of a series of cannons, each one of which seemed no more than an inevitable stage in a perfectly balanced equation, he had worked his three balls into a position where he was bound to lose a white on the next shot or end the run. He walked around the table surveying the position; his broad Creole face was wide-open in a smile of boyish glee, and he hummed the melody of "Sly Mongoose" with all the innocent bravura of a man in his bath. Making up his mind quite suddenly, he played a round-the-cushions shot that grazed one ball in its tiptoe passage and ended with his own ball hesitating on the lip of a pocket for a long fraction of a second and then dipping in. It was magnificent, and I spoke as much in relief from the tension and waiting as in admiration.

"Shot! My God, what a shot!" He started and peered into the dark beyond the table, cutting short the happy laugh that had been in the making. "It's me, Auguste," I said, laughing at him. "Brathwaite. That's fantastic billiards! *Ee ga'ce!*" The traditional St. Lucian exclamation used for everything from a good stroke at cricket to a drag-out fight in a film came to my lips more as a gesture of delighted camaraderie than as a tease. But he took it as a tease.

"Boy, when you play a shot like that I'll sell you my sister for six cents." He wasn't angry, but he was disoriented by the irruption of another human being into that world of calculation and coordination in which he had been insulated until I spoke. Perhaps he had been on the point of paying himself—aloud—some ridiculous unadult compliment, like "Beat that, Walter Lindrum!" and wasn't quite sure that the words had remained unspoken. I wanted to make amends because his playing had given me such pleasure.

"Auguste, boy, she'll have to die an old maid. As we say in Barbados, I ain't able, I can' able. That is master billiards. What I must do is to come to the club on Saturdays and bet on you. Nobody around here playing a game like that these days. *Sacré maman!*" If my penance was the slightest bit exaggerated, I knew it was because I could not stand the experience of losing contact with someone else that night. I didn't especially wish to talk to Auguste or to spend an evening with him; but if I had let him founder in the minuscule trough of resentment which I had perceived, from his fairly violent remark, to be in danger of forming, I would have felt jinxed, a precocious ancient mariner with an invisible albatross. He came out of it quickly enough.

"That is supposed to be patois you speaking? You say *sacré maman* as if it was something you learn in Cambridge! Come on, I'll give you a game. Hundred up, you can have forty start."

"No, finish your break. I counted thirty-seven already."

"Ah, ahh. That's all over," he said, splaying the balls all over the table. "Give you forty, you cue off. If I let you see me make a hundred break everybody in the club bound to hear. I'll never get anybody to take a bet against me!"

"Give me fifty!"

"I give you fifty and we'll have to play for money. Take forty and I'll take it easy."

He ran fluently into a hundred when I was stuck on sixty-three. We set up again and I reached eighty as a result of a series of flukes and much indulgence on his part. "You hold your cue all wrong," he told me. "You can't control it that way." He took my arm and set it in position. "Try now," he said, pushing my elbow through what seemed a marvelously symmetrical movement. I missed the object ball completely. "You'll never be a billiards player," he said softly. It seemed an irreversible judgment. "Come and have a drink in the lounge," he offered. It was his turn to mollify.

"That was a great fête at your place the other night," he said when we were seated. A foursome played bridge on a table under the deserted dartboard; its gooseneck lamp, twisted away from the wall for their benefit, threw their distorted shadow against the white wall behind

them so that the profile of a gentle little printer who was
dummy looked like a magic lantern ogre in the act of
gobbling up his unwitting companions. "A great fête,"
insisted Auguste. "Dam' nice people. Everybody very relaxed. A dam' shame the amplifier broke down. I was
really enjoying myself."

"I saw. What's her name? Angela? It's something like
that, isn't it?"

"Virginia." He couldn't meet my eyes. I laughed with
him. "'Virgin' for short, but not for long. Not bad. She
was a virgin when I was a very young man. She's crazy.
In the back of a Fiat 1500. I'm getting too fat for the
demands of present-day life. And I had a hearing in
Chancery the next morning at nine-thirty. No waffling.
All law. The dam' Master like a hawk behind me with
his nancy voice, 'Mr. Auguste, surely you can offer more
specific guidance than these vague, generalized references to Dicey on Tort. Is there no lesson for this hearing in recently adjudicated cases in West Africa?' A
wicked man. His wife is past it now, and he don't dare
do anything too obvious. All he can do is beat law books.
A wicked fellow." I laughed in commiseration; Mr. Justice Adeyemi, Master in Chancery, was known even to
the press as a special kind of tyrant; when he came on
the judicial bench some years back he was supposed to
have said, "Learned counsel may count upon me for intellectual rigor; I hope I can count upon learned counsel
for intellectual rigor." Learned counsel put about the
story that until *rigor mortis* set in, the only rigor
Mr. Justice Adeyemi could confidently offer to the world
was the intellectual kind. It was certain that after two
parties and a bout with Virginia, an early morning session with him was supererogatory punishment.

I bought a round, but could not escape until Auguste
had reciprocated. He talked about everything except
himself or Abike: Mostly we talked about the by-election

and Adu's unbeatable position as the independent who would be able to wave at meetings the documentary proof of the blandishments offered by both parties, a sort of Magna Charta of nonpartisan independence. I said nothing about Adu's new public relations officer, and I didn't mention Dacosta Payne's name. I was sure that Auguste would commiserate with me over the first.

"But what's Adu going to do with his independence when he gets the seat?" Auguste asked. Neither of us wasted any time on the hypothesis that he might *not* get the seat. "An independent in Parliament, if he don't own a newspaper, or bribe every reporter he can lay his hands on, he might as well be in Uzbekistan. Nobody going to know if he alive or dead. And he bound to sell out to one side or the other in the long run, otherwise by the time the next elections come round people asking 'Adumuyiwa? What's his last name?'"

"Maybe the big moment will be when it comes to selling out. If you're smart enough and you sell out in the *short* run, maybe it's not so hard to get a worthwhile price. A ministry, for example? If he handles it right, who knows, Adu could get away with it. I'm sure he'd make a very good minister. After that all he has to do is to pass the word around that he's still retaining his right to an independent voice; stage-manage a strategic quarrel with some of the big boys every now and then and he might end up leader of the party." I hadn't really thought it out before, but the brilliant formulation that three-brandy-and-sodas had created seemed quite watertight.

"Jesus, boy, you sound like a politician already! You been reading Machiavelli?" After a while he said, "You know, you could be right. Adu ain't no fly-by-night. He's been working up to something. I better get my ass to the campaign meetings, see if I can get a smell of what's going on. Imagine, I let you come to this country brand-new to give me lessons! Come on, let's have one on that.

But not here. How about the Imperial?'' But I demurred; Auguste, despite his complaints about the Master in Chancery, despite the long night and the long day he had had, despite our three drinks together and the others he must have had before I came, looked freshly washed and brushed, a man at the beginning, not clapped out at the end, of a cycle. I smelled on him the odor of readiness for a night out, and suspected that this was why he was here in the empty, echoing club, to wind up in leisurely fashion for a thorough change from domestic routine. Enough of my nights had ended in a stifling room-and-parlor in Surulere waiting for a sweaty girl to brush her teeth and strip down to brassiere and *lappa* while anopheles mosquitoes buzzed around my head and some lonely insomniac sang an Ibibio wedding song on the steps of the shack next door. Tonight I wanted my own room-and-parlor where the temperature was certainly the same as in Surulere but felt cooler because it was mine, just as the temperature on your own chair is always lower than on a chair somebody else has just vacated. Tomorrow I wanted to wake in my own sweat and my own smell.

Chapter Twenty-six

The man said, "Thank you for coming so promptly, Mr. Payne. It was rather short notice, I'm afraid." Payne was nagged by an indefinable sense of something like familiarity as the man spoke. He looked at him more closely. There was nothing to be seen but a pleasant-looking, young, freckle-faced, fair-haired man, obviously in his early thirties despite the thinning hair. Then Payne realized that what had caught his involuntary attention was the unmistakable burr of Barbadian speech beneath the canopy of proper English vowels.

"You're from Barbados, aren't you?" he asked.

"Yes," the man said shortly.

Payne was surprised at the pleasure he felt at this confirmation of his guess, at having ferreted out behind the official mask a fellow countryman, albeit a white one. There had been quite a few white Barbadians in the British administration over the years. While the majority cleaved to Barbados and to their traditional callings—agriculture, trade, the law—every generation seemed to produce a few who, as if responding to some inarticulate racial imperative, scurried off to the "Mother County" to pit themselves against "real Englishmen." Perhaps they could be considered as *boucs émissaires* who served to reassure the tribe that the years of expatriation and miscegenation had not leached out of the stock all the vital juices that had once helped Britannia to rule the waves. And who was more "more-English-than-the-English," the white colonial or the black colonial? A tantalizingly moot question.

"Well, isn't that something!" he said. "You can't hide the old Bajan accent whatever you do!"

The man looked at Payne a little oddly and then said, "You seem to be succeeding fairly well." A Bulldog Drummondism came to Payne's mind: "Deuced unfriendly!"

"My name is Proverbs," the man went on. This was really too much, Payne thought. He knew all about Proverbs. Funke had given him chapter and verse, but the one thing she had missed out on was the man's origins. Proverbs had come out of Funke's story rather well, an uncynical, uncertain, almost honorable young man who, so far from being straightforwardly venal, had fallen more than a little in love with Funke and had almost had to be argued into collecting his fleshly *quid pro quo*. Then she had had something of a job to persuade him not to cross that thin but quite unimaginary line that separates an excusable "fling-with-a-native-girl" from a full-scale "entanglement"; while the former was usually passed off by the colonial establishment with stag jokes about ebony and ivory, the latter tended to lead to transfers to Sarawak and much subsequent languishing in the doldrums of "deferred promotions." The Proverbs Payne was now seeing appeared to have put all that behind him and to be intent on playing the classic role of close-mouthed civil servant. Nevertheless, Payne tried once more.

"Weren't you in Education at one point?" he asked.

"Yes. Intraservice transfers are routine. Mr. Payne, I don't want to sound too abrupt, but we haven't much time. We ought to be leaving soon."

"Leaving? Are we going somewhere?" Payne was puzzled, but he gave Proverbs an indulgent little smile. The man deserved an "A"-for-effort for his British bureaucrat act.

"Yes. Will you come in my car, please?" Proverbs was quite peremptory. Hadn't there been a Proverbs high up in the Barbados Police Force? Payne felt menace, his old brass-knuckled sparring partner, tiptoe into the bright airy office of ASCOLAD (Assistant Secretary, Colony of Lagos Administration) which he had entered a few minutes before, at 9:30 on the dot, in response to an apologetic 9:00 A.M. invitation to discuss "some of the repercussions" of his proposals for middle-management training.

"Where on earth are we going? What's all this about, anyway?" Payne heard issuing from his mouth a voice that sounded like a particularly incompetent imitation of his own, the timbre wandering like a car with a broken steering rod. Proverbs stood and took a soft hat off a peg behind his desk.

"Look, I'm a fairly busy man, Mr. Proverbs. I don't have time to play games. And I don't expect this sort of thing from presumably responsible government officers. I thought I was coming here to discuss my training project, not take part in some obscure pantomime. If there's to be no discussion of the project, kindly say so in a direct manner. Then perhaps we could get our conversation onto something like rational ground." Payne's voice was now under perfect control. He had had to force himself to remain in his seat when Proverbs had arisen, to reassert his power over muscles which were seemingly ready to succumb to the tones of command in this younger man's voice, to the urgings of a yet unidentified fear. On his face there was a good reproduction of cold anger, and it had its effect because Proverbs now put his hat on the desk and sat down in his swivel chair again.

"Mr. Payne," he said, "all this is really nothing to do

with me. I had assumed that you had at least some vague notion of what this exercise was all about. Obviously I was wrong. I had better tell you exactly what my instructions are. I am to take you *in my car*," he paused to emphasize the last three words, "to meet somebody from Special Branch." Proverbs stopped again. He looked at Payne as if to see whether the announcement had set off some mechanism of recognition in Payne's mind. Payne's cold stare remained intact. "It's all rather secretive, quite out of my line," Proverbs went on. "If you absolutely refuse to come, I am supposed to say something to you." He stopped again, and continued to watch Payne.

"Something? What 'something'?"

"Only if you absolutely refuse to come with me. Those are my instructions." Proverbs stopped again and waited.

Payne said in his coldest voice, "Then you may take it that I absolutely refuse. Can we end the charade now?"

"I am supposed to say at this point, 'Remember Notts 'forty-six.' I'm sorry about the melodrama, but, as I said, it's nothing to do with me. I have my instructions from the Administrator himself, and you can be sure that in a Special Branch matter instructions originate even higher up. Shall we go?"

Proverbs rose again, took his hat and twirled it round and round his index finger. He looked inquiringly down at Payne, who remained sitting, legs crossed and hands clasped on his kneecap, for a full second longer. The look on his face had not changed and he seemed still to be staring at the space Proverbs had vacated. Then, abruptly, and with a kind of contemptuous boxer-like litheness, he sprang erect onto the balls of his feet and said, "Very well, then. Let's go. Where's your car?" Proverbs led the way through the back of the office and down a wooden stair between the two sprawling, green-painted, wooden buildings that housed COLAD. As they reached ground level, a breeze from the lagoon, coolly tingling with its

burden of Atlantic salt and spray, snaked past them and
ruffled the leaves of the poinsettia in the center of the
car-park. It made Proverbs think of Barbados, of beach
grapes and mile-trees, and that peculiar kind of vine-
grass that crawls irrepressibly along the island's east coast
in thin, sturdy lines, carefully skirting high-water mark.
He wondered what Payne was thinking about.

"It's nothing to do with me; it's quite out of my line."
Proverbs reheard the sound of his own words with a small
shudder of self-disgust. He had not only offended, Pilate-
like, against the canons of his own self-esteem: He had
also breached an essential administrative canon by which
the spokesman or executor of policy took, at least as far
as the outside world was concerned, the fullest responsibility. So he had been *irresponsible,* the *lèse majesté* in
the code of the British Public Service. The moral fibers
are weakening, boy; we always said that these colonials
don't really belong in an elite service like the Colonial
Service. Too close to the natives, what? I mean, they've
been subject to the same brutalizing influences for almost
as long, haven't they? Oh, some of them'll put up quite
a good show for a while, but when it comes to the crunch,
you see what stuff they're made of. This young feller,
whatshisname, Proverbs: Wasn't there something about a
little peccadillo with an African gal some time back?
Miss Addy-something, never get these native names
straight.

Oh, come off it, boy, Proverbs said to himself. Piss or
get off the pot. Either you're in it or you're out of it. But,
above all, don't waste time and moral energy ("moral!")
writing scripts for "them." And yet, he couldn't help himself; the obsessive game of wondering what "they" were
saying, thinking, about him continued sometimes in his
sleep, so that he would have incomprehensible snatches
of nightmares—not even full-scale productions—in which
there would be some inconclusive suggestion that he was

some sort of mountebank, an impostor. He had once dreamed that he had seen and yet not quite seen a report in the *Times,* a brief note in the social column announcing the annulment of the engagement of Mr. Robert Gordon Proverbs to the Hon. Cynthia Bell-Bowers on the intervention of Arbuthnot Herald, who had caused to be published in the *Gazette* a photograph of a coal-black woman believed to be Mr. Proverbs' mother. Another half-realized dream found him apparently selling schnapps and gunpowder to "natives" who seemed to be natives of no place he actually knew, men with rings in their noses and blue eyes, the color of whose skins always remained unrevealed. Yet Proverbs was sure that at the very deepest part of his mind there could be no uncertainty or guilt about the purity of his ancestry; from 1787, when the first Robert Gordon Proverbs of Tiptree, Essex, had landed in Barbados as a sergeant of militia with his ignorant but honest wife, a meticulous record of marriages and births had been kept in the rather splendid family Bible which his Aunt Millie had insisted on giving to him when he left for England. The record showd that the Proverbses had always contracted marriages within their own tight circle of militia, small overseers, and craftsmen, all with the same impeccable pedigree of church-going, puritan, petit-bourgeois, nigger-fearing rectitude. If one of his great-great-grandfathers had indeed strayed and brought a little bit of Africa into the Proverbs bloodline, they might all have been a little better for it; he remembered how Aunt Millie had only to hint at the existence of a little tarbrush in some "leading" family in Barbados for him to find them romantic and irresistibly fascinating.

And, indeed, those three or four families at the top of the pecking order in Barbados society who were popularly believed to be "wee-droppers," as the Jamaican expression went, undoubtedly were extravagantly endowed with looks, style, money, and an unfair share of brains.

These were the people with whom Greek millionaires stayed, whose children got crashing "Firsts" at Oxford, who kept racehorses in Barbados and at Newmarket, who flew their own Pipers for discreet weekends in Caracas, and who went to England every year for Cowes.

On the other hand, he couldn't seriously believe that his dreams had anything to do with wish-fulfillment; altogether, he was reasonably happy with the ethnic state to which the Lord had called him. So why was he tortured with this endemic uncertainty about his place in the scheme of things? Free, white, and thirty-one, with seven unblemished years of service in Her Majesty's Colonial Service, during which he had risen at a little better than average speed, possessor of a conditional pass in the Bar Finals which would be easily upgraded during his next leave so that he could, any day he chose, leave the service and return to Barbados to the safe berth awaiting him in his father's legal chambers, having "neither chick nor child," and owing no man—not even his father, who had said a hundred times that no child owed his father more than politeness: Wasn't he the very epitome of the petit-bourgeois dream, "His own man"?

Right now, silently chauffeuring Dacosta Payne back to COLAD to collect his car, Proverbs knew that all this watertight rationalization had brought him no nearer defeating the irrational upwelling of disgust and dissociation which had assailed him halfway through Payne's interview with the "somebody from Special Branch." He knew for a certainty that he was going to resign from the service at the end of his present tour of duty, and that he was going to live through the next seven months like a kind of zombie, performing his duties mechanically, marking time until release came. He knew all this as surely as he knew that what he intended was indefensible by any test of logic or self-interest that could be devised.

Looking at Payne out of the corner of his eye he realized
that he felt something very much like admiration for the
man—no, not "something like" admiration: admiration
without qualification. Payne was staring ahead through
the slightly muddy windscreen of the Hillman Minx with
an air of abstracted touristic attention to the landscape,
his left arm leaning lightly on the door-frame, his index
finger poking into his cheek. It was a picture of anything
except a man who had just been figuratively flayed
alive, totally stripped of the protective covering of self-
respect which every man, no matter how devious, how
catch-as-catch-can a life he has had, needs as much as
he needs his epidermis. It had been in its way a superb
job of work, as artistic as one of the better strip-tease
shows, and in terms of pure administrative logic almost
impeccable from every angle. And yet, Proverbs knew that
it was just this performance that had been the straw to
break the camel's back of his attachment to the way of
life that had been his for seven years. What was especially
perplexing to him was that up until that moment he had
not been aware that he had been so close to the breaking
point. Two hours earlier, when Payne was shown into his
office, Proverbs was already in possession of all the information he now possessed, having received the red file
by dispatch rider from the Administrator's residence at
11:00 P.M. the night before. He had been a perfectly
normal civil servant faced with a routinely unpleasant
assignment. Now, at 11:30 A.M. he was a renegade, a
recusant, ready to desert the Way, the Truth, and the
Light of public service.

His instructions had been to take Payne to a house on
the Ikorodu Road a few miles outside the center of the
city. They had driven in total silence (what was there to
say?) through the shouting streets and the manic traffic
of the city, through the scarcely less urban "suburbs" of
Yaba and Ebute Meta, and then for four quieter miles

along the road to Ibadan. Payne, watched politely out of the same corner of Proverbs' eye, was as composed on the outward journey as he was now, his face a lively, interested register of the scenes they traversed.

The rendezvous, described to him in his briefing as "a forester's hut," made him smile a small, disloyal, inward smile when he saw it. After traveling about two miles on a roughriding laterite track off the truck road, they came to a modern, low-slung bungalow in an immaculately swept clearing about half-an-acre in area. It was about as inconspicuous as an ice-cream cart in the desert, this aggressively European intrusion in the primeval forest of two-hundred-foot mahogany and black afara. An ostentatious black Rover was parked in the carport of the "hut," and a blue-painted police jeep stood at attention before the sloping verandah. Every villager for miles around would know that something extraordinary was taking place there this morning. "Discretion is the watchword," the Administrator had scrawled at the end of his minute. The meeting might just as well have taken place in the middle of the Carter Bridge.

Mike Fenton, Assistant Superintendent of Police (Special Assignments), a redhead who always looked brutally scrubbed, came to meet them.

"Morning, Gordon," he said as they descended. He paid no attention to Payne. "Get here all right?" Proverbs nodded. He had never particularly taken to Fenton, who had served in Kenya Police Force in the Mau Mau days and was given to a kind of bullying tolerance toward administrative officers that made Proverbs think of a sheepdog. "D.S.B. was sure that the only trouble you would have was navigational!" He patted Proverbs on the shoulder to make sure that he had got the point and escorted him into the "hut." Proverbs didn't dare look back to see whether Payne was in fact following; he felt he ought to have the courage of Fenton's assumptions. As

they reached the threshold, Fenton smartly tucked his
cane under his left arm, saluted, and announced in ringing tones, "Proverbs, ASCOLAD, reporting, Sir!" The
Director, Special Branch, turned out to be a man whom
Proverbs knew as a Brigadier in the Royal West African
Frontier Force. He was a jowly, gray-faced man in his
late fifties with a look of tired intelligence in his small,
brown eyes, and the stamp of the parade ground in the
erect set of shoulders. He was sitting on the room's one
sofa, wearing dashing mufti—cream silk shirt with regimental square at the throat, cream flannels, and suede
booties. He managed to make this quite comfortable get-
up look as if it was lined with sandpaper.

"Morning, Proverbs," D.S.B. said. "Didn't expect to
see me, did you? Line of duty, line of duty. Take a pew."
He waved to one of the two rattan armchairs which faced
the sofa and Fenton, who had fallen back, now justified
Proverbs' sheepdog image by moving behind Payne and
jockeying him without a word onto the far end of the
sofa on which D.S.B. was seated. Payne was evidently
a non-person here; until the time came to "deal with him"
he would not be dignified by direct speech.

"Now, we have here, Proverbs, one of the more interesting cases to fall into my lap since I've been in Africa,"
D.S.B. said, smiling at Proverbs. "Fascinating, really. It's
all been very instructive to me, I'll tell you that." Fenton,
standing against the wall where he could look down on
Payne and D.S.B., slapped his khaki shorts loudly with
his cane and barked a short laugh. "No, believe me,"
D.S.B. went on, "I've learned a thing or two from reading
up on this feller's career. Given me some ideas for my re-
tirement, I don't mind telling you," and he laughed a
more practiced, authoritative version of Fenton's bark.
"But enough of that. To business." He turned and looked
directly at Payne for the first time. "You are Wilfred
Dacosta Payne?" His voice was now the voice of an of-

ficer of the law. Payne nodded, his face taut with undecipherable emotion. "You'll have to speak up, man!" D.S.B. spoke with a vehemence that took Proverbs by surprise. "We're not running a pantomime here, d'you hear me?" Proverbs started slightly at the echo of Payne's own words. "ARE . . . YOU . . . WILFRED . . . DACOSTA . . . PAYNE?"

"Yes," said Payne.

"Very well, then. Now, just so that we don't misunderstand each other, Assistant Superintendent Fenton has a warrant for your arrest," and Fenton pulled an official document out of a capacious uniform pocket and waved it in Payne's direction, "your arrest under the Immigration Act 1927–60. If we consider that there is reason to execute the warrant, you will be held in Her Majesty's prisons awaiting deportation proceedings. Am I making myself perfectly clear?" Payne nodded, a marginal movement of the head, and D.S.B. exploded once more into a shout.

"SPEAK . . . UP . . . MAN!"

"You are making yourself perfectly clear."

"I warn you for the last time," D.S.B. said, heroically wrenching his voice back to normal pitch, "we are not playing games here. A number of things, a number . . . of . . . things . . . will depend on your conduct. If you should find any cause for complaint about the manner in which you are treated here, you will be, of course, at liberty to consult legal counsel. In due course. In due course." D.S.B. caressed his wispy mustache with the back of an index finger.

"Now, then, a person bearing the name of Wilfred Dacosta Payne, birthplace St. Michael, Barbados, British West Indies, was convicted at the Nottingham Assizes in September 1946 of the felony of fraudulent conversion and sentenced to six months' imprisonment. Are you and this Wilfred Dacosta Payne one and the same person?"

"That is a question which I will answer in the presence of counsel." Payne spoke very deliberately, his voice low and cool.

"A sea-lawyer, huh?" D.S.B. wrinkled his gray face to show amusement. "A.S.P. Fenton has a photostat of the judgment." Fenton pulled a document from another pocket and waved it. Payne did not look at him. "What we're trying to do, you see," D.S.B. continued, "is to make sure you understand that we mean business, *Mister* Payne. We have another photostat as well, concerning a suspended sentence in Leeds in 1948." Fenton conjured yet another document out of his braided pockets. "And then there is the matter of your war service." D.S.B.'s face seemed to take on a mauvish tint and became almost as taut and compressed as Payne's had been all along. It was as if the old man's mind was determined to suppress a shout but the muscles were offering the firmest resistance. "Your distinguished war career. Interpol says that you have described yourself in Switzerland as 'Flight Lieutenant, RAF (Retired).' You disgusting, shameless fruad!"

D.S.B.'s muscles had won the struggle. His voice, thin at best, broke now with the squeal of an alto saxophone whose reed is split down the middle. "Leading Aircraftsman Wilfred Dacosta Payne, reduced to Aircraftsman September 1943, on a charge of gross insubordination," and Fenton had a document in his hand again, making Proverbs wonder about the security implications of an Assistant Superintendent of Police wandering round with several highly classified papers on his person. D.S.B. went on, his voice a little calmer, "Aircraftsman Wilfred Dacosta Payne, dismissed the Service, March 1944, for embezzlement of funds placed under his control. Only the intervention of a sympathetic CO saved you from going to jail. What a bloody fool that man must have been! In any decent unit you would have been in jail and out of the service for the first offense! And this is the man who passes himself off as a former officer in Her Majesty's armed forces. For a man who is a proved fraud, chiseler, and really nothing more than a cheap crook, you've led a remarkably charmed life. Your so-called degrees: that 'M.Sc.' from Leeds. What is it, a Master's Degree in Solicitation? And your 'business management'; the only business management you've ever studied seems to be the management of the business of common prostitutes. With this background you have the nerve to come to Nigeria and pass yourself off as an 'industrial consultant,' incidentally committing perjury in a declaration to the Chief Immigration Officer in contravention of Sections 17, 18, and 31 of the Ordinance."

Proverbs knew that he was on Payne's side. He thought of the legal doctrine of false arrest and wondered whether Payne, in the university of freewheeling experience of which he was so brilliant a graduate, had learned about it. But, then, although the man was, technically, being coerced, according to common law, what could he do? If he resisted, Fenton had only to serve the warrant. This wasn't any longer the realm of law; it was an object lesson in the way power bent the law to its own uses. The law, and people: and, by an evolution which he did not at all understand and which he was quite determined not to examine now, in the short space of two hours he had switched from being an instrument of that power and had become the fellow victim with Payne of its operation.

"One thing is certain. You're a smart man." D.S.B. shook his head as if unhappy that he had to make the admission. "No doubt you've worked it out that there must be some reason for us to have brought you here instead of slapping the warrant on you and pitching you out of the country arse over hairpiece. But we're giving you a chance, one chance, because you may be of some use to us. When I say 'us,' I want you to understand that I'm referring to Her Majesty's Government, which has taken on the thankless job of trying to bring this country intact into the twentieth century. And you, Payne, of all people, can be of service. Instead of heaving you out of the country for the rogue and vagabond that you are, we're going to give you a chance to *serve*. Quite a paradox, ain't it? I know what I'd like to do with you if it were left to me. You'd better take over now, Michael. This is your end of this dirty business." D.S.B. nodded to Fenton who now moved from his at-ease position against the wall and took the twin of Proverbs' chair facing the sofa.

"Thank you, sir," Fenton said as he sat. "Now, this is very straightforward. We're asking your cooperation in an exercise which is of the highest importance to HMG and we're going to give you seventy-two hours to give us an answer. If your answer is no, I assure you that within another seventy-two hours you'd better be out of this country under your own steam or you'll be thrown out. I don't think you'll relish the latter procedure. It'll mean six or seven days in prison while the deportation papers are being prepared. We can't guarantee you VIP treatment while you're there. And the publicity. We'd make certain that you got plenty of that. Wouldn't be too flattering. Not flattering at all, to tell the truth."

"Well said, Michael, well said!" D.S.B. added, permitting himself a short bark of laughter.

"You follow me so far?" Fenton asked. Payne nodded wearily. Proverbs had the impression that Payne was concentrating every atom of his strength on the punishing task of maintaining the mask of cold detachment he had worn ever since they had left COLAD. Speech would have been a dangerous seepage of energy.

"Look here, man, I asked you a question and I want an answer for our records. A gracious nod simply won't do!" Fenton's rank was not elevated enough for shouting, but he made up in fierceness for what was lacking in volume, the words issuing from between his tight, thin lips as if under pressure from carbon dioxide.

"Yes," said Payne, "I follow you so far."

"Well, then, as I said, it's simple as pie. We want information on one of your cocktail party friends, the great nationalist firebrand Adumuyiwa. *Real* information, not just cocktail party guff. Between now and the date the election is announced we want you to supply us with a weekly report on our man, whom he sees, what he says, where he goes. We want you to use your closeness to him to give us a complete and detailed coverage. You know the kind of thing we mean. We've seen some of your so-called consultant's reports, so we know that you can write. And the reports will be in writing, and signed with your name." Fenton stopped and smiled. It was an obscene caricature of geniality and Proverbs was certain that he recognized its paternity. It came not from real life but from the cinema, Herbert Lom out of Sydney Greenstreet.

"Now, we don't want you going and getting any bright ideas about trying to fob us off with a lot of useless, inaccurate material. That wouldn't get you very far. As you can imagine, we're not quite so stupid as to depend on you alone for information. And we shall be checking your stuff, every line, every line, you can take it from me. The moment you try on anything we'll know it and we'll let you know it. Don't you think it would be rather interesting to see Adumuyiwa's reaction if someone passed him a photostat of one of your signed reports?" It occurred to Proverbs that the photostat was Special Branch's atomic bomb.

"Now, what's in it for you, you must be asking yourself. Simply this. You cooperate with us and your immigration permit will be revalidated for a period of one year from the time we receive your *written* agreement. And you make certain to keep your little nose very, very clean for the time you remain here. Then, out you go. Beyond that, no assurances. I think that's it, sir," Fenton concluded, turning to D.S.B.

"In a nutshell, Michael. Couldn't be clearer. That's all, then, Proverbs. Thank you for your assistance. *Mister* Payne here will communicate with you by 0930 Friday. A very good day to you, Proverbs."

Proverbs wished that he could speak to Payne. But now, on the return journey when there was so much to say, there was no way to begin. Payne, shut off behind his cold, opaque silence, could not possibly guess at the revolution that had taken place in his chauffeur's mind. And, at bottom, what difference would it have made if he had guessed? He couldn't be expected to put out flags of rejoicing because a white Barbadian British colonial civil servant had lost his faith in the mission of British colonialism. And this loss of faith, how would it stand up to rigorous scrutiny, anyway? Wasn't it really a kind of dandyism, the momentary revulsion of the meat-eater on his first visit to a slaughterhouse that is easily forgotten in time for him to enjoy his next mixed grill? If his repudiation of his career and, presumably, of the whole structure of beliefs and principles it was based on, was more than a finicky gesture, more than a passing milquetoast outrage, why hadn't he acted with courage—and logic! —during the inquisition on Payne? What, in fact, what in the name of hell and Aunt Millie was this journey that he seemed to have completed this morning? Where had it started and what had been its end?

It seems, he said to himself, using the cautious language of a minute, *it would appear* that to be white and quasi-British is too heavy a burden for me to bear, having special regard to the fact that to be white, quasi-British, and a colonial civil servant is *ipsis factis* to possess too much naked power vis-à-vis black colonials. *This* power does absolutely corrupt both its wielders and its objects, and I am apparently no longer willing to be the knowing agent of quite so much havoc, bearing in mind that a good proportion of the havoc in question is being wrought on myself.

So what are you going to do, migrate to another planet?

Je vais me mettre à cultiver mon jardin.

Oh, what a brave choice! And original, to boot!

Knock, knock!

Who's there?

Argo.

Argo who?

Argofuckyaself!

Chapter Twenty-seven

The by-election campaign was now in full possession of the city, displacing even the ever-present rainy season at the center of everyone's daily concern. The rain continued its annual ritual; once more it chewed potholes the size of manholes out of the causeway that led to the lone bridge between the island and the mainland, ferociously tying up traffic in both directions so that a trip that normally took a mere ten minutes now had to be budgeted for in terms of an hour or an hour-and-a-half. Once more we ran editorials about the need for a second bridge; a recurring conversation piece at cocktail parties was the native genius of the Italians and the Dutch for this sort of thing, and the insistence of English engineers that not even the Italians and the Dutch could do anything about the causeway. The Italians were still having trouble with some of the marshes around Rome, they said nastily, and the Dutch were living in a fool's paradise if they didn't watch the North Sea tidal movements more closely than they'd been doing these past few years.

But the by-election was more a thing of mood, a mood that produced new extravagances of gossip and speculation, as well as actual incidents. Some of them were trivial and even laughable, like the afternoon Olapeju was dropping me home in his new car and a small boy refused to move from the middle of an empty side-street that led into Alade Street. "Kill me!" he shouted in Yoruba, "kill me and see who'll suffer the most, you or me!"

"I wouldn't kill you," Olapeju shouted back without pausing to think. "We'll need people like you to be ministers twenty years from now!" Others were less jolly; there were daily news reports of people being beaten up by "henchmen" of one political party or the other (is it too late to invent a blunt instrument called a "hench," a cross between a halberd and a wrench?) and not a single case prosecuted in court because the victims either changed their stories at the last moment or told the police outright that they had better things to do than attend identification parades.

The mood was frenetic, like a carnival; everyone seemed to generate abnormal quantities of adrenalin; new jokes were minted every day; the Imperial did bumper business for no apparent reason; and in one night I saw three men drunk and incapable in the streets, a thing that I had never seen in Lagos before. There were more burglaries and petty thefts during the campaign than in any comparable period since the CID had started keeping records in the early 1920s. My Peugeot went into the statistics with both rear wheels stolen during a cocktail party.

The largest crowds converged on Adu's first meeting, held in the open air in defiance of common sense and the elements. We had spoken on the phone, semiofficially; I was making an inquiry on behalf of the *Sun* and at the same time satisfying my own deeper curiosity.

"Is it true you're holding your first meeting at Memorial Park?" I asked.

"Of course. Don't you believe what you read in the

newspapers?" It wasn't a very good joke, and it didn't sound too friendly. It was hard to put my suspicion into any concrete form, but it struck me that Olapeju might have received the same answer in the same tone. Was I being treated as a newspaperman, rather than the privileged acquaintance I imagined myself to be? It was only a suspicion; I maintained my own tone.

"But aren't you asking for trouble? I mean, it's bound to rain. You might get twenty minutes at the most if you're lucky and if you start on time."

"Look, Sinclair," it was a relief to hear him use my first name, "if I get twenty minutes, that will be a triumph as far as I'm concerned. In ten minutes I can say what I really want to say, and the people are going to flock to my meeting anyway. Lagos people are gamblers, to start with, and nobody likes sweating in a big unventilated hall. And we're starting on time. You dig?" My suspicion melted away completely; "you dig" was shorthand for our shared experience in Accra, and I was quite touched that he should invoke it now, even though the phrase, spoken with his strong accent and in that operatic basso, might have been mistaken for an inquiry about my preferred methods of tilling the soil.

Never having heard him speak, I chose to cover his meeting. He was right; the meeting which had one speaker and one chairman, Adu himself, did start on time, and was a smash success. There were a few stragglers limping in after he had begun, but a good couple of thousand were there before the start, ready to take the gamble inherent in coming at all, but unwilling to risk that the meeting should have been rained off before they arrived. There were no seats, just a brilliantly lit platform to look at and the sodden grass to stand on. There were probably more galoshes and umbrellas to be seen that night than on any other occasion in Lagos, except at the interregional football cup final. The rain gave

Adu precisely twenty-five minutes. But when the rush for shelter and cars and buses started he had already achieved his triumph.

He was on a perfect wicket and he knew how to exploit it. There was, first of all, the eminently provable fact that both parties had wanted him as their candidate.

"That does not mean that I am the best candidate available—although that is my private opinion," he dropped that marvelous voice at least a tone, and garnered a good belly laugh, "but you know what it does mean? That both parties are offering to the Lagos electorate people *they* consider to be second-best. What do they take the people of this city for? I tell you, it's pathetic. *Pathetic.*" He paused, and the word was taken up by a few people in the front rows. Stooges? A paid claque? Perhaps. "*Pathetic, pathetic,*" they chanted.

He talked about the way in which the by-election had been arranged, saying that there had been no need for it to be held in the rainy season; by law the Government could have waited another three weeks before making the formal move for nominations, and the campaign could have taken place during a drier period. "But you all know why it's being held just at this time, don't you? You don't know? Well, let me enlighten you. I ask you, who has the biggest party organization? The Government party." He paused and then repeated, "The Government party." Holding up his hands, he began to enumerate on his fingers. "They have loudspeaker vans. Loudspeaker vans. That is one. They have public address systems. Public address systems. That is two. They have enough speakers to hold meetings in ten places at one time. Speakers. That is three. They can call up on the telephone and say, 'Is that you, Afolabi? What are you doing? Eating with the wife and family? Well, we want a speaker in Isalegangan in twenty minutes. Good.' Afolabi has to go. Why? Because if he doesn't go he will lose his *garri.*" Everybody laughed.

"So, when one van breaks down at Apapa, what do they do? They send another van. Another van." He shook his head at the thought of such opulence. "As far as I know, those vans were bought with money that belongs to the party. That is as far as I know. As far as I know those vans were not purchased from Government funds. *As far as I know.*

"So who is in the best position to run an election campaign in the rainy season?" The crowd answered, "The Government party." Adumuyiwa held his hands up for Silence:"THAT"—pause—"IS"—pause—"WHAT"—pause—"THEY"—pause—"THINK." A long pause in which there was a silence so total that you could hear the frogs singing in the bushes and trees all around. "Adumuyiwa will show them. ADUMUYIWA WILL SHOW THEM!" The refrain was picked up by the crowd! "ADUMUYIWA WILL SHOW THEM!"

Then he started to attack the Government on its programs. "They have *no* program," he said, sadly. The schools were outdated, understaffed, and overcrowded. There was no program to train Nigerians for higher posts in the civil service, no thought of a program to bring them into the bigger jobs in commerce (had he been talking to Dacosta Payne?); Lagos hospitals were bus stops on the road to the morgue, no more. "And this their rainy season they love so much," he laughed, "you would think that after all these years they would try to do something about the roads in this metropolis, the center of this great country. Are they planning to have an election next year at this time again? Every year? Believe me, next year we'll have to bring back ferries if they go on like this.

"The trouble with both parties, *both parties,* my friends, because the only difference between them is their names, their trouble is that they have no *respect* for their *country.* They don't respect *Nigeria.* They respect *Britain.* They don't respect *Nigerians.* They respect the *British.* You

know very well what I'm talking about. They think that
the only people who really know what is good for Nigeria
are the British. So everything the *oyibo* says to them they
listen to. And everything the Nigerian people tell them
they ignore. That is why they have to have *British* civil
servants to interpret Nigeria to Nigerians. The British tell
them that Nigeria is too big and too complex a country to
be administered as one. So they say, 'Eh, heh! Oga, na
true!' And they split Nigeria into three. But only the other
day the British were administering Nigeria as one country,
right?"

"RIGHT!"

"So why is it that *we* can't administer our own country
as one country? Because those parties, *both* parties, are
listening to Their Master's Voice. Their Master does not
want a unified Nigeria, because a unified Nigeria might be
a threat to him one of these days. But those small boys
don't see this. Because they do not respect their country.
And they do not respect themselves. And if they do not
respect *themselves*, should you respect *them?* Tell me.
Tell me."

"NO! NO! NO!"

"So, who do you think is holding back our independence, the British? No, it isn't the British. They couldn't
do that by themselves. They cannot kill thirty-two million
people. They need help in their wicked work. And they
are getting it. From our own brothers. From our own
brothers. And getting it cheap. Cheap. A scholarship or
two to somebody's cousin, a few free trips to Europe, a
few OBE's, a few thousand pounds for houses on the lagoon with running hot and cold water and air-conditioned
bedrooms, a little piece of flag on an Armstrong Siddeley.
The Germans found a man like that when they captured
Norway during the war. He was a very valuable Norwe-
gian. For the Germans. You know his name? You know
his name?" He paused.

A single voice in the front rows said something that was not audible from where I was standing, but those around him heard, and soon there was the sound of chanting voices from which I made out the refrain: "QUEES! LEENG! QUEES! LEENG! QUEES! LEENG!"

Adu halted them with a two-handed conductor's gesture. "Eh, heh! Na him that! Quisling! Plenty Quisling here for this Lagos!"

Then he talked about the role of the truly independent politician. "They don't like people like me, and they will do their best to smash me. Why? Because I am eating my own *garri*. MY OWN *GARRI*." As the rain started its warning patter he shouted, "But Adumuyiwa will show them." And the crowd picked him up as they scampered, "Adumuyiwa will show them, Adumuyiwa will show them." It was almost too easy.

Back at the office, I had to wait more than an hour for the other reports to come in. They had stories of small audiences of party faithfuls, and long speeches that either recited the successes of the government or the grievances of the opposition, and they envied me my power to choose assignments and my acumen in choosing to cover Adu's meeting.

"If Adumuyiwa had four hundred people at Memorial Park tonight, they should stop the campaign now and give him the seat," Alapeju said. He had covered the Government party meeting in a hall that could hold five hundred but was more than half-empty. He refused to believe me when I estimated two thousand for Adu. "That's conservative," I added. "I counted lines across and down and multiplied, and then took off five hundred on principle."

"*Olorun!* It is a foregone conclusion. *O ti ton.* The matter is finished," he said, brushing one hand against the other in the familiar gesture of dismissal. I didn't think Olapeju cared one way or another who won, but he was disappointed at being robbed of the excitement of a real political contest. It was a professional reaction which I understood but did not share. I knew that I wanted Adu, who was, after all, the only politician I had ever known, to win. The more I saw of him the less I understood him. Right now, thinking about his performance at the meeting, I saw him as an actor—one who was his own director, scenarist, and producer, these being probably the only terms on which he would ever perform. Not so long ago he had been the austere cocktail party dogmatist; in Accra he had been quite debonair, an intellectual playboy of the more introspective sort. The only time we had ever really talked had been about his father, but in those conversations, by virtue of the very choice of words he had used to "explain" the old man, he had revealed perhaps more about himself than he had realized. The revelation of his tenderness—a quality which I was sure he did not wish to be broadcast—had delivered me into his hands with no reservations. And although I recognized the speech at Memorial Park as the work of a skilled, conventional demagogue, he would have had my vote if I had had one.

Chapter Twenty-eight

F*ade in* a sittingroom in a one-storied stone bungalow in the European quarter of Lagos. The time: 4:00
P.M. on a weekday. The bungalow is standard issue of
1936, white, low, and long, and barely functional. It has
no corridors so that one must traverse its two bedrooms
to reach the toilet and bath. Jalousies offer free entry to
mosquitoes in the warm season and to the chill morning
air during harmattan. The sitting room is too long to be
cozy and too small to be luxurious, and the uncovered
walk from the garage to the main entrance guarantees a
daily soaking during the rainy season. But the house suits
its occupant, Proverbs, very well. As a bachelor who
rarely has guests to stay, he has lived through his tour in
three rooms, and has a sturdy mosquito net which his
father bought him at Abercrombie and Fitch in New York.
He has bent the sitting room firmly to his needs, ignoring
all pretension to "decoration." So, there are half-a-dozen
small, low bookshelves disposed strategically around the
room where they serve as vase stands and magazine
rests, and supports for a turntable, amplifier, and two
boxy loudspeakers. As the scene begins, Proverbs
is seated on the blue-cushioned Public Works three-seater

246

mahogany sofa that faces the main door reading a fairly
recent *Life* magazine and half-listening to the George
Shearing Quintet's version of "September in the Rain." A
taxi comes to a stop on the gravel path before the door
and Funke gets out and pays the driver before Proverbs
reaches the door. Proverbs drops the magazine on the
floor but does not notice this fact.

PROVERBS: Funke, what's . . . ? Are you sending the taxi
away? (The taxi has already reached the street. Funke,
wearing a blue headscarf, a white shirtwaist, and blue
Gold Coast style wrapper that is mermaid-close at the
ankles, comes through the door, placing each leg carefully
before the other. There is a faint glaze of perspiration on
her forehead and she is smiling, but the smile is clearly
anything but a symbol of pleasure. Air hostesses wear that
smile as a VIP is sick for the third time while the
luncheon trolley is still in the aisle. Wives wear it when
their guess at the identity of their husband's mistress is
confirmed.)
PROVERBS: You should have telephoned. Suppose . . . .
FUNKE: *E'kason,* Gordon. How are you?
PROVERBS: Oh . . . good afternoon, good afternoon, Funke.
(She is inches from him, almost as tall as he, and he
kisses the cheek she offers. Then he touches her shoulder,
very gingerly, and steers her to the sofa and sits himself
on her left.)
   What's happening, Funke? What's the matter? Why
didn't you call?
FUNKE: Sofle, sofle, catchee monkey. Let me catch my
breath. I will tell you. I'm glad to see you. I'm glad to
see you. Where is your boy?
PROVERBS: Oh, Funke, you know he doesn't come back on
duty till six. He must be in his house. But you've come
like this, something must be the matter. You're not
thoughtless.
(She puts her hand on his forehead and strokes his hair.

The gesture is affectionate enough, but essentially automatic.)

Oh, Funke, what are you doing? You mustn't come and confuse me, now, of all times (he covers her hand with his own left hand) you mustn't, you know. I am glad to see you, but today isn't my day. Nor was yesterday. My God, I *am* glad to see you. (He removes his hand and so does she. Now they are both at ease. Proverbs remembers his manners.) A drink. Let me get you a drink. Vermouth and ginger, right? That same foul mixture? (She nods. Her smile has changed, it is now almost conspiratorial, as if they had been talking for hours about old stories known only to a very narrow circle. He goes into the dining section to the refrigerator and returns with Funke's drink in his right hand and a frosty bottle of beer in his left. They drink silently for a few seconds.)

PROVERBS: Now tell me what this is all about, what brings you here at four in the afternoon when God knows who might be in the place. Are you in trouble? Are you?

FUNKE: Sure, I'm in trouble. You know I wouldn't come here like this if it were not so. Plenty trouble. (She puts her glass on the side-table and claps her hands lightly together.) *Pata pata.* Trouble like peas!

PROVERBS: "Trouble like peas?" I thought your man was a Bajan. That's a Trinidad expression. Don't tell me you horning poor old Payne with a Trickyadian. The last thing he needs now is woman trouble.

FUNKE: Aiee! *T'olorun!* Don't make jokes about that, please! At this moment, if I see a naked man, I for done vomit! Yay! Please! Gordon, please, no jokes. (Her hands make a frantic, incoherent dance as she speaks, as if she were warding off a sudden swarm of evil spirits. Proverbs is taken aback by the vehemence of the display and gently pushes her arms down until they come to rest, crossed at the wrists, on her breasts.)

PROVERBS: Easy, easy. I'm sorry. Silly joke. All right. All right. Now, tell me. Tell me.

FUNKE: Trouble, my friend. Bad trouble. You know about it. Dacosta says you are part of it, but I know, I know that cannot be true. That is why I come. He says you are in this thing, but I know you, and I know what you can do and what you cannot do. So I know there is something missing, something he does not know. I want you to tell me. Everything, Gordon. Tell me from the beginning and I'm sure I will understand. Dacosta is so smart and yet every day I catch him missing things that seem so clear to me. I don't want you to misunderstand me, Gordon, you hear? I am not so stupid to believe that you can solve this thing, but I just have to know more, otherwise I will go mad! You know what we say in Yoruba: If you walk under a coconut tree and a coconut falls on your head, that is very bad luck, but it is normal. But if a coconut falls out of a mango tree that must be witchcraft. That is how I am feeling now, believe me. Can you help me, Gordon?

PROVERBS: You are unbelievable! What do you think I am, a priest? A miracle-worker? That's what you've come here for, a miracle. I can't even give you advice. Except that you should get as far away from Dacosta Payne as you can. But, of course, you'd never follow *that* advice. That's all I can tell you. Have you ever heard of something called the Official Secrets Act? (He shakes his head like a schoolteacher scolding a hopelessly wayward child.)

FUNKE: Don't talk to me about acts and official and all that civil servant business. You have no shame? You want me to report to the Administrator how you took advantage of a poor, ignorant bushgirl? How you frightened me because of my cousin and forced me to give you my body?

PROVERBS: Oh, shut up. (They are both laughing now.) We've been through all that already. Anyway, who would believe that the famous Funke Adedeji. . . .

FUNKE: AH-DAY-DAY-*GEE!* The man cannot even say my name right after he took advantage of me. A lawyer explained to me that you would be guilty of *constructive rape!*

PROVERBS: A lawyer? Are you telling me. . . .

FUNKE: (Mocking.) Oh, shut up! You must really be in a bad way if you could believe that. I can make jokes, too, not so?

PROVERBS: (His relief is obvious.) You'll have to apologize to me. That's something I really can't bear jokes about.

FUNKE: (Her hands clasped together in mock humility.) My deepest apologies, sir.

PROVERBS: That's exactly how you sounded the first day you came into the office.

FUNKE: Yes, *oga.* Your most humble and obedient servant. Now, will you please tell me what I have asked you?

PROVERBS: I can't. The whole thing is very hush-hush. They probably have their eyes on me already. All Lagos knows that we had an affair. It's not too hard for these people. . . .

FUNKE: What people? The Special Branch?

PROVERBS: This is impossible. I suppose Payne has really told you everything. It's their own bloody fault. They go to all sorts of lengths to cover up stupid little details, but the big boss thinks nothing of showing himself to Payne. How am I supposed to take it seriously? Funke, I still can't help you. I can't tell you a thing. Not as long as I'm part of the bloody charade, as Payne calls it. Funke, you really ought to go. It could be really terrible for me if some nosy bastard was to drop in and start putting two and two together.

FUNKE: (She stands now, arms akimbo, and looks down at him.) I am not going until you tell me what I want to know. You will have to tell me or I'll be here when Julius comes on duty this evening at six and I will be here when he goes off at nine and I will be here when he comes back tomorrow morning at six-thirty. I am not moving, *sh'ogbo?*

(Proverbs looks at her for a long moment and then shakes his head again.)

PROVERBS: (Quietly.) Jesus Christ, you mean it. Sit down. (She sits.) O.K., leaving out the Yoruba proverbs—"Yoruba proverbs"! How do you like that?—leaving out the tribal wisdom about mango trees and coconut trees, what is it exactly you want me to tell you?

FUNKE: Your people have frightened Dacosta very bad. They say they will send him out of the country unless he agrees to spy on young Adumuyiwa. Is that right?

PROVERBS: Go on. Just go on. Go on talking.

FUNKE: They have threatened to expose all kinds of things they say he did in England if he does not agree. And you were the one who took him to the meeting in the village by the Ikorodu Road. You told him to—what was it? Remember 1946. So you are in this thing, he says. Is that true? Are you plotting to destroy my man, your countryman? That is the first thing I want to know.

PROVERBS: I am "in this thing," as you say. The other question I can't answer. I simply can't say either yes or no. As soon as I open my mouth on one of those words I lose too much.

FUNKE: Lose what? This your civil service job? (She pronounces "civil service" "seeveel sahvees" and inflects the words with bitter irony.) I come to you as friend and you talk to me about seeveel sahvees? You think I come to hear about British palaver? When I was lying in your bed you did not talk about seeveel sahvees. You talked about love. And you were talking true. That time I believed you. I do not believe you now, you hear? You are lying. Why do you lie to me? When you tell me to go, I understand. But do not lie. When you lie to me you are saying that I am a whore or a servant, not a friend.

PROVERBS: Funke, that is all very well, and very sweet, but it has nothing to do with real life. I am *not* lying to you. Goddamnit to hell, I *am* a fucking civil servant and nobody forced me to be a fucking civil servant. It's all very well for you to tell me what you want from me for your man, but it wasn't so long ago that you were telling me that I have to live my life in the real world, remember? Now you're off on another track altogether, aren't you? Why? Because your current keeper is in trouble. And for that. . . .

FUNKE: "Keeper"? Are you mad? My "keeper" is Funke. You know that. Why don't you just call me a harlot, finish?

PROVERBS: Oh, Funke, don't let us get into a stupid semantic argument. Jesus Christ, of course you're a harlot. The worst kind of harlot, a harlot with a heart of gold. You're in all the cheap books. You're a harlot, you're a harlot, you're a harlot. A whore. Is that alright? A sentimental whore. (He chants, to a tune with a vague 1890s flavor.)

> A sentimental whore
> Is an inefficient whore
> And a blot on her ancient trade. . . .

(Funke attempts to throw her drink at him, but he is too quick. He catches her arm and holds it tight and works his way off the sofa.)

FUNKE: *Om'ota!*

PROVERBS: (Still holding her glass-waving arm.) The only way to deal with the natives. . . .

FUNKE: I'll kill you, Proverbs!

PROVERBS: . . . is with firmness and tact combined. Funke, please, don't you understand what I've been trying to say? I can't help myself, much less you or Payne. You don't believe me, you don't believe that I need help? (Funke relaxes her pressure on the glass and Proverbs relaxes his in turn. He sits again.)

FUNKE: I finish giving sympathy to white men. Your tribe is too powerful. (Proverbs falls sideways on the sofa and laughs raucously.)

PROVERBS: I'm only white nor' nor'east and I don't know a hawk from a handsaw.

FUNKE: What does that mean?

PROVERBS: Nothing. Nothing at all. I don't know what Payne is planning to do and I don't want to hear. But he's finished in this country. You must know that. They squashed him good. Squashed, not even smashed. Squash is the overwhelming verb that rules out any possible conception of resistance. Funke, there is just nothing anybody can do to help. Even if they wanted to help. By his very existence Payne has been on a collision course with the power boys here, and he's not equipped to deal with them. Who is? I'm sure that Wilfred Dacosta Payne can handle all kinds of other things—mass hysteria, a runaway horse, a rabid dog, the Chamber of Commerce. But not this. This is power. The real stuff. The steel in the concrete. He's finished. No escape. I'm sure *he* understands that. Why can't you? He seems to have told you everything. No secrets from his love. Admirable principle. So there you have it. In a nutshell, Michael.

FUNKE: You sound . . . drunk.

PROVERBS: I am not . . . drunk. One bottle of beer with the curry and one bottle of beer with you. Beer. It takes about eighteen bottles to really launch me. A spectacle to behold. Right now I am cold sober, but I won't deny that I'm intoxicated. A nice use of the language. I am suffering from the toxic effects of fear, uncertainty, and a touch of endemic schizophrenia, mild. . . .

FUNKE: Gordon, you are talking a lot of foolishness now. You are talking . . . like a madman. A real madman.

PROVERBS: But, girl, I *am* a real madman. Mad as shite! Haven't you noticed that every damned *ajerike* you know is a mental case? Man, we have madness at home like puppy have fleas. White and black alike. Our common bond. The only true national characteristic. I can't understand how they've missed it in all the textbooks so far.

"The West Indian, despite his richly varied ethnic and cultural background, has a highly developed national unity based upon the unique circumstance that all West Indians, without exception, are mad as shite." If you think I exaggerate, consider my Aunt Milly. A perfectly normal, middle-class Bajan white woman, reasonably well-educated, she's a teacher for that matter, reasonably contented with her spinsterhood and with running her own and my father's life. But you know when she really comes to life? At a sale! At any old sale at any old beat-up plantation house. She will change her teaching schedule to go to a sale. She used to drag me along sometimes in the vacations until I began to feel uncomfortable without even knowing why. She once paid a small fortune for a china po in which a member of the royal family may, *may*, have pissed in when he stayed in Barbados at the turn of the century. I have seen her almost come on herself when she touched it.

My father's house is full of stuff she's picked up at her eternal sales, and she can weep real tears when she talks about the disappearance of the old days and the old ways. But Aunt Millie was never a part of those old days and old ways, not Aunt Millie and not any Proverbs I ever heard of. And she knows that better than anybody else. She is the one who kept the family Bible. My father was probably the first Proverbs to go into a great house by the front door. He was the first "professional man" in the family, so they sometimes invited him for bridge or a funeral. The only land we ever owned was a couple of small housespots around Bridgetown, but to hear Aunt Millie talk you'd think she'd grown up on her grandfather's estate surrounded by faithful servitors. It isn't that she actually *lies*, but she's so wholehearted in her lusting after other people's heritage that you'd have to listen very carefully indeed to realize that the prince's piss hadn't actually dripped into the famous po right there in a guest-room right next to Aunt Millie's nursery back in the spacious, gracious old days. But Aunt Millie at least confines her madness to the narrow circle of family and friends.

Back home we even tolerate public madness. Institutionalize it. We have Land Ships. Yes, Land Ships. That's right. We have people who get together in groups and call themselves *ships*. They appoint captains and admirals and commanders and commodores and even able seamen, and make elaborate uniforms for themselves and employ British naval language and etiquette, and what do they do? *They walk from place to place*. That's all. All dressed up, shouting orders back and forth along the line. Regularly, once a month, with a general flotilla maneuver at Christmas. Hundreds of able-bodied men and women and youths. And it never occurs to anyone that they ought to be locked away in a home for the mentally incapacitated, or at least examined by a competent psychiatrist. And there's your Dacosta Payne, with his impeccable upperclass public school English accent? God, at least my dear departed mother was English. How did you ever come to get mixed-up with a bunch like this?

FUNKE: So all this talk just means that you are not going to help me, not so?

PROVERBS: Exactly what is it you want me to do, to give up my career, to throw it away for your sake? For the sake of the memory of a few dozen historic fucks? You want me to give you chapter and verse of something which I am bound by oath to keep to myself? It wouldn't do you or Payne any good even if I did. The only person who would stand to gain from my criminal revelations would be Adumuyiwa, and that doesn't help your man, does it? And what would happen to me, then? I'd have to resign, even if they didn't find me out, and that means a return to the sugar-cane garden I haven't visited lo these many years. What would I *do* in the garden? Christ,

I can't even cultivate it. Haven't the training. Law practice? The word would soon go round that young Proverbs had blotted his copybook in Afrikar, what? Gone
native, frightful shame, had a promising career in the
service, threw it up for a woman, bewitched doubtless,
basically not a *sound* fellow. Would you like to see Adu
win the election?

(Fade out.)

Chapter Twenty-nine

I had my background piece ready in ten days. It was easy. All the businessmen I interviewed "for background only" had been infected by Dacosta Payne's enthusiasm for the scheme and most of them were dying to see their names in print preceded by adjectives like "dynamic," "pioneering," "innovative." I was inundated with pictures of general managers, regional managers, counterpart training officers-designate, and potential candidates for the scheme; in the time I was actually on the story I received more invitations to buffet suppers given by the English business community than I had got in all the time I had been in Lagos. (Cocktail parties were normally considered quite good enough for journalists.)

To my surprise, I heard nothing from Payne and, after waiting a few days more, I called his office to see how things were going. He wasn't in. "Out of town for a few days," according to his secretary; she was *perfectly* sure that he would call me as soon as he was back. When another week went by without a word, I called again somewhat anxiously. A story of that kind couldn't keep indefinitely in Lagos, and like any self-respecting journalist I wanted to keep my "exclusive" exclusive. There was

257

no answer from his number, and all the exchange would
say was that the line was in order. Then I checked on his
house and got an out-of-order signal. This time the operator, indubitably Nigerian from all the evidence of intonation but internationally delphic of utterance and par-
simonious of information, told me: "I confahm that that
numbah is out of sahvice."

It is still a little embarrassing to recall that my first reaction was that of a journalist; at the smell of "a story,"
Brathwaite the sometime pupil and friend gave way to
Brathwaite the reporter and columnist. I went into the
editor, told him about Payne's "coup," and handed over
the copy I had up to then kept locked in my desk. I suggested he put Olapeju on to the story.

But I suppose that Brathwaite the friend hadn't altogether disappeared, that it was partly he who tried to
find Funke—and quickly discovered that she; too, was out
of town. I found out that she hadn't been seen for more
than a fortnight; a brother of her police superintendent,
who worked in the Inland Revenue, gave me a couple of
names of people who might know where to find her, and
volunteered that he had heard that "there was something on" with Dacosta Payne, but would volunteer no
more.

It was surprisingly easy to track Funke down; Lagos
seemed to be full of people with whom her secrets were
not safe. I was told by one of her former protégées that
she was staying in a town in the West, which I shall call
Afin, where she had relatives, but that she was living in
a house by herself. Within fifteen minutes of arriving in
Afin I found her. Her refuge was an unpainted lathe-and-
plaster house about four hundred yards in from the trunk
road that passes through Afin on its way to Ibadan. Surrounded on all sides by the poor mud-and-thatch cottages
of road workers, public works messengers, and roadside

vendors of the one-stick-of-cigarette-and-two-kola-nut variety, it was as inescapable as the first skyscraper in Lagos.

I have never learned much about Funke's background. When I arrived in Nigeria she was already in full spate, and since she seemed to be the black sheep of no particular family I assumed that she was the result of some kind of social parthenogenesis, a kind of Aphrodite from the provinces who had sprung full-grown from the foam created by what the sociologists call the drift to the urban areas. Now, here in Afin, it seemed that she had a place and a family to whom she could turn for shelter.

It was she herself who answered my knock, coming on to the little verandah at the front of the house and pushing the door shut behind her.

"*Ki lo fe?*" she said, abruptly. Yoruba custom, deeply embedded in habits of language, demands that the stranger be greeted "properly"; and the elaborate formulas of courtesy are so automatic that they come close to being instinctive even among the most sophisticated of city-dwellers. "What do you want?" would be uttered only after the "proper" remarks about the weather and at least one apology about the state of the road. Funke was clearly under great strain. She stood watching me, waiting for me to speak, her legs challengingly apart, dressed in nothing but a *lappa* that went slightly more than once around her body, covering her from armpit to kneecap and loosely tucked in near her left breast.

"I'm a friend of Dacosta Payne's. Sinclair Brathwaite. I think you've seen me before at his house. I've heard he is in some kind of trouble. I'm trying to find him," I said, dropping the phrases down one after the other in the desperate cadence of the stammerer. She had really unnerved me by her aggressiveness.

"*Ori e o baje!*" She was shouting. "Weytin do you, my

friend, your head no good? You dey come ask me for your friend? You think say if he get trouble, na *Funke* go know wey side he dey?''

My God, I thought, she's right, of course. I had sought her out on the banal principle of *cherchez la femme* like any tenth-rate detective—or journalist; but this, after all, was Funke, a specialist in skinning men but no taxidermist. If it was obvious that Dacosta Payne was in trouble, then it was obvious that Funke would be the last person to offer him a helping hand: It simply wasn't her style.

And yet . . . instinct told me that there was something; why *had* she left Lagos, for one thing? Why was she being so aggressive? Why was she pretending not to know me? And, inconsequential as it might seem, I found it odd that she should speak Yoruba and then pidgin to me when I knew that she could speak perfectly good English. It was no more than a feeling; but after driving forty-five miles to find her I wasn't going back to Lagos without some kind of satisfaction. And, anyway, she had to know *something* about what was going on.

I decided to play it sentimental.

"Look," I said, "I'm a *friend* of Dacosta Payne. We're cousins as a matter of fact; he's related to my mother." Perhaps it was the word "mother" that did the trick. Nowhere is the mother an object of such awed devotion as in a polygamous society.

"You are from Barbados, too?" she asked, but from the way her body had relaxed after my last speech I knew that I had won. I nodded.

"I know you. Come in," she said simply, and turned and walked through the door.

The sitting room into which she led me reminded me of nothing so much as one of those weekend beach houses that are rented out to the holidaying middle classes on the east coast of Barbados. In one half of a large room

there was a perfunctory suite of four mass-produced
Morris chairs and a settee, in the other half a dining
table with four upright cane-bottomed chairs, with an anti-
quated refrigerator groaning away in a corner beside
them. It was already 11:00 A.M., but the dining table still
bore the traces of breakfast in the shape of a porridge
bowl, a coffee pot, a loaf of computer-sliced bread, a dish
of melted butter, and a bottle of honey.

Funke waved me to a seat and, turning her back on
me, leaned over and unwound and rewound her *lappa*
around a body that was evidently nude. It was a gesture
that was more familial than coquettish. I was truly accepted. The maneuver over, she moved in an instinctive
housekeeperly gesture in the direction of the dining table,
and then stopped herself as if realizing that she was in
the presence of a friend who would not—or should not—be
bothered about the disarray that was so evident there.

I literally couldn't take my eyes off her. Never had I
heard even the bitchiest of Lagos women ask about
Funke the classic bitch question: "What do they see in
her?" It was only too obvious. It was the body, of course,
an extravagant thing on a scale nearer to poster art than
to real life. She was tall, as tall as I, statuesque, a sculpture of mahogany curves and smoothness. But it was the
face, which I had casually judged to be "good-looking"
the two or three times I had seen her, that now held me.
There was a flatness at the eyes that was oriental, but
the high cheekbones were those of the Benin terra cottas;
down the cheeks ran the single slash of the Ondo mark,
giving to the whole face a quality that was at once exoti-
cally savage and classic. You suspected, perhaps from
something in the eyes and from the slight pout of the
lower lip, that all her life had been one of sexual challenge, that she took as much pleasure from men as she
gave, and that she was probably too familiar with ecstasy
to be capable of love.

I had been looking at her frankly, and she seemed to have *paused* to let me complete the examination. "You finish?" she asked in a voice that was both mocking and complacent. I was quite unembarrassed. I nodded.

"Omowale is at Alapa. He is under observation," she said. There was no identifiable emotion in her voice, but she looked directly at me, waiting, I knew, to see my reaction. Alapa, about three miles from Afin, was the site of the most modern psychiatric hospital in Africa.

I had been expecting something fairly shattering. This was almost a relief. But it would have been impolitic to show this—to show anything at all—for I wasn't yet quite sure exactly where Funke stood.

"What happened?" I asked, neutrally.

"He had a breakdown. They say it isn't very serious, but they want to keep him for a few weeks. It is only in the last few days that he begins to recognize me." Up to then she had been standing over me, anxiously scrutinizing my face as if searching there for an omen. Now she suddenly moved away toward the table, stacked the crockery in a tray, and disappeared into a passageway behind us.

A moment later she reappeared and joined me on the settee. Putting one electric hand on my knee she said, "He has to go away. He must not stay in this country. He must go as soon as he is better." She must have seen the sign she wanted for her tone had softened and she spoke to me now as to a fellow member of the club, the exclusive international sodality of those who had been smitten by the Dacosta Payne magic. She started to tell me the whole story.

She didn't know all the details; she hadn't been precisely an intellectual companion. But she did know about the Payne Plan and perhaps, in the ultimate intimacy of the bedroom, he had been able to unload his whole freight of anxiety and excitement and anticipation over

it. What seemed clear was that he had managed to engage Funke more deeply than any of her previous lovers,
possibly because he was more articulate and himself
more engaged than any of them.

One evening about three weeks before, she told me, he
had come home and without even a greeting had handed
her an envelope, and had gone to his room. She saw that
it was from the firm of solicitors headed by Sir Femi, and
contained a formal letter signed by Sir Femi himself as
well as an enclosure. The letter stated that on the instructions of his clients the Nigerian Businessmen's Association, Sir Femi was transmitting to Mr. Dacosta Payne
the attached note, and was informing Mr. Payne that
copies of the note had been circulated to the Private
Secretary, Government House, the Immigration Department, and to members of the Council of the Association.
Such circulation might well be construed by the courts as
publication, in the terms of the Defamation Act, and it
might be that Mr. Payne would wish to contemplate legal
action as a consequence. Oladairo, Rawson, and Adedapo
looked forward to hearing from him.

The enclosure was a *curriculum vitae* of Dacosta
Payne, which included a reference to a six-month jail sentence at Nottingham for fraudulent conversion in 1946
and a suspended sentence for living off the immoral earn-
ings of a prostitute in Leeds in 1948. The *curriculum
vitae* noted that no trace could be found of the American
Institute of Business Management of which Dacosta
Payne claimed to be a member.

Payne didn't go to work the next day, or the next, or
the next. He didn't speak a word to anyone, not even herself, for a fortnight. Incredibly, she stayed with him, fed
him, and continued to try to communicate with him.
When he did start to speak again, she said, it was nearly
always declamatory, to an unseen audience: He spoke
sometimes in what she thought was French; sometimes

in a gibberish mixture composed of .the few Yoruba words he knew, of sounds she didn't recognize, and of Nigerian pidgin; sometimes in English. "I have come back, my people, I have come back," he would repeat over and over again when he spoke English; and among his gibberish speeches she often heard the Yoruba expression, "*Omobawale, omobawale*"—"the prince is come back." It was then she decided to have a psychiatrist see him.

Irony is too much with us. For once Dacosta Payne had been playing it more or less straight; for once this promoter *par excellence* was promoting something other than his own immediate financial interest; for once his interlocutors genuinely had nothing to fear from him; and it was this one time that he came a cropper.

He was gone within a week of my meeting with Funke at Afin. I had tried to visit him at Alapa, but the director was adamant that the only visitors allowed were those whom that patient had specifically asked to see. I suspected that it was more likely a case of the director's trying to shield Payne from representatives of the milieu in which his breakdown had taken place. "Breakdown" was the word he used to me on the phone to describe what had happened to Payne. "A simple breakdown," he said, "what you might call a collapse of the adaptive system in the face of overwhelming pressures." If it sounded rather simplistic over forty-five miles of crackling wires, I excused it as the kind of professional baby talk that specialists seem to consider appropriate when dealing with laymen. "He'll be all right as soon as he gets out of this country," he added. "There's no reason why he shouldn't be leading a useful, productive life before very long."

"Any chance of my seeing him before he goes?" I asked.

"I'm afraid not," was the reply. "We'll be seeing him

straight on to the boat. Just in case, you know. . . ." It was hard to imagine a Dacosta Payne shorn of *danshiki* and cavalry-twill trousers and supported by white-coated attendants; but this was precisely the picture that the director's terse remark had produced. I felt sad and impotent and—it must be admitted—faintly, guiltily, relieved. I had no confidence that I would have been able to deal with a diminished Dacosta Payne and could not help feeling just the slightest bit thankful that I had not been put to the test.

Chapter Thirty

Adu drove negligently and almost mechanically on this road so familiar, so often traversed that a very elementary computer could have taken over from him and reproduced his responses: fifty-five mph through the swampland leading to Ikoroja, with four descents to forty-five mph at points where the engineers had arbitrarily introduced gentle curves more to break the monotony of the journey than because of any topographical necessity; twenty mph through the town itself with its compressed confusion of minuscule markets; then a dead stop; then a right-angled left turn; first gear past the cemetery, second past the police station, third past the experimental agricultural station, top in open country again, and up to the inevitable fifty-five through the flatlands where pallid rows of cassava ridged the red earth, and then up again into the cool, Anglo-Saxon greenery of kola-nut groves. Automaton-like, Adu went through his repertoire of well-rehearsed gestures and did not see the paralyzed beggars squatting in their paper-clip poses by the side of the street in Ikoroja, their flour-bag *danshikis* burnished almost to the color of the earth by months of unlaundered wear and by the accumulation of kola-nut juice inconti-

266

nently dribbled from their slack mouths. He did not see the policeman, immaculate in his starched khaki shorts and rigidly putteed socks, with his boots casually slung over one shoulder, stubbornly ignore an altercation ten feet to his left in which a matronly Amazon, serene of face, beat a man as big as herself across the side of the head with a stout wallaba stick while she lightly waved a six-month-old child before her as a shield. Nor did he really notice, as he approached Ile-Oja, the marvels of black afara and mahogany reaching phototropically to heaven and making a cool, green cavern that ran for fifteen straight miles to the point where you made a sharp left turn to go to Alapa. (Payne, traveling the same road a fortnight before, had seen many such things because he had never seen them before and was unsure whether he might see them again.)

Once through Ile-Oja he did see the new roundabout, since it was only his third time past this prodigious piece of *oyibo* engineering which had transformed a simple crossroad in agricultural Yoruba country into a complex piece of free-form asphalt-and-cement sculpture that had taken many an unwary Ibadan-bound traveler on a three-hundred-sixty-degree circuit back to Ile-Oja. Exiting safely from this modish trap, Adu moved with caution along the Alapa road, for this, too, was unfamiliar. A few years before it had been an uneven laterite track traveled only by the hardiest of mammy-lorries in search of out-of-the-way—and thus juicier—fares, and by the Land Rovers of the pioneer rubber plantation which ACG had established in the area. Adu also saw the monotonously regular stands of mature rubber trees, uniformly erect and uniformly scarred, and realized that he felt a vague resentment at their presence—their *alien* presence!—in this landscape. These were *oyibo* trees that did not belong to the Egba earth. As the thought formulated itself he laughed out loud. He knew that the trees had been

brought from Malaya, a land of brown men, not white.
And not even his father was so antediluvian in his nationalism as to resent the importation of means to increase his country's wealth. So where had the thought
come from? How was it that somewhere, not particularly
deep in his unconscious, he felt offended by the intro-
duction and harnessing of these richly productive *tropical*
trees? Perhaps it was the word "plantation" which, particularly at a time when he was on his way to visit
Dacosta Payne, had raised a subliminal cloud of atavistic
images of white men lovingly transporting exotic plants
to virgin lands, and brutally transplanting in their wake
the millions of human beings, *black human beings*, they
thought they needed to make the plants flourish and
prosper for the greater glory of the white world. "Plantation" was chained in his mind to "black slaves."

Alapa was on a high plain, a good five hundred feet
above sea level, three or four square miles of cool grazing
land full of little indentations and thorn-tree-shaded
bowers and lakelets in which rainwater had seasonally
lodged for centuries. It had attracted the cow-Fulani as
an ideal stopping-place on their marathon journey from
the arid plateaus of the north to the cities of the coast;
over the years by beating, killing, raping, and plundering
the peaceful Yorubas they had finally established over
the area an objective dominion that came to be buttressed
by the subjective power of juju as memories of pillage
and defeat were transmuted into a self-sustaining legend
that said: Death walks on the plains of Alapa and sickness
dwells in its waters.

Here, in the first flush of postwar guilt about their colonial possessions, the British had decided to build what
Colonial Office propaganda described as the most
modern psychiatric hospital in Africa. Given more or less
carte blanche, the planners had designed a lavish compound of modernistic palaces fit to harbor six oriental

potentates and their retinues; the technicians had brought in electrocardiographs, electroencephalographs, electrotherapeutic equipment, pneumatically operated beds, confinement rooms padded in the latest synthetics, surgical equipment for prefrontal lobotomy, the *dernier cri* in x-ray techniques and laboratories, and a vast library that featured everything from holographs of Freud's earlier lectures to the diaries of Vincent van Gogh. Soon after the official opening the journalists and photographers had descended upon Alapa and both *Life* magazine and the *National Geographic* had carried special coverage of this extraordinarily thoughtful contribution of the West to the social development of Africa. Later it was discovered that one or two things were missing: The British had omitted to train Nigerian psychiatrists and psychiatric nurses, and therefore had to bring in British staff at horrendous cost to the Nigerian taxpayer, just to "get the project off the ground." Further, because of the juju, no Yoruba worker would go near the place and cleaners, attendants, gardeners, maintenance men, and launderers all had to be imported from the North or the East. Also it was somewhat difficult to recruit patients, as the families of the mentally disturbed all heard sooner or later about the juju and were unwilling gratuitously to expose their already fragile charges to yet one more doubtful psychic influence.

Adu drove through the tall iron gates and gave his name to the Ibo gateman. He was directed to the center block, which he reached after driving a good half-mile, through lawns immaculate as a golf links, on a cement road that was certainly good for another hundred years. His destination was the pivot structure of a beautifully proportioned crescent of five three-story buildings. He parked and walked through an uninhabited vestibule that was furnished—down to the posters of far-off places—like an airlines office. Except that what these posters celebrated was not idle, picture-postcard vacations, but the hard-won triumphs of medicine and administration and education in backward countries fortunate enough to have fallen into British hands. On a center door marked "Director" a handwritten sign said, "Knock and Come In." Adu obeyed. A big white man about forty, with a great springy shock of dark brown hair going handsomely gray at the temples, sat behind a shining white desk in a large room that was all white shelves and white filing cabinets and bathed in mid-morning light that streamed in through white net curtains. The man was an older version of men Adu had seen in Durham trooping onto rugby fields on Saturday afternoons—innocent, overgrown boys gleefully setting forth to savor the permitted weekly ration of brutality. He pictured this man as a generous prescriber of electric shock treatment, and felt a surprising *frisson* of concern for Dacosta Payne. But the big man greeted him with a big smile, a friendly display of perfectly maintained teeth.

"Mr. Adoo. . . ." The director halted and smiled more widely. "Forgive me. Even for a Yoruba name, yours is a fairly difficult one. Do sit down. I recognized the name, of course, when the gateman rang you through. Alapa isn't all that far away from the civilized world. I've been keeping a disinterested eye on the by-election campaign. Now, then. You've come to see Mr. Payne. A very interesting case. I always insist that visitors, especially when they come for the first time, should have a word with me before they see the patient. You'll understand why, I'm sure. For one thing, it may not be, ummh, convenient for them to receive visitors at a given moment. Mr. Payne. Ummh. He's causing us a great deal of concern. A great deal of concern. Oh, nothing for his friends to worry about. He's fine, really, no question of a psychosis, so far as I can see, no violence, nothing of that sort. But he's a great puzzle to me. Professionally. I have the feeling I'm close, as close as this!"—he made a pinching gesture with thumb and forefinger—"to a definitive diagnosis, and it then slips away again. Two weeks I've been at it now, observation, interviews, tests, a bit of empirical therapy, but at the end of it all I still have the sense that there's something which just eludes me. And it doesn't help that both my colleagues are away, one on home leave, the other ill. All I know for certain now is that your friend needs psychiatric help, that he's definitely unwell. But unless I can arrive at something of a firm diagnosis there isn't a great deal I can do in a positive way to help him, do you see that. And then, on top of all this I have our friends from the CID who want to tell me that Mr. Payne is malingering, that there's nothing wrong with him. I've had to be very firm with them. As a matter of fact, there's at least one of their people who definitely strikes me as being in need of psychiatric help himself, but I decided that it would be a little provocative to come right out and say it! Now, if you don't mind, I'd like to ask you one or two questions. I know that as a friend your answers are likely to be, shall we say, a little less than objective, but that's a kind of bias that we can make allowances for. First of all, has he had, to your knowledge, similar break-downs in the past? That's the key question."

Adu, dizzied by the onslaught of words, wanted simply to turn and drive back to Lagos. He had been at best half-hearted about the expedition to Alapa and still thought it a little ludicrous that he should be responding to a call for help from Payne. And yet, as the director spoke, a new image of Dacosta Payne had been forming in his mind; the Payne he would be seeing was not the Plasticine Man he had portrayed to Tola, but an actual man, human and, specifically, black, beleaguered by white institutions in a country where he ought to have been able to feel reasonably secure from that particular species of harassment. *"Omowale,"* incarcerated in this elegant *oyibo* mausoleum, was being batted back and forth like a shuttlecock between the egregious director and the Criminal Investigation Department. The situation had its quota of cheap irony, just right for one of those itinerant groups that travel in Yoruba-land making instantaneous operettas out of the current week's gossip.

"I'm sorry, I can't help you," he told the director. "Mr. Payne and I have only met a few times and I know very little about his health. He asked me to come to see him on business and that is why I'm here." He had a sudden, surprising anxiety that by this admission he might have failed some basic directorial test and might now be unable to see Payne. "I can still see him, I hope?" he asked. "Of course, of course," the director said, not hiding his disappointment. "He specifically asked to see you, and we always respect the patient's wishes as long as there is no medical objection." He rose and escorted Adu to the door from where he pointed to the building at the extreme western end of the crescent. "He's on the second floor. I believe his lady friend is with him right now. I'm sorry you weren't able to be of assistance, but ours is a profession where disappointment is routine. Go right ahead. I would only ask that if by any chance you've brought any stimulants, I'm thinking of spirits in particular, please refrain from offering it to him." Adu had not brought any "stimulants" but he didn't bother to answer. He was recalling a sign at one of the zoos in London: PLEASE RE-FRAIN FROM OFFERING NOURISHMENT TO THE ANIMALS.

He found Payne installed in what could only be called a suite, with bedroom, living room, and a fair-sized kitchen, plus a wide balcony facing north away from the direct onslaught of the sun. When Funke opened the door to his knock, Adu saw the patient lounging in a deck chair on the balcony with a pile of books beside him on the floor. He was wearing a flamboyantly patterned *lappa* and yellow Moroccan slippers and looked to be in perfect physical and mental trim.

"Hello, Adu," Payne said. "Welcome to the loony bin. And thanks for coming, after all. I wasn't absolutely sure that you'd want to exert yourself to quite this extent on my behalf. Sit down here." He pointed to the twin of his deck chair. "Scotch? Or is it too early for you?"

"What kind of man are you?" Adu asked, an involuntary grin on his face. "I've just been warned by the director not to give you what he calls 'stimulants,' and two minutes later you're offering me Scotch. Well, yes, I'll take one. He's not my doctor." Payne laughed.

"With water. That's all there is. For propriety's sake we'll have to drink it out of cups. Funke, don't forget to bring some saucers and teaspoons in case someone should come in. It's these little details that count, you know."

"Well, well. I do not know quite what I expected, but it certainly was not this. What are you really here for? I understood that you were more or less in confinement and more or less on the run from the police. But I find you installed like an *oba* and apparently in the best of health. What's going on exactly? Why did you ask me to come?"

"To tell you the truth, old boy, several things are going on at the same time. You like my quarters, I notice. I think this place was meant to be the Nursing Tutor's flat, but since they have few nurses and no tutors young Dr. Freud out there didn't need much persuading to let me have it. I'm not a believer in avoidable discomfort, as you have probably guessed by now. For the rest, we'll come to that by and by. Cheers."

Funke, a very subdued version of the woman Adu knew, had returned with the drinks and sat silently in an upright chair in the corner of the balcony. Glancing at her in the hope of some clue to the almost surrealistic labyrinth of Payne's troubles, Adu saw only undisguised distress, a Yoruba mother in the third week of mourning her dead child when the tears and screams have all been drained away and nothing is left but unadorned, unarticulate, life-diminishing grief. Adu looked away again very quickly.

"Yes, a number of disparate things are happening, Adu," Payne said, his drawling voice sounding to Adu's ears even more affected than ever, "but, fortunately, not all of these things need concern you. I didn't ask you here to give you a rundown on *my* troubles, let me hasten to say. Not because of any access of altruism, but simply because there is no way in which you can help me. But I thought I ought to pass on one or two little gems of information which have come my way before the curtain is brought down on the short and happy life of Dacosta Payne in Nigeria. Don't you like Hemingway?" He gestured downward to the pile of books on the floor and Adu saw that the top two were *Death in the Afternoon* and *For Whom the Bell Tolls.* The books immediately brought to his mind an image of a bald and still beautiful Ingrid Bergman whom he had adored in sleazy London cinemas at two-and sevenpenny a time. But did not care for Hemingway because he found it impossible to care for a so-called artist who systematically excluded black people from his concept of humanity. Still, he wasn't altogether surprised that Payne, whose whiteness stopped barely short of his epidermis, should speak admiringly of him.

"Don't you find it extraordinary," Payne went on, "that so many of the artists beloved by the marvelous democracies of the northern climes turn out to be nothing but fascists? It's a gorgeous paradox. Ought to make an excellent subject for a thesis, except that the examiners would surely blow a fuse. But, then, I don't suppose you give too much thought to that sort of thing. You're too busy trying to get your hands on whatever bits of power our imperial masters have graciously left lying around.

Perfectly right, too. Theorists are masturbators; the pragmatists shall inherit the earth. Forgive me, Adu, I've had nearly three weeks here in which to expend my substance on speculation of one sort or another, whereas you come very three-dimensionally out of your three-dimensional election campaign. But, all the same, haven't you wondered what kind of person Hemingway would have turned out to be if he had been black? What would have happened to that urge, that power, all caught up in the vise of his skin? No pun intended. I'm sorry. I'm getting carried away. You are probably sitting there wondering exactly which dread mental disease I'm suffering from. Right now it's nothing more serious than a spot of nervous logorrhea."

"Well, I really would like to know what's going on. I am no doctor, but it's obvious that you are no more sick than I am. What are you up to? What are you doing here?"

"Oh, taking a small respite from some of the nastier aspects of what is sometimes called real life."

"You mean there is really nothing wrong with you?"

"That's what all madmen say, isn't it? All the same, when the wind is southerly, I think I know a hawk from a handsaw. *Hamlet.* No, Adu, in all seriousness, I'm here because it seemed my best chance of putting a stop to a series of events that was beginning to, well, overwhelm me. A time came when I had to cry: Enough! and run like hell."

"If I understand you, then you're deliberately pretending to be . . . mad. . . ."

"Mentally ill. Disturbed. Watch your language."

"Mentally ill. And you've managed to fool a trained psychiatrist and the staff at a mental hospital?" Adu was pulled up short by the gentle mockery in Payne's look and realized that he had spoken with considerable vehemence. He laughed a little shamefacedly.

"Lèse majesté!" Payne laughed with him. "All you pro-
fessionals hang together, don't you? You're shocked that
a mere layman dares to pull a fast one on one of Her
Majesty's bonded, *London-trained* trick cyclists. You'd be
surprised what you can do with an up-to-date edition of
the *Britannica* and a little imagination. I bet I could even
be an insurance broker for two weeks! And you mustn't
forget, the poor old director is frightfully short of practice,
no patients to speak of apart from a few straightforward
psychotics and epileptics. You can't blame the man for
showing a fair amount of enthusiasm when he's suddenly
confronted with something a little more subtle. As far as
I can judge, my stay here has been eminently satisfactory
for both parties. Except that he keeps feeding me drugs
which have a tendency to knock me out about four in the
afternoon just when I'm getting into the meat of a good
read. But, then, there's a price for everything." Adu
burst into outright laughter now, great involuntary spasms
that pounded against his ribs like hydraulic hammers. He
had to put his glass on the floor as it threatened to leap
out of his hand. As he straightened up he saw teardrops
poised on Funke's lower lids, two bulbs trembling on the
dark flesh like raindrops on a rose petal, and he stopped
laughing abruptly, resentful at Payne the prestidigitator
who could simultaneously provoke such opposite reactions
in his hearers.

"Is it not risky to drink alcohol on top of the drugs you
have been receiving?" Adu asked now. But what did it
really matter to him?

"Oh, I've checked up on that. It appears that the main
risk is that the alcohol may make the drugs pass through
the bloodstream more quickly than they should. Dimin-
ishes their effectiveness." Payne's smile was one of un-
adulterated small-boy mischievousness. "This Scotch
may in fact be the only *bona fide* therapy being dished out
in the establishment. All the same, since I don't know

exactly what my friend may be pulling out of the pharma-copoeia, I might just turn out to be wrong. Terribly wrong. But whatthehell, whatthehell . . . Archy the Cockroach. In the circumstances it's a risk that I think I'm entitled to take. Drink up. It's almost time for refills." It is impossible, Adu thought, to be comfortable around this man. You can't even rely on his jokes.

"I've been changing, Adu," Payne went on. "Extraordinary. My friends of a few years ago wouldn't recognize me now, I'll wager. A mutation has been taking place. Bloody irreversible, it seems. Up until a couple of years ago I was so sure that the world owed me a living, as the Yanks have it. I mean a good, splashy, wide space in the universe where I could move slow, fast, stand still, pirouette, drive, surface, hibernate, gyrate, levitate, the whole bloody bag of tricks, with nothing to hold me back except the constraints of my imagination. And I must say until I came to this country the world was really doing very decently by me, all things considered." Payne's inability to suppress, even in his language, a kind of stubborn ebullience seemed, in the circumstances, obscene.

"What about Nottingham?" Adu asked sharply. "We know all about that, you know. Your *oyibo* friends in the Administration have put out a very interesting dossier about you. Just a few days ago, to a selected group. Makes good reading. I must day, Nottingham cannot be one of the chapters you enjoyed."

"Oh, they've done that, have they? I had no idea they were quite so desperate. But you mustn't get the wrong idea about Nottingham, you know. I look on that as a period of postgraduate training." Payne smiled a wide, happy smile. "A crash course in reality, Adu, with special emphasis on the nature of power in all its aspects, monetary, physical, sexual, psychological. Six months in prison is a *sine qua non* for living in these years of grace. Especially for a black man. Beefs up your sense of values no end. Believe me, Nottingham did me no harm at all. Anyway, that's all water under the bridge, as they say. All the same, it has a kind of bearing on my being in this place and also on what I asked you here for. As you clearly know, I've been having a spot of trouble with the Administration. Needless to say, all is not as it seems. The main thing, though, for you is that I was able to learn that right now you are the number-one target of the political secret service. In a roundabout way that's one of the reasons I'm here. They want your hide. Badly. Desperately, I would say. You've obviously frightened the life out of them, and it would appear that in my modest way I've caused them a headache or two in the past few months. Unfortunately for me I'm something of a sitting duck as far as they're concerned, and they picked me off with considerable ease. You're a different proposition by far, and they've been going to incredible lengths to get you. I do hope I'm making myself absolutely clear on this. The trouble is that I haven't too much to offer you by way of proof. You'll just have to take my word for it. . . ." Payne stopped speaking and turned his palms upwards in a half-ironic gesture of surrender. Adu, speechless at the turn Payne's declaration had taken, simply looked at him, waiting for him to go on. After nearly a minute of silence it was clear that, for his part, Payne was waiting to hear from Adu.

"Do you really mean to say that this is why you asked me to come here, to tell me that the people in the Administration don't like me?" Anger transformed Adu's English words into a liquid cascade of Yoruba sound. *"O ma she o!* You really take me for a fool. But I suppose I *am* a fool. Only a fool would have come in the first place. I should have known it would be a waste of time. My God!"

"Do tell me why you *did* come?" Payne said. His voice was tight and insultingly languid and cool. "Do you know, I never expected to see you. I gave you two weeks. After that I was packing up. After all, you've never made any pretense of liking me. Why *did* you respond?"

"Why I came? Oh, because of Tola, if you really want to know." Adu had not wished to say this, but the combination of anger and his discomfiture at the blunt way in which Payne had boarded him pushed the truth unwarily out of his mouth.

"Tola? But she scarcely knows me. How . . . ?"

"She knows your countryman, Brathwaite. Even before I received your message she had spoken to me. Brathwaite is very upset."

"Brathwaite, oh, yes, he thinks I'm really stark, raving bonkers. I worked out a whole scenario for his benefit. But I still don't understand."

"It is of no importance, I am here. You sent me a message and I came. Now I see that you have worked out a whole scenario for my benefit as well, but I do not think it is very successful. It is much too obscure for me." He started to rise.

"*Joko!* Sit down!" Funke, up to then a silent server of drinks, exploded into a shout. Her eyelids flashed moistly in the sunlight and Adu saw minuscule rainbows by the bridge of her nose. "You do not have to take Dacosta's word. There is a *white* man who knows." The adjective sang out at him like a whip. "When you return to Lagos go to Proverbs of the Administration Office and he will tell you. Proverbs. A white *ajerike*." Adu felt Funke's vehemence like a new presence on the balcony. As he sat down again it was as if he had been pushed back into his chair by this woman who not only had not moved but was sitting, arms folded over her stomach, in the same passive mourning pose as before. Turing to Payne he also saw that Funke's remark had taken him by surprise.

"Proverbs?" Payne was clearly at a loss. "He knows, of course. He was in the thick of it. But I scarcely see him in the role of advocate for Dacosta Payne." His voice was strengthening with each word as a muscle is strengthened by tension. "And he certainly wouldn't talk about stuff that is bound to be highly classified." That smile, which was half a frown, lips slightly downturned and eyebrows slightly raised, was back again. But Adu knew Payne had been caught unawares, and this was a new dimension. That smile was all style and bravado.

"What will Proverbs tell me?" he said, looking at Funke. "That the political service has been shadowing me ever since I started my campaign and maybe before? It is the same as if he would tell me that there is a traffic light at the corner of Gbamgbose and Broad Streets. It is not news."

"He will tell you that they forced Dacosta to spy on you and to give them weekly reports on everything you did and said for the last two months."

"Funke, what are you saying? Do you think I have not known that Payne was a spy from the very beginning?" Payne laughed out loud and in the same fraction of a second the back of Funke's hand was a flying flat bludgeon alongside Adu's cheek, the force of the blow knocking him off the flimsy aluminum chair. His glass described a bluntish arc and smashed against the wrought-iron balustrade, the remains of the drink seeming to hang in midair for a ridiculously long fraction of a second before it cascaded onto his supine chest. Payne was up quickly to hold Funke round the waist with one arm while he clapped the other hand to her mouth. The words he was stifling were only too legible in her eyes.

"No, sweetie, none of that," Payne said very softly, "none of that." Immediately he released her and she went quickly inside. Adu was now upright again, wiping away at his shirt. He stepped gingerly through the small field of broken glass that winked wetly in the sunlight and with one foot on the metal threshold said to Payne, "I must go."

"Yes, I suppose so. Thank you for coming anyway. The scenario seems to have got distinctly out of hand. I'm sorry if you feel you've wasted your time. That wasn't my intention. I'll see you out."

"Oh, you don't have to 'see me out,' Payne," Adu said with some annoyance. "Why do you always have to play the part of an English nobleman? As long as I live I shall never understand you. Will you tell me something before I leave? Why did you laugh when I said that I had known all along that you were a spy? Why is that so amusing?"

"So 'live and laugh, nor be dismayed. As one by one the phantoms go!' Edward Arlington Robinson. And I think it was Charles Lamb who said 'Anything awful makes me laugh. I once misbehaved at a funeral.' Is that enough of an explanation?"

"It is no explanation at all. I just wanted you to know that I was not deceived."

"You had my number."

Adu ignored the sarcasm. "Don't forget that I know a little about you West Indians. You are not to blame for your history, but it is your history."

"We just love the smell of the white man's ass."

"That is not my language."

"But it expresses your feelings. It isn't quite my language either. But some years ago in London a young Trinidadian used the phrase and I find it both picturesque and accurate. Up to a point. Tell me, aren't you even the slightest bit curious about what Proverbs might have to say to you? Or is he untrustworthy because he's a West Indian like me? Or, who knows, perhaps there's an algebra that makes a white West Indian the equal of a black African, history and all that?" Payne stopped speaking as they both saw Funke emerging from the bedroom. She was walking toward them quite slowly, her head slightly bowed and her thighs held close together like royalty, as if she were waiting for them to break apart to let her through. But neither of them moved, and she came to a deliberate stop before them. "The party's over, darling," Payne said, reaching out a hand to her shoulder. "Mr. Adumuyiwa has to return to Lagos on urgent private business." Her expression was impregnably sober and Payne, seeing it so, did not continue.

"I am very sorry for what I did just now," she said to Adu. She was now no more than two feet away from him, and she was looking so directly and intensely at him that he felt a small, involuntary muscular spasm of something like physical fear, and an urge which he recognized as irrational to glance quickly down at her right hand to see if she was carrying a knife or some other lethal weapon. "Dacosta is not a spy," she went on. "He is a fool. But please go to see Proverbs when you get back to Lagos. It is very important for you. Not for Dacosta." She switched her gaze briefly to Payne, and Adu saw in her face a kind of maternal anger. "It is very important for you. Not for him. He should have left Nigeria a month ago, but for some things his head is not good."

"I still don't understand why Proverbs would talk," Payne said. For the first time he was betraying irritation. "I just don't see a conscientious civil servant stepping that far out of line. Not even a white colonial buckra johnny."

"He will speak," Funke insisted.

"How do you know, sweetie? You haven't been near the man for months."

"I have seen him," Funke said. She turned abruptly and went once more into the bedroom.

"So what will Proverbs tell me, that you were coerced into spying?" Adu asked, but there was little conviction in his voice.

"God only knows," Payne said shortly.

"I wish I had some idea of what you are really after, Payne."

"What I'm after? Oh, Christ! Would you like, in thirty pithy words or less, a summary of the Dacosta Payne philosophy? Try this. I consider that it is the moral duty of the slave to kick his master in the ass as frequently and as firmly as he can manage. To do him in, if at all possible. I try to live my life on that rigidly moral plane."

"Everything is a joke to you."

"Believe me, that was no joke, Adu."

"Give me one straight answer, please. What is it that I have to fear from the British? According to you. Tell me that. All you have done so far is to drop vague hints. Now, please give me something more specific."

"How specific do you want me to be? The British want you stopped. They don't want you, above all things, to win the by-election. And they mean business. I would go so far as to say that they're desperate. Otherwise, why should they bother to rope me in to do what any half-wit lance corporal could do just as well? And now that I've managed to slip out of their grasp they've taken the trouble to circulate a poison-pen dossier about me. Doesn't that strike you as the action of desperate people? I can't give you chapter and verse, but I know that a suspicious amount of money has recently gone into the Government party's bank account. That's the sort of thing that Proverbs would know about. If he's really prepared to spill the beans, you're in for a tolerably interesting session with him, I promise you. Is that specific enough?"

"Yes, yes. If Proverbs confirms what you say, then they've more or less handed me the election on a silver platter."

"I hope so."

"Thank you, Payne." Adu hesitated, head lowered, searching for the right words. The situation was so *conditional;* he was almost ready to believe Payne and if he believed then he was deeply in the debt of this unfathomable clown, dandy, butterfly-man. And if he didn't be-lieve him, then he had no business thanking him. Raising his head he saw Payne, half-smiling, wink slowly at him.

Chapter Thirty-one

Dear Professor Selman:

I was delighted to receive your card, even though it caused an access of guilt—happily, not of clinical proportions!—at my own silence since my posting here.

The work here is pretty much run-of-the-mill, in that the bulk of people who are sent to Alapa correspond, to most intents and purposes, to the classic categories of mental illness. However, I recently stumbled on a case which had a rather interesting clinical configuration; although it was some months ago, I am still turning over in my mind the possibility of writing it up for the *Journal of Psychiatric Medicine*. The difficulty about this is that I was the only qualified observer; hospitalization was comparatively brief in duration; and gravest weakness of all, even if I am right about my hypotheses, and I am convinced that I am, I have so far not had the good fortune to come upon even one other subject with a comparable condition. All the same, I am sure that you will be interested to hear about it in outline; you may have some thoughts after reading this which you may wish to pass on to me. I am sure that this would be valuable for the future.

The subject is a man of thirty-five, West Indian of African origin. Highly articulate, a specialist in business management, who lived in Nigeria for just under a year as the head of a small consulting firm. As the result of what appears to be a major business setback he underwent a breakdown and was sent to me at Alapa. By all the accepted definitions his behavior must be described as psychotic. A simple description, based on my own observations as well as on the evidence of his common-law wife, would be of a series of symptoms beginning with: (a) total withdrawal; for a fortnight he did not open his mouth to communicate with even his "wife." (b) delusionary behavior: He constantly described himself as a "prince come back to Africa," and spoke to me of royal blood that had been sold in "the first social revolution to hit Africa, the slave trade." (As I said, a very articulate man!) (c) hallucinations; he made recurrent claims during the first week of his stay in Alapa of being "monitored." In one tape-recorded conversation with me he said:

> I have been under surveillance since 1946. In the early days when electronic technology was in its infancy and reserved for military purposes, the surveillance was physical. I was incessantly "TAILED" wherever I was, by a series of rather comical men, none of them over five-feet, eight-inches tall. They were all, curiously enough, blond. There was some respite when I was in Nottingham, in the sense that they put a blonde woman to shadow me. We eventually became good friends and through her I got to know of the nature of the conspiracy and of the techniques which were being used against me. With the increasing use of electronics, the surveillance changed in character. Since about 1950, I would say, a close watch has been kept on my thoughts and I can only assume that two-way equipment is being employed, since they have become fiendishly accurate in *predicting* my plans and my thoughts. When I say "two-way" I mean equipment that is not only able to

report on me but that is capable of interfering with my own thought processes. It is quite clear to me, for example, that my whole Nigerian experience was inspired *from outside,* since so much of it goes completely against the grain of my own life-style. . . .

The patient had no previous history of mental illness, although he jokingly spoke of the "endemic neurosis of blackness." There is no evidence of hereditary predisposition to mental illness. In "normal" circumstances of stress he has never felt the need to have excessive recourse to alcohol (a line of inquiry which was suggested to me by a recent paper on alcoholism and stress by Coleman in *Am. J. Psychiat.* 112).

So far, you must be saying to yourself, all I have done is describe the conditions for a classic case of mild psychosis; and, indeed, this was my first reaction when the case was brought to my attention. However, there were two aspects of the patient's condition which persuaded me to look a little deeper: The first was the quite extraordinary degree of lucidity which he manifested. In the first week, for example, the rate of occurrence of lucid behavior to hallucinatory or delusionary behavior was in the ratio of 10:1; by the second week it had risen to the astounding figure of 27:1. By the fourth day of the third week constant observation could turn up no evidence whatsoever of maladaptive behavior.

To what extent this was the product of therapy or of an extraordinarily resilient adaptive mechanism, I would not venture to guess. The therapy employed was the following: (a) traditional psycho-therapy, including unsuccessful attempts at hypnosis (the subject being highly resistant: the very idea of hypnotherapy had the effect of shocking him out of the maladaptive syndrome); (b) experimental pharmacotherapy, i.e., 150-400 mg. of Thorazine daily for seven days, beginning four days after admission, followed by an observation period of four days, followed by *ad hoc* administration of benactyzine hydrochloride (dosage on lines suggested at p. 140, *Danish Med. Bull.* 2 1955).

The second reason for my hesitation in accepting the case as "typical" came out during our psychotherapeutic sessions. Bearing in mind Johnson's famous definition of a delusion as being "essentially a disguised expression of an overwhelming trauma *actually experienced by the patient*" (my emphasis) and his comment that the content of the delusion usually reflects a "real assault" on the patient's psyche, I attempted to elicit from him memories of "actual assaults." He was, generally speaking, totally unhelpful, until one day, toward the end of the second week, he volunteered that "he had been criminally assaulted by Nigeria, materially, psychologically, and most of all culturally." Resisting the strong temptation to dismiss the remark as one more flippancy, I pursued this line. He said, *inter alia* (excerpt from the tape recording):

> We West Indians are cultural virgins in a world of practiced rapists. They pile on top of us, not even having the decency that gang rapists usually observe, of waiting until the previous rapist has had his orgasm. We face the world, my dear doctor, covered in the stinking sperm of yesterday's faceless attackers. . . .

At first it was exceedingly difficult to establish a continuity between this trauma and the current psychotic disturbance. The connection came by accident: Later that same day I was browsing through some official papers and came on a still confidential report by a Nigerian psychiatrist who has been investigating behavior problems among Nigerian students in Great Britain. Out of this report two words leaped to my attention: "cultural shock." I know as well as anyone that this is uncharted ground; the conclusions of the report I refer to are exceedingly tentative, and the use there of the expression is made almost apologetically. But it is not by diffidence that new categories of illness are discovered, and I fancy that it is not my business to dismiss my own intuitions, particularly when they are paralleled by the work of other researchers. Proper diagnosis, as you never tired of telling us, is the key and the only key to proper therapy.

What do I posit? I can hear you asking the old question. Well, after all the brave words in the previous paragraph, I must confess that I am still fearfully tentative. But if enough evidence is forthcoming in the next few years, I hope to be able to posit the existence of a *definable psychoneurosis*, consistent in configuration (the syndrome would combine depressive, delusionary, and hallucinatory phenomena), socioculturally determined, of course, with a narrow class-culture span. The symptoms would be acute in most cases, but almost invariably symptomatic behavior would be of comparatively short duration.

What I am saying amounts to this: There is a mild psychoneurotic condition which we can call for want of a better expression "cultural shock"; it can occur even within what might appear superficially to be a cultural continuum (after all, the Dahomeans refer to Nigerians as "les Anglais"!). The condition to which I refer, although paralleled in some ways by other manifestations of psychic maladjustment, is essentially *sui generis;* the objection of "inadequate observation" cannot apply here, since *I categorically posit a sharp disturbance/recovery curve!* Why should not recovery be quite as abrupt as the onset of illness itself? Neither logic nor experience militates against such a possibility.

As to therapy, once again I admit total blankness; have you followed the great chlorpromazine/reserpine debate in the United States? Kinross-Wright has been very caustic in a recent issue of *Dis. Nerv. Sys.,* and I guard a cautious and skeptical detachment about the whole matter, reinforced, needless to say, by the difficulty we have here in getting hold of the most fashionable pills! My impression (and I admit to a total lack of scientific justification for it) is that the condition may yield to a combination of psychotherapy and pharmacotherapy; instinct is stubbornly against any resort to insulin shock or any other forms of purely physical therapy. It would, however, be highly disingenuous of me to pretend that I have any systematic evidence on the therapeutic side. All my excitement is reserved for what I feel in my bones is a small diagnostic breakthrough. Do let me have your most critical reactions to this admittedly sketchy and scientifically unrigorous description of what I am secretly and with considerable hubris, I admit, beginning to call the Dacosta Payne syndrome. . . .

Chapter Thirty-two

Payne left Lagos on the Monday of the last week of the by-election campaign. It is a week I shall never forget. To my surprise, the fact as much as the circumstances of his departure profoundly depressed me. I found it practically impossible to resist the feeling that an important part of my own life was coming to an end. It was totally irrational: At bottom, I felt no more than sorry for Payne, sorry that his laboriously crafted shell had so ignominiously cracked, sorry that his last, uncharacteristically honorable enterprise had been the one to attract the most capriciously destructive thunderbolt of all. But Payne had long ago ceased to move me in any way, and at the time of his downfall even Olapeju could scarcely have accused us of being friends.

Yet, in the middle of that morning the worthy editorial I was writing (on the need for Government to consider reducing the extraordinary number of public holidays in Nigeria) suddenly struck me as almost obscenely pointless, and I left it dangling in mid-paragraph and walked out on to the third-floor balcony to look down on the rain-slick galvanized roofs around and the sodden laterite alley that led to Ayo's Bar and Refreshment Center. I had no diagnosis for my state of mind—symptoms: (1) simple moroseness; (2) burning pains of disgust at the existence of a direct line of causation between my pontifications on rampant holidays and my monthly emoluments; (3) general unease externalized by my chain-smoking of rope-like Tandems; (4) recurring split-second visions of coral sand beaches populated by black, brown, and beige girls named Patricia and Marilyn and Bette who spoke giggling Caribbean English and nothing else. Nostalgia? Not pure nostalgia, at any rate, and anyway, why?

I loitered on the balcony, smoking, chewing kola-nut, and spitting into the rain until suddenly it was twelve o'clock and I was fifteen minutes away from the daily editorial meeting. I finished off the editorial at a good mindless clip and was sitting in my chair in the conference room at 12:15 on the dot to suffer the predictable jokes—the only holidays we had at the *Sun* were Good Friday and Christmas Day—and was in my car on the way to 10 Alade Street by 12:45. Miraculously, Monday, who made no effort to hide his resentment at this breach of custom, was actually at work ironing. My radio was giving forth at full blast the famous last record cut by Njemanze before he was chopped to pieces by some or all of the eleven men who were hanged for his murder, an appropriately plaintive Ibo lament for something or other. After he had pointed out heatedly that today was his ironing day, Monday agreed to try to find me something to eat.

I ate the leaden omelet he made me, lying in bed and working away at suppressing my malaise just as you work away at keeping your eyes in focus when that brandy-too-many has begun to assert itself. That evening, as on many evenings in the past three weeks, I would not be seeing Tola. But I would be seeing trusty old Auguste. The campaign, a presence as positive and plaguing as the weather, had somehow brought us back together just as it was prising Tola and me apart. In classic grass-widower tradition I had started frequenting the club in the evenings. There Auguste tutored me, despairingly and in short order desultorily, at billiards. But tonight he had arranged a match, a handicap foursome, to test my shaky game in competitive conditions, perhaps to give me a little confidence or, just possibly, to encourage me to abandon the game definitively. Having often wondered why Auguste continued to desire my company, frequently to the point of soliciting it, after I had more or less taken a woman from him and certainly never shown to him one-half the consideration he unfailingly showed to me, I had come to the conclusion that he was probably a desperately homesick man who did not wish to go home, that the "small-time" planter who was supposed to be his father was either a figment of his imagination or else a piece of biologically accurate history who had no social existence for his son. This was the merest speculation: But I thought myself reasonably well-equipped to speculate about fellow West Indians.

Auguste knew perfectly well that Tola was now deep in Adu's campaign and, although he never mentioned the fact, I suspected him of making a deliberate effort to distract me. So that these days I was often as eager for his company as he seemed to be for mine. As I lounged on my bed, half-pleased at my truant status, half-annoyed at my inability to understand why I should be suffering this access of fashionable *Weltschmerz,* I found myself thinking that the evening would bring a change and looking forward to my session with Auguste.

The match was swift and, for our opponents, devastating. I had breaks of seventeen and nineteen, my two highest public scores ever; and Auguste shot: four, zero, forty-three, thirty-seven, and then an olympian sixty-one that totally silenced the dozen or so buzzing spectators and drew drinkers from the bar to gasp and applaud.

With my forty handicap we had won halfway through his last break, but everyone wanted to see him complete his inspired run. The enemy had barely passed the hundred mark when we reached our two hundred. We were served what seemed gallons of congratulatory alcohol and floated from the club to the Imperial on a wave of euphoria and triumph.

Since the beginning of the campaign, Auguste and I had visited the Imperial a good half-dozen times. He never took Abike there, but twice we had been joined by Virginia, she of the *Dispatch* and the Fiat 1500. She had sat with us, had a laconic couple of drinks, and then taken Auguste back to her flat, everything about her saying that she had nothing else on that night and she might as well.. She looked me over the first night and gave me a sign which she was polite enough to hide from Auguste that said, "Actually, I wouldn't mind a tumble with you, unless you're playing the old loyalty game." I was, and I told Auguste about it the next time I saw him. "I know," he said without emotion, "she told me on the way home."

An Abike was a thousand times to be preferred, he argued, to a Virginia. "Even to live with, when you get down to it, man. Conversation. That's all the edge Virginia got on Abike. Plenty conversation. For two fucks she'll give you the entire history of the Yoruba race. Very literate. But you have to hand it to the pro; when she tired and you come home itching for a piece, you getting value, let me tell you!" Mostly he talked of Abike the way a man would talk of a wife who is a slight—very slight—social embarrassment, but still a wife. At other times, particularly when we were at the Imperial, she became in his conversation little more than an indentured laborer, but one who was giving total satisfaction to the holder of the contract. When I was tempted to be cutting about this example of his insensitivity I held myself back (my current experience with Tola was giving me a diploma course in several kinds of restraint); after all, I might have had my own Abike had things been only slightly different, and what would my lines have sounded like? He and Abike had struck a very special bargain, and I was less and less inclined to laugh at it or make judgments about it, as it became more and more obvious to me that there was no factory specification for what was produced by the joining of men and women. When you "got value," you got something you valued: Who the hell was I to assume that Auguste had a less admirable set of values than I?

"And, let's face it, I know exactly where Abike is right now," he said on one of those evenings. "How many men you know can say that about their wives, not to speak of their girlfriends? Boy, as sure as I'm sitting here drinking brandy and soda, right now that girl ironing my shirts or putting lime and salt on some meat for tomorrow lunch."

He was on the defensive most of the time that we talked—that *he* talked; I do not recall ever bringing up the subject—of Abike. His statements were all questions, in a way. There seemed, however, to be one recurring question: Do you, Sinclair Brathwaite of Barbados, journalist, graduate of Cambridge, *copain de mon pays*, do you find it all that ridiculous that Leon Auguste of Vieux Fort, St. Lucia, son of a respected, small-time planter, barrister-at-law of the Inner Temple, should have living in his house one of the best-known prostitutes from one of the best-known bars in the city? The true answer was, of course, that I didn't care a thimbleful worth of dogshit; and there were moments, as I practically squirmed under the weight of my uneasiness about Tola in those late, selfish hours when the glass in your hand is a time-machine mirror in which you see only tomorrow's hang-over, when I could cheerfully have given him the true answer. But I was also learning that truth was sometimes worse than relative. It was sometimes downright, bloody irrelevant.

"So, hey, I hear your man Payne gone," Auguste said as we were having our first beer at the Imperial after the billiard match. He was always abreast of the latest in *movay-lang*. "What happen, he outsmart himself at last?" When I had related to her the last stages of the demolition of Dacosta Payne, even Tola had shown more sympathy than this, indeed more than I had expected; and I found Auguste's mocking comment unfeeling, particularly coming from a fellow West Indian. But euphoria triumphed. I had no brief for Payne, and it seemed naive to expect Auguste to share my own faint sense of loss which had its roots exclusively in my own experience.

"Why are you so hard on the man? As far as I know he never harmed you. Anyway, he's gone. And I suppose you're right when you say he outsmarted himself. But he wasn't a bad man, you know. When I was a student he was very kind to me. *Requiescat in pace*."

"Alright, alright," he said, holding up his hands in a mime of surrender, "me ain't getting in Bajan business. But I wouldn't mind if he'd willed Funke to me. Now that would be a legacy, eh boy? I'd be calling for probate tonight!"

After a few more drinks, Auguste was ready to "capture" one of the Imperial girls and put a proper lid on the evening. He declared himself "basodee" when I demurred, and I think he was a little horrified when I finally convinced him that I was being, without the slightest sense of strain, faithful to Tola, that neither the new girls at the Imperial nor the remembered delights of the old could persuade me to go back to 10 Alade Street accompanied.

"Why? What are you trying to prove, boy? Don't you know you're going to die by yourself? I never hear such stupidness," he ended, scolding me in the accents of a

Creole father. I couldn't explain beyond saying that I didn't want, these days anyway, to wake up beside any other woman. I knew exactly what I meant; it was a matter of textures—the texture of Tola's voice, harsh in its unique way; of her body; of her gestures. Not to have this at the moment of waking in the foreday morning was a just bearable discomfort; to be confronted with different ones would be a disappointing and almost literally disorienting experience in every particular. I would feel as if I were in the wrong place with no way of escaping, in a wrong and hostile place; out of this dislocation and the irrational terror of those first vulnerable, paraconscious moments, I was afraid that I might even harm some poor girl. Auguste would probably not have believed me.

"What about a short-time, then? We'll take two of them to your flat, and I'll drive them back?" When I still refused—it seemed to be an undertaking that would require an output of effort wildly disproportionate to its benefits—he slammed his hand down on the metal table and said, "Well, Mother of God! What get into you, boy?" A glass, my glass, fell to the floor, clinking once against the table edge as it turned over before it crashed; the noise brought an anxious Festus to our table, his face bunched up with concern, ready to share our troubles. For a moment I was scared that my "problem" was about to be thrown open for general debate in traditional Imperial fashion. But Auguste was laughing; he simply ordered another drink, and went back to discussing the campaign.

I saw him next in the hospital, two days later; a slight fracture of an arm and two surface cuts in the head that had not required stitches had nevertheless earned him a vast yardage of bandages, so that his smile on seeing me, no different from the smile he would have worn at the Club or the Imperial, made him appear like a caricature of those unfailingly brave and unfailingly cheerful war-wounded heroes I had thought existed only in Robert Taylor films. I tried my best not to laugh, but it was difficult since I knew from the Ward Sister how unserious his injuries were and what had caused them. Abike had left him, taking with her two lorry-loads of "effects," most of which were Auguste's—all the food in the fridge, his record-player and most of his juju records, sheets, towels, pillow cases, and a hand-tinted picture of himself in his LL.B. cap and gown. He had had the misfortune to arrive in the house when the second consignment was being packed, and the movers, three huskies from the thieves' kitchen in Isaleko, had given him a mild beating to keep him from inhibiting their work. You couldn't help feeling sorry for him; but it was hard to suppress the little ground swell of laughter that lay beneath the surface of distress.

He perceived my struggle and absolved me by laughing himself.

"Boy, you're right. It's dam' funny when you get down to it. Dam' funny," he said when I sat by his bed. "The nurses are giving me hell." He laughed again, the loose swaddling on his head bobbling and slipping with the throb of his muscles. It looked, suddenly, quite unhilarious. I knew that he took no joy in his predicament; he was simply trying to throw up this light screen of mirth as a protection against the world's mirth, as a man armed only with blank shot may fire first at bandits armed with real bullets.

"Don't laugh, man," I said urgently. But then I didn't know how to go on; it wasn't in my place to instruct him on how to keep his dignity, so I ended, weakly and insincerely, "You shouldn't be exciting yourself like that."

"Nonsense! I'm coming out tomorrow. Don't mind all that," he went on, pointing to the bandages. "They get on in here as if the Crimean War was still on. They ain't heard about elastoplast yet." He laughed at the joke he had certainly made to every nurse or doctor who had come near him. I said no more, and he began to talk about the incident. He spoke quite quietly now, as if my silent appeal to his dignity had by some kind of osmotic process got through to him. He told me that he had actually recognized one of the men, a familiar character from the magistrate's courts.

"Have you told the police?" I asked.

"For what? You must be joking. You know anything about those petty courts, all the bullshit you have to go through? You think I want to face all that?" And the laughter? I asked myself silently. But I was doing Auguste an injustice. "Boy, one of these days that fellow is going to come up to me in the street and say, 'Oga, I beg you, oh, make you no vex with me.' I know that kind of man. Next thing you know he'll be round by my house six o'clock in the morning with a big jar of fresh palm wine, begging me to take it. Man, that's better than sending the poor bastard to jail for two years. I know what I'm talking about." I believed him.

"What about Abike?" I asked. "The police will be after her."

"They won't catch her, boy. She gone north!" He gave me a gleeful slap on the leg, his pale, yellow, turbaned face opened wide by a smile that would have been more appropriate on the man who had actually organized Abike's escape. "They can't catch her. Anyway, I ain't bringing charges. Let me tell you something." He leaned over closer, although we were alone in his air-conditioned private room. "You see your man Payne? He had the right idea. This ain't no dam' country for West Indians. I'm getting the hell out as soon as I catch myself. O-U-T, out. You hear?" I cannot say why I knew he was lying.

Chapter Thirty-three

The night before Polling Day, at about eleven o'clock, the rains stopped. The office was in the crowded, noisy, half-festive state that always accompanied a big "pull"— the cancellation of a national edition that has already come off the presses. There were more subeditors and reporters and photographers around that humid evening than one saw in normal times: The enormous breach of settled daily production routine a pull brought on seemed to act as a magnet for any member of staff who was not actually on a sickbed; it even brought out part-timers and special feature writers and others who had the most tenuous of connections with the paper, possibly because it gave them a dramatically heightened sense of participation in important "events" which, translated into nine-point linotype Times Roman next morning, became merely "news."

Only half-a-dozen of the editorial staff had actually been called in for the "election pull"; I was among them because the Adviser had been toying with the idea of an editorial pull as well. The newsbreak was the issuance at 10:00 P.M. of separate but identical communiqués by NANI and the Freedom Party stating that they were with-

300

drawing their candidates from the by-election and that they—identically and separately—endorsed the candidature of Mr. Adumuyiwa Adumuyiwa who would therefore be returned unopposed.

There was no editorial pull. Changing a front page is easy enough on a rotary press, but inside pages were a different proposition. And, more crucial, London had long ago made it clear that it didn't care for too frequent editorial surprises; the Adviser probably didn't quite feel up to telephoning the African Region Director at his home, a dormitory suburb in Sussex, to get a go-ahead.

But I didn't leave. Tola had, in any event, gone out with Adu on the vitally important last-minute tightening-up tour of the wards. By now they would doubtless be celebrating in the kerosene-lit house of a ward leader in some obscure part of Lagos. But even if they were in fact within walking distance of the *Sun*, they would still be locked in an esoteric world into which I had no entrée. And here at the *Sun* there was already in train the orgiastic professional process of analysis and speculation and argument which would carry on through the night until the casts for the front and back pages were tapped into place on the rotary machines, probably to adjourn to the Imperial for a late reprise.

For analysis there was, first, the communiqué itself, Exhibit Number One:

"The Executive of the National Alliance for Nigerian Independence meeting this evening in special session has decided to withdraw its candidate from the by-election for the vacancy created in Lagos South by the death of Alhaji Babatunde Ribeiro, M.H.R. The Executive informs all members of the National Alliance for Nigerian Independence that the Party warmly and freely endorses the candidacy of the Independent Nationalist, Mr. Adumuyiwa Adumuyiwa, and invites them to vote in his favor should polling take place tomorrow as originally envisaged in the Writ issued by the Chief Federal Electoral Officer. The Chief Federal Electoral Officer has been informed of the decision of the Executive of the National Alliance for Nigerian Independence."

That was all. The communiqué had been sent to press and radio, and neither party was available for clarification. But there was clarification to be had, for the simultaneous action of the parties legally put an end to the election and involved the Government, so that the Government Information Services had to issue their own release and be available for comment. Their release, handed to the press about 10:30 P.M., merely repeated the information in the NANI and FP releases, adding that the Governor-in Executive Council had officially rescinded the election writ. Mr. Adumuyiwa Adumuyiwa would therefore be returned unopposed in the Lagos South constituency.

But that was reckoning without Olapeju. He had got a hint of what was in the air from one of his NANI friends about seven in the evening, and had started telephoning right away. British officialdom, some of whom had been dragged out of leisurely dinner parties in Ikoyi for the meeting of the Executive Council, were unanimously short-tempered, bitchy, and vituperative.

"By the time they were ready with the handout I had already talked to Shofoluade from the Legal Department," Olapeju said. (A year ago the gentleman, a senior parliamentary counsel, would have been *Mr.* Shofoluade; but Olapeju was progressing.) "The legal position is straightforward. By the terms of the Representation of the People Act 1951 when the Chief Federal Electoral Officer receives from the Governor-in-Executive Council notification in writing that there is only one candidate for a vacancy, he is empowered to declare the candidate returned unopposed." Olapeju liked to use precise-sounding technical language. It made me think, unkindly, of the eighteenth-century dandies whose spotless ruffles and French perfumes sat rankly on unwashed skins and reeking underwear. I was not in a charitable mood.

"But that briefing! You would have thought that the black people had stolen something from the *oyibo!* The Chief Information Officer was almost rude to us. He kept talking about 'you people' at every turn, and I did not really know if he meant the press or all the black people in the world or just the backward black people in Lagos. 'You people should be able to understand the game NANI and FP are playing better than we,' he said when we asked him what provoked the withdrawals. 'Perhaps you people don't really want to work the two-party system.' *O ma she o!* I am sure that he was in bed with his dog-faced wife when they called him out to the ExCo meeting!" This sally was greeted with loud, raucous laughter from the dozen or so of us who sat on chairs and desks and upturned wastepaper baskets in the newsroom while two subeditors tried to devise seventy-two-point Bodoni headlines and eighteen-point subheads and to rewrite the original lead and change the back page, all the while keeping more than half-an-ear on the passionate goings-on around them. For Olapeju's exposition was merely the English-language centerpiece of a boisterous, multilingual chorus of amazement and delight and disappointment—not all the *Sun* staff loved Adumuyiwa unreservedly.

"And the candidate," a voice broke in, "has anybody found him?"

"No chance," said the man of the moment. "His PRO left a message at GIS saying that he would make a statement at ten o'clock tomorrow." His PRO had not yet any message for me. "Ten o'clock. Ministerial time. He has not even taken the oath of office and he is acting like a minister already!" Olapeju was absolutely in his element. He had heard it first and, sweet as the kudos of tomorrow's byline would be, tonight's basking in the warm light of his colleagues' attention and curiosity was perhaps even sweeter.

"But, believe me," he went on, "before the harmattan comes, that man will be a minister."

"Yay!"

"*Ori e!*"

Shouts of unbelief, queries about Olapeju's sanity, more laughter.

"An independent? By October not even Chukuemeka," our Ibo chief sub, "will be able to spell his name."

"The only Yoruba names Chuks can spell are those of the women he has to pay for their services at the end of the month. Na true, Chuks?" Chuks pretended to be engrossed in his style book.

"Let me tell you," Olapeju said, waving his half-full beer glass in the air but spilling not a drop, "this Adumuyiwa is not a lightweight. As my name is Abiodun Olapeju, he will be flying a ministerial flag on his car before Olapeju and Jesus Christ celebrate their birthdays. Do you think this is a West Indian carnival? Why have *both* parties withdrawn? Why have they issued an identical communiqué? Don't you know that this is the first time the two parties have agreed about anything since the last increase of salaries for members of Parliament? They do not love Adumuyiwa, you can be sure. So there must be another motive. It is not money; you have never heard of anybody rich enough to bribe *both* parties. It is not love, it is not money. What is it? I will tell you. It is fear. Fear. They must have come to the conclusion that Adumuyiwa was going to wipe out their parties at the polls tomorrow. Wipe them out. We all thought he was going to win, but NANI and FP must have been afraid that he was going to win by a landslide. And that would ruin them throughout Lagos. And Lagos is where the money is, *abi?* If you can smash FP and NANI in Lagos South, you can do it in every other constituency. The others are too easy. So there was nothing left for them but to shelter from the storm. They chose the best way out. When you withdraw you are not defeated. But think of the power that gives Adumuyiwa. Within two weeks the Government will come to him offering a small ministry, Interregional Affairs or Agriculture. He will laugh at them. Two weeks later they will offer him something a little bigger. Aviation. He will laugh more. Then perhaps Health. He will not stop laughing until they reach Commerce and Industry or Finance. Then he will accept. I give them until Christmas. It may be before. Anybody who does not believe me can give ten pounds to Chuks to hold until Christmas. I will do the same." Olapeju pulled out some notes from his wallet and made to walk over to Chukuemeka. But nobody moved with him, and the buzzing of rival conversations had stopped.

"What about our *ajerike* friend? What does your money say, Sinclair?"

"Don't look at me. I said almost the same thing a month ago."

"*Koburu!* I am glad that you have become an expert in Nigerian politics. But, of course, you have good connections. For all I know, you may be one of Adu's backroom boys. We have to pay more attention to the Member from Barbados from now on, gentlemen. If the Honorable Brathwaite says it is so, it is so. *O ti ton.*"

"Hey, listen," somebody said. "*O ti ton,* indeed. The rains have finished." We all realized that we hadn't heard that finger-drumming sound for more than an hour. We trooped out onto the balcony and saw a nearly full moon riding brightly and arrogantly in skies that had been washed miraculously clean of all but a few straggling sirrus clouds looking like the tails of lost kites.

"Our big-voiced friend could not want a better omen than that," Olapeju said, his own voice dropping several tones down from the schoolmasterish bark he had been using all evening. Nobody thought to laugh at his sudden solemnity.

Chapter Thirty-four

Adu was shot on the Marina the next morning as he was on his way to meet the press at the office of the Chief Information Officer. The bullet, a thirty-two caliber Smith and Wesson, coming through the windscreen at a high angle, hit his right breastbone and lodged in the flesh. "Off the top of his head" the police ballistics expert guessed that the shot had been fired from a perch in an almond tree along the Marina by a "chap who looks to be pretty handy with small arms." Tola, who was in the car with Adu, was unharmed. The bullet was quickly extracted —the shooting had taken place, luckily, not more than a hundred yards from the hospital emergency entrance— but Adu was detained for forty-eight hours for "observation." By lunchtime Sunday he was out. A short release was given to waiting reporters by his PRO, whom I hadn't seen or heard from in three days.

The release said:

> Mr. Adumuyiwa Adumuyiwa, MHR-elect for the constituency of Lagos South, was discharged from the Colonial Hospital at midday today after superficial surgery and treatment. Mr. Adumuyiwa will be convalescing for a few days, and proposes to take the

oath of office before the end of the present week. Although still suffering slightly from the effects of shock, he is not in pain.

Mr. Adumuyiwa wishes to thank all those who have sent him messages and flowers and other tokens of good will, and above all to assure his constituents in Lagos South that he will actively commence his duties as their representative in the Federal Parliament within a few days. A meeting with the press will be arranged as soon as practicable.

Later that evening the police picked up a man known in the Thieves' Kitchen as "Jeep" who had served with the Royal West African Frontier Force in Burma during World War II, and who was reputed to be a specialist in cannibalizing and repairing—and stealing—Jeeps and Land Rovers. On Monday he was charged with attempted murder, possession of an unlicensed firearm, grievous bodily harm, and assault and battery.

Since Tola had not called me, I didn't see much point in calling her. Early Monday evening, however, I received a call from Miss Matilda, who asked me to tea at four the next afternoon. Before she hung up she also asked why I hadn't called Tola or gone to see Adu in the hospital. I realized that I truly didn't know the answer to either question, so I told her it was all very complicated and that we would talk tomorrow.

I was three minutes late for my tea with Miss Matilda and got the telling-off I expected. She had never accepted that time was an abstraction: "Four o'clock" was a very personal compact with life and my arriving at 4:03 was a gross breach of faith and almost a direct insult. After properly scolding me she said that I would have to wait until Bola had brewed a fresh pot of tea. She had already finished her first cup when I came into the Victorian drawing room where she sat in her high-backed mahogany rocker, silently cursing me, I assumed, for the unreliable young whippersnapper I was. The shutters on the west side were closed to keep out the fierce afternoon sun and she seemed, sitting there stiff-backed in the near-gloom with her hands folded neatly on her lap, not so much old as lost, a little fuzzy-headed lady marooned in some warp in time.

"I'm sorry I'm late, Miss Matilda."

"You're late for many things, young man. You're late for Tola, you know that? You know you have lost her?" I hadn't really known it until Miss Matilda pronounced the words, because lovers seem to know nothing, the subsistence of love being something alien to the condition of cognition. And yet there was some groove in my mind which was already prepared for the smooth entry of this piece of information, so perhaps I *had* "known" something.

"Can I ask a stupid question, Miss Matilda? Does *Tola* know it?"

"Oh, it is not a stupid question at all. She is very confused. These past weeks I am not sure that she has known what has been happening to her. I have seen her confusion. But that does not help you. With you, it is finished."

"You asked me to tea to tell me this?"

"Yes, of course. She cannot tell you. Not yet."

"Why hasn't she given me a hint? She hasn't been near me for days now. Why hasn't she talked to me?"

"Why didn't you call her this weekend? She does not talk to me about her life, but each day she asked if you had called. I don't think you have acted with too much intelligence, if you want me to tell you the truth. What did you mean when you told me on the instrument that it was 'complicated'?"

"I suppose I knew it wouldn't do any good. When she didn't get in touch with me for three days it was as good as if she'd sent me a message."

"And you did not go to see Adu in the hospital because you were afraid of what you might see. Well, I suppose I have some responsibility in the matter. I do not concern myself with other people's affairs, but I thought you would be good for Tola. You have been. She has improved much since she has been seeing you." I had "improved" her for somebody else's benefit. In international trade this is called "value-adding," and there are classic formulas for computing compensation. What was going to be my reward? "But she will marry Adu. Sooner or later," Miss Matilda went on. And when he becomes Prime Minister I can point with pride to the indentations in her Dior dresses and say to the spectators nearest me: I have been *there*. What had I really thought during these past few weeks, and particularly the last week of the campaign, when she didn't come once to Alade Street? That she would come back to me intact as soon as the member had taken the oath? I hadn't been thinking at all. Incoherent, nameless bacteria of doubt had been accumulating within me and at last I had got a lab report.

"Adu is 'good for her' too?" I asked. I knew I was being crude and indelicate, as well as unkind to Miss Matilda, who was clearly trying to do me a favor, to soften the blow. But the pictures were beginning to form: Adu, until now almost as much as an abstraction as the campaign itself, was jelling into an image of a male with a penis that was about to be—had already been?—inserted into that place in Tola which was so inherently, so totally, so permanently private to me, that I might almost have invented it, husband and admitted previous lovers notwithstanding. The known and possessed was about to be—had already been?—converted into an unpossessable stranger. The present—Good Jesus CHRIST!—was being palpably converted into the past. *This* is what they call *loss!*

"Yes," said Miss Matilda, the issue-less surrogate materfamilias. "I think he will be very good for her. She has to put some order into her life, or she will end like me. A relic living in a relic. This house is always here, waiting."

"Oh, please, Miss Matilda. Has your life been all that hard? You can't have too many regrets." It was an idiotic and arrogant thing to say, and I knew it as soon as the words had left my mouth.

"The past is not to be regretted. It is the present I regret. I am here *today*. I came back from Cardiff. I have no children. I left Bengt to his roots and I came back to mine. Perhaps it was easier in those days to pay attention to that sort of thing, I don't know. But I told you before, the first time I met you, Tola is very much like me."

"Are you saying that God ordained that Yorubas should stick with Yorubas? Isn't it too late for that?" I was going to talk about the West Indies and the Carolinas and many other places but she sensed my bitterness and quickly put her hand out and took my wrist.

"No, no. I am talking about *Tola*. I am trying to help you to understand her. I may not know her as well as I think, but I know things about her you would know only if you were a member of the family. Tola and I are the same, *omole*, home-children. We always come back home. It is something in the heart that does not change. It is what brought me home forty years ago. It is what makes Tola live here instead of getting her own flat." (Is it what shocks her automatically awake at five o'clock in the morning regardless of when we have gone to bed and takes her to the Alatishe house for breakfast? Thank you for the reference, Miss Matilda; shouldn't the Egbe Omo Oduduwa design a special mark to be placed—say, on the inside of the thigh—on all *omole* so that unwary Danes and West Indians may avoid pointless entanglement? Especially West Indians. It would be a service to all the black peoples of the world. Here endeth the lesson. Amen.)

Chapter Thirty-five

Private Mail Box 727, Lagos, Nigeria
Personal and Confidential

Mr. Charles Moeltke   22nd July
Special Assistant
Office of the Assistant Secretary for
African and Middle Eastern Affairs

Dear Charles,

By now you will have seen the Consul General's report
on the recent events here and will have the advantage of
a detailed appreciation of what took place. I shan't try to
kid either you or myself that I have anything to add to a
professional report of that kind, even though I have, of
course, no idea of what Grant has written, having made
a point of keeping as far away from him as possible.

I have already informed you of the small initiative which
I essayed and I must say that I was pleased by your reaction. These things are so much a matter of judgment,
and a tyro—especially an amateur—is bound to be less than
confident about his judgment in these matters. With our
friend's success in the election—I hope Grant has clearer
information on the background than I have been able to

312

glean—I can uneasily but confidently foresee his early arrival at a position of authority. What I cannot guess at this point is whether he may then be moved to act against me. Please be assured that, if he does, you will not be involved in any manner; I certainly shan't require any assistance from your end.

My main purpose in writing you this letter is to convey as forcefully as I can what seems to be the lesson to be learned from this experience. As I understand it, the informal assignment you gave me is the first of its kind, and is a long way from having the Department's full blessing. Speaking as an amateur, I would like to impress upon you with all the force at my command that the time has come to put an end to amateurism in our policy toward this country. A consulate in a consulate, and with the best will in the world cannot go much beyond its mandate. Informal observers like myself have their uses, but are in double jeopardy, especially at this stage of the country's political evolution, from burgeoning nationalism on the one hand and British jealousy on the other. There is too much happening here for the conventional diplomacy to handle, especially with the constraints imposed by our relationship with the British. In other words, Charles, it is time to bring in the pros, otherwise we shall be caught badly napping when the crunch comes. And, believe me, with the private information I have about the oil potential here, plus the demographic and geographic factors, yesterday is not a moment too soon. As Mr. Drysdale used to say when we were at Andover, *verb. sap. sat.*

Warmest regards to Dorothy and the boys.

Sincerely,
Myron Dryfoos

Chapter Thirty-six

Bjornsgatan 7710,
Uppsala,
17th August

My dear Adu,

Your letter brought me great joy, much of it selfish. As
you can imagine, by the time news of the incident filtered
through to me here, a flesh wound had been transformed
into a bullet in the brain (the least sensational version I
heard) and it wasn't too difficult for me to see a line of
causation stretching all the way back to Alapa. I am
really delighted to learn that not only was the damage
slight, but that you have already taken your seat in
Parliament . . . .

You put a very difficult question to me when you ask
if, in my judgment, the British could have been at the back
of it. I have two conflicting judgments: On the one hand,
if they really, desperately wanted to get rid of you, they
would have done it by now—they have *all* the trumps.
And my impression of their secret operation in Nigeria
drawn from my one brush with the Special Branch people
is an impression of doggedness rather than of ruthlessness.

On the other hand, who the hell knows? I am sure there are people in that unit who would as soon shoot a black man or have one shot as they would kill a fox, possibly with less remorse. Who is to say that on a particular day the "smash-the-wog" boys weren't in the ascendant? When I first heard the—wildly distorted—news, I went through the possibilities very rapidly and found that I had no completely convincing guess, so I settled for the easy way out: some nut who had some obscure grudge against you as well as a gun. But from what you say, "Jeep" not only admits to the shooting but says he was paid to do it, and he must have got his instructions from someone who knew you would be passing on the Marina at about that time. Ergo, the "lucky nut" theory has to be ruled out.

There is, of course, the possibility that either (a) the wog-smashers prevailed and they did undertake to silence you but failed and have therefore been discredited and called off; or (b) they may just conceivably have wished only to frighten you. When the trial takes place, it may be possible to rule out or confirm hypothesis (b) on the basis of the evidence Jeep gives.

I have not seriously considered the possibility that one of the political parties may be involved, because I think I am safe in saying that there is nobody in the leadership of either party who would dare—or care—to go beyond the traditional head-cracking that I understand goes on at election time. That said, my list of candidates is exhausted.

You will forgive this rather morbid speculation which I have put on paper only because you specifically asked my view. I have had plenty of time for speculation in this sun-cured country. (Can you imagine it? If you forget to draw your blinds when you go to bed at, say one A.M., the sun, the sun! wakes you at two A.M. The Creator seems to have indulged some of his more surrealistic fantasies in the North.) A young professor here chanced on two of my papers on management and productivity and invited me to chair a summer seminar which he had organized. The pressure the University got from the British Embassy here to have nothing to do with such a notorious character seems to have made them all the more keen to have me: They take the concept of academic freedom with exceeding seriousness, though not quite so seriously as they take sex in particular and amusements in general. My part here is, to say the least, not strenuous. There is talk of offering me a special fellowship for a year, but I am trying to soft-pedal the idea. I have other plans in mind, and besides, the thought of spending a year in the midst of all this Aryan earnestness rather frightens me. I have been earnestly admonished to report any suspected instance of color prejudice to the authorities; I have been equally earnestly invited to inform the administrative director of the seminar (a lovely bint in her mid-thirties with cotton-candy hair) should I find that my sexual needs are not being met.

Actually, I think at the end of the seminar I shall revisit Italy and Germany in a new capacity, adviser/interpreter/manager to a group of West Indian musicians whom I found half-stranded in Stockholm. They are brimming with talent, but don't know one end of a contract from another and haven't the faintest idea how to survive in Europe. Needless to say, some so-called manager has been bleeding them dry, and I think I'm going to try to give them a hand.

I was very flattered by your interest in the so-called Payne Plan, which is simplicity itself. Since you insist, I am sending you by separate post some of my background notes. I hope they can be of help.

Ta-ta for now. Lots of luck.

Yours ever,
Dacosta Payne

Chapter Thirty-seven

Adu held his press conference on the day after my tête-à-tête with Aunt Matilda. I itched to see him. Not the MHR-elect with the bandages and the sling and that bronze-gray color that comes to the face when you've lost a great deal of blood. I wanted to see the body and hear the voice that had displaced mine in the atmosphere called Tola. She had eventually phoned me, a hoarse, tense voice brought to me by courtesy of Alexander Graham Bell which said that she was writing me a letter because she did not have the courage to see me face to face, the voice disappearing at this point as a result of a severe loss of induction caused by the replacing of the receiver.

I had no more courage than Tola, so I stayed in the office and waited for Olapeju to return to inform us that Adu had not so much forgiven as dismissed Jeep; if he were to be found guilty, he had stated, he should be most accurately considered to be no more and no less than an exploited urban peasant whose inherent Nigerian values had been comprehensively corrupted by colonialism. In reply to a question, Adu said that he would refuse to give evidence against Jeep unless subpoenaed, and made

a plea to leading Nigerian counsel to undertake the man's
defense free of charge. (Sir Femi Oladairo's name was
entered the same day as counsel, and we all assumed
that *somebody* was paying him.)

Adu refused to speculate on the identity of the person
or persons who might have engaged Jeep to take a pot-
shot at him, reminding the journalists with a smile that
Jeep had been *charged,* not convicted. He seemed to take
the attitude that what had happened on Saturday was a
clear case of Providence playing at tabloid journalism.
What had happened on Friday was *history.* History required him to offer his public thanks and congratulations
to the two parties for having transcended the "monkey-
see-monkey-do" role which British colonialism had foisted
upon them. History also required that he should reaffirm
his independence of both parties. It was this independence, and the recognition that the parties had belatedly
given it, that was the key to his election to Parliament.

"The man was magnificent," Olapeju said. Adjectives
like that would never be printed in the *Sun,* and Olapeju
had a number of them to get off his chest. "Whatever I
have said about him before, *t'olorun* he is an authentic
nationalist. The only one."

"But what about the shot? Why they shoot am? You're
not writing anything about that?" Chukuemeka asked my
question.

"An irrelevance, my friend. Don't you understand that?
I am talking to you about a man who is going to bring
something very new into Nigerian politics. Nobility, Nobility, *sh'ogbo?*" Olapeju's long foxy face seemed to have
taken on some of the nobility he was distributing so
royally. Perhaps he was quite serious, I thought, realizing
with something like jealousy that it was absolutely not
open to me to share the exaltation that had fallen upon him.

"You're talking like a revivalist convert, Olapeju, not
like a journalist," I said a little acidly. "Next thing you

know you'll be down at Bar Beach at dawn on Sunday in a white *agbada.*"

"You want to hear something, Sinclair?" he said, wagging his index finger very close to my face. "If I want a revival in my country, no *ajerike* is going to stop me, you hear? I thought you and Adu were so close. *O ma she o!* He has taken your titi, is that it? *E pele!*" I knew he was just lashing out at me in a general way, but the lash had landed on exactly the right spot, and it silenced me. It is not possible for a journalist to weep in his own newsroom at midday in high summer.

"Listen, listen," he said confidentially, putting his hand on my shoulder in the friendliest way. The heat of a second before had dissipated as soon as it was released. "I really think the whole shooting business is woman palaver. I know it's nothing to do with you. You West Indians are too civilized. But what about Bijou? You don't think she will just stand by and see her man captured by a glamorous intellectual and do nothing about it, eh? That's my theory. But, *egbo,* I tell you it is irrelevant. The big thing is, Jeep *missed.* We have Adu. Believe me, he is going to turn Nigerian politics upside down. Upside down!"

"Commerce and Industry by December?" Chuks asked.

"Fifty pounds! FIFTY POUNDS! I will steal the money to bet you. I will give you . . . I will give you two-to-one! Are you betting?" Olapeju still had his copy in one hand, but the passion that had returned with the mention of his wager made him fling the yellow quarto pages in a cascade onto the floor as he frantically searched for his wallet. "I have seven pounds here now. I will have fifty by four o'clock. You wish to bet?" His excitement seemed to have compressed his vocal cords, and instead of the shout his brain was surely calling for, a sort of squeak issued from his mouth. He cleared his throat and tried again. "Four o'clock! Four o'clock!" It took him a full second to realize that there were no bettors in the room.

"Sofle, sofle, Mazi Olapeju," Chuks said, "you no go get my money. I ask you a question, that is all."

"You are just a bunch of jokers," Olapeju said, bending down to collect his story. Once again his paroxysm had passed as quickly as it had come. "I will win my bet. You will all buy me whisky at Christmas. You will beg me to drink it." He was smiling his rodent smile and shaking his head. "I will be very gracious. I will drink your Christmas bonuses to God! Let me go from these ignorant people. The white man waiteth to see my copy."

Chapter Thirty-eight

On Saturday, two days before the preliminary investigation was scheduled to begin, the police announced that Jeep had escaped from prison. On the Monday they said that there was strong evidence that he was in Dahomey, extradition procedures were being initiated. (From then until the time I left Lagos, eight months later, Jeep's name did not appear more than once in the newspapers and scarcely more than half-a-dozen times in those conversations at which I was present.)

On Saturday, too, Tola's letter arrived. I had been playing an unserious game of cricket that afternoon and had made an inspired twenty-three and taken three lucky wickets for a team of alcoholic foreigners, blasphemously called The Lord's Eleven, and had then taken part wholeheartedly in a noisy, beer-drinking British sunset sacrament. The letter, lodged between floor and door at 10 Alade Street, appeared to my alcohol-and-fatigue-inflamed eyes like a message of revelation coming from another world, and I picked it up very carefully and placed the heavy rag-bond envelope on the little dresser until I should have had time to wash my hands and splash tepid water on my face.

The letter said:
    Sinclair:
        Even in a letter there is very little I can say. I
    love you. Please don't dismiss that.
                                                    Tola.
It was beautifully typed on a fine onion-skin paper with
the words "Mango Lodge, Lagos" embossed in a Palace
copperplate jobbing face. The message was as clear as
the light on the road to Damascus. The word "love" was
a foreign word, a word of foreigners, by foreigners, and
about foreigners. It was nevertheless a pleasant word,
not to be dismissed. Especially not to be dismissed if one
was oneself a foreigner.

By every possible criterion of common sense, decorum,
and animal self-preservation I should have left Lagos immediately. I had the sensation that my life was being
crushed between forces which I did not understand into
a shape I did not wish. (I think I got the image from one
of those newsreels local cinemas eagerly accepted from
the United States Information Service to flesh out their
meager programs: A film I had seen on the technological
paramountcy of the U.S. showed as a *pièce de résistance*
a giant machine that could reduce an entire motor car
to a compact polygonal gob of steel.)
    But no convincing escape route offered itself. I was
tentatively propositioned about a job in a prestigious
news agency in London and suddenly, as I was in the
midst of working out the financial pros and cons, another
movie image came to mind, an image of myself as a species of tumblewood rolling insentiently, perpetually, in an
infinite vista of assignments, jobs, flats, agencies, countries, a vista studded with sand-dune Tolas that offered
temporary purchase but no sustenance. In the end I told
the agency's area manager that I was very interested, but
could not, for personal reasons, move just yet.

So I stayed on. We bought Olapeju his Chivas Regal in late November. The harmattan had not quite reached Lagos yet, although our correspondent in Ondo said the nights were already becoming "cold"—75 degrees Fahrenheit—and the days dusty-dry. Adu accepted the portfolio of Commerce and Industry. He said at a press conference that he did not plan to revolutionize the Ministry overnight, but he did have a few immediate changes in mind. The first was the establishment of a Training Division, for which he obtained at record speed a senior man from the British Board of Trade as Director. The Division's terms of reference were published as a White Paper which appeared soon after the Christmas parliamentary recess, and which Adu brilliantly defended in his maiden appearance on the Government Front Benches. The speech was in all essentials the Payne Plan. Funke had a forwarding address for Payne in Milan and I dropped him a card to give him the ironic news. I didn't hear from him, although I knew he was in touch with Funke, who claimed that he was traveling with a group of West Indian musicians between Rome, Milan, and the resorts around Lake Como. It seemed a bizarre mutation.

Auguste took six months' leave back in St. Lucia soon after he came out of the hospital. He said he would be "looking the place over" with a view to going back permanently. I still didn't believe he would leave Nigeria for good. Finally I had come to understand what he refused to understand: Lagos suited him, and he, Lagos. The orphan in Auguste had found an accommodation in the disorderly, sometimes brutal, universal mother in Lagos. He was not an expatriate as Payne and I were expatriates, and one day some village was going to ask him to accept the cap of an honorary chief. Perhaps the resistance he was displaying was genuine and necessary, like the palm-wine tapper's straining against the rope that holds him to the tree.

When he turned up in February, a good month before his holiday was due to end, protesting· that he had felt himself "a stranger" in St. Lucia, I was not surprised. "Man, my old lady dead and gone," he said half-plaintively. "The boys I was at school with spread out all over. The ones who still in Castries only drinking Mount Gay from five o'clock till all hours and screwing the same old whores we used to screw when we were in high school for seventy-five cents. The only difference is that it's five dollars now. And the same three old men dominating the legal profession. As far as the ordinary St. Lucian concerned, if your name ain't Probyn, Deschatelets, or O'Malley you ain't a lawyer, don't care how many degrees and how much experience you got. I figure I'll hang on here another two-three years and then make another rounds home to see how things going. Then I'll *really* make my move." Virginia had gone to meet him at the airport. In his absence she had conspicuously spent a great deal of her time with a young NANI minister whose wife and six children had remained in Port Harcourt. None of my pigeonholes could accommodate that woman.

Since the election I had gone through the routines of sleeping, waking, working, playing billiards at the club, sampling the girls at the Imperial, weekend trips to Ibadan to hear my academic friends talk or to Cotonou for a change of nightclubs and girls and language. I had gone on an assignment to Fernando Póo and had found a tribe of prosperous, traveled, trilingual black men with homes in Santa Isabel and Barcelona who drank Fina La Ina from Baccarat crystal at sunset on filigreed iron balconies and were called "Don," who had demanded that I interpret for them the strange events in the Gold Coast where men to all appearances like themselves had taken the *"paso tan peligroso y ilogico"*—so dangerous and illogical step—of becoming independent from the European power that had held them in tutelage. Bijou had dropped out of circulation and was variously rumored to be in Dakar or Freetown or Bathurst.

As the harmattan came and went I watched Adu making the transition which I had glibly predicted but still found hard to credit, from Jeremiah to Jesus, from critic of the machine to major prophet and teacher and leader. March, "small rains" and stifling heat rising in rainbow waves from the tarmac, brought escape. The company had bought a newspaper group in Trinidad, and I was asked if I was interested in the job of Sunday Editor. Before my forty-eight hours of consideration were up, Olapeju knew about the offer.

"So when do you expect to be in Port of Spain, *egbo?*" he asked, swinging one leg like a pendulum as he sat in his traditional half-assed position on my desk. There was obviously no point in trying to dissemble, so I said I hadn't yet made up my mind to take the job. This was untrue. I had made up my mind the moment the offer was made, but I felt that Olapeju, who was sure to get my job when I left, deserved at least twenty-four hours of uncertainty.

"I don't know if I could live in the West Indies again," I said twisting the knife a millimeter or so. He was genuinely shocked.

"But that is your home! You mean you do not want to go home? My God, if it was me I would not even hesitate. I wouldn't need forty-eight hours. And the money is good, not so?" The money was indeed good, as he knew. Through his "connection" with the Adviser's secretary he had probably seen the original letter from London with the details of the offer. "And, anyway, your circle is breaking up." I looked at him with raised eyebrows. "Oh, ho! You think I do not know about the little group you have been living in these past months?" He stood up as if for greater dramatic effect. "The *oyibos* who just *love* Africans, like Dryfoos and his superannuated bobbysoxer of a wife, and the detribalized Yorubas like Mrs. Ayodele, Virginia from the *Dispatch*. I know, *egbo*, I know."

"And Adu Adumuyiwa, your hero. Is he detribalized, too?" I didn't realize how violently angry I had become until I saw him back away from me in a jerky one-step, his hands raised before him like a man apprehending imminent physical danger.

"*Je, je* my brother! Make you no break my head!" he said. I felt foolish, and eased back from the edge of my chair where anger had brought me. "Alright. We are all detribalized. Na so. Each time I go back to my father's house I know that. Olapeju self is detribalized *pata pata*. *Abi* from the time you can understand one word of English you are detribalized. But is it not true that your group has broken up? Adu and Mrs. Ayodele are gone, Bijou is starting a business in Freetown, the Dryfoos' are about to be deported. . . ."

"Jesus Christ, Olapeju, will you stop talking shit?"

"*Egbo*, it is the truth. You did not know? Our friend the Minister of Commerce and Industry is having their residence papers withdrawn."

"Olapeju, I don't believe you. You're really getting too dam' creative now. Don't you know that Adu and Myron Dryfoos have been friends for years? Since you claim to know so much about my so-called circle, you ought to know that."

"To God, Sinclair. A friend of mine in the Cabinet Office told me last night that the recommendation to refuse renewal came straight from the Minister himself. That is the truth."

"What is supposed to be the reason?"

"My friend could not tell me. Under the Act the designated Minister is not obliged to give a reason for a refusal. The decision is subject to review by the Governor General, but these days it's a formality. The GG doesn't want some Minister to get up in the House and accuse him of protecting Europeans."

"But haven't you asked yourself what Adu would want to get Myron out of the country for? He's just an oil executive, after all. The place is crawling with them."

" 'Just an oil executive,' you say? Have you ever looked up his name in *Who's Who in American Business*? I suppose you would say that John D. Rockefeller, Junior, is just a New York banker?"

"Olapeju, I still don't see what that has to do with it. In fact, if he's a multimillionaire, that would be all the more reason for keeping him here."

"I don't know any more than I have told you. Some people last night were saying that it may be woman palaver again, some old story between Mrs. Ayodele and Dryfoos. That's just talk, *sh'ogbo?*"

I burst out laughing, and when he asked what was so funny I refused to explain. It was about time that Olapeju got something comprehensively wrong.

Chapter Thirty-nine

When he said that Trinidad was "home," Olapejū was wrong again. Not too wrong, though; the house of your father's twin brother can be very much like home.

Trinidad, an island in which I had never lived, was enough like home and enough unlike home to be a delight from the beginning. St. Paul would not have cared much for it. As in his Greece, people were forever asking each other, urgently, pantingly, "What's new?" And when they weren't asking they were searching. The newest thing was identity, and you could see bevies of searchers everywhere, heads down, ears pricked up, at street corners, in the pick-up taxis from Diego Martin to the city, at cocktail parties, in the Löwenbrau bar near my paper's offices, even in Parliament. Every now and then somebody claimed that he had found it. On the strength of this alone a number of painters and dancers acquired enormous followings for short periods until it was announced that somebody else had truly and definitively discovered it.

Roopnarine would have none of this. "When you nine-teen and you wake up one morning and find you have a wife and a baby son, you don't have much time to waste looking 'bout for a abstract noun, let me tell you. Man,

328

the only identity problems somebody like me could have is with the kinda people who think all Indians is coolie. And even that don't bother me. Identity? Man I got identity to burn. Trinidadian. Creole. Brahmin. You want to borrow some?"

Roopnarine was quite new, a West Indian in the West Indies who was running away from nothing and in search of nothing, a homegrown adult of a kind that I had never known as an adult and, I suppose, had not conceived of as possible. A meat eater, a beer drinker, a frequenter of brothels, a paterfamilias emeritus—Vidia, the doctor, twin air-hostesses, and a PPE student on a government scholarship at Balliol were all eminently self-supporting—he was a "self-made" journalist who had taught himself to write "in self-defense, man," when the eldest child had won the first of a series of scholarships at the age of ten. He pretended to be happily rid of parental responsibilities, and to be totally immersed in the life he was now free to live, irreverent, truly irresponsible—"the children would never let their mother starve, and me, I couldn't starve if I tried. I have at least four Chinese restaurant owners in this town owing me for plugs in the paper and for telling visitors that they sell the best Chinese food in the world outside San Francisco."

But his face gave the lie to this picaresque image; it was darkened and runneled by vicarious exam fevers and by a too close appreciation of the perils of air travel; to see him walk on his thin bowlegs with his head carried at that tellingly introspective inch below the perpendicular was to know him for the congenital worrier and bearer of other peoples' burdens that he was.

His stoop and his conversational English seemed to me of a piece, a banner aggressively marked, "Trample on me!" If someone actually tried, as once occurred in my presence when a new English recruit to the staff made the innocently imperial assumption that Roop was the obvious man to send for a paper-cupful of water, Roop would straighten up physically and linguistically and it was the trampler who found himself flat on his back.

"A cup of water, Mr. St. John-Prestwick? Certainly. But I don't recommend the water here; local standards of cleanliness are pretty poor, you'll find. I've a better idea. Here's fifty cents. Run round the corner, over there where you see the Löwenbrau sign, and buy yourself a cold beer. Foreign, of course, the local stuff is horsepiss. Would you bring me a box of matches if there's any change?"

This was the man whom the management assigned to be my deputy on the *Weekly Star*. At the beginning he was no more than correct, and predictably suspicious of this younger man who had come straight into a top job on a transfer dictated from headquarters. Perhaps he had expected me to trample, or try to, but when I didn't and when I wrote what I hoped was a sympathetic but unsentimental series on current Nigerian affairs, I knew I was on the way to total acceptance.

"I thought maybe that you was one of these kiss-me-ass back-to-Africa boys who was coming back to tell we how to run the West Indies," he said afterwards, when he had well and truly integrated me into the void, which he vociferously claimed not to exist, that the absence of his children had clearly created.

He was very skeptical about my plan for the next series: six articles, ending the week before Carnival, on the place of carnival and calypso in the life of Trinidad.

"Man, you must be mad! You come here to tell Trinidadians about Carnival? First to begin with, all-you don't even have carnival in Barbados. And then, even if you was a *Brazilian*, no Trinidadian going to listen. All-you Bajans fast, yes?" But as he spoke he was already succumbing to the professional challenge of the thing. "A Bajan and a Creole Indian writing about calypso. That is gall father! Let we try."

We tried. As a first step he tracked down material for me in defunct "little magazines," in books, in learned journals, even in the newspaper's own badly preserved and uncatalogued back numbers. From there we went to talk to the survivors of earlier generations, old journalists, old promoters, old mistresses of old-time calypsonians, and even a handful of old-time calypsonians themselves, living, according to their luck, on the fringes of senile respectability or senile destitution. His own experiences and ideas and prejudices accompanied all this "objective" research like a running counterpoint.

"A calypsonian is by definition a whoremonger," he dogmatized. "I ain't asking you, I telling you. The only question is which comes first, calypsonian or saga boy? My answer to that is saga boy come first. I talking about the good ones, because anybody can put together a couple easy rhymes, steal a old melody, and it have enough coonoomoonoos in this world that he can catch a beer or a rum from them from time to time and he gone home and tell everybody in Tunapuna how he is big calypsonian down in Port of Spain. I have a feeling the good ones don't even know they're calypsonians until something irrelevant happen to start them off. Like a tess lost a girlfriend or he lost all his money on a horse race, and all of a sudden he listening to the radio or a jukebox and he hear the Mighty This or the Mighty That singing, and right there he know that he only have to spend a few minutes thinking and he can come up with something better. And it does turn out that he right. You *have* to be a saga boy, and you *have* to be a Trinidadian."

Roop held the view that the great calypsonians were the only true West Indian poets. "All that crap they does write in these little magazines, you call that poetry? Either they trying to imitate some American or English poet, or they turning out a bunch of introspective nonsense, 'Look, boy, is suffering I suffering, but elegant for so, yes?' There should be a law that no West Indian should be allowed to write an iambic pentameter until he write one halfway decent calypso. You have to be a poet of the people first!"

By this time the pre-Carnival season was in full swing. Most of the labels on the jukeboxes were handwritten, a sure sign of the fast turnover in nine-day wonders, and three or four definite contenders for the title of calypso king could already be identified, including a new singer called Lord Beguiler.

"Beguiler could be the man this year, yes," Roop said one day. "Leh we make a rounds by the New Ca'iso Tent tonight and hear how he shaping." He went on to talk about Beguiler, about whom nothing much was known, except that he had spent a fair time in England, probably as a merchant seaman, and had come back to Port of Spain just a few months before Carnival with some small fame as a result of a calypso called "Beguiler Is a Beast," which had climbed fairly high on the English hit parade.

"The boy got something," Roop said. "I hear this Beast thing a couple times last year, and it call to mind some of the good old-time calypsonians, Lion and Killer, and them. But where he beat them, to my mind, ain't so much that he up-to-date in style and all that, because every half-ass calypsonian nowadays making records with echo chamber and amplified guitars and jazz-up arrangements. What Beguiler have is the *line*, man, the line. He taking a line and bending it and stretching it and filling it with assonances like if he was one of them post-Victorian poets." By now I knew Roop well enough not to be startled by the reference.

"The boy really clever; if you hear that Beast song you bound to take off your hat to him. He singing about how he is a savage from darkest Africa, and he have to start the day with a sacrifice, but is only farm-fresh English chicken he using. First he does clip their wings, then he does strip them down, and then he does eat them raw. I don't have to dot the i's for you; but maybe the English didn't catch on. Anyway, I hear they was playing it on the BBC on 'Housewives' Choice.' "

He laughed the sad, almost reluctant laugh I now knew well, the stifled, unpracticed guffaw of a man who has only recently been able to afford the luxury of laughter.

"As a matter of fact, the boy in trouble right now," he went on. "The police arrest him at a bar in Cocorite over a girl, they say. He supposed to be a very fast man with a broken bottle, and they say he ain't too fond of white people. Anyway, he out on bail now, and I willing to bet he have a calypso on the case already. I think maybe we should do a little interview with him after the show. From our point of view that's the man with everything. I mean he modern, and yet you can see that he got roots in the old tradition. I hear he driving a Mercedes some company give him on credit; he building a house with swimming pool and thing, on credit, too. This must be the first calypso singer to have he own lawyer, and yet he can't keep out of whorehouses and it look as if he can't keep out of the police station. The boy brand new, but you can still see the old pattern coming out."

The New Ca'iso Tent was the most modern in town. In the off-season it served as the assembly hall for one of the largest unions in Trinidad, a prestige affair in the American union tradition, with cantilevered roof, seating for a thousand, and—this the mark of true affluence—a plenitude of modernistic toilet facilities.

" 'Nice' people love to come here even if the calypsonians mostly second-rate. At least they sure their wives could go to the toilet in comfort," Roop explained as we sat in the front row press seats and watched the common herd being tortured by the sports-shirted ushers. The proceedings had already begun, and a thin Indian boy, holding onto the microphone as if afraid it might otherwise

do him grievous injury, was singing a dreary single en-
tendre song about a battle he had with a hairy monster at
the dead of the night.

"It even have Chinese calypsonians these days," Roop
observed in a low voice; and, indeed, one did come on
later to sing a self-regarding and strictly nonessential
ballad about the problems of being a Chinese calypsonian.

"All this is just preliminaries," Roop told me in the
first interval. "People does come to hear one or two
singers, although sometimes, once in a blue moon, one of
these young ones does come up with a hit. But tonight it
look to me like is strictly Beguiler, Lord Fantasy, and
maybe Exciter might spring a surprise." Exciter had been
much in evidence as master of ceremonies, introducing
his colleagues and competitors with remarks of varying
snideness as to their chances of beating him for the
crown, and making cutting remarks about late-comers,
especially those who had to run the long gauntlet down
the aisle to the cheaper seats.

The interval over, Exciter reappeared leaning over the
wooden barrier that enclosed the stage, and speaking
through a negligently held hand-mike, "Ladies and gemmen," he intoned, "did you ever hear of a English calypsonian? Well, I in the business all these years and this is
the first time I ever run into one. The New Ca'iso Tent
takes great pleasure in introducing the London Beast
himself, the one and only, ever-popular, Mighty Beguiler.
He is going to sing for you his latest composition, and I
understand his lawyer is in the audience to take it down
word for word to be used as the defense case in a forthcoming trial. From what I hear, Beguiler may not be in
the competition this year. Certain people planning for
him to do his singing in a cage. But meanwhile give the
Beguiler a big hand, ladies and gemmen, and lend an ear
to his new calypso, 'UNTOUCHED BY HUMAN HAND'!"

The ten-piece band broke into a fast jump-up rhythm,
a voice was heard through the public-address system

shouting, "Taint me, taint me, I never touch the Yankee
man!," and a tall, spade-bearded, black man, wearing a
well-cut gray italianate suit, and swinging a ten-gallon
hat in one hand, appeared at the wooden barrier.

The beard was new to me, but the rest was Dacosta
Payne.

> I don't know your worship, I don't know.
> Don't ask me, your worship, who beat up the
>   Yankee so.
> The last time I see he, he was getting in the police
>   van,
> And up to then I swear, your worship, he was
>   UNTOUCHED BY HUMAN HAND!

The chorus came first, and then Beguiler/Dacosta Payne
moved into the narrative: He had been sitting in a bar
sipping a lemonade and waiting for a friend. It was a low
bar, full of people with whom he ordinarily didn't associ-
ate, in particular a number of ladies whom he understood
to be "businesswomen," although he was not certain
what kind of business was meant. It was very noisy, and
he presumed that the ladies were discussing contracts in
their line of business. Suddenly a well-dressed white man
came in, escorted by some Trinidadian men whom he took
for tourist guides. What was a man like that doing in a
place like that?

> Could be a anthropologist
> Checking on the local practices
>   because he had heard that
> Anthropology,
> Could only be practiced in black people country.

Anyway, he didn't pay too much attention, and the next
thing he knew a fight broke out, and as a supporter of
nonviolence he retired to a corner to wait for the whole
thing to blow over. But the police arrived

> and started to act ignorant,
> catching onto the guilty and the innocent

and that was where he found himself being hustled into a police van. And back into the chorus.

The audience, which had been little more than polite in their applause for previous singers, now went wild; by the time Beguiler was ready to sing the fourth chorus they were singing with him. In the back row people were jumping in the aisles. Everyone, including Roop and me, was shouting, "Encore," although a traveled wit near us preferred *"Bis!"*

"As of now," Roop shouted in my ear, "that is the calypso king, and that song is the Road March for this year. The others might as well don't bother. What I tell you, man?"

It was true. Even a total stranger would have been able to sense the great, swelling pressure of unanimity that washed over the audience in the tent. The wit and rhythm and the dipping melody had sharpened and sweetened our awareness of the poetry of our daily existence; and the disrespect for what we still considered, deep in our hearts, "the white man's law" was now codified and slotted precisely and unforgettably into our consciousnesses, and it was Beguiler who had done it for us. For months—perhaps for years—to come we would be singing this song, or remembering snatches of it; without question this was the song we would be calling for from the steel bands on Jouvert Monday morning when, exerting our right to possess ecstasy before death possessed us, we would make the annual march of weary triumph through the streets of town, greeting the dawn as if it was our first and might be our last.

The applause and the shouting went on, and Beguiler stood at the rail, sweating under the fluorescent lights, smiling, a look of exhaustion and achievement on his face like that of an athlete at the end of a race, fanning himself with his Stetson, waiting until the shouts of "Encore" should die down to sing the encore we wanted.

"That is a giant, yes," Roop said, and I noticed that he was sweating almost as much as Dacosta Payne.

"Roop, Roop, I know that man! He's a Barbadian called Dacosta Payne," I said stammeringly in between little uncontrollable spurts of laughter. I had had that kind of seizure only once before in my life—listening to some new jazz records at a friend's house one afternoon soon after the end of the war. I had heard the music of Dizzy Gillespie and Charlie Parker for the first time, and had to be pummeled on the back and shoulders for a good five minutes before I could recover. Luckily, Roop's instinctive reaction was to slap me hard on the back a few times, and the paroxysm ended.

"Wha' wrong with you, boy? You frighten me to death! Eh, eh! Come leh we go get a beer. Me throat kinda dry."

"Roop, did you hear what I said?" I asked more calmly. "I know Beguiler. He's a Bajan I used to know in London and Nigeria. Dacosta Payne. That's his name." I started to laugh again, and Roop shook me sharply and made me stand up.

"Look, boy, if you ain't feeling too good you hads best go home. We can do the interview another time," he said in his kindly paterfamilias voice.